By Xenia Melzer

GODS OF WAR
Casto
Love and the Stubborn
Ummana
Braving the Storm

Published by DSP Publications
www.dsppublications.com

BRAVING THE STORM

GODS OF WAR: BOOK IV

XENIA MELZER

DSP PUBLICATIONS

Published by

DSP Publications

5032 Capital Circle SW, Suite 2, PMB# 279, Tallahassee, FL 32305-7886 USA
www.dsppublications.com

Braving the Storm
© 2017 Xenia Melzer.

Cover Art
© 2017 Aaron Anderson.
aaronbydesign55@gmail.com
Cover content is for illustrative purposes only and any person depicted on the cover is a model.

ISBN: 978-1-63533-675-7
Digital ISBN: 978-1-63533-676-4
Library of Congress Control Number: 2017950125
Published November 2017
v. 1.0

Printed in the United States of America

∞

This paper meets the requirements of
ANSI/NISO Z39.48-1992 (Permanence of Paper).

For Andrea, my first fan who wasn't blood-related.
And for my readers. You guys rock!

ACKNOWLEDGMENTS

As always, I have to thank many people for getting this book out. Since my family already knows how grateful I am, I want to thank my editors, Anne Regan, Liv, and Kelly, for their help and support. I can only imagine how hard it is sometimes to deal with a nonnative writer. I'm sure your patience and kindness will be rewarded with a few extra karma points. I also want to thank everybody at Dreamspinner who help make not only my books, but every writer's books, look as good as possible. Without all the people in the background who compose blurbs, set up blog tours, and generally make it all run smoothly, getting a book out would be a hassle. So thank you. I know what you do, and I appreciate it!

SUMMARY OF BOOKS ONE-THREE

A LOT has happened in the lives of Casto and Renaldo so far. After being taken prisoner by Renaldo, Casto has fought his master at every turn. Their explosive relationship has seen many ups and downs that would have broken weaker men. The worst came when Renaldo fell for the schemes of Damon, a priest of the Good Mother, who convinced him that Casto had been unfaithful. In a fit of rage, Renaldo sent Casto to the mines in order to kill him. But thanks to Sic's courage, the scheme was revealed and the magic spell clouding the divine brother's sight broken. Casto has returned to his master's side, no longer as a slave, but as his lover, heart, and future husband.

To bring Casto down, Damon had used Sic by blackmailing him into bringing Damon a cloak pin that would prove Casto's guilt. When Sic finally finds the courage to tell Renaldo what has happened, he is punished for his treason. Noran wishes to see his apprentice dead, and it is only thanks to Casto's interference that Sic is allowed to live. Deeply hurt by Sic's deed, Noran starts losing control of himself and tortures Sic cruelly by using the young man's love to force him into absolute subservience.

Daran, on the other hand, is more than happy with his two masters. He has overcome his shock after Kalad was almost killed during the battle of Ki't and knows now without a doubt that he belongs to Aegid and Kalad for the rest of his life.

The divine brothers have found out that the followers of the Good Mother, who had infiltrated the Valley, had been trained in Medelina. Now the Wolf of War wishes to get his revenge on the city.

They decide to go to Ummana, where Casto claims the throne and becomes king, not only of the Twin Cities, but also of the Alliance. That way, Canubis and Renaldo get their revenge on Medelina and Casto his on the council of elders and his father. Before he leaves, Casto installs his sister Anesha as queen of Ummana.

But their mission also claims sacrifices. When Noran is poisoned, Sic offers his own life to save his master, only to find out that he is a Luksari, a creature of pure magic. After he is rescued, Noran gives Sic his freedom and Sic finds a family and happiness with Jago, the master of the royal smithy, his wife, Cassia, and their little daughter, Heljia. He decides to stay in Ummana, although parting with Casto almost breaks his heart.

After the barbarians have left Ummana, Sic is visited by Ana-Isara and she marks him as the last Emeris, thus forcing him to follow his gods into the North.

Daran gets more than he has bargained for. In a foolish attempt to impress his masters and express his gratitude toward them, he becomes a spy for Casto. This dangerous game almost costs him his life and it is only thanks to Casto's foresight that he survives.

Now the Pack is back on its way home to the Valley.

PEOPLE OF ANA-DARASA

THE VALLEY
Lord Canubis, the Wolf of War
Lady Noemi, the snake witch and wife to Canubis
Lord Renaldo, the Angel of Death
King Castolus of Ummana, husband to Renaldo
Lysistratos, "Lys," Emperor of the Storms

THE EMERIS
Lady Hulda, the Mother Superior of the Sisters of the Night
Lord Wolfstan, armorer of the Pack and husband to Lady Hulda
Lord Aegid and Lord Kalad, the desert brothers
Lord Noran, master smith
Lord Bantu and Lady Cornelia, siblings
Sic, Luksari

OTHERS
Daran, slave of Aegid and Kalad
Frankus, master of the sauna
Sar'reff, demon of chaos

UMMANA
Princess Anesha, Casto's sister
Captain Aktan, leader of the Royal Guard
Jago, master smith
Cassia, Jago's wife
Heljia, daughter of Jago and Cassia
King Erac of Medelina
Lady Vespia, ambassador of Medelina

BACK AND BEYOND

1. BITTER TRUTH

IT WAS the third day since their departure from Ummana. Canubis had taken the first watch, eager to have some time on his own, alone in the darkness with nothing to distract his thoughts. He still didn't know whether he should be pleased about this year's unusual campaign or if he should write it off as a failure. Their original mission had been a success, no doubt. Not only had they gotten their revenge on the followers of the Good Mother in Medelina, they had also seen to it that the lives of those worshipping the old hag in the vicinity of the Confederation were going to be a lot more uncomfortable from now on. It was all thanks to his brother's heart, and that was where the problems started.

Canubis liked Casto, not just because he was Renaldo's missing part, but also for his stubborn and unbending personality. Once you got past his defenses, the young man was easy to like. He was also a king who had shown impressively what he was capable of at any time of the day. Canubis didn't feel threatened; his own dominance was too absolute. It was his nature, after all, just like Renaldo's nature was the fire, wild and untamed. He was worried, though. It was hard to read Casto, and Canubis still wasn't entirely sure if he could rely on the capricious blond like he had to.

Then there was all that trouble with Noran. The Wolf of War had silently watched the affair Renaldo had with the master smith shortly after he joined them. Since he himself had rarely said no to anybody before he met Noemi, he didn't have the right to interfere. When Noran had chosen Arja, Canubis had still held back. From his point of view, it had been a minor incident with little to no significance whatsoever. Well, he had been wrong about that one. Now he had to deal with an Emeris who was so riddled with guilt, he was hardly capable of performing his duties. Canubis wondered whether he should have a word with Noran. On the other hand, Hulda seemed to have taken this in hand. Interfering with her was unwise, to put it mildly. Besides, leaving the whole business to her made life easier for him.

Their latest addition, the demon called Sar'reff, was another problem he hadn't decided how to deal with yet. His sudden appearance had at least shed some light on Lys's nature, and so far, that was the best he could say about him. Canubis wasn't too keen on having two alien creatures who did not answer to his power inside the Pack. There was nothing he could do about Lysistratos, since he was irrefutably linked to Casto, but the other one was a different matter. Noemi thought it was a good thing to have him here, a notion her husband didn't share. If push came to shove, Lys would always side with Casto, and he was unpredictable. Most likely, Sar'reff would follow the stallion's example, since he hadn't found his anchor yet. And probably never would—putting him out of his misery might even be an act of mercy, just as Renaldo had suggested.

Losing the Luksari had been a low blow. Given the circumstances, they had to be grateful for getting out of their debt toward the young man almost unscathed, but the whole thing still left a bad aftertaste. Of course, it was hard to recognize a Luksari—not even Ana-Aruna was always dead-on—and there had been that damned spell, but still. He and Renaldo had not only not recognized what Sic was, they had also subjected him to their wrath and left him to Noran. It was the worst blunder Canubis had ever made in all his years as a leader. And now, of all times, when they had gotten so close to finally completing their ranks. It was infuriating. And stupid. If only—

One of the wolves who had been lying at his feet perked up. A single rider was approaching. The Wolf of War drew his sword, his eyes piercing the darkness.

"Whoever you are, come out and show yourself or I'll kill you."

There was a rustling in the bushes and then a thin, familiar voice answered.

"Please, don't do that, Master. It's me, Sic."

The smith emerged from the shadows, leading an unhappy horse toward the warlord.

"I'm sorry, I didn't mean to sneak up on you, but this one here isn't used to the wolves and she's kind of edgy."

Canubis indicated the predators to leave them alone and take up their posts a little farther from the camp. Once the wolves were gone, the mare calmed down enough for Sic to step closer.

"Thank you, Master."

"Sic, what brings you here? I'm thrilled to see you, but, to be frank, I expected to never meet you again."

The young man evaded his gaze.

"Can we go to the camp? I'd better show you."

Canubis furrowed his brow but followed the smith back to the fire in the middle of the camp. He could tell there was something strange about the young man, probably the awakening of his Luksari nature. At the fire, Renaldo was waiting for them. He had felt his brother's surprise and was curious about the reason. When he beheld Sic, his eyes widened.

"Sic! What are you doing here?"

The Luksari stepped into the light, his eyes shyly cast downward.

"Some things have happened, and now I want to ask your permission to return to the Valley with you."

"Something bad? You don't look very happy."

Thrilled about the prospect of getting Sic back, Canubis had to concentrate on not showing his excitement. The smith looked so crestfallen, his reason for returning had to be something serious.

"After you left, I had a visit from Ana-Isara. She kissed me."

Stunned silence followed these words. Then Canubis rushed forward.

"Show me."

Demurely, Sic took off his riding coat and opened his tunic. The warlords stared at the black runes glowing on the unmarred skin, unable to believe their own eyes. Here stood the last Emeris, the one they had been waiting for so long—it was too good to be true. Renaldo reached out to touch the signs with an expression of sheer awe on his regal face.

"This is so amazing. And so perfect." He hugged the smith gently. "Welcome to the family, brother. It's good to have you finally here."

"My brother is right—I'm glad we're now complete. Welcome, Lord Sic."

The oddly formal words made Sic realize how drastically and completely his life had changed. All of a sudden, he felt exhausted.

"I'm very tired, Masters. May I rest?"

"Of course. This must have been difficult for you."

Canubis patted his shoulder. "Go and have a good night's sleep. We can talk tomorrow."

"Casto will be thrilled. I can't wait to see his face." Renaldo radiated happy excitement, which made Sic feel even more miserable than before.

Then again, seeing Casto was the one thing he was actually looking forward to. He went to lie down and hesitated. On their journey to Ummana, things had been painful but clear. He had helped the other slaves to set up camp, served Noran as his personal toy, and then slept on the ground in the master smith's tent. It was not a place he wanted to visit right now, so he directed his steps toward the area where the common slaves slept. A heavy hand on his shoulder stopped him.

"What do you think you're doing?" Renaldo sounded apprehensive.

"I wanted to lie down. But if there's anything you want me to do, Master…."

"No! You don't have to do anything. And you're most certainly not going to sleep with the slaves. Come with me. You can have my place."

Sic was close to panicking. Having the aloof Angel of Death treat him like a treasured friend was too much after all the strain he'd had to endure. Desperately he tried to find a way out, but Renaldo was already dragging him toward his own tent. He shoved the struggling smith inside, pressing a finger to Sic's lips.

"Shh. Casto's sleeping, so try not to make too much noise. My furs are right next to him. Now take off your boots and rest. We'll talk about everything tomorrow."

Sighing, Sic obeyed the commands of his god, too tired to argue with the empty air, for Renaldo was already gone. Casto was sleeping soundly, his soft blond hair surrounding his face like a halo. He looked very young and vulnerable in his sleep, nothing like the stubborn, arrogant, and short-tempered man Sic had come to call his friend. When it came to hardships, they both had gotten more than their fair share. Being with Casto again was the only good thing he'd gotten out of the bargain with Ana-Isara. He was still afraid of her sons, and he dreaded having to deal with Noran again. It was too confusing, too painful. If he had still been a normal human, he could have evaded the master smith somehow, but now that he was an Emeris as well, there was no way he could ignore him. Sic would have to address his issues with his former owner, and the sooner, the better. The mere thought terrified him.

Well, there was nothing he could do right at the moment, so he took off his clothes, made himself comfortable on the furs, and was asleep before he even noted the velvet softness of his covers.

THE NEXT morning Sic woke with a start. Casto was looming over him like a hungry vulture, his face only a hand from the smith's nose.

"So you're finally awake. I thought you'd sleep the entire day. Why didn't you wake me when you came here?"

Sic smiled weakly. Talking to his friend again made him feel all tingly inside.

"Because a certain god who has the means to make my life unbearably miserable told me to let you sleep."

"Why would you listen to him? He's like a mother hen, so just ignore him."

"I can't do that, as you well know. I don't have your guts."

"I'm not that brave either, just annoyed as hell. He's really getting on my nerves. Now back to the issue at hand. Why are you here? I mean, I'm thrilled, don't get me wrong, but I do remember your reasons for staying in Ummana, and they were substantial. So what made you change your mind?"

Sic's face darkened.

"Not what. Who. I got a visit from the Empress of the Dead. Seems like we'll be staying together for quite some time."

It took a few moments for the words to sink in, and when they finally did, Casto's face was a sight to behold. Different emotions flickered across his features, among them joy, pity, regret, and fear. It moved Sic deeply to see how completely his friend understood him and how he felt with him. Finally, the king hugged the smith, his voice a harsh whisper.

"I can't say I'm sorry. I know how hard this must be for you. But I just can't say I'm sorry. For that, I'm too glad."

"I know. And you're the only one permitted to say so."

They were still basking in the intimate moment when Renaldo came barging in. Sic couldn't remember ever seeing the god so jittery with excitement.

"What are you two waiting for? There're lots of people out there who wish to welcome the new Emeris to the Pack. So get going. Get going."

"Easy, Barbarian. Sic has just woken up. He hasn't had breakfast yet."

"He can eat later. Now come!"

Renaldo grabbed Sic by the hand, dragging him into the morning light like an impatient toddler would his mother. In front of the tent, they were all gathered. Up front were Noemi and the Emeris—Hulda, Wolfstan, Kalad, Aegid, and Noran, although the master smith stayed back when the others approached their new brother. Behind them came the warriors and then the slaves. They all wanted to greet, or at least catch a glimpse of, the last Emeris. Sic was buried under an avalanche of hugs, kisses, and salutations. It was Canubis who rescued him in the end.

"It's enough! Sic has gone through a lot, and we still have to get back home before the winter storms set in. So while he eats his breakfast, it would be nice if the rest of you could put down the camp and prepare our departure."

THE JOURNEY back to the Valley was peaceful; no highwayman was crazy enough to go after the heavily armed baggage of the divine brothers. Sic spent a lot of his time with Hulda, who introduced him to the rules that would shape his life as an Emeris from now on. If he wasn't with the beautiful killer, he rode next to Casto. Most of the time, they kept their silence, simply enjoying each other's company. They didn't need words to understand each other. In the evenings, when the slaves erected the camp, the Angel of Death took Sic aside to teach him the basics of fighting. Sometimes Aegid and Kalad would accompany him and act as sparring partners. Renaldo was satisfied with Sic's progress.

"You're a fast learner, Sic. And you're talented. Soon you'll be able to stand your ground in any fight—except against me, of course."

Sic bowed demurely at receiving such praise.

"You're very gracious, my lord."

Renaldo put his hand on the young man's shoulder.

"You know you don't have to call me 'lord' anymore? At least not all the time."

"Yes, but I have to get used to the thought first. Not long ago I was worth even less than the dust beneath your feet. My sudden ascent is still confusing me."

The powerful warrior laughed out loud.

"You're not the first one. Believe me, you'll get used to it. In a hundred years' time, we'll think about this day and have a good laugh."

At the mention of his immortality, Sic still felt uneasy. He didn't want to imagine what it felt like to have all the time in the world. Right now he didn't want to think about anything at all.

When they were only a few days' ride from the Valley, Canubis sent a messenger to announce the happy news about their latest addition.

"We want the last Emeris to have accommodation befitting his rank," he had told his brother with a broad smile. Renaldo had reciprocated the smile. Both gods were in an exceptionally good mood, since the time of waiting was finally over for them.

The welcome to the Valley was as effusive as could be expected in view of such good news. Cornelia and Bantu had prepared an elaborate feast during which Sic was officially introduced as the eighth Emeris. A shower of gifts rained down on him, and his spartan rooms in the main house filled up quickly, a fact he mainly owed to Aegid. The intimidating giant had excellent taste and was eager to decorate Sic's new home.

More important to Sic than the pleasant housing was the small forge Renaldo had built for him adjacent to his chambers. Through a newly installed door, he could enter his working space any time he wanted. Since his rooms were facing west, away from those of the other Emeris, he wouldn't disturb them even when he started working early in the morning or stayed late into the night. Sic was so happy about this, he even managed to forget about Noran for a couple of minutes each day.

The master smith kept away from him. Even coincidental meetings were rare, although Sic longed to see his master's face. He hated himself for still loving the monster who had hurt him so much. The contradictory feelings tore him up inside, constantly gnawing at him, making his thoughts go round and round without ever coming to a solution. Even the peace in his smithy was disturbed by this emotional whirlwind.

Only during the training sessions with the Angel of Death was Noran completely erased from his thoughts for some time. The god was working him so mercilessly, he had trouble standing on his own two feet after each lesson. This overwhelming exhaustion helped him to stop his useless pondering, at least for a while.

Another reason for worry were the slaves he had received during the feast as part of a welcoming gift. The two men and three women still saw the traitor in him he had been at his departure in spring, and they acted accordingly. Not being able to bring himself to punish them didn't help his case at all. He was still musing how to solve this problem on his own, because he would rather die than ask any of his new brethren for help, when Casto took matters in hand. How his friend had found out about it, Sic didn't want to know, but it reminded him never to forget that Casto was far more than met the eye.

One day, his capricious friend waited in front of Sic's door with an elderly slave at his side.

"Sic, may I introduce Gweris to you? She's been working for Renaldo for ages, and from now on, she's going to take care of you. You're so busy at the moment, nobody can expect you to keep your slaves in line as well. Gweris is going to do that for you."

The slave bowed to him respectfully. Her voice was a soothing, congenial alto.

"My Lord Sic."

"Gweris. I'm honored to meet you. Please, come in."

The slave entered the room. Her friendly green-brown eyes narrowed when she took in the chaos inside. Her voice was stern when she talked to her new owner.

"Where are your slaves, Master?"

Sic blushed. "To be frank, I don't know."

With a last scornful glance, Gweris pushed the two young men out of her way.

"I understand. I'm going to take care of this."

Her tone of voice indicated that those on the receiving end of her wrath would regret their abhorrent behavior quite deeply. When she was gone, Casto's shoulders slumped forward.

"I admit, she's a bit scary, but she's also the best."

"Scary? You're kidding me, right? I almost lost control of my bladder, that's how terrified I am. Have you seen her eyes? She's almost as bad as Cassia. I think Gweris has only spared me right now because she was too busy being furious about my slaves. How can anybody own a woman like her?"

Casto grinned.

"Because she chooses her masters, which is the reason I brought her to you. Even Renaldo treads carefully around her. She's going to bring your servants to heel."

Embarrassed, Sic glanced at the ground. "How did you know?"

"I'm your friend, Sic. And a king, heart of a god, and not stupid. I can sense it when you're upset. This is a problem with which I can help you, so I did."

The underlying message in these words was clear. The king also knew about Sic's other problems, even though he wasn't able to offer useful counsel. His voice was very gentle.

"Perhaps you should talk to somebody who understands what you've been through. Once you think you're ready, I'm sure Cornelia will gladly listen to you."

Lost for words, Sic embraced Casto. He thanked the Mothers for blessing him with such a wonderful friend. It was up to him to prove that he was worthy of such grace.

In the meantime, Kalad and Aegid were sprawled on their huge bed, Daran lying between them, sleeping soundly after hours and hours of strenuous lovemaking. In order to celebrate their safe return to the Valley, the desert brothers hadn't held back when they enjoyed their delightful slave. Aegid was drawing lazy circles on the thief's still-hot skin, musing about how perfectly the three of them fitted together. Daran stirred a little in his sleep and the giant's fingers stopped their journey, not wanting to wake the young man. Instead, the warrior regarded the makeshift collar their slave was wearing. Because of the attack by Sar'reff, the original one had been damaged beyond repair. Until they could get a new one, the desert brothers had given Daran one of their old stock, which did not fit as well and had a clasp made of steel, not gold. It wasn't a satisfying solution at all, but now they were back home, they could get the young man a new one.

"What do you think, Kalad, should we go for a golden one this time? We still have that bag of pebble-sized emeralds somewhere, and I think it would suit the little thief very well."

"There's no need to concern yourself about such things, Aegid. We don't have to get Daran a new collar, for we're going to sell him in the near future."

Kalad's voice was level, as if he were stating a mere fact, not a decision with far-reaching consequences. Aegid sighed. This wasn't entirely unexpected, for he had known his desert brother for too long. It still was unwelcome, though. He was just about to open his mouth when Daran stirred again, making a mewling sound deep in his throat. Kalad looked grim.

"Let's move this discussion elsewhere."

They both got up stealthily and left the bedroom without making a sound. As soon as the door closed behind them, Daran's eyes snapped open. He had been just awake enough to hear about his masters' plans to sell him. It was like somebody had punched him in the guts. A long time ago, Daran had faced and accepted the fact that those two men were the center of his life, that he would always be theirs. And until now, he had thought they felt the same way about him. Nothing in their actions had ever woken any doubt in him, which made the blow even worse. Obviously, their feelings for him did not run as deep as his for them, and there was very little he could do to prevent his fate. But he could at least try. Maybe if he showed them how serious he was about being a good, obedient, and faithful slave, they would reconsider their decision. Daran clung to that thin straw of hope while tears of misery streamed down his cheeks.

In the main room, Aegid was glaring at Kalad. He usually followed the spry warrior's lead in everything, but this was an entirely different matter.

"Why in the Mothers' names do you want to sell him now?"

Kalad was tense. He had expected opposition, but the giant's fierceness came as a shock.

"You know why, Aegid. We have no choice."

"I'd say it's already too late. Face the truth, Kalad. We've fallen in love, and we've fallen hard. There's no turning back now. Besides, he's perfect for us. We've never had a lover who accepted our bond as wholeheartedly as Daran does. He's emphatic, intuitive, downright dirty when it suits him, and he's got the same humor as we do. There's nothing wrong about him. It's as if he was handcrafted just for us."

"I'm aware, Aegid. Which is why we have to end this now. End it before we get in too deep, before our world starts revolving around him."

"But it already does! And you know it. Back in Ummana, when he was on that stupid mission, you were even more worried than me, and when he was almost killed… we both were devastated. If that's not in too deep, then what are you afraid of?"

Kalad reached out for Aegid, resting his forehead on the huge man's chest. He sounded lost now, almost like a child.

"I just can't lose him, Aegid. I just can't. You know what it's like, how we all will suffer. And I don't want that. Call me selfish, but I don't want the drama. I don't want the pain. I most certainly don't want to watch the love of our lives wither and die while we can do nothing but stand on the sidelines. Until now, the two of us were always enough. Can't we go back to that?"

Aegid sighed deeply. Of course he understood his brother. He, too, wasn't too keen on all the complications a serious relationship with a human implied. But he had a nagging feeling that it was already too late. Daran had been with them for five years, enough time to fall deeply in love. And fallen they had. There was nothing that wasn't adorable about the little thief. He was intelligent, alluring in his own rough-hewn way, and simply outstanding in bed. Never before had the warriors enjoyed a sexual partner who was as willing, submissive, and—at the same time—demanding as Daran. He respected the bond between his masters, didn't try to get in between or play them against each other like others had tried before him. On the contrary, he seemed to be thrilled to have two owners instead of one.

And Daran always knew what his masters expected of him; he always behaved perfectly. So letting him go wasn't an option Aegid had ever considered seriously. Of course, it was their own fault. They should have gotten rid of Daran the moment they realized things were getting out of hand, but it had been too comfortable, too exciting to be with him. And now their tardiness had gotten back at them.

"What do you think we should do?"

Kalad's gaze hardened. As much as it hurt, there was only one answer to this question.

"We part ways with him. Better now than in the next year. The pain will only get worse."

Aegid sighed. He knew this was the best solution for all of them, Daran included, but he didn't want to lose the thief. So he tried reasoning with Kalad.

"How do you want to do that? Just letting him go? You know he's not fit to survive on his own."

Irritated, Kalad took a step backward. He, too, didn't really want to part with the thief, but unlike Aegid, he was terrified of the pain waiting for them should they keep Daran. It was better to let him go now than to receive the wound later, when it would leave even deeper scars.

"I'm aware of that. I want him well off, which is why I thought about sharing him with others. He'll learn to use sex as a weapon, and we can get used to the idea of not having him around anymore. Once he's learned to get by without us, we'll find him a rich lover outside the Valley. Given his looks and talents, it shouldn't be a problem."

"Sharing him, just like that? What if he doesn't give his consent?"

Kalad stared at his brother. He had never thought about that possibility. If Daran didn't want to, there was no way they could get him used to the touch of other people.

"I don't know. What do you think?"

"We could still sell him. I've been approached by various people who were interested in buying him—and willing to pay a hefty price for that privilege."

The brothers shared a look. There was no way they could ever bring themselves to simply sell Daran, no matter the sum. What this meant if their slave refused to start serving others as well, they didn't want to think about. It was too much like what they were wishing for from the bottom of their hearts.

"WELCOME, SIC. Casto has already mentioned that you wanted to visit me."

Cornelia's soft voice was like a balm for Sic's tumultuous thoughts. He had hesitated for more than three days over whether he should talk to the Emeris or not. In the end, he had chosen to do so simply because things couldn't get any worse than they were now. His thoughts were constantly circling around his former master, and he was getting tired of the torture. Whether Cornelia would be able to help him, he didn't know, but Casto was right. He had to talk to somebody who at least understood what it meant to be hurt like that. Nevertheless, he was still terrified of revisiting the past again. Not even Casto knew about the worst things Noran had done to him. All Sic wanted was to forget. It helped that the scars on his body were gone, but the ones on his soul couldn't be so easily cured, not even by Ana-Isara.

Some nights, he woke up screaming and covered in sweat because a faceless stranger was torturing him sadistically. They were the things his master had done to him, but when he woke, he craved Noran's presence.

All he wanted then was to be held and comforted by the master smith. The contrariness of his feelings, the equivocality of his own thoughts, nourished fears that threatened to consume him. He was no longer able to see the wonder and beauty in small things, like a leaf tinted by autumn. His ability to take pleasure from things apparently mundane to others was diminished by an overwhelming fear that held his heart in a squeezing grip. Cornelia was probably his last chance to change things.

"I hope my visit is not inconvenient?"

Cornelia's rough features brightened in a friendly smile. Sic didn't know much about this woman, except that her singing voice had the power to move even stones to tears. She was responsible for the smooth operation of all the daily affairs in the Valley, as well as looking after and taking care of the countless slaves who didn't have one specified owner but served all the mercenaries. She was also the only Emeris who never showed up for the Spring Ceremony and who didn't have the slightest interest in any sexual flings. Given what she had been through, this was understandable. Now she motioned him inside.

"No, it's not. Come in, I'm going to make some tea."

Sic watched in silence as the Emeris put a kettle on the iron stove, filled a small linen bag with various herbs she took from heavy glass jars lined up in the cupboard, and then poured the boiling water over it. She placed two cups with spoons and a jar of honey on the table, and sat down.

"I assume you wish to talk to me about the things you've endured at Noran's hand. Am I right?"

Sic felt crimson invading his cheeks. This was going to be even harder than he had imagined.

"Only if you want, my lady. I know how painful this is."

Cornelia smiled again, but this time there was a darkness underneath which made Sic flinch. She poured him some tea and pushed the honey toward him.

"Take plenty. Discussions like this one need lots of sweetness to help bear the pain."

Obediently Sic stirred two generous helpings of honey into his beverage before he looked up. He didn't know where to start. Fortunately, the Emeris took the decision from him. She started to tell her story in a dispassionate voice, as if the horrible things she had endured had been done to somebody else.

"I was twenty when it happened. Because of my looks, I hadn't found a husband yet and was completely inexperienced. I had resigned myself to staying unmarried for the rest of my life. Since I had my brother and my music, this wasn't bad at all. I was genuinely happy.

"Then the marauders came. Back then, times were difficult. There was always a war going on somewhere. There was always an army marching past. Our village was so tiny and poor, it usually stayed unnoticed. The men who ambushed us had just lost a battle. They had managed to escape from the slaughter and were drunk from all the fear they had felt, all the terrible things they had seen. They passed our village and decided to revenge themselves on us.

"It was harvesting time, so most of the men and a good portion of the women were out in the fields. The few who had stayed behind had no chance whatsoever against the invaders. They killed the old folks and the children without mercy. The smallest ones hadn't learned to walk yet. Then they herded us women to the square. We were six, they were thirty. We didn't stand a chance.

"They raped us, again and again, mutilated our bodies beyond imagining, and crushed our souls. In the end, I was the only one who survived, but it was a close call. And sometimes I wonder whether those who died weren't the luckier ones. I'm carrying the scars on my body and soul with me, and they remind me every day what I had to endure."

Cornelia fell silent for a moment, her hands trembling.

"All this happened a long time ago, and yet it still hurts to talk about it, although I know that those who did this to me have long since become dust."

"Have you forgiven them?"

A strange light appeared in her eyes, a light that terrified Sic, for it made Cornelia's face look like that of a creature born from nightmares.

"Forgiveness is a big word. I'm still not sure what it truly means and if I'm able to offer it. Those men hurt me both physically and mentally, but they couldn't destroy who I am, for I was too strong. So in a certain sense, I have triumphed over them. But if I will ever forgive them—I don't think so. If they were still alive and I could get my hands on them, I'd probably do things to them that would make their crimes appear harmless in comparison. Once you've gone through what we had to endure, you have to learn the meaning of forgiveness and mercy anew. I'm not sure if I really want that."

Perturbed Sic stared into his tea. "Can something like this be forgiven?"

He looked up when Cornelia caressed his arm.

"I guess it depends on the kind of person you are. I assume you don't know whether you should forgive Noran?"

"It's complicated. He's not a stranger, nobody I can hate wholeheartedly. He saved my life when he bought me from Dalwon. For more than eight years, the better part of my life, he was the center of my world. Admittedly, he was never easy, but he was always fair toward me. I was never punished without reason or treated cruelly like Dalwon used to do. Noran had been really kind. He deserved my gratitude and love.

"When I betrayed him, it was only just that I was punished brutally. What I did cannot be forgiven. And yet he allowed me to stay alive…."

"But?"

"But he had no right to abuse my love for him to make me compliant. He forced me, took me against my will, but the worst thing was that he made me grateful for it. In the beginning, I was just glad he still acknowledged me.

"When he started becoming crueler, I began to hate him, or at least I thought it was hatred. But why do I crave seeing him? Why do I want to hear his voice so badly? I would give everything if things could go back to the way they were before my betrayal. I can't stop wondering whether it was my fault in the end. I don't know much about his past, but Hulda told me Noran has been betrayed before. What I did must have been like a blow to the face, especially after he had started treating me so well. I forced his hand, and I abhor myself for it."

Sic was crying now. The tears streamed down his cheeks and fell into the tea and on the table. Cornelia got up and took him in her arms.

"Shh, Sic. It's fine. Let the pain go. Let everything go. You have all the time in the world, so take it."

For a long time, they sat there, Sic cradled in the arms of the Emeris. The sun had started going down on the mountains when the smith finally calmed down. Cornelia caressed his cheeks soothingly.

"I don't envy you, Sic. The men who raped me were strangers, and the only thing I ever felt for them was hatred. Your relationship with Noran is a lot more complicated, and I only begin to understand how difficult this must be for you. To be honest, I don't know what I should tell you." She paused. "Except that you have to forgive yourself first before you can even think about forgiving him. Things have changed drastically for you, Sic. Yes, you did betray Noran, but you did it out of love. No matter the outcome, your actions were not designed to deliberately hurt him and he had no right to do to you what he did. He should have been able to see past the obvious and acknowledge how hard this has been for you. Instead he acted like a child, lashing out at the one person who loved him unconditionally. That is his sin, not yours and you should not take on that burden in addition to your own. In the end, you have to follow your heart in this."

The young man looked up.

"My heart says I love him, no matter what he's done. But Cornelia, he has never told me he loves me. He admitted that he wanted to destroy me. I'm in love with a man who doesn't give a damn about me."

Again Sic started to cry, deep, throaty sobs, after speaking out loud for the first time what agonized him so much. Cornelia watched him helplessly. She realized there was no helping the young Emeris, that nothing she could say would change anything. She patted his shoulders.

"Perhaps you should try getting your mind off him. You're a man, so you don't have to be on the receiving end during sex. Not being the victim, but the one in control, could help you gain a new perspective."

Sic stared at her with bloodshot eyes.

"You mean regarding the Spring Ceremony?"

"Not necessarily. Renaldo and Canubis would understand if you refuse to participate."

The smith's shoulders slumped.

"I could never do that to them. It's the first Spring Ceremony with all the Emeris present, the first time they'll hold the ceremony as full-fledged gods again. I know how unbelievably important this is to all of you."

"You're a good man, Sic. Yes, it is important for us all. I haven't been in the Valley for as many centuries as Aegid or Kalad, but I've been here long enough to know how tiring the waiting has been. We all can feel the shift, and we're all very excited. Still, you should listen to your heart. You're going to live for a long time, Sic, and no matter what the poets may tell you, time does not, as a rule, heal all of your wounds. This is something you have to do yourself."

Overwhelmed by misery, the smith slumped forward.

"So what should I do?"

"Try something new. Escape your old ways. Go to Aegid and Kalad—they've tons of experience with noncommittal sex. I'm sure they'll be able to help you. Try it. Even if it doesn't work, you can still say you made the effort. Don't get caught up in this monster of a relationship you have with Noran. Things will sort themselves out once you gain a little perspective. And let me stress again how important it is for you to forgive yourself."

She smiled warmly. "Of course, you're always welcome to visit me. I like you, Sic. You're a good, gentle man. Usually I'm only this relaxed around my brother."

Confronted with such trust, Sic bowed low to his new sister.

"You're very kind, my lady. I'll gladly accept your offer."

"THE TIME has come, brother. We've our first opportunity to quit Daran."

Aegid's face was dark when he spoke those words; he was still not happy about Kalad's plan but didn't have a better idea.

"Who?" Kalad's voice sounded strained. He wasn't happy either. Since the night they had decided to part ways with Daran, his mood had hit a new low point every day.

"Sic. I just talked to him, and he asked for our help. He wants to deal with what Noran has done to him, and he wants to start by finding out what it feels like when he's in control during sex." Aegid sighed, not happy at all. "It's almost as if the Mothers have orchestrated this. Sic is inexperienced and friendly. We can be absolutely sure Daran won't be hurt. And he's our brother-in-arms, so he's family as well."

Kalad straightened. He knew there wouldn't be a candidate better suited for their plan than the new Emeris. "Let's go ask Daran."

The young thief had just returned from a riding session with Casto and was exhausted. When he saw the serious expressions on his masters' faces, he knew something was off. His heart started beating loudly in his chest for fear they would tell him he was already sold.

Kalad spoke first. "Daran, we want to ask you something. It's very important, so listen closely. Do you understand?"

Dazed, the young man nodded.

"As you know, Sic has gone through some horrible experiences concerning the bed. We want to help him get over his trauma. If you agree, we would take you to him tonight. It's a great responsibility, since he's inexperienced. He's going to need your help and guidance. Do you think you can do it?"

No! Daran wanted to shout in their faces. He couldn't do it. The thought alone of anybody but his masters touching him made bile rise in his mouth, yet he knew he had to give his consent. If he didn't want the brothers to sell him anytime soon, he had to demonstrate his absolute obedience to them, even if it meant lying. When he answered, he refrained from looking at them.

"This is kind of unexpected, Master, but I'm going to do it. Lord Sic is very friendly, and he deserves happiness."

Aegid and Kalad exchanged a look. They hadn't thought Daran would give his consent so easily, and they felt a painful sting when they realized the young man wasn't as committed to them as they were to him. Anger flared in Kalad's eyes, but Aegid raised a warning brow and his brother contained himself.

"That's very generous of you. Take the rest of the day off and make yourself presentable. We want Sic to be as comfortable as possible."

With his gaze still cast down and his heart beating like a war drum, Daran retreated. The desert brothers stayed in the main room, both busy getting their emotions under control and telling themselves that everything was fine, that they were glad about how things were turning out.

It was the biggest lie ever.

A SHARP knock pried Sic from the draft he was pondering. He was planning to make a special dagger for Casto, a small token of gratitude for all the things he had done. Sighing, he went to get the door, a little miffed about the disturbance. Kalad stood in front of him, a cheerful smile on his face and Daran waiting behind him.

"Sic, may we enter?"

"Of course. Please forgive me, Mas—please excuse my rudeness. I didn't expect a visit so late."

Kalad's brow arched. It hadn't escaped him that the last Emeris still had problems embracing his new standing.

"I've been talking to Aegid, and he's told me about your problem. We discussed it, and here is your solution."

He grabbed Daran's wrist and pushed him toward Sic.

"You already know Daran. He's well-behaved and glad to help you. Whatever you're asking for, Daran will be thrilled to give it to you. Isn't that so, little thief?"

The young man looked at his owner, full of love.

"Whatever my master wishes."

Kalad patted the young man's cheek before he turned to the door.

"Enjoy yourself, Sic. Don't hesitate about anything. This night is yours alone."

Despite the cheerfulness in the desert warrior's tone, Sic could sense an underlying tension, which left him insecure about what to do. Before he could react, Kalad had vanished through the door. Embarrassed, Sic regarded Daran, who had, until recently, outranked him by far and was now standing in front of him with his gaze demurely cast down.

He wore dark green linen trousers that hung low on his hips. His naked torso was slick with oil, the well-defined muscles highlighted by the light of the candles. As usual, he had his long hair in a braid. A hint of kohl accentuated his expressive brown eyes.

Sic had the feeling the young man wasn't comfortable, but was afraid to confirm it, since he wasn't sure it wasn't him projecting his own feelings of insecurity. Daran moved slightly, and Sic approached him hastily.

"Are you all right, Daran? Do you want to sit down? Are you thirsty? Or hungry?"

The thief looked up, amusement and something darker and more dangerous sparkling in his eyes.

"No, I'm fine, Lord Sic. I'm waiting for your orders."

"Orders?"

"How you want me to be."

"How I want you…. To be honest, Daran, I don't have the faintest idea. What do your masters usually do with you?"

Daran shrugged. Again Sic got the impression that the young man was trying hard to suppress his true feelings, to maintain a façade, but before he could confirm his hunch, the thief answered him.

"Whatever they please. When they're already aroused, they don't waste time on formalities, and just order me to undress. When they're in the mood to play games, I make a little show of stripping for them, and in turn they take their sweet time teasing me. It's entirely up to you."

Sic tried to make up his mind.

"What do you want, Daran? How do you wish to be taken?"

Hastily the young man lowered his gaze. Still, Sic had caught a glimpse of the crimson in his cheeks. The feeling that Daran didn't really want him, that he hated being here, was overwhelming for a moment.

"What I want is irrelevant. You've heard my master—this night is for you. I'm whatever you want me to be."

Somewhat reassured by those words, Sic approached the thief slowly. Carefully, as if he was afraid to burn himself, he reached out and touched Daran's face. Then he leaned in to kiss him, only to stop a hand from the slave's face. Whatever the young man had just told him, there was no way he was here voluntarily. Sic reared back.

"I think we'd better not do this. Thank you for offering such an opportunity to me, but I simply can't do this. You can leave, Daran."

The thief looked up in surprise. The tiniest hint of relief tainted his voice. "You're sending me away, Master? Have I made a mistake or offended you? If so, then please punish me and allow me to make up for my blunder."

"You didn't do anything wrong, Daran. I'm just not ready for this yet. You can go back to your masters. Tell them I'm grateful."

Slowly Daran turned to the door. It was obvious he was torn.

"As you wish, my lord."

After Daran had gone, Sic fell down on one of his lounges with a sigh. He did not know whether he should be relieved or sad about what had just happened. Mainly he was glad he was no longer responsible for making the night a success. Still in turmoil, he decided to get back to his drafts. There was a tricky problem still waiting to be solved. He had just begun with a new sketch when the knocking started on his door again, this time a lot more aggressive than before. It seemed as if his work wasn't meant to be done tonight. He only hoped it wasn't one of his brothers-in-arms again, trying to help him.

It was Aegid *and* Kalad, both enraged, dragging a contrite Daran so brutally into the room that he fell on his knees in front of Sic. Kalad didn't bother with any polite conversation.

"Sic, what has this piece of trash done to make you send him away? Speak freely, because we'll use it as measurement for the severity of his punishment."

Taken aback by the sudden outburst, Sic raised his hands. The desert brothers' wrath had obviously not much to do with Daran's behavior toward the new Emeris. Where the problem really was, Sic couldn't tell, and so he tried to smooth things over as best he could.

"Kalad, please, calm down. I assure you, Daran's behavior was blameless. It's my fault, and I'm sorry you underwent all this trouble. I'm just not ready. Your slave really tried to help me."

The furious warrior turned to the kneeling thief.

"Is that true, slave? Have you been obedient?"

"Yes, Master. At least, I tried. Perhaps I wasn't convincing enough, I don't know. Please, forgive me."

"Kalad, I assure you, he's done nothing wrong."

The Emeris's features softened a little.

"Stand up."

Trembling, Daran obeyed. Imploringly he looked up at his owner, who extended his hand to caress his face.

"I'm sorry, little thief. It seems I've punished you without reason."

With his eyes closed, the thief leaned into his master's touch.

"You own me. It's your right."

Fascinated, Sic watched as all fearful tension vanished from Daran's body while he completely gave in to his master's gentle hands. Aegid stepped close to Sic, his voice soft. Something had just changed; the smith could feel the shift in his bones. Whatever was going on between Daran and his masters had calmed down considerably, at least for the moment.

"If you want, we'll show you how much fun sex can be."

Taken by surprise, Sic turned to the giant.

"You would do that for me?"

Aegid chuckled good-naturedly.

"Of course. You're our brother. We're glad to be of help. Besides"—his eyes lit up in amusement—"sometimes we like having an audience. Relax and enjoy the show."

With this he went to his brother and Daran, slung the young man's braid around his wrist, bent his head back, and started kissing him. Kalad left his slave's mouth to his brother's ministrations, his hands stroking lovingly over Daran's torso, his lips fastened on the thief's right nipple while he got rid of his trousers. Daran's member came up hard. Groaning, he rubbed himself against Aegid, who was now entering him with two fingers. Helpless in his lust, the thief hung between the strong bodies of his masters, willing and ready.

Sic's breathing hitched, his own erection waking in reaction to the open display of lust in front of him. This was indeed different than everything he had experienced so far. Daran showed no hints of fear or shyness toward his masters; on the contrary, it was obvious how utterly he trusted them. He offered himself without fearing the strength of the brothers.

Now Kalad guided the young man toward one of the lounges. Daran knelt between his owner's spread legs and started licking his penis hungrily while Aegid stepped forward, his own impressive erection standing up like a terrifying weapon. His big hands parted Daran's backside, and he entered in one graceful thrust.

Sic realized he had held his breath in fearful anticipation. Full of awe, he watched as Daran took his master into his body, not in pain but with a content whimper, as if this was all he had ever wished for. Given the size of Aegid, Sic had assumed he would hurt the slave, but Daran only showed lust, not pain.

The warriors poured their essence into the willing body of their slave; then they changed places and everything started anew. After they had found their relief a second time, Kalad pulled Daran up, and his hand closed heavily around the young man's hardness.

"Which one of us shall make you come, slave?"

Daran whimpered lustfully, his answer hardly audible. "I'm yours. It's not my place to decide."

Satisfied with this answer, Kalad shoved his tongue into Daran's ear. "Good boy."

Aegid grabbed the young man's face with both hands and started kissing him passionately while Kalad entered him at the same time. He took him with hard thrusts that would have forced Daran to his knees had it not been for Aegid holding him upright. The desert warriors made their slave orgasm twice. Then Aegid sat down on the lounge again, dragged Daran with him, and held him down. Kalad turned to Sic.

"Did you like it?"

The smith nodded with big eyes. He was so fascinated and aroused, he was unable to speak. Kalad grinned knowingly.

"Then come. Take off your trousers."

Shivering with excitement, Sic obeyed. His hands were trembling. With an encouraging smile, Kalad took his hand and led him to the kneeling Daran. His fingertips skimmed over the trembling cheeks that were presented so boldly. With two fingers, Kalad slid into the slave, who started groaning.

"As you can see, the boy wants it badly. He can't wait to serve you, isn't that right, little thief?"

"Master, please take me."

Daran's voice was choked, his anus twitching excitedly. Again Sic had the feeling that he was making a mistake, that Daran didn't want him, but he shook it off. The slave had given his consent, and his owners had offered him so generously; why should he reject their kindness?

Hesitantly, he placed his hands on the young man's hips. Kalad was standing right next to him, cheering him on.

"Very good. Now enter him. Daran is very tight, so you'll have to use some force, but rest assured, you're not hurting him. You've seen how he's taken Aegid in without any problems."

Sic nodded, gathered all his courage, and thrust.

It was exquisite, tight and wet and wonderful. Daran's muscles contracted rhythmically around him, holding him like a velvet fist, waiting for something Sic didn't understand.

Kalad's hand fell down heavily on Daran's left cheek, leaving a red mark on the soft skin. His voice was sharp.

"Pull yourself together, slave. This is for Sic, not for you."

A groan escaped Daran's throat, and his entire body seemed to tighten; then the twitching stopped and he relaxed. Kalad stroked the slave's back as if he were a dog.

"Very good, little thief."

He turned to Sic.

"He's all yours. Take him in your own time, the way it feels good for you. He's already had his fun, so don't feel bad for him."

Gratefully Sic nodded toward his brother-in-arms before he concentrated on the young man in front of him. The physical feeling was magnificent. Sic had never felt so alive before. Taking Daran was like drinking very old wine; it left one slightly tipsy and completely relaxed.

If it hadn't been for the nagging feeling in the back of his head that he was making a terrible mistake, Sic would have labeled this moment as one of the best in his entire life.

Aegid and Kalad left him hours later. Hours during which they had taken Daran again and again, hours during which they had showed Sic what a skilled lover could do to a willing partner. When they left, Aegid was carrying the exhausted Daran in his arms.

Sic was worried about the young man. "Is he all right?"

Kalad grinned saucily.

"Of course. He'll be a little sore tomorrow, but we'll let him sleep in so he can recover. Everything's fine, little thief, isn't it?"

Tired, Daran lifted his head, and his brown eyes lit up.

"Of course, Master." He turned to Sic. "Lord Sic. I wish you a good night."

Sic gulped. What he had seen in Daran's eyes sent shudders down his spine. The thief had most definitely not wanted this. And he, Sic, had taken him against his will, although he had sensed the truth right from the start. Quickly he glanced away.

"I wish you a good night as well, Daran. And thank you for your kindness."

The desert brothers left Sic's chambers with their tired slave.

2. CRIME AND PUNISHMENT

RESTLESS, SIC tossed around in his bed, threw aside the fur he had used for a blanket, only to grab it again a short time later. For more than two hours he had been trying in vain to find sleep, but whenever he closed his eyes, he was confronted with Daran's smooth features and the reproach in his dark eyes. He had made a terrible mistake; there was no way around it. In hindsight, he should have known from the start. The entire situation had been beyond bizarre. For one, why would the desert brothers even think about sharing their precious thief with somebody else? Until now, anybody who had so much as stared at the young man for too long had been subjected to their glares and open displays of displeasure. And Daran—he was so completely theirs. How could he ever agree to get involved with somebody else? Sic doubted that what had happened the previous night had just been an act of kindness toward him. Something much more complicated was going on, and such was his luck that he had been sucked into it.

Annoyed, he sat up. There was no way he would be able to find sleep, so he might as well start working again. The sketches for the dagger meant for Casto were still on the drawing board, since he hadn't found out how to pleat the steel to get the pattern he was aiming for yet. He stared at the drafts with an empty gaze, his thoughts digressing, returning to Daran and the previous night, which somehow had made things even worse than before. Sic regretted deeply not having sent the desert brothers and their slave away when he had the chance.

The sun was already high in the sky when Sic finally decided to take action. He gathered a present that he hoped would show Daran clearly how sorry he was for what had happened. Then he went to the chambers of the desert brothers. His knock was answered by Daran, who looked bleary, as if he had just gotten up. Nevertheless, he greeted Sic demurely.

"Lord Sic, good morning. What can I do for you?"

The smith swallowed hard.

"May I bother you for a moment? I'd like to talk to you."

Wordlessly, Daran stepped aside. He closed the door and stood expectantly in front of Sic, still avoiding his gaze.

"I'm sorry about yesterday, Daran. I was an idiot."

"I don't understand, Master."

At the sight of Daran, who looked so guilt-ridden himself, Sic wished, not for the first time in his life, that he could turn back time. As gently as he could, he said what he had to say, hoping to do the right thing at least now.

"I know you didn't want me. I could sense it. And yet I took you, and I regret it deeply. I had no right to do so. This is for you."

He offered the flat package to the thief.

"It's not meant as a bribe. What I've done can't be compensated with material goods, I know that all too well myself. But it should remind you that I owe you. Whatever you need, you only have to tell me, and you can be sure I'll do anything to help you. And should you decide to charge me for my despicable behavior, I'll understand."

Speechless, Daran stared at the last Emeris. He didn't know what he had expected, but surely not this. His voice cracked when he answered.

"Lord, it wasn't your fault. If anything, it was mine. I agreed to sleep with you. There was no way you could have known."

"But I did, Daran. I saw it in your eyes. I'm so sorry."

Tentatively the young man stepped forward and placed a hand on Sic's arm.

"Master, it really is fine. You didn't hurt me, I even had my fun. Nobody has come to harm."

Sadly, Sic took the thief's hand in his.

"No, Daran. You have come to harm. Why did you give your consent?"

Blushing, Daran looked down. "My masters really wanted to help you. And I don't want to disappoint them, which is why I acquiesced to their wish. It was my own decision."

"Do they know about the sacrifice you've made?"

Daran shook his head. "No. All I want is to obey them, to please them. Don't fret it, Lord. Everything's fine."

"You're very generous, Daran. I thank you from the bottom of my heart."

The young man smiled crookedly.

"As I said, it was my decision. If there's anything to forgive, I've done so."

Sic regarded the thief for a long time, pondering all the strange and utterly crazy things love made people do. Then he kissed Daran's hand.

"I'm your friend, Daran. Now even more than before last night. You can rely on me. And don't worry, it's never a mistake to love. And whom we love—well, that's not up to us to decide."

"You're a wise man, Lord Sic. I thank you for the present. Although it really wasn't necessary."

Thinking he had at least expressed his regret in a befitting manner, Sic left Daran. At first he thought he would return to his smithy, but his feet kept wandering aimlessly through the Valley while his thoughts raced in his head.

Even though Daran had been so generous to take on most of the blame, it didn't change the fact that he had ignored the thief's needs in favor of satisfying his own. He had been an Emeris for only a short time, but it seemed as if he had already lost all empathy for those who'd outranked him not so long ago. Sic was disgusted with himself. He knew all too well what it felt like to be forced, to be a prisoner to circumstances. The ugly truth was that he had known exactly what he had been doing, justifying it by thinking it was his right. Because wasn't he an Emeris, some kind of demigod, if the prophecies were true? What did he care about the will of a slave, who had even given his consent?

It was despicable to think along such lines.

A steady hammering pried him from his musings. He was standing in front of Noran's smithy, which had been his home for more than eight years. As aimless and tumultuous as his mind might be, his body knew where it belonged. The hammering stopped. Sic became aware that he was being eyeballed by everybody present, starting with the youngest apprentice up to the seasoned fellows. It was too much. He started to turn away, to leave this place where nobody had ever been his friend, where he had experienced only envy and hatred. At the same moment, the door to Noran's private rooms smashed open and the master stormed out with a thunderous expression on his face.

Without thinking Sic knelt down, since he knew that mood only too well. Noran was close to a formidable rampage. His dark voice reverberated through the smithy.

"You damn bunch! Get on your knees and show Sic the respect due to an Emeris. When you're done, leave. I'll deal with your lack of manners tomorrow."

It was a bizarre situation, each smith honoring Sic while he got up again. He was relieved Noran wasn't angry about him, although he didn't know how to behave.

When the last fellow had left, they stood in front of each other in silence, the quiet between them spreading like blood from the corpse of a freshly killed enemy. Noran finally managed to speak.

"I'm very pleased to see you, Sic. Is there anything I can do for you?"

Sic looked up. The words coming from his former master enlightened him as to what he wanted.

"Would you allow me to watch you while you work, Master? Just like old times?"

The smith's features softened.

"I'd be happy to, Sic."

Relieved, Sic followed Noran into the familiar gloom. The sound from the smithy, the soft rustling of the coals in the forge, the tingling when steel brushed against steel, the glugging of water in the big buckets used for cooling—all this was like a soothing embrace. He felt a deep calm rising inside him, one he hadn't known since his betrayal. Not even the anvil to which he had been chained during the last eight months could disturb the peace he felt.

He was finally home.

With a satisfied sigh, he sat down on the spot where he had used to watch his master after he had fulfilled all his duties.

Noran was working on a sword, and Sic admired the virtuosity with which the smith created a lethal, elegant weapon from a crude lump of metal. The master's exuberant strength was like an exquisite piece of art that Sic would never grow tired of looking at.

The sun had already set when Noran finished his work. Sic got up, insecure. The hush that had been soothing until now was about to tip to the opposite once more. Again it was Noran who took the initiative.

"Are you feeling unwell, Sic? You look haunted."

For a moment the young man hesitated, then decided to admit his disgrace.

"I'm desperate, Master. I've done somebody an injustice and don't know how to make up for it."

"First of all, you don't have to call me 'master' anymore, Sic. We are equals now. And second, you did an injustice? I don't think so, Sic. You're not capable of such things."

Intently Sic examined his fingertips. He didn't react to Noran's announcement about them being equals—at the moment, he had more pressing problems.

"I was capable. I've taken Daran, the slave of Aegid and Kalad, against his will."

Sic felt Noran's stare burning holes into his nape. The master's voice was raw.

"I don't believe you. You would never do something like that! Tell me what happened."

Sic took a deep breath. "I had asked the brothers for help. They wanted to show me how physical contact with somebody else can be fun."

When he saw the pain in Noran's eyes, he regretted his choice of words immediately. He had never thought he would be able to cause another being such agony.

"Please forgive me, Master. I didn't mean to—"

But Noran stopped him with his hand held high.

"It's okay, Sic. This is my sin, and it's only just that I'm reminded of my mistakes on a regular basis. The two wanted to help you?"

"Yes. Kalad had brought me Daran, but I didn't know what to do and sent him back. Later, both of them came to me again and showed me how to handle him. Which was odd, since they're usually so jealous about anybody who has contact with Daran."

"This doesn't sound as if Daran was opposed to it."

"He wasn't. At least, he said he wasn't. But I'd seen it in his eyes, how much he resented me, although his mouth told a different story. And yet I took him, because I thought it was my right. Because I wanted it."

"As far as I can tell, the fault lies with Kalad and Aegid. He's their slave. They should know when something is amiss."

Sic shook his head. Noran was missing the point here.

"It doesn't change my responsibility. Do you know what the worst part was? It wasn't even fun. My urges were satisfied and it felt good, yes, but there were no emotions, no bond. All I could think of was you, Master."

Noran made a croaking sound.

"Sic, I'm so terribly sorry. I would give my right arm, even my life to undo the terrible crimes I committed against you. I regret deeply how my sin is still haunting you."

The master smith's reaction gave Sic the courage to keep on talking, to bare his soul a little more to the man who was both his nightmare and his savior.

"It is indeed haunting me, your sin. But that's not what I was thinking about while I was with Daran. I was fantasizing about what could have been between us, what I had been wishing for so eagerly. I had the feeling I was betraying you—us—all over again."

"Sic, you can't be serious, not after everything I've done to you. And I assure you, you can't betray me, because for that to happen, I'd have to have a right over you, which I don't. I thank the Mothers on my knees for the smallest place you may offer me in your life, but if you throw me out, you don't have to justify yourself. Not to me, certainly."

His master's voice sounded so desperate, Sic felt himself moved and encouraged to share the confusion of his feelings with the person who had caused them.

"Master. You're my world. You've been the center of my life from the day you saved me from Dalwon's grasp. Everything I do is intended to please you. Even when you punished me so cruelly, I was still hoping to gain your forgiveness. As much as I may resent it, nothing will ever change that. I'll always be yours. And now I don't know what to do, and it's eating me up inside."

Speechless, Noran stared at the love of his life. He would have never dared to hope to hear such promising words from the young man. Overwhelmed by this unexpected, completely undeserved mercy, he sank to his knees. When he tried to take Sic's hands in his own, his former slave made a hasty step back, his body suddenly tense. Noran lowered his hands, desperate to convey his feelings to him.

"I swear on everything dear to me, Sic, you'll never regret this. I will never hurt you again or do anything you don't want. From now on, I'm going to treat you like the precious treasure you are, I promise."

Taken aback by this outburst, Sic retreated even further. This felt somehow right; he wasn't uncomfortable, just very anxious, for it was happening so fast. If he wanted this to work, they had to slow down the pace.

"I believe you. I really do. But I'm going to need time. Too much has happened this year that I still haven't come to terms with. Before we can reshape our relationship, I have to deal with my new status and all the change it brings, otherwise I won't be able to decide what I really want. Perhaps we can start by no longer avoiding each other?"

Noran slowly got up. This was beyond what he had hoped could transpire between him and Sic. He was eager to show the young man his willingness.

"Whatever you wish, Sic. This time, you're the one to set the terms. I will no longer avoid you and will try to behave normally around you."

Sic smiled shyly.

"That would be a nice start. I'm not going to lie to you, Master. I want to forgive you, but I don't know if I'll ever be able to do so. First, I guess, I have to learn to trust you again."

Noran tried hard not to appear too forward.

"You don't have to forgive me. If I were you, I probably wouldn't be able to do it. I'm already thrilled that you're even considering it."

"Then we can start anew?"

It was an anxious question, one that showed how deeply the cuts between them ran. Noran was aware of the monstrous task lying ahead, but the mere fact that he had been allowed to take the first step on this long journey made him giddy with joy.

"Yes, we can start anew. Let's see where time will take us, okay?"

Pure relief flooded Sic. This day, which had started out as a complete failure, had suddenly brightened up considerably.

"I thank you, Master. And I wish you a good night."

"I wish you a good night as well, Sic."

The last Emeris left the smithy lighthearted and, for the first time in weeks, at peace with himself.

"DARAN, GET your pretty ass over here right now!"

Kalad sounded so irritated, Daran hurried to do his bidding. Since he had overheard his masters' discussion about selling him, the moods of the two warriors had taken a turn for the worse on a daily basis, although Daran tried everything within his power to please them. This only served to confirm his fear that his masters had grown tired of him and wanted to get rid of him as soon as possible.

Kalad had just come back from an errand. His gaze was fixed on the package Lord Sic had brought only a few hours ago. When he remembered that discussion, Daran felt his heart constrict with reproach. The smith's guilty conscience, the agony he was going through because he thought he had done to Daran what he himself once had to endure, had overwhelmed the thief. In his desperate attempt to please his masters, he hadn't thought about the consequences of his actions. While he had tried to calm the Emeris, Daran had understood for the first time why Aegid and Kalad abhorred lies so deeply—they never amounted to anything good. Now Daran was getting the uncomfortable feeling he would be paying the price for this particular lie in the near future.

"What's that?"

Kalad eyed the package with suspicion, as if it would burst into flames at any minute. Daran raised his hands in a soothing gesture.

"It's a present from Lord Sic."

The warrior's forehead wrinkled.

"For us?"

"No, for me."

Kalad's lively eyes drilled into Daran's bent neck.

"Why would Sic want to give you something? Yesterday was good, but not good enough to merit a present."

Trembling, Daran reached for the worn collar around his throat; then he knelt down, anticipating Kalad's rage when he heard his next words.

"It's not a present, per se, but a plea for forgiveness."

"Daran." Kalad's voice had now a threatening undercurrent. "If you don't tell me right now what's going on here, you're in deep shit, and that's a promise."

Daran gulped, afraid of what was to come. He had never seen Kalad so furious before.

"Lord Sic has given me this present as a symbol that he owes me. He was very upset because he'd taken me against my will."

A long silence followed these words, a silence filled with all kinds of emotions—Daran's fear, his regret about having lied, and his terror of being abandoned. Kalad's fury about the lie, about the fact that Daran had given his consent in the first place, about the love he felt for the thief that had taken deep root in his heart. The irritable tension that had been building up during the past days finally found an outlet.

"You said it was your pleasure."

"I lied. I only complied because it was your will."

The desert warrior let out his frustration in a roar; then he grabbed Daran, yanked him up, and slapped him hard.

"You worthless, despicable piece of shit! How dare you? Strip!"

Shivering all over, Daran obeyed. His master's fury terrified him. He had never seen Kalad like that; it was as if he had lost all control. As soon as Daran was naked, Kalad seized him, pushed him face-first against the wall, and chained him there. Then he got a whip. Until this day, the worst punishment Daran had ever received from the hands of his masters had been the twenty slaps on his backside after their first time together. All the more brutal felt the bite of the whip, which Kalad handled with merciless cruelty. Daran bellowed in pain but didn't dare to beg for forgiveness.

After an eternity, Aegid returned to the chambers as well. Questioningly he turned to his brother.

"Why are you whipping Daran?"

"That's for the scrawny little rat to tell. Go on, you worthless street mongrel! Tell Aegid what you did!"

The order was heightened by three brutal strokes on Daran's thighs. Aegid stepped toward Daran, bent his head back, and regarded him quietly. Daran felt tears streaming down his cheeks, his voice was nothing more but a sobbing sound. The pain caused him to see Aegid's face only in blurred lines.

"I've lied to you and your brother, Master. I didn't want to have sex with Lord Sic. I only did it because you wanted me to."

Aegid's milky-blue eyes narrowed in anger, and his face hardened. Grimly, he turned to Kalad.

"Hand me the whip."

If Daran had thought he knew the meaning of pain after Kalad had punished him so cruelly, he was now taught better. Aegid whipped him methodically, peeling the skin off his back until thin trickles of blood streamed down the thief's legs. Only when Daran was close to losing consciousness did the furious man stop. Disgusted, he threw the whip aside.

"For the night, you stay like this. We'll decide about your fate tomorrow."

The desert brothers left their desperate slave alone.

Crying, Daran hung in his chains, trying to ignore the searing agony in his back and not think about his disgrace. He had wanted to stop his masters from selling him, but it seemed as if his thoughtless actions had brought about the contrary. He didn't expect the slightest mercy from their side.

THE NEXT morning, Aegid and Kalad found their slave riddled by guilt. Like a heap of misery, he cowered at his owners' feet after they loosened his chains. In between his sobs, his pleas were hardly understandable.

"Please, forgive me, Masters. I'll do everything you want, I'll bear any punishment. Just please, forgive me!"

"Do you have a choice in the matter?"

Kalad sounded contemptuous. Whimpering, Daran huddled even more.

"Of course not, Master. I'm so sorry. Please, show some mercy."

"Why should we?"

Never before had Aegid sounded so uncaring and dismissive, as if his voice had turned to ice.

"We have given you a home, Daran. We have fed, clothed, and protected you. We've always been good to you, and we never asked for things you didn't want to give. You had privileges only few slaves can enjoy, and yet you go behind our backs and lie to us, knowing how much we hate it. Why?"

Crying like a child, Daran pressed his forehead to the ground.

"I didn't want you to sell me. I heard you talking about it. But there's no way I can ever belong to anybody else but you. It's simply impossible. I thought if I did everything you asked of me, you would change your mind and keep me. I'm solely yours. I hated it when Lord Sic touched me and all I wanted to do was run away, but for you, I endured it. I love you so much."

Now that he had bared his misery to his masters, Daran started sobbing again. Aegid and Kalad exchanged a long, loaded glance. Last night they had been too agitated to think clearly; their rage about Daran's betrayal, about his willingness to lie to them, had ruled their emotions. Now that they had learned the truth, they felt embarrassed. It had never crossed their minds the explanation for Daran's strange behavior might simply be his love for them. Because of a misunderstanding, they had forced their precious thief to do something he didn't want to. At the same time, they had also violated the laws of the Pack by forcing Daran to have sex with Sic. That he hadn't told them no only made it worse because, in their opinion, they should have known. There was no denying they had messed up badly.

Carefully, so as not to wound him any further, Aegid lifted Daran up.

"Shh, little thief. It's fine."

"I'm so sorry, Master. So unbelievably sorry!"

"We know, Daran, we know."

Gently, Kalad swept a loose strand of hair from Daran's face.

"Come, we better take you to the bath."

In the flickering light of various candles, the brothers stared at what they had done. Kalad was worried.

"This looks bad. We overdid it. I better get Noemi."

"I agree with you, brother."

After Kalad had gone, Aegid turned to Daran, his face tense with worry and regret.

"I'm sorry we punished you so harshly. It was over the top."

Shyly, Daran glanced at him.

"I'm your possession. It's your decision, Master." He hesitated a moment, then went on with a voice thin from pain and fear. "I really didn't want to lie to you, Master. But I was so afraid. The mere thought of living without you…." Daran stopped. The idea was too terrifying.

Aegid placed his hand on the young man's cheek.

"You little idiot. We could never sell you. We love you too much to do that. We were very hurt when you agreed to serve others as well."

"I hated every single moment. But if that's the price I've to pay for staying with you, I'll do it."

Sadly, Aegid shook his head. "There will be a price to be paid, Daran, quite a high one. We all will be paying it. But I can assure you, you'll never belong to anybody else but us."

Despite the searing pain in his back, Daran managed a weak smile.

"I thank you, Master."

In silence they waited until Kalad returned with Noemi. The snake witch placed her cool hands on Daran's shoulders without commenting on his wounds. A tingling sensation ran through his body, and then all traces of his punishment were gone. Full of respect and awe, Daran bowed in front of the fragile-looking woman.

"I thank you, lady. You're very kind."

The witch chuckled warmly.

"It's fine, Daran. I can only advise you to never anger your masters like that again."

"I'm not planning to, lady. Once is more than enough."

Again that deep, warm chuckle before Kalad escorted the healer outside. When he returned, Daran glanced insecurely at his masters.

"What are you going to do to me?"

After a few moments of loaded silence, Kalad grabbed Daran's wrist; his voice sounded amused. He was definitely back to his old, easygoing self.

"We're going to have a very, very long talk with you, little thief. About trust and obedience and how you owe us both. I'm afraid you won't like it, but it's only fair after what you've put us through."

"Before that"—Aegid started to take off his tunic, his tone full of warmth again—"we're going to wash off all this blood. You look like a slaughtered pig."

"Once you're back to your old, clean, and delicious self, we're going to fuck you silly."

Kalad's hand was resting on Daran's back, his lips close to the thief's ear. Daran gulped. With a wolfish grin, Aegid took his hands and pulled him into the water while Kalad pushed him forward. The giant embraced him tightly, his enormous muscles tense when he carried Daran into deeper water.

"We're going to introduce the concept of make-up sex to you. It kicks in whenever we have an argument, just like now."

In a daze, Daran let his masters wash him. He didn't resist when they first took him in the water, then on the floor in the bathroom, and later on their bed. Only when he was completely exhausted—after all, he hadn't slept a wink the previous night—did they allow him a break. Aegid got a platter full of food, placed it next to the bed, and took turns with Kalad to feed Daran.

The thief was so overwhelmed by his owners' sudden kindness, he didn't know what to say. When he finally had gathered the courage to speak up, his voice was thin and insecure.

"How can I thank you, Masters? Why are you being so generous with me?"

Kalad shoved an apple slice into his mouth.

"We're generous because what's happened is our fault as well. If pressed for details, I'd say more than half of it. We should have known something was off, that you weren't being your usual self. But we were so eager to get you out of our lives, we didn't notice it."

Affected by these words, Daran lowered his gaze. The apple was stuck in his throat.

"So you're really going to sell me? Can you at least tell me what I did wrong?"

Aegid kissed him lovingly.

"We won't sell you, I already told you that. And you didn't do anything wrong. If anything, you were too perfect. We had never planned to fall in love with you. When we chose you, we only wanted to keep you throughout the winter, as a pastime."

"But you've been so delectable, so easygoing, we kept you around. It was an oversight on our part. And when you took on that stupid mission for Casto and we almost lost you, we had to face the fact that we had fallen in love. We had no choice but to part ways with you."

"I have to go because you love me?"

The desert brothers managed to look contrite. It was Aegid who tried to explain in more detail.

"As we said, it wasn't planned that we fall in love with you, and until the incident with Sic, we still thought we could end it without being hurt. Since you so readily agreed, we assumed you weren't as attached to us as we thought. And yes, we do admit this was wishful thinking on our part, even though it annoyed us."

"I still don't understand. Why is it so bad that you're in love with me? It almost sounds as if you're regretting it."

Kalad took Daran's hand, his fingers massaging the young man's palm.

"No, we don't regret it. It's just—Daran, we're immortal, and you're not. This kind of relationship always ends badly, and we didn't want to do this to you. The coming ten, twenty years are going to be bliss, that much we can promise, but then you'll gradually realize that you're growing old and it's going to weigh you down, especially since you'll be confronted daily with the fact that we don't. It's going to be a difficult phase for you to come to terms with, if everything goes smoothly. And then we'll have to watch you die slowly, every day a bit more. We're going to lose you in the end, and it will break our hearts. That's what's going to happen.

"We're really sorry to subject you to something so cruel, but we love you way too much to let you go. You're bound to us for the rest of your life."

There was a long, shocked silence after these words had been spoken. When Daran answered, his voice was gentle and full of conviction.

"Don't be sorry, Masters. You saved me from an existence that would have led me to the gallows sooner than later. I owe you the best five years of my life so far. I understand your fears, and I'm not going to tell you it won't be difficult, but no matter what's to come, nobody can take from me what you've given me so far. I'm really grateful and truly happy. I love you."

Moved deeply by those touching words, the warriors leaned in to kiss their beautiful, courageous slave. Their hands started exploring his sensitive spots once more, and only a short time later, they drowned their fears in sexual fulfillment.

"SO, WHAT did Sic give to you?"

Kalad was leaning on his right arm, his eyes sparkling with ill-concealed curiosity. Daran whimpered.

"Please, Master. I haven't slept all night and I'm sore from all the sex we had. All I want is some rest."

"Forget it."

Aegid smirked while his arm snaked around Daran's waist. "As you should know by now, he's unbearably curious. View it as part of your punishment."

Sighing, Daran left the bed.

"All right, all right. I'll get it. I haven't opened it yet."

"You've gotten a present and left it wrapped?"

Kalad obviously had problems getting his head around such an alien concept. Daran grinned at him in amusement before he turned serious again.

"I felt too bad. It was my fault Lord Sic was so miserable. The thought of looking at the proof of my stupidity wasn't alluring at all."

"We're going to talk about that later. I'm sure we'll find a way to compensate Sic for the inconvenience you caused him."

Grateful, Daran bowed to Kalad, who shooed him away.

"Come on, what are you waiting for?"

Daran got the package and placed it on the bed.

"You can open it, if you want, Master."

Kalad shook his head.

"It's your present. Come on, hurry."

"You better get going, little thief, before my brother here explodes from the excitement."

"Shut up, Aegid. As if you're not interested in what's in there."

His heart beating wildly in his chest, Daran opened the clasps holding the lid in place. Once it was removed, all three of them stared at the contents, lost for words.

Nestled in the white silk cushion lay the most exquisite golden belt the men had ever seen. Woven from thousands of little loops, it almost seemed like a cloth. At both ends of the belt, an emerald gleamed on the silk.

Sic had given his masterpiece to Daran.

Kalad was the first to regain his speech.

"I can't believe it."

Awed, Aegid touched the golden plaiting with his fingertips.

"Our brother is not only talented beyond all measure, he's also more lavish than anybody I know."

Daran was trembling.

"I can't and I won't accept this." Determined, he reached for the lid. "I'm going to find Lord Sic right now and give him back the belt."

Kalad stopped him before he could get up.

"No, you won't do that. Or do you wish to insult our brother-in-arms?"

"Of course not. But there's no way I can keep his masterpiece. Not when it was my fault to begin with."

"It's not that easy, Daran. A present like that, especially when it's given as a symbol for a debt, can't be handed back. Even if you forgive Sic— which I assume you've done already—it still remains in your possession. It's not a pawn, but a symbol."

"So what am I supposed to do now?"

Aegid grinned saucily.

"Wear it. We want to see how you look."

Daran rolled his eyes.

"Is that all you can think about?"

Kalad embraced him from behind, his hands resting on the thief's thighs.

"What else should we think about when you're lying in our bed so gloriously naked, like a ripe, plump fruit we only have to pick?"

All his blood gathered in Daran's loins. Without thinking, he offered himself to the brothers, as it had been his destiny from the day he was born.

3. TRUST

Sar'reff was perched on one of the branches of the mighty oak tree growing next to the stables. He liked this place, where he was able to watch the buzz of daily activities without being a part of them. Meeting the demon king had been a lucky coincidence for which he was still grateful. Since he had encountered the Emperor of the Storms, his sanity, as well as his powers, had started to stabilize. He was still far from the state he had been in when he'd first come to this world, and it was entirely possible he would never get it back completely, but the haze clouding his memory was gradually lifting, and for the first time in decades, he dared to hope again.

Before he had followed the call to Ana-Darasa, he'd had no concept of time or even of himself. The steady pressure coming from the passing of days, weeks, and years had been the main cause for his inexorable slide into madness. It remained a mystery to him how those creatures the emperor called inferior managed to go about their business as if they weren't aware of their slowly decaying bodies. They were so fragile, so short-lived, and yet stronger than him, who was barely able to stay focused in the face of all the laws that ruled this world.

A noise in the distance made him look up. Lys was coming back from his daily ride with his anchor. Until he'd met the emperor, Sar'reff hadn't cared much about humans; to him, they were nothing but blobs that barely lived long enough to merit his attention. But the people staying with Lys were different. Of course, the anchor stuck out. Even Sar'reff could sense the connection he had to the demon king, although he doubted the boy knew what it really meant. So far, the stallion hadn't decided to enlighten his rider about all his secrets, and Sar'reff would be damned if he dared to utter a word. Apart from the fact that he still found it difficult to speak at all, he didn't know what to talk about with the anchor anyway. To him, the boy with his arrogant attitude, his stubborn strength that veiled the vulnerability of his soul, and his ruthless, demanding stance seemed even more out of place than Sar'reff himself was.

Interestingly enough, though, the anchor wasn't the only outstanding person in the Valley. There were a lot of other interesting people as well. The two gods were powerhouses, brimming with energy very much like the one he knew from the other side. They were swords that cut reality into the pieces they needed. Then there was the shining one. Sar'reff never tired of looking at him, even though his light was so blinding. It was fascinating how pure magic could be contained within a shell that was comprised of nothing but thoughts and ideas. Now and then the magic would leak out, allowing glimpses of its vastness, only to be reined in by a smile and a friendly deed.

Meeting the snake witch had come as another pleasant surprise, since the snakes were known in his realm as well. They tended not to stay for too long, for they preferred the solidity of real worlds, but when they needed to rest, they went into chaos. The one who could bend time was intriguing. Sar'reff found it comforting to know that even this absolute force, which bothered him so much, could be altered and controlled. Then there was the dark one, who wore the shadows like a coat, attracting them without knowing it. Sar'reff was wary of him, for his power was precariously balanced. Only one little push and it could tip either way. Compared to this menace, the desert brothers were like a ray of sunshine, although this was mainly due to their attachment to the thief. The thief. Sar'reff didn't know what to make of him. He seemed to be only human, but there was something about him… like an undercurrent in a peaceful lake. It could drown you before you knew it.

Now Lys had arrived at the stables. His blond rider slid down his back, his cheeks flushed by the cool air. He was greeted by the fiery god, whom everybody respected, if not feared, except for the boy. Which was probably the reason the god loved him so much. Finding somebody driven by the same fire, somebody so perfectly matched—it had to be the greatest blessing.

Lys whinnied imperiously, beckoning Sar'reff down the tree. The demon sighed. It was time for training.

"WHAT'S THE matter with you today, Sic? This is the third time I was able to break through your defense. When Renaldo sees how inattentive you are, he'll flay you alive."

Sighing, Sic lowered his sword. He was aware he wasn't at his best today.

"I'm sorry, Casto. I'm distracted."

"What's the matter, Sic? You've been keeping to yourself the past few days. I hope you know you can tell me anything?"

The smith gave in. Except for Noran, he hadn't told anybody about the incident with Daran; he had been too ashamed. And the desert brothers hadn't said a word about it either, mostly due to the fact that they were too busy enjoying their reconciliation with Daran. It was hard to face Casto and tell him the ugly truth.

"I did something despicable. When I talked to Cornelia, she suggested it would be a good thing if I tried sex as the dominant party. So I asked Aegid and Kalad for help, and they offered Daran to me."

"They did what?"

Casto didn't know what shocked him more—the fact that Sic had seriously contemplated such an outrageous action without consulting him first, or that the desert warriors had even thought about sharing their precious thief.

"I know. If I hadn't been so overwhelmed by their offer, I'd have been more suspicious, but so much has happened, I'm still scattered all over the place. Anyway, they brought Daran to me and after some hither and thither, the four of us ended up spending the night. I had a feeling Daran wasn't as willing as he had claimed to be, but I got swept away by the mood. Basically, I took him against his will. When I realized what I had done, I went to ask his forgiveness, which he was gracious enough to grant me."

"This is so bizarre, I can't believe it."

"Trust me, it happened. Whatever the problem between the three had been, they've solved it now. Ever since that night, I haven't seen any of them, which can only mean they're busy making up."

Sic shuddered delicately. After everything he'd witnessed, he almost pitied Daran. Kalad and Aegid could be pretty intense, to put it mildly.

"Given your tense face, I assume this is not what bothers you."

"Well, it does, but not as much as what happened afterward. I was completely riled up, not knowing what to do. Somehow, I ended up in front of the smithy and spent the day watching Noran while he made a sword—just like I used to."

"I won't like what you're going to tell me now, will I?"

"No. You won't. We talked and somehow, I ended up making an overture of peace. I don't say everything's good between us now, but we won't be trying to avoid each other anymore."

Sic didn't dare look at Casto; he could almost feel the rage rolling off the king in waves.

"Don't tell me you've forgiven him. That's not what I intended when I sent you to Cornelia."

"I know. And no, I haven't forgiven him. I don't know if I ever will. Talking to Cornelia was very therapeutic for me. It helped me gain perspective, and I was able to forgive myself. And as much as I regret what has happened to her, I don't want to end up as lonely as she. Before that happens, I'll try everything to escape this vicious cycle. I mean, we're not talking about a lifetime of hatred and animosity that I could probably bear somehow. Since we're both Emeris, chances are we'll be trapped in the Valley together for centuries, or at least until the Good Mother is defeated. I can't and won't imagine eternity in a constant state of alarm for fear I could meet him unprepared."

"Believe it or not, I think I can understand your reasoning. So what's the plan now?"

"We agreed to try to act normal around each other, like brothers-in-arms should. It'll surely take some time until this ceases to be awkward, but it's a step forward."

Casto sighed deeply. He didn't like what he had just heard, mostly because it was logical and prudent. There was nothing more frustrating than when reason reared its ugly head.

"Are you going to forgive him?"

Sic hesitated long enough with his answer to stoke Casto's fury.

"Don't tell me you're considering it! You know he doesn't deserve it!"

"I know. And I didn't say I will. I just don't know myself. This is so messed up, all I want is to get out of this situation. And you're one to talk! You forgave me even though I almost killed you."

Casto shook his head dismissively.

"There wasn't anything to forgive to begin with. Once I thought it over, it was crystal clear, so why should I have held a grudge?"

Sic leaned his head against Casto's shoulder. No matter what the king said, becoming Sic's friend had been an act of incredible kindness. It was just like Casto to dismiss his own noble gesture.

"You forgave Lord Renaldo, didn't you?"

"No, he didn't. He just decided to let it slide. Isn't that true, Casto?"

Renaldo's voice made Sic jerk up in surprise, whereas the king didn't so much as blink. How Casto always knew when his mate was close remained a mystery to the smith. Now the mesmerizing blue eyes lit up in a way Sic had never seen before. There was a hint of regret, as well as anger, and a faint trace of amusement. Once again Sic realized how complicated and difficult the relationship between god and heart was.

"Why do you even ask when you know the answer already, Barbarian? I think we all know by now I'm not the lenient, forgiving type. And what you did was most certainly unforgivable."

Renaldo smiled sadly at Sic.

"You see how it is, Sic. You can count yourself lucky. You've been singled out. Now, would you two care to explain to me why you're sitting around, chatting like old men, when you should be warming yourself up for training?"

"It's because Sic is about to do something really stupid—or, to be more precise, has done so already."

It was hard to interpret Casto's tone. He wasn't entirely angry, nor was he truly amused. And the sarcasm underlying his words made Sic shiver. Renaldo stared at Sic, demanding an explanation.

"Tell me what the problem is. *He'll* just play games."

Casto pouted but didn't object. Sic glanced from god to heart, looking for a way out of this dangerous situation. When he found none, he started retelling the whole story again. The Angel of Death listened intently, not disturbing him once. When Sic had finished, he looked him straight in the eye.

"I can't see where the problem is. So you've decided to grant Noran the opportunity to earn himself a second chance with you. That's very noble. Not what a certain someone we both know would ever contemplate, but it suits you."

Casto glared at his mate. He had been in a foul mood all morning, and Sic's little confession hadn't helped to improve his state of mind. Being teased by the Barbarian almost made him snap.

"That's not the point. I always knew Sic would forgive that despicable piece of trash sooner or later. I just didn't think it would be so soon. It's hardly been five months since the last time he forced you! So far, I haven't seen him seriously repenting. All he does is run around with puppy eyes, wallowing in self-pity because he has finally realized what an ass he is. And you all fall for his act!"

"No, we don't."

Renaldo's face was grim.

"But I've known Noran for quite some time, and I can assure you, he *is* repenting. And he's changing. When I look at him these days, I can even find glimpses of the man I once deemed worthy of sharing my bed."

Sic could feel the storm brewing. Noran was a sore topic to begin with, but when Casto was reminded of how the master smith had once shared carnal pleasures with the Angel of Death, he lost all reason. By now, a vein in his forehead was already throbbing dangerously, and his eyes had darkened into black, menacing holes. It was time to intervene before lightning struck.

"So you're saying I did the right thing?"

Renaldo smiled.

"Yes. Not only for your own peace of mind, but also for the rest of us. It is rather awkward when the two of you meet, and since you're one of us now, this will happen on a regular basis. The sooner you get over your animosity and establish at least a professional relationship, the better for all of us. You have my approval. And since we're at it, have you decided about your colors yet? The Spring Ceremony is nearing, and it would be nice if you had your own ceremonial robes by then. Of course, Canubis and I are buying."

Sic opened his mouth to respond but was too shocked to know what he should say. He had deliberately forgotten about the Ceremony, which terrified him almost as much as the idea of having sex again. It was just like the Angel of Death to bring it up now, when his defenses were low. After all, he was a predator who would instinctively strike at the weakest point of opponents and friends alike.

"You really don't have to, Lord Renaldo. And no, I haven't decided yet."

"Then it's about time. Even our best seamstresses need at least two weeks to make something acceptable. And now, you two, get your lazy asses moving. It's time for some serious training."

MORE THAN two hours later, when Sic had left them alone after the merciless exercises, Casto cornered his mate with a stern look on his face.

"You really are a heartless bastard."

"I guess you're referring to my little remark about the Spring Ceremony?"

"Little remark? You practically forced him to take part, and after everything he's gone through."

"He can decline anytime. It's not compulsory, as you well know." Casto snorted.

"And you know as well as I do that Sic won't ever go against your will."

Until now, the Angel of Death had worn a mocking expression, but it turned serious all of a sudden.

"And he shouldn't. What he can do is voice his opinion. As an Emeris, he has to learn how to do that. His new status comes with lots of privileges and a whole bunch of duties. Serving us well is one of them, and it entails the self-confidence to stand up for what he wants or deems right. Until he's learned to do that, neither I nor Canubis will stop pushing him."

Casto frowned. He couldn't deny what his mate had stated. It was indeed important for Sic to learn how to be a lord; his problems with his slaves were proof of that. Still, seeing his friend cornered like a sewer rat woke protective instincts in him he hadn't been aware of until now.

"I understand. But you're still a bastard. It's all so new to him. You could cut him some slack."

"But I won't. And I may be a bastard, but that's what makes the two of us so compatible. Birds of a feather…."

"Are you implying I'm a bastard as well?"

"I've seen you in action. If I had needed any more proof, Ummana would've provided it. You're just like me and yes, I do mean it as a compliment."

"You can take that compliment and choke on it, Barbarian. I'm done with you for today."

With that, Casto stormed off. Renaldo watched the retreating figure of his beloved heart in mild surprise, for he hadn't expected to get off so lightly. Perhaps it was because he had worked the two young men so hard. The Angel of Death straightened up. Without any doubt, there would be an aftermath to this skirmish, tonight in bed, and he could hardly wait for it.

NORAN WAS busy sharpening a sword he had finished the day before when one of his gods graced him with his presence. He bowed respectfully and waited with his gaze cast down. Since he and Sic had started their careful, shy approach to a polite acquaintance, his relationship with Renaldo had also eased somewhat. But he still avoided meeting his former lover more than necessary. The guilt he felt when he imagined how deeply he had disappointed the Angel of Death was too much. That the powerful warrior had refrained from punishing him until now only increased the burden on Noran's shoulders.

"Can we talk?"

"Of course, my lord. Please follow me."

Noran led his god into the private rooms, where he offered him some wine. The Angel of Death declined politely. He regarded the master smith intently and for so long that the bulky man started to shift uneasily.

"Are you displeased, my lord?"

As if he had been pried from a trance, Renaldo looked up. Smiling, he shook his head.

"No, not in the least. I'm just overwhelmed. I hadn't seriously expected to ever meet the old Noran again, but here you are, almost as good as old. I'm really glad."

He patted the smith's massive biceps.

"You and Sic are making progress, aren't you?"

"Baby steps, my lord. But I'm grateful for every little thing. Considering what I deserve and what he's offering me, I'm a lucky man."

"Indeed you are. Sic is probably the most generous man I've ever met." Renaldo looked at Noran directly. "Which leads us straight to the point. What are you planning to do, Noran? And I mean in the long term."

The master smith sat down next to his god. It was a question he had been pondering ever since Sic had made his generous offer.

"I guess I'm still hoping to win him back, one day, in a distant future."
Renaldo nodded.

"I assumed as much. But what will you do if this is all you'll ever get? I know how much you love him. It reeks of obsession. Will you be able to handle rejection?"

"If you're asking if I'm going to repeat the mistakes of the past, I can reassure you, my lord. There's no way I'll ever let anything so abominable happen again. And if I'm really rejected, well, I may be absent from the Valley for prolonged intervals of time, to deal with the pain."

Renaldo leaned back against the wall. He was satisfied with this answer.

"And what are you going to do if he allows you to get closer? Somehow I get the feeling that might be as dangerous as the other option."

Wistfully, Noran stared at the ceiling.

"Should Sic ever grace me with his trust again, I'm going to woo him properly. I will take my time to prove that I'm worthy of being with him. I will do everything in my power to make him happy."

"Sounds good to me. But you'll have to make a bit more of an effort. As things are now, you're in no shape to woo even a stone. I mean, you never were what I'd call a natural charmer to begin with, and in the past century, you've taken a turn for the worse. You should really work on your social skills."

Noran stared at his god in disbelief.

"Are you trying to tell me you're fine with me going after Sic?"

Renaldo smiled as he had done on the day they first met, the open, friendly gesture of a young man who hadn't had a bad experience in his life before.

"I'm trying to tell you a lot more. It's called subtext, but since you're not getting it, I'm going to be more direct. I'm willing to forgive you, Noran. Not right now—it's still a little too early for that—but in the near future. And not just the thing with Sic, but also the incident with Arja. For that, I'll even take part of the blame, since I didn't speak up when I had the chance."

Dumbfounded, Noran could only stare at his god. This sudden turn of events was more than he would have ever dreamed of. Trembling, he went down on one knee.

"Thank you."

It was only two words, and yet they conveyed more than an entire speech would have been able to express. Renaldo grinned, satisfied with how things had turned out. Then he helped Noran up.

"Don't mess up again, brother."

ABOUT TWO weeks before the Spring Ceremony, Daran was standing in front of Sic's rooms, accompanied by his owners. Kalad and Aegid had conferred about how they could repay the smith for what Daran had done for a long time. In the end, they had come to a conclusion that was honorable, yet highly unattractive. Nevertheless, Sic was an Emeris, a brother-in-arms. It was inevitable to indemnify him properly. Which was the reason they had brought their thief like a lamb chosen for sacrifice. When Kalad knocked, it wasn't Sic who opened, but Casto. The king looked at them in surprise.

"Kalad, Aegid. Nice to see you. Sic hasn't mentioned anything about expecting guests. Come in."

He stepped aside invitingly.

"We haven't announced our coming."

Kalad sat down on a divan next to a small table with golden inlay. He declined the wine Casto offered him and Aegid.

"It won't take long."

Casto regarded the desert warriors and their thief sharply. Something was wrong, and since he didn't want Sic to have yet another unpleasant surprise, he decided to find out what.

"What's the matter with you? You're as tense as a father who's planning to sell off his only daughter to a stranger."

Kalad opened his mouth to answer Casto when Sic entered the room. He stared at his guests, momentarily taken aback; then his gaze darkened. Daran, who had watched the smith closely, hurried over to him and knelt down. Confused, Sic looked at Kalad, whose face had become serious. When he had seen the three men, Sic assumed they had come to incriminate him, something he deserved after what he had done.

"We're here because of Daran's abominable behavior."

Kalad sounded strained; it was obvious how much he resented what he was about to do.

"You're our brother, and we know how much grief our slave's lie has caused you. We have already punished him severely, but you, too, have a right to castigate him as you deem fit. For the next week, Daran is yours. You can do to him whatever you wish."

Silence descended on the room, only to be broken by a whistle from Casto. The king was grinning with malicious glee.

"So you *are* selling off your only daughter…."

Kalad and Aegid were too tense to react to this banter and simply ignored it. Sic was staring wide-eyed from Casto to the desert brothers and then to Daran, who was still kneeling in front of him, his head demurely bowed. A smile brightened the smith's features, and he bent down to help the thief up.

"So you're mine for the next week?"

"Yes, Master. I'll do whatever you ask of me."

Sic stared into the big brown eyes, which looked back at him despondently. He was almost able to grasp the fear and remorse coming from Daran. And he understood him only too well, for he himself had once been willing to do everything for his master's love. Luckily, there was an amiable solution to this loaded situation. Gently Sic caressed Daran's cheek.

"Since you've got to do whatever I wish, these are my orders. The entire next week, you're going to serve my brothers, Lord Aegid and Lord Kalad. You will do everything in your power to please them, for they are my dear brothers-in-arms and two very special persons I want to be happy."

"Lord." Daran's voice was a mixture of disbelief and surprise. Smiling, Sic motioned him toward the desert brothers.

"Come on, go over. I'm sure they know better than me what to do with you."

Seeking help, Daran glanced at his masters, but they were too stunned to react. Kalad approached Sic with his mouth set in a determined streak.

"Daran has inconvenienced you, to say the least. It's only just you make him pay."

Sic shook his head.

"Strictly speaking, I was the one who inconvenienced Daran, and he was so generous as to forgive me. How can I do less? Moreover, you only wanted to help me, and in a certain sense, you've done that. If I hadn't experienced that night, I'd probably still be moping, unable to change myself. Thanks to you, my situation is already improving. All I want is to end this regrettable incident for us all. If Daran can forgive me, I'll do the same."

Aegid hugged the smith silently; his brother followed his example.

"You truly are generous, Sic. We'll never forget this."

"You're my brothers. Did you really think I could lay a finger on Daran when I know how much you love him? Despite that, we're friends."

He turned to the thief.

"I've neither forgotten how you forgave me so readily after that dreadful night, nor how you've always been friendly to me even when none of the other slaves bothered to do so."

He took Daran in his arms.

"I never want to hear another word about this topic, agreed?"

"Agreed, Lord Sic."

Daran's voice was thin but full of relief. His exuberant imagination had shown him the most horrible things Sic might to do to him to punish him for his lie. In hindsight it was, of course, nonsense, for the smith was a gentle, kindly person. Still, the days since his owners had told him how they planned to reimburse their brother-in-arms had been unpleasant.

"Now I'd take some of that wine."

Kalad's relieved voice disturbed Daran's train of thought. Casto took out five wine cups, but when he offered one to the thief, he shook his head.

"I have no right. But if you allow, I'll serve you."

He reached for the jar to refill the Emeris' cups. Over the bent head of their slave, Casto winked at his masters.

"Daran, it's nauseating how perfectly well-trained you are. Can't you be a little bit more disobedient? Or at least defiant? Just something that shows me you're alive and not some puppet on a string."

"Leave him alone, Casto. It's not his fault that he's perfect."

The blond made a face. Mischief sparked to life in his eyes.

"Is that why you gave him such a nice, shiny new collar?"

Upon these words, Daran unconsciously reached for the new jewelry around his neck. The old, battered one had indeed been replaced by one that looked more like an adornment fit for a princess and not like a symbol for slavery. It was still made from leather, like the first one he had gotten, but the material was hardly visible underneath the thick layer of emerald splinters attached to it with thin golden threads. The clasp was golden as well, with an emerald the size of a large coin sitting on top of it. Among all their other treasures, the desert brothers had found the aforementioned bag of jewels after some frantic searching.

"The presents we bestow on our slave are none of your business, Your Highness. You're just jealous you've never gotten anything like it."

Kalad watched with amusement as his god's heart grew angry. The mesmerizing blue eyes darkened dangerously, and the sensuous lips trembled slightly.

"As if." The words came out like a hiss, and things might have gotten out of hand if Aegid hadn't drained his cup and then shooed his desert brother and their slave out of the room. As soon as they were gone, Casto cooled down. Sic knew he would never tire of watching this quick display of emotions.

"Well, that was something."

"Do you think I was wrong? Did I handle the situation poorly?"

"No, certainly not. I mean, Daran wasn't at fault at all. Neither were you, by the way. Those two arrogant bastards are to blame, and they know it. You made it too easy for them."

Sic couldn't help but grin.

"What would you have done?"

Pure malevolence made Casto look like a very handsome god of revenge.

"I'd have kept their precious thief for the entire week—without letting them see him. Just for fun, of course."

"You truly are wicked, Casto. I'd never be able to do such a thing."

"You're not the first one to tell me that, my friend. Makes me doubt my impact on others."

Sic knew better than to follow this path of conversation. Instead, he started talking about other, much lighter topics.

4. SPRING CEREMONY

GROANING, RENALDO closed his eyes when his lover's lips engulfed the tip of his member. Casto was taking his time. He enjoyed torturing his mate, a just revenge for the sweet agony the Angel of Death had invoked in him during the course of this evening. But Casto never got to enjoy his fill, for when the warrior had enough, he simply grabbed him, turned him around, and entered again deeply. Casto resisted in a playful manner, willing to turn what had been meant to be an aftermath into a wild pairing again. Renaldo chuckled happily.

"Have I told you how glad I am you're no longer a mortal?"

"Not today, but you do mention it quite often—especially in bed."

"That's because I can't get enough of your new stamina. You've always had remarkable endurance, but now…."

"You only say that because I'm putting up with you."

"And because I don't have to hold back. No matter what I'm doing to you, you endure it—you even enjoy it."

A wave of heat flared between them. Casto pressed his naked ass against his mate. His voice was savage, coming from a place so deep within it almost hurt letting it out.

"You know how much I like it when you're losing control."

A growl was the answer, and the movements of the god grew faster. Both men gave in to the rush that overwhelmed them whenever they let all restraints go.

Later, Casto leaned on his mate's broad chest. Renaldo's right hand was resting on his lover's thigh while he held a cup of wine with his left. Now and then he would take a sip and hold it against Casto's lips as well.

"What's going to happen now that we've found all the Emeris?"

Renaldo put down the cup. His voice was implacable.

"We're going to obliterate the Good Mother."

"I assumed as much. I'd only like to know more details."

"We don't really know. We were still young when Mother took our hearts. We had just arrived in this world. We have yet to find the full extent of our powers. It'll take some years until we really know what we're able to do. The Emeris, too, have to get acquainted with their talents. Sic's arrival has turned all of them into demigods. What exactly this entails, we don't know. For the time being, we'll continue to wage war, although we're going to concentrate on the areas where the Good Mother has the most supporters."

"So it won't be boring?"

"Certainly not, my own."

Lost in thought, Casto traced his mate's abdominal muscles with his fingertips. Renaldo took his hand and kissed it.

"Please, don't worry, my own. So far I haven't felt the urge to enslave you completely."

"Yet you do know my thoughts."

"That's not difficult. I know you pretty well by now, and even though Hulda claims differently, I do have a certain empathy. I know your worries."

"You know what troubles me most? That the thought of belonging to you entirely is starting to lose its horror. Seems like I'm getting used to it."

Renaldo's eyes lit up. Then he created a picture in his mind—Casto, chained with the leather cuffs, his arms behind his back, his upper body resting on the bed, his rear stretched up invitingly.

The young man's breath hitched. Silently he got up to fulfill his god's will.

HEART POUNDING wildly in his chest, Sic stood in front of the door that led to Noemi's realm. He still doubted the wisdom of what he was about to do, but he was running out of time and options. Today had been the final fitting for his official new robes, all in blinding white, and the Spring Ceremony was drawing nearer. He was cornered like a rat, his only way out being the snake witch. Sic lifted his hand to knock.

"Come in."

Noemi's voice was warm and friendly, as always. When she saw who her unexpected guest was, the smile on her face deepened.

"Sic! What a pleasant surprise! What brings you here?"

Shyly, Sic sat down on one of the chairs the witch indicated. Noemi looked at him expectantly.

"Given how you're fidgeting, I assume you want to ask me something difficult?"

Grateful, Sic looked up.

"Yes. And I don't know how to start."

Her tiny hands closed around his callused ones in a reassuring manner.

"I'm a healer, Sic. There are few things that can shock me, and I'm pretty sure you aren't capable of performing them. A certain pair of desert warriors, yes. But not you."

In spite of the seriousness of the situation, Sic couldn't suppress a snicker. It was too easy, picturing Kalad and Aegid doing something outrageous. The statement also reassured him. There were worse things than what he wanted from her.

"I wanted to ask you if you could mix me a drug for the Spring Ceremony. One that shuts down my mind so I can't think about what's happening."

Noemi's eyes widened.

"So you're planning to participate? If it's so hard on you, why don't you refuse? You know you have the right, don't you?"

Sic evaded her gaze. The situation was complicated, and it seemed as if he had no choice but to explain it.

"I know. Nevertheless, your husband and his brother are expecting me to come. It's hard for me not to do their bidding, especially when I know how much it means to them."

Noemi made a dismissive gesture.

"They're both grown men. They can live with disappointment. It's no reason for you to force yourself into doing something that requires the use of drugs in order to bear it."

"It's not just that. Lady Noemi, what was it like when Ana-Isara kissed you?"

Noemi furrowed her brows. She couldn't see where Sic was aiming with this question. Yet she could sense how agitated he was.

"I guess it's been different for all of us. And me, well, I wasn't alone when I met her. Shaa-Azar is always with me. It was still very intense. This feeling of inevitability. Knowing that your fate is chosen and there's nothing you can do to alter it. Of course, I was already madly in love with Canubis at the time, so from my point of view, everything was fine."

Sic sighed deeply.

"I had a choice. I could have said no. And not because Ana-Isara would leave me one, but because there's something inside me that can defy even her. I don't know what was worse, realizing I was chosen or knowing I had the means to say no."

Noemi stared at Sic open-mouthed. Like everybody else in the Valley, she knew little about the Luksari. Even the snake hadn't been able—or willing—to tell her more than she had deduced from touching the young man. Considering what she knew, Sic's statement wasn't as outrageous as it seemed at first glance.

"You allowed her to kiss you."

"Yes. I *allowed* it. Not because I wanted to, but because I was terrified of what I could be. I've experienced firsthand how power can be abused, what it makes of people. I don't ever want to become like that or go through the same misery. I just can't."

"And so you choose not to be disobedient even though you can't stand what's happening to you."

Pity made the witch's voice even gentler than before.

"I think I can understand you. Being singled out is never easy. Shaa-Azar was with me from the day I was born. As a child, I never thought twice about it. Only when I grew older did I start to understand the implications. It was hard. Accepting what I was, embracing the snake with all the power and responsibility it brought—it took me a long time, and it cost me dearly. Only when I met Canubis could I finally make my peace with fate. I know my words surely sound like mockery to you, but you have to come to terms with who you are and what powers you wield. There won't be any peace for you until you manage to do that. I'm sorry."

Sic felt tears streaming down his face.

"How long will it take me? For how much longer do I have to live like this, insecure and frightened, unable to breathe freely?"

Noemi embraced the smith and patted his back.

"I don't know. It's up to you. Just never forget, you have a family now, one where all the members are not only special but also willing to help you. You're not alone."

She let go of him and turned to one of the shelves where she kept her medicine. After a few moments' contemplation, she selected a small vial of tinted glass.

"You take two drops on the morning of the Spring Ceremony and then another two during lunch. Just before you attend the feast, you take five drops, preferably with wine. It'll make you feel tipsy and light-headed. Your body will be relaxed enough to feel pleasure while your mind will more or less sleep. You'll still be able to interact with others, but it'll be like a haze. Chances are, you won't remember much of what is going to happen."

Sic stared at the vial as if it could save his life.

"Thank you. Thank you so much! I can't tell you how grateful I am."

Noemi patted his shoulder, her face grim.

"Don't mention it. Even though it goes against everything the Spring Ceremony stands for, I can understand your reasoning. Just don't make me do this ever again."

The young smith kissed Noemi's hands reverently.

"I won't. I promise. Just this once."

"Yeah, just this once."

Somehow, the snake witch didn't seem convinced.

"WOW, CASTO, you look stunning!"

Daran was gaping at the blond in awe. Casto glared back at him with so much menace it made the thief stagger back.

"Shut it! I'm not in the mood!"

"Daran, don't look so frightened. You know what he's like at the Spring Ceremony. Your well-meant compliments will only serve to make him angrier."

Noemi nudged the young slave carefully, so as not to damage the silver powder all over his body—or the golden on her own. They both looked at Casto, whose defiant glare was in stark contrast to his elaborate getup. He truly was a magnificent sight, the ideal of a human being with his elegantly toned muscles, the velvet skin glowing from gold dust, and the perfect features brimming with barely concealed displeasure.

"Then may I compliment you, my lady? You look stunning as well."

There was only the slightest hint of mischief in Daran's voice, barely recognizable for those who didn't look for it.

"But of course, Daran. And I do thank you for your generosity. Also, let me give the praise right back. Seeing you like this makes me wonder how Aegid and Kalad can bear being separated from you for even a minute."

The witch's eyes sparkled in amusement; she was enjoying this immensely. Casto pointedly turned his back on them.

"I can really do without your mockery. This is bad enough as it is, I don't need you two to rub it in."

"Why are you so opposed to it? I mean, you get to feel good, don't you?"

"I don't know about you, Daran, but I think the idea of being dragged along the lines of dozens of drunken mercenaries ogling me with lust in their eyes only to be fucked unconscious at the banquet table more than a little repulsive. As much as I like getting down and dirty with the Barbarian, I just hate it when I have an audience."

"Oh, I don't know. It can be quite stimulating—being watched, I mean."

Casto shuddered.

"This only shows how much those two lecherous fiends have already corrupted you. And you were such a nice boy to begin with."

"Don't give us too much credit, Casto. Daran was never as innocent as he may have seemed."

Kalad and Aegid had just entered the room to pick up their thief. Both men looked impressive in their dark green robes with white rabbit fur at the seams. They had hardly glanced at Noemi and Casto; their gazes were fixed on Daran, whose body responded quickly and proudly. Casto rolled his eyes.

"Hurry, take him with you before I have to vomit. All this lovey-dovey is hard to stand."

"Admit it, Casto, that's what you're missing with Renaldo."

Kalad hastily ducked out of the king's reach.

"I guess we better get going."

Aegid fastened the golden chain to Daran's collar and then led his smirking brother and their gorgeous thief outside. Casto murmured some colorful curses under his breath before he started pacing the room again. Noemi watched his movements with mild interest. In the beginning she had thought she could help her capricious brother-in-law, but now she knew better. Just like his relationship with Renaldo, Casto himself was highly complicated. Trying to understand him was like trying to understand the weather—there was always room for unpleasant surprises. Suddenly the king stopped dead in his tracks, his head turned toward the door. Only moments later, the divine brothers entered the room. Noemi smiled and went to her husband, who kissed her briefly on the mouth before putting the chain on her. His eyes were full of love.

"My precious jewel, you're so beautiful, I can't find the words to describe you."

"Thank you, my lord. As always, you're truly gracious."

Meanwhile, Renaldo had approached Casto like a hunter would a shy deer.

"My own. I know telling you how unbelievably good-looking you are is a waste of time, but I simply have to."

"Blah, blah, blah. Just cut it out, Barbarian. Put that damn chain on me and then let's get this over with."

"Charming as always. But I won't let you ruin my good mood."

With that, the Angel of Death fastened the chain on Casto's collar. Then he turned to his brother, who was grinning broadly.

"Let's go. As you can hear, my mate can hardly wait."

SIC WAS standing nervously next to Bantu at the high table in the main hall, his fingers constantly kneading the cloth of his robes. As Noemi had instructed, he had taken the drug. It had made him feel tipsy all day long, and the last five drops had put him into a daze. He was still aware of his surroundings, but in an absent kind of way, as if he wasn't part of what was happening. His body felt heavy, though not relaxed enough not to be nervous. Sic only hoped to get through the evening as smoothly as possible and before the effect wore off. Bantu nodded to him encouragingly, trying to reassure him. Sic managed a grateful little smile before he started fidgeting again.

Now the big doors swung open and the gods entered. Sic couldn't help but stare. Canubis and Renaldo were intimidating enough during daily affairs, yet that was nothing compared to the auras of pure dominance they were giving off as they proceeded to the high table. Perhaps it was because he was seeing it for the first time. Perhaps it was because this was the first Spring Ceremony they celebrated as fully fledged gods again. In any case, Sic couldn't help but kneel down, as did all the other Emeris and everybody else in the hall. The gods of war had finally come into their right.

When they reached their places, Bantu and Kalad handed the divine brothers each a cup of wine. They prayed for the blessing of Ana-Aruna and

Ana-Isara, reciting the old chants with so much vigor it made Sic shudder. After they had all sacrificed some of their blood to the goddesses, the feast started. Until now, Sic had only known the Spring Ceremony from tales. He quickly decided the truth was even more outrageous than the stories. From the corner of his eye, he watched as Aegid and Kalad bent Daran over a chair. The giant entered him smoothly while his brother enjoyed the thief's oral ministrations. Canubis had Noemi sitting on his lap, his member buried deep inside her. Casto's upper body was resting on the table, his legs spread wide to accommodate his mate. Later, Sic couldn't tell what had jolted him out of his drug-induced daze. Perhaps it was the sight of Noemi and Casto, who were usually so proud and independent and who were, at this moment, so completely under their gods' will. Perhaps it was all the other pairings going on around him, all of which only knew the goal of finding relief. Or it was the intense aura coming from the Wolf of War and the Angel of Death.

Sic suddenly felt oppressed, as if a heavy weight had come to rest on his chest, keeping him from breathing. All his fears bore down on him at once as his mind started working clearly again. The sounds of people having carnal sex all over the hall overwhelmed him, bringing back memories of the terrible agony he had come to connect with intercourse. It was almost as if he was back in the smithy, on that fateful day when Noran had coaxed him for the first time. There had been so much pain in his heart and mind. Cornelia had been right. Some things just could not be forgotten; they were etched into his being, impossible to remove. Giving his consent to attend the feast had been a grave mistake. Even though he feared his own powers, he should have been selfish about protecting himself. Now it was too late, and he was trapped in a nightmare.

Sic was close to a panic attack when the female approached him. She wasn't bad—young, average looks, with a hungry gaze. It was obvious she had chosen Sic as her next partner, even though the insides of her thighs were already tacky with the essence of her former encounters. Desperately, Sic tried to get out of this situation. There was no way he could have sex with this woman, no way he could have sex with anybody in the hall, no matter if they topped or bottomed. While his mouth opened to tell the woman to go find somebody else, her face suddenly paled. Hastily she withdrew back into the crowd. When Sic turned around to find the reason for her sudden terror, he stood face-to-face with Noran.

Panic rose inside Sic. Dealing with the master smith was not an option in his current state. But before he could retreat, Noran stepped even closer. His mouth was level with Sic's ear, his voice a harsh whisper.

"Don't be afraid. I just want to help you. I swear, I'm not going to do anything to you. I won't even touch you. If you don't want to participate in the feast, you better come with me right now."

Sic stared at the orgy that was gaining more momentum by the minute and decided Noran was right. With a short nod, he followed the master smith, who led him into a dark corner with a small table and two chairs. One of the chairs was hidden so deeply in the shadows it could hardly be seen. Noran placed Sic there. He himself sat on the other, more prominent chair, and chased anybody who came too close away with a threatening glare. Shielded like that, Sic started to relax slowly. Since the drug was obviously completely gone from his system, he was able to process his surroundings again. It was so overwhelming, he almost heaved. Noran looked at him sharply.

"Are you feeling unwell? Should I get you something to drink?"

"No, Master, I'm fine. It's just a little too much."

"Not master. Noran. Why are you here anyway? I thought I'd die when I saw you at the high table."

"I didn't want to disappoint the gods. Lady Noemi gave me something to help me through this, but apparently it didn't work as planned."

"This is stupid, Sic. Since you're here, we have to wait till midnight until we can officially leave. Do you think you can do it?"

Sic stared at Noran, who was so obviously worried for him, and felt a calmness he hadn't known for almost a year wash over him.

"As long as you stay with me, I can do it."

Shyly, Noran smiled at his former slave.

"I won't leave you alone, no matter what."

KNOWING HE was protected, Sic managed to relax. From the shadows he watched the mercenaries and their slaves indulge each other and wondered about the raw energy building up in the hall. It had to be a feast for the goddesses.

Sic's gaze wandered back to the high table. Hulda looked as majestic as always while she sat on her husband's lap, controlling both their movements. The killer always enjoyed physical contact, and the naturalness with which she took what she wanted and gave what her partner needed made Sic believe in beauty again. Even Bantu, who was always so composed and quiet, had chosen a young man who was shivering with pleasure beneath him. When the smith's gaze reached the desert brothers and their thief, he blushed and looked away hastily. Casto used to call them lecherous, but that was too friendly a term to describe what he had just seen.

And then Casto. Although his friend hated the Spring Ceremony with all his heart, he still indulged in it. The way he and Renaldo were going at each other was like a dance, or, more accurately, like a choreographed fight. A sight of beauty with imminent danger; fascinating, yet deadly. Not for the first time did Sic wonder about the different faces love could show.

He glanced at Noran, who was still discouraging anybody who got too close to their little place in the dark. The master's back was tense, and Sic could only imagine how hard it had to be for Noran to hold back his own urges only to stay with him. A wave of gratitude washed over Sic as he realized how much he was treasured by the grumpy master smith.

At midnight, Noran nodded toward Sic.

"You can leave now. You've fulfilled your duty."

Sic stared at the hall full of horny people he had to cross in order to get back to his rooms and shook his head.

"I think I'd rather stay a little longer, if it's all the same to you."

"But you're uncomfortable."

"I am. But there's no way I can make it through the hall. I'd rather be here with you."

In a tired gesture, Noran wiped his eyes.

"It's fine, Sic. I'm going to accompany you. Nobody will dare lay a hand on you."

Again a wave of warm gratitude washed over Sic. Shy, but determined, he reached for Noran's hand. When their fingers entwined, a prickling sensation ran through his body. The master smith stared at him blankly for a moment, then jolted back to reality.

"Let's go."

IN FRONT of Sic's chambers, Noran let go of the hand he felt was the most precious thing he'd ever touched. He didn't know what to say or how to get out of this awkward situation. When he had come to Sic's aid, it had been on pure instinct. He had never thought it through. Sic looked up at him and smiled. It wasn't the open, blissful smile he had shared with his fellow smiths in Ummana, or the relaxed one he usually wore around Casto. It was a new kind of smile, one Noran had never seen before on the thin lips. It spoke of all the hardships its owner had endured, but also about the blessings he had received. It was a mature smile full of hope for the future.

"Thank you, Master. Noran. You were my saving grace in there. I'm sorry I ruined the feast for you."

"You didn't ruin it for me, honestly. If I had the choice between the Spring Ceremony and spending an evening with you, I'd always choose the second."

The smile deepened.

"Would you come inside and watch over me till I can sleep? I'm still a little shaken, and your presence is soothing me."

"Of course, Sic. It is my pleasure."

Again Sic reached for his former master's hand. His voice was nothing but a whisper.

"I think I'm ready to trust you again."

"Sic?"

"It'll take time, but I can feel it again. The love I had for you. It still needs to grow, though."

"Sic."

Noran sank to his knees, unable to believe what the love of his life had just offered him. After his conversation with Renaldo, he had been depressed, since he had known there was no way Sic would ever give his consent for Noran to woo him. It was an impossible hope he had nourished deep in his heart, another pain that was just punishment for what he had done. And now his precious treasure was offering him so willingly what he had been convinced was forever lost. He pressed kisses on the young man's open palms.

"I can wait, Sic. I'll wait as long as it takes. And I'll do everything. I swear."

Sic smiled again, still a little insecure and wistful, but for the first time since Ana-Isara's kiss, he felt he had done the right thing.

"Then please, watch over my sleep."

With a happy nod, the master smith followed his love into the chamber.

WHEN THE first rays of the morning sun lit the mountains around the Valley, Lord Renaldo, the Angel of Death, picked up his beloved heart, King Castolus of Ummana, and carried him back to their chambers. Casto was far too exhausted to register what was happening to him. He simply enjoyed the feeling of floating in the air and of being utterly safe. In the bedroom, Renaldo put his mate down and kissed him lovingly. Then he got up again to meet his brother. Together, they walked into the Valley.

Under their naked feet, the snow vanished, and the cold was replaced by the familiar, pleasant climate of the Green Lands. A tantalizing scent entered their nostrils. The grass under their feet was soft and warm and the sky a brilliantly clear blue. On a rise they met their mothers. Ana-Isara was as pale and deathly as always; her sister, on the other hand, was flushed and warm. The Green Lands were Ana-Aruna's realm, so she was the first to speak.

"The time has come, sons. Ana-Darasa has chosen her gods."

"So you're leaving us?"

Canubis's voice was calm; both he and Renaldo had known this day would come.

"Our presence is no longer necessary. Even though you haven't regained your full power yet, you're still the rightful masters of this world. We would only be a hindrance to your growth."

Ana-Isara sounded sad. Tears like silver pearls shone in her eyes. In a soothing gesture, her sister took her hand; she, too, was crying, but the moment the tears left her eyes, they turned into colorful butterflies that flew into the sun like little jewels.

"We're very proud of you. As soon as you've beaten the Good Mother, you'll form this world to your liking. But don't underestimate her. The Good Mother is going to fight you till the last moment, and she doesn't know any honor."

"We are aware of that."

Renaldo sounded grimmer than he had intended to. Ana-Aruna caressed his cheek with a sad smile.

"Our harbinger of death. The power of your fire will consume all doubt."

Ana-Isara hugged Canubis.

"Beware. Your fight is going to last for many years to come. In the end, the threat will come from the sea, this much we can tell. Our leaving means there will be a vacuum. The power's going to go to you and those who follow you, but she's going to steal some of it. The Good Mother will gain power as well."

"It won't benefit her. We're going to destroy her."

Canubis spoke with the calm determination of a true leader. His brother nodded in agreement.

"Are we going to meet you again?"

The sisters shared a look. Ana-Isara answered, her voice full of regret.

"When time ends and everything returns to the beginning, then we'll be reunited. But it's going to be long until then. Not even we can see the end."

The brothers nodded. The thought of living for so long was no longer disturbing, now that they were gods again. Time, which had been dragging on them heavily now and again, had lost its power. They were not only the masters of this world, they were eternal.

"Take good care of the light. He's going to bring you the worthy servants."

Canubis furrowed his brows. Some of the suspicions he'd been having seemed to prove true.

"Sic?"

The Mothers nodded.

"Luksari. We doubt there will ever be somebody like him again. He's precious in more than one respect."

One last time the Mothers embraced their sons; then the gods of war turned away, ready to face their fate. Ana-Isara's voice echoed in their ears when they returned to the Valley.

"Those serving you will still be welcome in the Green Lands. The gate won't be closed."

With those comforting words in their ears, the Wolf of War and the Angel of Death returned to their home.

NEW BEGINNINGS

1. MARKET DAY

"I can't believe it! How can you be so unbelievably stubborn?"

"You dare call me stubborn? Of all people?"

"The way you're behaving, stubborn is a compliment, Barbarian!"

"Watch it, Casto! I'm starting to lose my patience here."

Aegid and Kalad stopped dead in their tracks. The fight they were witnessing just now was growing more heated by the minute. A wise man kept his distance when Lord Renaldo, the feared Angel of Death, got into an argument with his irascible heart, King Castolus of Ummana. Although the two had been married for more than a year now, their fights had not eased. Sometimes Aegid got the impression they were getting worse. This was not a problem per se, since the mercenaries loved a good show as much as anybody else. No, the real crux was that Casto still hadn't managed to control the fire inside him. Usually Renaldo did that for him, but when they were enraged like now, chances were high that Casto would inflame something. Kalad shook his head.

"Sounds pretty serious. Let's return at a later time."

He was about to turn around when Aegid stopped him.

"Daran is somewhere close. We can't leave him alone."

A determined streak hardened his quirky brother's lips. When it was about Daran, Kalad was willing to do anything. They had come to the stables to watch their beloved thief during his riding lesson. Now that spring was slowly chasing the winter out of the Valley, the children of the desert could dare to venture outside again. But it seemed as if the lesson hadn't even started yet. Hell-bent on protecting their most precious possession, the desert brothers got closer to the source of all the excitement.

Renaldo and Casto were standing face-to-face, their handsome features full of rage. The face of the Angel of Death was frozen into its usual immobile mask, in which only the glaring eyes revealed his emotions, while Casto's cheeks were tinged by a soft red that could have made him appear vulnerable were it not for the tense jaw muscles and the threatening black of his eyes. As pleasing to the eye as both men were, there was no doubt that this beauty was merely a thin veil under which the untamed passion could barely be hidden. Aegid thought it was beyond ironic how contradictory the inside and outside of his god and his heart were. It was as if light and darkness had been unified in these two.

Meanwhile Kalad had spotted Daran, who was huddled in a corner, his expressive brown eyes big with horror. The wall behind him was stained with a soot mark, which was pretty fresh by the looks of it. While Aegid hugged the thief protectively, his brother hissed at the squabblers.

"Damn it, you two! Can't you control yourselves? You've frightened Daran!"

Renaldo and Casto turned around to face Kalad. For a moment, embarrassed silence ruled. Obviously they had forgotten everything around them.

Casto was the first to regain his speech. "I'm sorry, Daran. I neither wanted to hurt nor frighten you. It's all the fault of the Barbarian."

"My fault? Daran, you've been here all the time! I'm sure you can confirm that this is all Casto's doing!"

Whimpering, Daran buried his face in Aegid's broad chest. He hated being part of this skirmish. His voice was barely audible. "I'm truly sorry, Master, but I was too scared to remember one word you said."

"Then I'm going to refresh your memory! This incautious idiot"— Renaldo stabbed his index finger threateningly in Casto's direction—"is seriously planning to go to the market in Kwarl all on his own."

"I've explained it to you countless times, Barbarian, it's perfectly safe. It's the big spring market next week. I want to sell some of our horses and see whether I can find a good stallion for my breeding program. What in the Mothers' names could happen?"

"You still need to ask? You're not going—that's my final word!"

A wave of heat made Kalad's braids fly, but before Casto was able to snap at his mate, the desert warrior intervened.

"That's why you're fighting? Because Casto wishes to visit the market?"

"It seems you're not aware of the gravity of the situation, Kalad." Renaldo's voice was pointed. It was obvious that he was miffed.

"Damn, Renaldo. He's not planning to travel to the end of the world. And Lys is surely with him, isn't he?"

"I can only repeat what I said earlier. Casto won't go."

"As if I'll let you hold me back! I'm not your slave! I'm a free man!"

Fast as an attacking snake, the Angel of Death turned around. His eyes were two small slits, his lips pressed tightly together.

"You're my mate, which makes you a lot more than just my possession. I'm your lord and god, and if you don't stop challenging me right now, I'll punish you accordingly, *slave*."

Even Kalad reared back a little, not ashamed by his accelerated heartbeat. When in this mood, Renaldo was beyond terrifying, something that didn't seem to faze his beloved mate in the least.

"Don't you dare think I'd be impressed by this, my *god*. If I want to go, I'll go."

"Damn it, Casto."

Renaldo grabbed the young man's wrist in a crushing grip, but as always, Casto refused to show any signs of pain. With a bland expression, he stared into Renaldo's gray eyes until he let go of him again.

His arm slung around Daran, Aegid approached the two squabblers.

"Why don't you escort Casto, my lord?"

"I don't have the time."

Aegid sighed. This short sentence was probably the core of the problem. Even though they had decided to stay in the Valley this summer, there were still countless tasks to fulfill. This meant Renaldo didn't have the time to indulge his capricious husband as they both might wish, which resulted in Casto getting bored. When the King of Ummana wasn't occupied, he tended to find things to do—things the Angel of Death rarely agreed with, resulting in situations like this one. And such was his bad luck to be dragged right into it.

"What about we go with him? Would that put your mind at ease?"

The Angel of Death thought about it.

"A little. So far you've never disappointed me. I'm going to think about it."

"Splendid. Perhaps we can focus on the really important things now." Kalad grinned at Casto, glad the thunderstorm had been put off for the time being. "We want to see what Daran has learned."

After a last, calculating stare at his mate, Casto nodded in agreement. Again Aegid found himself fascinated by how easily the king was able to control his emotions. No matter how heartfelt his tantrums were, Casto never lost sight of the big picture. Without a doubt, he had already displayed all possible variants of this argument in a corner of his complicated mind and decided to hold the matter in abeyance. Which didn't mean he would forget even the smallest detail. It was only a short reprieve before he resumed the battle at a later, more convenient time. Renaldo, too, seemed to have decided to leave the matter alone. He even pressed a reconciliatory kiss on Casto's forehead, a gesture that made the young man roll his eyes derisively.

ON HIS way back to the training hall, the Angel of Death met Hulda, dressed in black leather, sauntering toward him with a bow slung over her shoulder. As always, the killer was breathtaking: her long blonde hair was braided, the lavender eyes glinted mockingly in her regal face, and the leather clothing accentuated her alluring curves. Although Renaldo loved only Casto, he felt a throbbing in his loins when he looked at Hulda. There was no man in the world who remained unperturbed by her enchanting sensuality, a fact she was aware of only too well and that she often used to her advantage. Her full lips parted into a beaming smile.

"What is it, Renaldo? Are you remembering old times?"

The Angel of Death smiled back a little sourly. Both he and Canubis had shared the mother superior's bed on a regular basis before she had finally chosen Wolfstan. What had always fascinated Renaldo most was the naturalness with which the killer enjoyed physical intimacy. Hulda never tried to please in bed. She knew what she wanted, took it without regard for anything else, and expected her partners to do the same. She knew neither regret nor false morals. Everything both parties agreed on was allowed, and at the end of the night, there was no room for guilt. The Mother Superior of the Sisters of the Night was a remarkable woman in more than one respect.

"Maybe. We had some intense fun, didn't we?"

Her soft fingers caressed his cheek slightly.

"Indeed we did. Now tell me, what have you been fighting about, you and your precious heart?"

"Is it that obvious?"

Hulda only cocked an eyebrow.

"Fine. He was stubborn and I lost my temper."

"How can that be? I mean, this has never happened before! You're a fine example of self-restraint and Casto always listens to reason. You both must have experienced a rather black day."

"Cut it out, Hulda. I'm perfectly able to make fun of me by myself."

"But not even half as effectively as I can do it. Admit it!"

"I told you to stop. Just help me."

The killer looked up at him in a calculated display of mock innocence.

"How should I help you? He's your mate. And I don't even know what this is all about."

"Casto wants to visit the market in Kwarl. Since we're staying in the Valley this summer, he's eager to do some breeding work."

"I fail to see the problem."

"I can't go with him."

Hulda sighed. Now she knew where the bone was buried.

"Let me guess, you forbade him to go and he lost it."

Renaldo's silence was answer enough.

"Why are you doing this, Renaldo? Casto is a grown man, a warrior of great ability who, before he met you, was perfectly capable of taking care of himself. Kwarl is only a two-day ride from the Valley. Why shouldn't he go?"

"Because something could happen to him. And I wouldn't be there to protect him. Hulda, I've almost lost him once, and through my own hand, to top it off. I simply can't stand it when he's not close by."

The killer slung an arm around her god, her voice very soft. She knew what she had to say wouldn't please Renaldo—especially since he had already realized the stupidity of his action himself.

"You have to stop caging him. Since the Spring Ceremony, you've been acting like a hen with only one chick. Casto has been remarkably patient until now, but if you don't pull your act together soon, it's only a matter of time until he gets on Lys's back and leaves you out of principle."

The Angel of Death tensed. He didn't like Hulda's words in the least.

"You always want him to trust you, to submit to you completely. But when it's your turn to do the same, you chicken out. I know how hard it is for you to relinquish control, but if you don't learn to grant your heart some small freedom soon, you'll be smothering him."

"So you think I should let him go?"

"It's Kwarl. And Lys will be with him. What in the Mothers' names could happen?"

Renaldo sighed.

"I don't want to start thinking about it. But you're right, I've got to stop patronizing him. Thanks for your counsel."

"As always, it was my pleasure, my god." Condescendingly, Hulda patted Renaldo's cheek. "And now excuse me. The stags won't wait."

For a moment, the Angel of Death allowed himself the pleasure of ogling his sister-in-arms's swinging hips; then he returned to his tasks. Although he knew how right the killer was about his heart, he could feel everything inside him rebelling against her words. The mere idea of allowing Casto to leave the Valley on his own made his fire blaze. His heart was his, and his alone. Casto had no right to disobey or even leave him. Renaldo suspected his overbearing possessiveness was a result of the Mothers leaving them. Now he and Canubis were the masters of this world, at least unofficially. The Angel of Death had always wondered what it would feel like to get his full power back, but he would have never dreamed it could be such a painful process. His fire had always been a burden, elevating him above everybody else, just like his beauty did. After he had acknowledged Casto as his heart, he thought he would be able to control the lethal heat inside him, but now he knew it was impossible. The fire wasn't just a part of him; it was his very nature, something he would never be able to resist. And like the flames, which consumed everything in their way to live on, he needed Casto to keep going. Possessing the king was an instinct that ensured his survival. At the same time, Renaldo was painfully aware that this was a sure way to grow apart from—and ultimately lose—his alluring mate. Hulda was right. Casto had been unaccustomedly patient with his husband, but after today's argument, his heart would definitely cease being so understanding. It was time to change.

"Daran! Damn, you're dreaming with your eyes open!"

Kalad's angry voice pried the thief from his musings. After he had been the involuntary witness of the argument between Lord Renaldo and his heart, he hadn't been able to concentrate on his riding lesson. It had been so bad that Casto had ended the lesson earlier than planned. Aegid and Kalad had been very understanding and had brought Daran back to their chambers. But the loving care of the desert brothers, which usually calmed him down, couldn't reach him today. If Daran was honest, it hadn't been the fight that had left him so confused, but the mention of Kwarl, the city of his birth. During the five years he had been serving his masters, he had never wasted a single thought on the place, since he had realized quite soon that the desert brothers were his true home. In addition, his memories of the town were not only happy ones. His life there had been dangerous and full of hardships, and he had often felt alone. But when Renaldo had spoken the name of the town, the memories had attacked him like a pack of hungry wolves, and now his thoughts were moving in circles. He was so fixated, he didn't even register when he tried to pour the entire contents of the wine jug into Kalad's cup. Guiltily he stared at his master's ruined clothes.

"I'm so sorry, Master! Please forgive me!"

He wanted to hurry and get a new tunic as well as a rag, but Kalad stopped him with a determined stare.

"Daran, look at me! What the heck is wrong with you?"

Before the thief could answer, Aegid placed his right hand on his shoulder.

"In case you're still upset about before, don't fret. I think Casto was rather glad to cancel the lesson."

Embarrassed, Daran stared at the ground.

"That's not it, Master. I just can't stop thinking about Kwarl."

Frowning, Aegid loosened his grip.

"What about Kwarl?"

Daran lowered his head in silence. In the hush, Aegid slapped his forehead.

"Damn it, Daran. I'm sorry! I've completely forgotten that Kwarl is your home."

"The Valley is my home. Kwarl is just the place I was born."

Kalad embraced the thief.

"Would you prefer to stay here when we accompany Casto?"

"I don't know." Daran tried to suppress his sobs but failed. "I just don't know. Part of me wants to stay away from the place for the rest of my life, but another part would like to see the town again. And that's really strange, because until today, I haven't even thought about it. Only when Lord Casto mentioned the name did the memories return."

Kalad took the thief's face in both hands. "Do you regret having gone with us?"

Daran's elegant fingers gripped his master's wrists almost desperately. "How can you ask something like that? I thank the Mothers each day for letting me meet you. You are my life."

The thief's openness touched his masters. With a smile, Kalad pressed a kiss on the soft lips of his slave. "I can feel how distressed you are. I think it would be best if Aegid and I help you to relax. After all, it was a tiring day."

Daran tried to answer, but at that moment, Aegid slung his arms around his hips. Knowing well there was no escape now, he let his masters drag him into the bedroom.

EMOTIONALLY HIGH-STRUNG, Renaldo entered his rooms. After the fight this forenoon, he didn't know what to expect. Everything between a humble plea for forgiveness, a continuation of their argument, and smoldering sex was possible. It all depended what Casto had decided on during the day.

His capricious mate had made himself comfortable on some cushions in front of the cold chimney and pointedly ignored his husband when he entered. Renaldo closed his eyes for a moment. So Casto wasn't angry enough to spend the night with Lys in the stables, but still so agitated as to provoke another fight. Experience had taught Renaldo not to react to the silence.

First he went into the bath to wash the day off his skin. Then he returned, poured himself a cup of wine, and sat down next to his heart. That Casto let all this happen without comment was encouraging, if only a little. Still silent, the Angel of Death sipped his wine and enjoyed the flavor while he contemplated how to start the conversation without igniting the next fight. His pondering was interrupted by Casto's calm voice. The king sounded stoic. It was obvious he had resigned himself to the circumstances, even though he didn't like them.

"If it is your will, I'll stay in the Valley, Barbarian."

Renaldo sighed heavily. Casto's sudden, reluctant submissiveness only reinforced his decision.

"No, you won't. You'll go to the market. But"—he raised his finger in warning—"you're going to take Aegid and Kalad with you. This will reassure me, at least a little."

"Where does this sudden change of heart come from?"

Renaldo placed a forefinger under Casto's chin and caressed the young man's cheek with his other hand.

"I'm aware that I kept you on a tight leash. You've been surprisingly lenient with me, for which I'm grateful. But it's time for me to get over my puny fears. You're a grown man and capable of looking after yourself."

A mocking smile appeared on Casto's lips.

"Let me guess, you've spoken to Hulda. It sounds like her."

"Doesn't make the words untrue, though."

"So it's fine if I go?"

Renaldo sighed.

"No, it's not. But I'll still allow it."

The king's mesmerizing blue eyes lit up. Gently his fingertips traced his mate's cheeks.

"I thank you, Barbarian. I know how hard it is for you to relinquish control, and I promise to be careful."

"I know."

An alluring smile parted the lips of the Angel of Death.

"So, are we going to make up?"

Casto felt his pulse going up. He hated himself for it, but when Renaldo looked at him like that, his entire defense crumbled to dust. Initially he had planned to punish his dominant mate by ignoring him tonight, but the hungry glint in the gray eyes overwhelmed him, together with the fire awakening deep inside himself. He slung his arms around his mate's neck, their lips connected, and the night turned to ashes.

"SIC, YOU need to do me a favor!"

Cheeks tinged a healthy crimson from running in the morning air, Casto dashed into his friend's smithy the next day. Sic was sitting on the only chair in the room, looking totally flustered. The king stopped dead in his tracks, forgetting about his own needs for the moment.

"Sic! What's the matter?"

The smith looked up, tears streaming down his face while a happy grin dominated his lips. He held out a sheaf of paper to his friend.

"I got a letter from Jago and Cassia! It has just arrived!"

Now Casto, too, had to grin. This was indeed happy news.

"How are they? What's going on back in Ummana?"

"They are doing well. Heljia is growing just fine, and Cassia is back to working as a midwife. Jago is drowning in work and money because Anesha has rescinded all the new laws the council had passed. Now the smiths are getting a fair share again, and it seems my work is selling adequately as well. Oh, and guess who is Cassia's latest and most prominent client? It seems as if your sister is pregnant. Jago writes it's an open secret that—"

"Aktan is the father."

Casto sounded smug. Sic stared at him open-mouthed. He had gotten used to the king's empathy by now, but this managed to surprise him.

"How did you guess?"

"I didn't have to guess. He's the only logical candidate. Aktan is not only captain of the Royal Guard, but also the bastard brother of Lady Evienna, the current head of the Murreano family. Like the Donai, Krapati, Sylves, and Ereat, the Murreano belong to the oldest, most influential families in Ummana. In order to free herself from Erac, Anesha has to find strong allies on which she can rely to a certain extent. And Evienna is going to fight tooth and nail for her niece or nephew to inherit the throne. From a tactical point of view, this is an ideal match."

Sic shuddered. Casto's birthplace was indeed a snake pit where sentiments like love or trust were nothing but shattered dreams. Casto, who had picked up on Sic's sudden change of mood, directed their dialogue back into happier territory.

"So Jago and Cassia are fine?"

The smith beamed.

"It seems so. They sent me a little painting of Heljia, and it's amazing how much she has grown in these few months. I also got quite a long list of orders from Jago. He says he has to fight customers off whenever they get wind of a delivery from or to the Valley. It's flattering."

"No, it's not. You're simply that good. Something I've always known."

"Thank you, Casto. And now tell me what you need from me. You're here for a reason."

The king regarded the smith intently.

"I need a favor from you. Can you please accompany me to Kwarl? I'm leaving tomorrow morning, and Renaldo has made Kalad and Acgid my watchdogs. Of course they're going to take Daran with them, and there's no way I'll survive all the mooning without somebody else to distract me. Plus those two can be pretty annoying when the mood strikes them. So please, come with me!"

Sic couldn't suppress a knowing grin. It was indeed nauseating to watch the desert brothers together with Daran. The three men were so perfectly matched and so syrupy-sweet to each other, as if they had walked out of a fairy tale. And watching two seasoned warriors like Aegid and Kalad fuss over Daran as if he was a newly hatched chicken, only to ravish him most lecherously the next moment, was disturbing, to put it mildly.

"So going alone wasn't an option?"

Sic couldn't help but tease his friend a little. Casto shot him a dirty look.

"Don't go there, Sic. I'm still too pissed to think this is funny."

"Don't do anything stupid, please! And if you do, keep me out of it."

"I never do anything stupid. Don't worry, I'm going to comply to the Barbarian's will. So are you coming with me?"

Sic sighed.

"Of course I am. How long is this going to take? I do have work, you know."

For a moment Casto felt a pang of guilt for cornering Sic as he had just done, but then he imagined an entire trip with only the desert warriors and Daran as company, and his chin hardened in determination.

"Well, it's a two-day ride to Kwarl. Selling the horses and finding a good stallion will take two to three days. One more for all the minor things, and then the trip back. About a week, I'd say."

"That's pretty long. Well, I guess it's fine. I do have some things I need, and getting out doesn't sound too bad. I'm in. And now please excuse me. I have some packing to do."

"Thank you, Sic! You're a lifesaver! See you tomorrow at dawn!"

WHILE HE was busy packing, Sic's mind pondered an entirely different problem. He didn't know whether he should tell Noran about this trip or not. Ever since the Spring Ceremony, their relationship had been progressing smoothly. Meeting the master smith was no longer awkward; he even looked forward to it now. When Sic had problems concerning work, he never hesitated to share them with Noran, who could usually provide a solution. Regarding work, they were meeting on equal ground, and it made Sic ecstatic to be acknowledged by his former master. He was still shy about physical contact, even though his reluctance was less and less grounded in fear, shifting toward a weird mixture of insecurity and anticipation. It felt like falling in love all over again, making him both happy and anxious. Noran's own insecurity and reticence didn't help at all. He had left control over their relationship and its progress entirely to Sic, who had no clue how to handle things. Most of his life, Noran had been the one to make all decisions for him, and as his slave, Sic had been content with that.

Now even a simple thing like talking about a trip was an almost impossible task. Sic rubbed his eyes. After all the pondering he had done, the whole problem still boiled down to one thing: what did he want? By now, he had learned to ask himself this question and answer it truthfully, even though it might hurt sometimes. And what he really wanted was to talk to Noran about the trip. Filled with new determination, Sic left his chambers to meet the master smith.

Noran was less than pleased to hear about Sic's traveling plans, but he managed to hide his consternation. Like Renaldo, the smith was deeply worried about all the things that could go wrong on a trip like this. Knowing Aegid and Kalad would be with the two young men wasn't enough to put his mind at ease. But there was no way he could object to something his precious treasure had decided to do. Sic was still timid and had considerable problems voicing his will. He needed encouragement, not opposition. And so Noran gritted his teeth and put on a friendly smile, although his inner beast wanted nothing more than to tie Sic down and forbid him to go.

"Kwarl is nice at this time of year, and the market is a sight to behold. I'm sure you're going to have fun."

Sic regarded his former master sharply. He had known Noran long enough to know when something was off. And now his finely tuned senses were shrilling like crazy.

"You don't like it, do you?"

For a moment it seemed as if Noran wanted to deny the statement; then his shoulders slumped forward. Part of their agreement was to be honest to each other.

"No, I don't. To be frank, I'm strongly opposed. I'm surprised Renaldo has given his consent."

"Not voluntarily. As far as I understand, he could have either agreed and have Aegid and Kalad accompany his heart, or he could have forbidden it and Casto would have gone all on his own."

"Sounds just like him. He really does whatever he pleases."

Grumpy admiration resounded in those words. Sic grinned.

"Makes it more interesting for all of us." He paused for a moment, choosing his next words carefully. "May I know why you are against it? Kwarl is not exactly enemy territory."

Noran sat down heavily on one of his ancient chairs.

"No, it's not. Most probably the worst thing you'll encounter will be some pickpockets when you're in the market itself. And the journey is not worth mentioning, since it's so close to the Valley." Noran hesitated. "It's just—well, it's a miracle you're standing here, talking to me, after everything I've done to you. I know I haven't got the slightest right to tell you what to do and what not. Still, the mere idea of you leaving the Valley makes me feel uneasy. And if something happens, I won't be there to protect you."

Sic stared at Noran for a long time. Then a smile stole over his face.

"I'm glad. I'm glad you're being so honest with me and that you're harboring fears and worries similar to mine. This gives me hope for the future. I'm still going, though."

"I figured as much. And since I can't change your mind, would it be okay if I gave you a list to do some shopping for me?"

Relieved about how well things had turned out, Sic extended a hand.

"It would be my pleasure, Master."

2. TRAP

Fascinated, yet slightly intimidated, Daran stared at the city that had once been his home. During the past five years he had spent in the Valley, Kwarl had changed profoundly. The marketplace had been extended to make room for the increasing number of merchants dwelling in the city. For this, some houses on the western end had been obliterated, and as a consequence, the market had swallowed up a part of the thieves' quarters. Daran felt a twinge of sadness; he had loved the small alleyways and winding backyards that had provided ideal cover from the guard and other thieves as well. He could imagine how unhappy the masters of this shadow empire were about the changes. On the other hand, more merchants meant more chances to get a share of the riches. Daran sighed, glad these kinds of musings were no longer his problem.

Casto had finally found a place where they could stable their horses. Since their departure from the Valley, the king had been in a splendid mood and was so friendly and forthcoming, it spooked Daran. He simply couldn't understand why it was so important for Casto to demonstrate his independence. For Daran, the main reason to come to Kwarl had been that he didn't want to be separated from his masters for any length of time. Lord Sic, who was riding with them as well, put up a cheerful front, but he seemed to be distracted. Daran suspected he was missing Lord Noran, although he would probably never understand why. Perhaps it was because of Lys, Casto's intimidating warhorse, that the king didn't miss his husband. The close relationship between horse and rider had always impressed Daran, and on their way to Kwarl, he had the chance to witness it at close range. The most exciting thing was when Casto talked to the stallion. From what he was saying, it was sometimes possible to reconstruct the entire dialogue, and Daran had realized very soon that Lys was even more intelligent than he had thought possible. In addition, he was always ready to dish out a nasty comment on his rider's actions, which made Daran like him quite a lot.

As soon as Casto's feet touched the ground, the first merchants started streaming toward him with greedy looks on their faces to inquire about the price for this outstanding horse that drew all eyes with its majestic posture alone. The king indulged in the negotiations with such enthusiasm and skill that his ancestry was clear without any papers to prove it. Lord Sic excused himself; he had a long list of items he wanted to get as soon as possible. Kalad and Aegid stayed with Casto but did allow Daran to wander around by himself.

"Be careful not to be kidnapped by barbarians."

Kalad's broad, salacious grin made Daran blush. He didn't have to be a seer to know what he would be doing tonight.

"And stay here at the marketplace. If you want to make a trip into the city, we'll do that tomorrow."

Aegid's admonition still ringing in his ears, Daran ventured into the hurly-burly of the market. His owners had given him a wallet heavy with gold and silver to spend at his leisure. Overwhelmed by such generosity, even though he should have been used to it by now, Daran kept the wallet close to his body. He didn't plan on spending more than just a few silver coins for some sweets. He vividly remembered the stall of Mother Gwen, who had slipped him a candy once in a while when he had still been a child. For him, the taste of her sweets was equivalent to happiness, and he only hoped to find her in the chaos of the market. And he was lucky. Mother Gwen and her stall were still at the same place as back then. And like the old times, many a rich customer was standing in line to purchase a bag of sweets. Mother Gwen's skills were famous beyond the walls of Kwarl. When it was his turn, Daran bought two bags of honey candy and a box of chocolate. Aegid was addicted to sweets of any kind, and Daran hoped to make him happy. Mother Gwen had barely changed during the last five years. She was still an impressive, good-looking woman, even though the first gray had started to tint her auburn hair, and the fine wrinkles around her dark brown eyes and full mouth were proof how much she liked to laugh. She regarded Daran sharply, and then a smile appeared on her face.

"You're Daran, aren't you?"

The thief reciprocated the smile from the bottom of his heart, happy that one of the few friendly persons from his past remembered him.

"I wouldn't have thought you'd recognize me, Mother Gwen. It's been some time."

"Stupid boy. I rarely forget a face, especially when it's as beautiful as yours. You're looking great."

"I was lucky."

"Good for you! How long are you going to stay in Kwarl? If you have time, come and pay me a visit. You know how much I love to hear a good story, and I bet you've got some great ones to tell."

Involuntarily, Daran lowered his gaze. He was a little uncomfortable all of a sudden.

"Indeed I have, Mother Gwen. I'll try to make time for you."

Happily, she patted his cheeks with her warm hand before she turned to her next customer.

Thoughtful, Daran put a candy in his mouth. The taste brought back memories he had deemed forgotten. And meeting Mother Gwen had upset him more than he wanted to admit. The emotions overwhelming him were confusing. He couldn't understand why he still felt so much for his birthplace. Daran was so lost in thought, he didn't realize how close he had come to the outskirts of the market. A man elbowed his way ruthlessly through the mass of people and pushed him hard.

"Watch where you're going, you idiot!" The man glared at him. He wore a long, dark coat with the hood deep over his face. Daran was just about to murmur some kind of apology when the stranger took his upper arms in an iron grip. Their faces got so close, Daran could smell the other man's foul breath.

"I can't believe it! Daran?"

Confused, Daran stopped trying to wrench free. The stranger was laughing now.

"It is you! I hadn't thought I'd ever see you again!"

With awkward movements, the man pulled the hood away from his face. It took a moment before Daran recognized him.

"Gar? Is that you?"

"Of course, stupid. Who else?"

Imploringly, Daran looked at his friend from childhood days. Gar was two years older than him and had always been like a brother. When they were still little, they had played together in the streets; later they had started begging as a team. Gar had even started taking him along to bigger burglaries, but in the months before Daran left Kwarl, they had lost contact. Gar had developed a deeper interest in women, and his business had become shadier. When he looked at his former friend closely, Daran could see the traces of hardships engraved in Gar's features. Living at the edge of society had made him age faster. He had the appearance of a man in his thirties, not somebody who had just left twenty behind. A hard streak had formed around his mouth that Daran didn't remember, and the once-cheerful eyes were now full of resignation. A wave of gratitude washed over Daran when he realized his owners had saved him from more than just death on the gallows. Without their care, he would now be like Gar, aged before his time, weighed down by destiny, and robbed of all hope.

"You look well."

As if he had read Daran's thoughts, Gar regarded him intently. "It seems you fared way better than I did."

Slightly flustered, Daran evaded his gaze. "I was very lucky."

"I'd say so too. But you know, let's go somewhere and have a beer and a chat. There's too many people around here."

Sadly, Daran shook his head. "I'm sorry, that's impossible. I have to be back soon."

Gar furrowed his brow. A shadow danced across his face, turning it into a hideous grimace for a moment, only to soften up immediately. His tone was mocking.

"Don't tell me you're too noble to be meeting with your old friend."

Startled, Daran's eyes widened. "No, of course not! You have to believe me!"

"It's fine, I'm just making fun of you. Come on, just one beer."

Desperately Daran tried to find a way to decline the offer. He had no intention whatsoever of accompanying Gar, but if he didn't want to insult his childhood friend any more than he already had, he was left with no choice.

"Please, Daran. It's my treat."

With a sigh, Daran gave in. He knew he was going to get into trouble with his masters, but if he didn't follow Gar, the man would surely stalk him, and Daran did not want Aegid and Kalad to find out what kind of company their slave had kept. Given the choice, he preferred the beating he would surely get for his disobedience over the disgrace of the warriors finding out. With a last longing glance at the market, he followed Gar into the shadows of the thieves' quarters.

"YOU'VE ALWAYS been a sight to behold, but now you seem to be glowing from the inside. Whatever has happened to you, it must have been spectacular."

Embarrassed, Daran stared at the mug standing in front of him. The stench in the bar assaulted his nostrils, and the smell coming from the swill the owner of the bar dared to call beer made him nauseated. To satisfy Gar, he pretended to take a sip, but not a drop passed his lips. Life with Aegid and Kalad had made him particular.

"As I said, I was lucky. But let's stop talking about me. How did you fare?"

Gar's gaze darkened. "Definitely not as well. You know, life was never easy for us. Speed and cunning alone are not sufficient if you want to get by. The older you get, the more brutal business becomes. I've survived until now, but it wasn't a stroll."

Daran nodded emphatically. He knew all too well about the harsh reality Gar had been describing. It was a world where the strong were always right, a world where law and order had no place. Sometimes he wondered how the Valley, which was led by the will of two gods of war, was different from the streets of Kwarl, but given the choice, he would always prefer his masters over life as an outlaw. He shuddered. It would be better to return to said masters right now, before his punishment reached an extent he wouldn't be able to bear.

"I'm sorry, Gar. It was nice talking to you, but I really have to go."

"You haven't finished your beer yet."

"I'm not really thirsty. Goodbye, Gar."

Daran was about to leave when his friend's hand landed heavily on his arm. "Daran, stay."

The desperate tone in Gar's voice alerted Daran. "Gar, what's going on?"

His childhood friend evaded his gaze. "I'm truly sorry. I had no choice."

"Gar! What are you talking about?"

"Well done, Gar. You may leave now."

The voice made Daran freeze, for he knew it all too well. A hand landed heavily on his shoulder, and he winced. That hand had beaten him so often, he knew its weight and structure by heart.

"Egand."

His voice was hoarse. Gar retreated with a guilty expression.

"I'm so sorry, Daran. I had some unsettled debts with him, and if I hadn't handed you over, he would have killed me."

Daran didn't reply. It hurt too much to be betrayed by this man he once had thought of as a brother. Egand grabbed his shoulder impatiently and forced Daran to turn around. His stepfather had gotten old since the last time they met. The years had intensified the cruel streak around his mouth and the scornful look in his eyes. His hair had thinned and taken on a washed-out gray color, and his burly frame slumped a little, but he still emanated danger. Now his lips contorted into a sadistic smile.

"If it isn't my poor lost stepson. When I heard the rumors about you being back in Kwarl, I couldn't believe it. But here you are, handsome as ever and dressed like a prince."

Daran rolled his eyes. He didn't have time for shallow games. "What do you want, Egand?"

His stepfather's eyes narrowed in anger.

"What do I want? How about the money you owe me? I'd been feeding and clothing you for ten long years, providing a roof over your head, and just when you reached the age to repay my generosity, you vanished into thin air. I turned Kwarl inside out to find you. Where in the Mothers' names have you been?"

"As if you'd be interested in that. Concerning your 'care,' I always had to earn my keep. I don't owe you a thing."

Egand chuckled with malicious glee. "It seems the little doggie has grown some teeth. But I'm warning you, think twice whom you growl at, you ungrateful piece of shit."

"I'll growl as much as I like. If you don't have anything else to say, I'm on my way."

"Not so fast, boy." Egand's dirty fingers dug into Daran's upper arm. "You can leave when I decide so, and at the moment I want you to stay. Since you've obviously been doing well, you're going to share your riches with me. Then you can leave."

Daran was speechless for a moment, and then he started to laugh.

"My riches? Could it be your eyesight has become poor in your old age? Do you see this?" Daran gingerly touched the collar around his neck. "I'm a slave. I don't own anything. Strictly speaking, not even my body. How am I supposed to share with you?"

"A slave? Do you want to make a fool out of me? Your shirt is made of the finest linen, your jerkin and trousers are chamois leather, your boots are made from mountain deer leather and, as far as I can see, lined with rabbit's fur. I don't know a single master who would adorn a slave like that."

"My masters like to dress me up. It heightens their status."

"And who are these ominous masters?"

Daran was torn over whether he should tell Egand. But then he decided it would be better to have his cards out in the open. Perhaps his stepfather would even let him go.

"If you must know, they're lords from the Valley. It was they who took me away from here. I wanted to steal from them, and in exchange for not handing me over to the guards, they kept me as their slave."

"And I'm supposed to believe this?"

Egand's voice was meant to sound derisive, but Daran could feel the insecurity that had taken hold of the man. Every child in Kwarl knew how foolish it was to challenge somebody from the Valley.

"I don't care whether you believe me or not. All I'm saying is, if I don't return soon, they're going to look for me, and then we're all in deep trouble."

Egand appraised his stepson closely. Daran could almost hear the thoughts in the man's head. On one hand, Daran was a most welcome, promising prey. On the other hand, it was akin to suicide to meddle in the affairs of the lords from the North. After some agonizing moments, greed triumphed over reason. Egand's gaze hardened.

"I think you're just trying to fool me. You're coming with me, and then we'll see whether your 'masters'"—he spat the word out sarcastically—"will stoop to saving you. If they do, I'm curious as to how much they're willing to pay for you. Until then, I'll take this. Just think of it as an advance."

With this he wrenched the wallet from Daran's hands and gave the two men, who had been staying in the background until now, a sign. Despite his efforts, they grabbed Daran and began to drag him outside. When he tried to wrestle free, Egand knocked him out without batting an eyelash.

"I WONDER what's keeping Daran. It's not like him to make us wait."

Aegid scanned the crowd with worried eyes, as if his will alone could make the thief appear again. Kalad put a hand on his arm. He, too, was worried. The sun had already started to go down, and Casto had retired to their accommodation for the night. After an entire day of ruthless negotiations, he was exhausted but satisfied. He had managed to sell all the horses he had brought at top prices and was looking forward to finding a suitable stallion for breeding. The desert brothers had wanted to wait for their thief and were growing more restless with every minute he didn't appear.

"Shall we go looking for him?"

"I'd prefer to. Unfortunately we haven't brought any of the wolves with us, but in this chaos, they'd probably be unable to follow the trail."

Determined, they went to the best inn in Kwarl, where Sic and Casto were waiting for them. Seeing their strained expressions, the king knew immediately that something was amiss.

"Where's Daran? Is he still not back?"

"No. And we're getting worried. He's always reliable."

Kalad's heart was in these few words. Casto put on his boots again.

"We'd better go looking for him."

"It's fine, Casto. You and Sic better stay here. We can do this on our own."

"Do you really think we'd let you search for your thief all alone? Of course we're going to help, won't we, Sic?"

The young smith smiled broadly despite his exhaustion. "Who can say no to you, Casto?"

The king turned to the desert brothers in triumph. "How do you wish to proceed?"

Aegid regarded the eager faces of his brother-in-arms and his lord with heartfelt gratitude.

"At this time, there shouldn't be too many people left on the market. We'll spread out and start asking questions. Daran is noticeable enough to make an impression. Somebody must remember him. We'll meet again in an hour at the place where you sold the horses today."

The two young men nodded, and Sic placed a soothing hand on Aegid's arm.

"We'll find him, I'm sure. I bet it's nothing bad. Perhaps he's just forgotten the time."

Kalad's face was dark. "No matter what, he can look forward to some serious punishment once he's back. We won't let this slip."

"First we have to find him. Then you can think about his punishment."

Casto's voice was gentle. He understood the worries of the two men all too well. The obsessive love of the desert brothers for their thief was the target of good-humored banter almost as often as Renaldo's affection for Casto. And everybody in the Valley admired Daran for keeping the balance between his masters without favoring one of them. For two men who were as inseparably connected as Aegid and Kalad, a partner like that was as rare and precious as a blue diamond. Perhaps even more, since it had taken them more than eight hundred years to find him. Determined not to lose this treasure, the four warriors got on their way.

It was Sic who returned with good news to the place they had agreed on. He was accompanied by an older, yet still striking female whose lively eyes seemed to take in even the most mundane details. Sic introduced her with a slight bow.

"This is Mother Gwen. She's got a stall for sweets in the market and has known Daran since he was a little boy. Mother Gwen, these are the Lords Casto, Aegid, and Kalad."

The proud woman made a movement that could be interpreted as a curtsey; then she turned directly to the desert brothers.

"So you're the good fortune that's befallen him."

"How did you manage to deduce this so quickly?" Casto was impressed. Mother Gwen treated him to a smile, which reminded him of Hulda. It was full of motherly warmth but also a tiny bit condescending, as if he were a small boy who had just asked a foolish question. The king felt crimson creeping into his cheeks.

"It's not as hard as you might think. I can feel the worry surrounding these two. Also, you're too young to bind him like he is."

"What do you know about Daran?" Kalad sounded gruff. He was frustrated that they hadn't been able to find out anything substantial.

Mother Gwen turned serious. "Not much and nothing good. This morning Daran visited my stall to buy some sweets. Sometime later, he was seen with a man called Gar. Gar is a friend from childhood days and was always Daran's hero. Rumor has it they went into a tavern called the Golden Hat. It's a bad place where thieves and cutthroats meet."

"Why would Daran go there? We forbade him to leave the market, and he always obeys our commands."

Aegid was enraged, but Mother Gwen only shrugged her shoulders.

"How would I know? But you shouldn't forget that this is the place Daran grew up, and Gar was the closest thing to a brother he ever had. Perhaps he thought he had no choice. Anyway, Egand, too, has been seen in the Golden Hat, which makes things complicated. He's Daran's stepfather and still harboring a grudge because the boy managed to give him the slip five years ago. If he has him, you might as well give up."

"This Egand—he's the man who beat up Daran." There was a dangerous tone in Kalad's voice. He sounded like an angry wolf shortly before it charged.

"Egand has done a lot to Daran, including things he'll surely never tell anybody about. The only reason Daran could still be alive at the moment is Egand's greed. He's probably found out by now that Daran is no longer poor. He's going to try to get his share of the wealth before executing his revenge."

"Where can we find this Egand person?"

Mother Gwen stared at the four warriors long and hard. Then she shrugged again.

"I'll tell you where his lair is, but be careful. Egand is ruthless, unpredictable, and crazy enough to challenge you. Plus he's at an advantage since this is his territory. If you're not careful, he can become a danger to you."

"Don't worry about that, Mother Gwen. You only tell us where we can find him."

The determined air around Kalad as well as the lethal glint in his eyes, convinced the woman that these men were capable of winning against Egand. She described the way to his hideout down to the last detail before bidding them farewell.

"Good luck on your mission. Once you have Daran back, tell him hello from me." An impish smile appeared on her lips. "He owes me more than just one good story."

"We will. And I will personally see to it that he pays his debt."

Aegid bowed gracefully to their informant, before the warriors went on their way.

DARAN WOKE because of a searing pain in his arms. Still dizzy from the blow he had received, he blinked rapidly. Obviously he had been tied quite effectively, since he was unable to move his arms and legs and felt cool steel around his neck. Egand didn't want to take a risk. Slowly his surroundings slid into focus. The shadows of unconsciousness were driven away by the flickering light of some smoky torches, which cast their irregular light on the stone walls. Daran had been placed under an arch, and in the distance he heard water dripping. He smelled a mixture of sewage, stale beer, excrement, and cheap perfume. It was a stench Daran knew by heart. They had brought him to Egand's main quarters, a desolate place in the underground of Kwarl, which once had served as the city's cistern system. When the city grew, the citizens had started to get water from outside, and the underground system with its countless tunnels and caves had been first neglected and then forgotten, until Egand had ventured down. From here his stepfather controlled the thieves' quarter with an iron fist. All those who had a run-in with the law found a safe haven here, because the guard didn't dare to come into this labyrinth where even the rats were vicious. Daran closed his eyes in despair. Nobody had to tell him how serious the trouble was he had gotten himself into. He had to escape as fast as possible if he didn't want his masters to follow him down here.

The mere thought that Aegid and Kalad could see with their own eyes in what shabby surroundings he had grown up made Daran's insides churn. Of course, they already knew about his shady past, but knowing something and seeing it were two entirely different things.

"I see our guest of honor has finally woken up."

Egand's mocking voice startled Daran from his gloomy thoughts. He turned his head to look at his stepfather, who was giving him a cold and calculating smile.

"Your masters seem to be taking their time. Perhaps you want to come clean and tell me the truth about how a worthless piece of shit like you has managed to become so rich?"

Daran saw Egand weighing the wallet in his hands with a thoughtful expression.

"Do you even know how much money this is? If you're indeed only a slave, then you must mean a lot to them. With this kind of money, I could live comfortably till next spring."

"Then take the money and let me go. You've caused enough trouble, stepfather."

Egand's expression darkened. Without warning he administered two vicious kicks to Daran's ribcage.

"Shut up! You must know the only reason why you're still alive is because of the profit I'm hoping to get from you." His dirty fingers grabbed Daran's chin and turned the young man's face to one of the torches. "Although, even if your masters don't show up, I'll probably let you live. There's lots of money to be made with beauty such as yours, and should you be disobedient, I can still sell you to the highest bidder. By now you should be used to being a slave."

Cold shudders ran down Daran's spine. Egand was dead serious about this matter, and for the first time since he had met his stepfather again, Daran felt something like fear creeping into his heart. He didn't know how to react and was furious at his own weakness. Abruptly Egand let go of him, condescending laughter erupting from his mouth. He was just about to mock Daran further when a boy of about thirteen years approached him with a pale, haunted expression and whispered urgently into his ear. The mockery in Egand's face turned into triumph.

"Seems like you didn't lie. Four noblemen are on their way here."

He bent down to open the chains around Daran's feet and then the one on his neck.

"Let's go and greet them like they deserve. I warn you, Daran— one wrong word and I'll have them killed on the spot."

Daran felt a gut-wrenching fear overwhelming him. "Please, don't harm them. I swear, I'll do anything you ask of me. Just let them go."

"They mean a lot to you, your masters, don't they?"

Although Egand's voice was full of derision, Daran managed to look straight at him. This was the truth, and there was no reason to be ashamed of it.

"They are my world."

It was only a simple sentence, spoken with absolute conviction. Even Egand was taken aback for a moment before his natural sadism took over again.

"How absolutely heartwarming. If they die, it's your fault."

Brutally, Egand dragged Daran to the middle of a room whose ceiling arched almost one and half paces above them. The visitors were coming through the main tunnel, so his men were waiting in the three smaller ones branching off into the less-frequented parts of the labyrinth. Egand would not let chance take the rein. Although he acted all high-and-mighty, the ruler of the thieves of Kwarl was deeply shaken. The animalistic instinct that had kept him alive for many years and had brought him to the top of Kwarl's underworld was going off like crazy. Until now it had always been worthwhile for him to trust his gut feeling, and now this instinct was telling him he was in serious trouble. The wisest thing to do would be to let Daran go right now, leaving him to the warriors without putting up a fight, and try to make his escape while he still could.

But he would be damned if he let his useless stepson get away unscathed. The sudden disappearance of the young man had made him the butt of countless jokes, and even today, five years later, people gossiped behind his back how Daran had managed to give him the slip. Daran's escape had caused him so much trouble, Egand felt sick just thinking about it. He would have the scrawny rat pay, no matter the cost. Besides, what could four warriors who were strangers in the city do against him and his men? Determined, he reinforced his grip on Daran's upper arms while his eyes tried to discern the dancing shadows in the main tunnel. Then he heard a noise, and just like that, the four warriors entered the heart of Egand's empire.

They were led by a slim man of about one ell and two and a half spans. His raven-black hair was done in countless braids, his body was slim yet muscular. He resembled a cat of prey, moving with the natural grace of a born predator. His brown eyes were lively and shot dark glances through the room. Behind him came a giant of a man, towering over the first with almost an ell and four spans. His hair was white, his eyes covered by a milky substance that made Egand think the man was blind. The dark skin was covered in tattoos, strange, runic symbols of which the outlaw didn't recognize even one. Compared to his companion, he appeared to be more composed, but the look in his eyes was just as furious.

When his gaze fell on the third man, Egand's breathing hitched. Although his hard life had dulled him in every respect, he was still blinded by this warrior's beauty. His wheat-blond hair framed his noble, harmonious face like a halo of light. Mesmerizing blue eyes dominated the imperious features, which were completed by a sensuous mouth. The young man's body was lean, with long muscles that rolled gracefully beneath the smooth skin. This man moved with the elegance of a dancer; it was obvious he had absolute control over his body and felt comfortable in his skin. But it wasn't this harmony that made the hair on Egand's neck stand up. It was the aura of danger surrounding the handsome stranger, the impression that his beauty was only camouflage for the lethal strength inside.

Compared to this, the fourth warrior seemed almost mundane. He had short-cropped, light brown hair, smiling green-blue eyes, and a friendly, open face. His sturdy muscles showed that he did hard manual labor on a daily basis. If there hadn't been a strange, intimidating openness about him, he could have been mistaken for a simple servant.

All four men had their hands on their weapons and looked around with suspicion in their faces. The one with the braids talked directly to Daran.

"Daran! The Mothers be praised! Are you all right?"

The thief kept his gaze down. "I'm fine, Master. I'm sorry for having made you worry."

"We'll talk about that when we're back home. Who is that man?"

"My name is Egand. I'm the master of Kwarl's underworld—and Daran's stepfather. So, you're the men who have kidnapped my poor son and made him a slave. I wonder how you're going to reimburse me for this."

The eyes of the warrior with the braids narrowed dangerously. Before he could answer, his giant companion placed a placating hand on his shoulder.

"Leave it to me, Kalad." He turned to Egand.

"I'm so pleased to make your acquaintance. Before we get on with this rather unpleasant business, allow me to introduce my brothers-in-arms. Just so you know who you're dealing with."

Despite the obvious threat, Egand managed a derisive smile. "I can hardly wait."

A strange expression flashed across the warrior's features, a mixture of reluctant respect, anger, and determination. With a slight nod, he turned toward the stunning blond.

"This is Lord Casto, husband to Lord Renaldo, the Angel of Death."

Ignoring the hushed silence in the darkness of the three tunnels, the giant spoke on.

"Next to him is Lord Sic, Emeris in the Valley. This"—the warrior gestured toward the leader—"is Lord Kalad, Emeris in the Valley. I am Lord Aegid, Kalad's desert brother and an Emeris as well. Concerning your accusation that we kidnapped Daran, I have to disagree. It was his decision to become our slave. He preferred serving us over the loss of a hand and life under your domination."

Still shocked about whose displeasure he had invoked, Egand stared at the warriors. If they were telling the truth—and he didn't doubt it any longer—then they knew how to handle the weapons they were carrying only too well. Even his thugs, who had been hardened in countless brawls and street fights, wouldn't be able to win against fighters like these. Desperately he tried to find a way out, but the only thing he came up with was a very stupid move that showed how much the situation had slipped from his control.

He grabbed Daran even harder with his right hand while he drew a dagger with his left. Then he pressed the blade against his stepson's throat, right above the collar, until a thin trickle of blood appeared.

"I've heard enough. If you don't want me to slit his throat, you better scram."

"If you so much as harm a hair on his head I'm going to kill you with my own hands, scum."

Kalad's voice was stony and monotonous. Daran shuddered in Egand's arms. Only once before had the warrior talked to him like that, and he would never forget the punishment he'd had to endure afterward.

As if he could sense Daran's distress, Egand's grip hardened even more. "This may be, but then he's dead. I can see how much he means to you, so you're not going to risk it."

"Maybe. But we won't leave without him either." Absolute conviction tinged Aegid's voice.

"It seems to me we have reached an impasse." Casto stepped forward with a smile that didn't reach his eyes. "Obviously, none of us will give in, so let's consider our options."

He held up his index finger.

"Firstly, you make good on your threat and kill Daran. Let's even assume you manage to escape. As far as I can see, this underground system is pretty widespread. This means you buy yourself one, perhaps even two days, depending on how good you are. After that, you're at Kalad's mercy." Casto shook his head. "Believe me, not a desirable option. And don't make the mistake of thinking you can escape us. Until now, nobody has managed this."

A grim smile played around the boy's lips, as if he was talking about a fact he had experienced firsthand.

"Secondly, we retreat. Then you're going to kill Daran. Don't try to deny it—I can see it in your eyes. I've seen too many monsters in my life to not recognize you for what you are. So we're not going to leave without Daran.

"Thirdly, you leave him to us. In return we'll spare you and those men lurking in the shadows." Casto turned his head as if he was thinking about a complicated problem. "Then nobody comes to harm. We'll even allow you to keep the money you've stolen from Daran. How about it?"

Egand's inner voice urged him to accept the offer, knowing this was his only, and last, chance to get out of this mess unscathed. He nodded slowly.

"I do accept."

The dagger was taken away from Daran's throat and the ropes around his wrists were cut loose. Then Egand pushed him in the direction of his masters. The thief didn't hesitate for a second. He ran toward Kalad, who embraced him hungrily while Daran hid his face on the broad chest of his owner.

"I'm so terribly sorry, Master."

Gently Aegid pulled the sobbing young man into his arms.

"It's fine, little thief. Now everything's fine. We're just glad nothing has happened to you."

When Egand was confronted with such openly displayed affection, he felt a nameless, night-black fury rising inside his heart. Daran had no right to be so happy, no right to be loved like that. He had to pay for his sins toward Egand. There was no way he could be allowed to go unscathed after he had made such an utter fool of his stepfather. Egand's common sense was buried under an avalanche of hatred and envy. All he could still see clearly was Daran's back, the spot he had to hit to erase his annoying stepson forever. Anger made him fast. He grabbed the dagger by the hilt and threw it with deadly precision. A crunching sound resonated when the weapon found its target, when it buried itself in Daran's back and penetrated his heart.

TIME SEEMED to stand still. All noise, even the smallest rustle, died, frozen in the improbability of what had just happened. The sudden silence was ripped apart by a scream so hollow it made everybody present shiver. It came from two people, and the despair resounding in it was overwhelming.

"Nooooo!"

Kalad and Aegid were holding their thief in their arms, staring into his clouded eyes as life left his body. A sad smile appeared on the open face.

"Ma—"

He couldn't speak on. His body went limp in his owners' arms. Kalad made a whimpering sound; tears dripped from Aegid's eyes onto the lifeless body of their beloved. Everybody was staring in morbid fascination at these two powerful warriors so completely caught up in their sorrow. Their pain was like an invisible barrier, keeping everything out. There was only room for these three men and the love that had bound them. A love that had lost its home.

Suddenly, as if in silent agreement, Kalad and Aegid lifted their heads, their gazes locked on Egand, their eyes burning with insatiable fury.

"You'll pay for this!"

Gently they placed Daran's body on the ground before they approached Egand, who wasn't able to move a single muscle in his body. Frozen in fear, he awaited the destiny he couldn't escape anymore.

3. SAND AND LIGHT

IN THE Valley, Renaldo jolted awake, covered in sweat. He could feel the danger his heart was in. Casto's tense excitement was like a knife leaving bloody cuts in his soul. Without thinking, he reached for his sword before he remembered that his heart was in Kwarl. But the feeling of urgency was steadily increasing, and so he put the weapon aside to get dressed in order to leave the Valley immediately.

He was just slipping into his boots when Canubis entered the chambers. He, too, had been woken by a feeling of urgency, only in his case it had come from Renaldo.

"What's going on?"

"Casto. He's in danger."

He didn't have to say more. While he was putting on his coat, Canubis turned toward the door again.

"I'll get the horses ready. Do you want anybody to come with you?"

"Wake Noran. If Casto's in trouble, Sic won't be far."

Canubis nodded in agreement. If push came to shove, the master smith would be a fierce and determined ally. Ever since his relationship with Sic had started to progress so remarkably well, he had started turning back into the man they had both once welcomed into the Pack. Canubis felt at ease knowing Noran would have his brother's back.

"Anybody else?"

"No, I don't really know what's going on, so speed is of the essence."

"What a pity he took Lys."

"My words exactly. The sunrise is only a few hours away, so if we push the horses, we can be in Kwarl this evening. Ghost and Demon may not be as fast as the black beast, but they're still superior."

"They are the horses of gods. What else did you expect? I'll go and wake Noran."

About half an hour later, Renaldo and Noran were galloping out of the Valley. The master smith was so worried, his face was frozen in a grim mask. Renaldo knew the pain his brother-in-arms was enduring, which was why he decided to apologize.

"I'm sorry, Noran. I should have never allowed Casto to go on his own."

A weak smile flitted across Noran's face.

"Somehow I got the impression that a ban wouldn't have impressed Casto at all."

The Angel of Death sighed.

"Probably not. But I do have some means to make him obey."

"But you don't like using them."

"Of course not. I love Casto's independence. And you're one to talk. If you had pressed your point, Sic would have stayed here. He listens to you."

A wistful smile appeared on Noran's face when he remembered that particular conversation.

"Not as much as he used to. He's making remarkable progress. Who am I to hold him back?"

The sadness in Noran's voice made Renaldo perk up.

"You know Sic is going to forgive you completely, don't you? He probably already has."

"I know. And it makes the burden that much heavier. For reasons I'll never understand, I've been given a second chance. I'm not planning on screwing up again."

Renaldo sighed. He could understand his brother very well. Noran had taken on grave culpability when he had treated Sic so horribly. That the young man was even contemplating to forgive him was a worse punishment than showing him anger or contempt. This way, Noran was painfully aware of the responsibility he had taken on. Still, the master smith had never been happier in his entire life. Renaldo shook his head. Love did strange things to humans—and gods as well.

"One day you'll have to forgive yourself. You owe it to Sic."

Noran grinned crookedly.

"I will. But not anytime soon. I thought I'd wait till your heart decides to forgive me."

Renaldo couldn't help but guffaw.

"You know that could take a long time? Casto is terribly vindictive."

"I figured as much. And I can't say I don't understand him." Noran turned serious again. "The way I behaved towards your heart was abominable. You forgiving me is more than I could have hoped for. I don't expect Casto to grant me the same mercy."

"Don't fret about it. He will forgive you, if only because of Sic. It's just going to take some time. Like one or two centuries."

Noran did not respond to this banter, since it was unpleasantly close to the truth. Casto wasn't a man who forgave easily, and the two of them had never been on friendly terms to begin with. Even now, the overbearing, arrogant attitude of the king made Noran's fingers twitch. Casto was exactly the kind of person he couldn't stand at all. The only thing that made him a little more accepting of the young man was the ferocity with which he loved and protected Sic. It was probably the only thing the two of them would ever have in common. Since it was useless to ponder such fruitless thoughts, Noran tried to concentrate on the road. If Sic was truly in danger, he had to get to Kwarl as fast as possible.

CASTO AND Sic were standing protectively over Daran's corpse, their swords at the ready. Although nobody had made a move until now, it was only a question of time till Egand's men would decide to attack. Aegid and Kalad had almost reached the master thief, and their fury was like a shield protecting them from any possible attack. Sic touched his cheek with his left hand. Then he stopped, irritated, his fingers fumbling over his skin.

"Casto."

"What is it?"

"Don't you feel it?"

Surprised, Casto turned to his friend.

"What am I…?"

At that moment he, too, realized it. His skin was itching as though something like tiny needles was scraping it.

"Sand?"

The king was so surprised, he forgot for a moment where they were.

"Where's it coming from, all of a sudden?"

"I'm afraid I know." With his chin, Sic indicated the desert brothers, who had now grabbed Egand's arms. Where Aegid and Kalad were standing, the sand, which hadn't existed only a few heartbeats ago, was getting thicker and thicker, obscuring their outlines to a blur. Soon only Egand's shrill cries indicated where the warriors and their prey were standing. In the side tunnels, Casto heard the clinking noise of weapons being heedlessly dropped because their owners felt the burning desire to get away from this spooky place. Casto still kept his sword at the ready, just to be on the safe side, but he lowered it since he didn't assume there would be any more resistance or even an attack.

Speechless, he and Sic watched as the sand started whirling around Aegid, Kalad, and their prey in accelerating speed. Casto only knew the infamous sand spouts of the Hot Heart from the reports of merchants who had lost entire caravans to this phenomenon. Those terrible eddies made of hot air and sharp-edged grains of sand could arise within minutes and go for miles before they vanished again. Casto had heard of caravans that had been completely wiped out, with only bones left to prove there had once been life.

Up close, the sand was even more terrifying than the king had imagined. The only reassuring thing was that the storm was strictly confined. Whatever the desert brothers were doing, their pain had not taken away their self-control. Nevertheless, it was creepy to see what kind of power they commanded. Ever since the Mothers left the Valley, they all had been waiting to discover what kind of powers the Emeris would develop. It seemed as if Aegid and Kalad had taken with them the worst nightmare their home had in store. At the moment, Casto couldn't ponder the consequences of this, but he stored the thought somewhere in the back of his mind to examine it later. It was a habit from his days in Ummana and had helped considerably to ensure his survival back then.

Egand's screams stopped; only now and then did the king think he could still hear a muffled whimper full of pain. Then the sand collapsed on itself and vanished as if it had never been there. Aegid and Kalad stood alone. There was no trace left of their enemy. Only a few pale bones were lying on the ground, but they looked so old, Casto wasn't sure whether they were really from the master thief. With their shoulders slumped by grief, the warriors returned to Daran's lifeless body. It almost seemed as if they weren't aware of the importance of their deed.

As gently as possible, the brothers wrapped the thief in Kalad's cloak; then Aegid picked him up as if he were a newborn. Sic and Casto followed their companions with bowed heads. The loss they had just experienced weighed heavy on their minds. Sic was crying openly; he had really liked Daran. Casto, too, was full of sorrow, but it was mixed with anger. When they reached the entrance to the tunnel system, he turned around to take a last look at the cursed place that had robbed them of something so precious. His eyes were blinded by rage and before he knew it, he had already connected his mind with the torches still burning down there. With a guttural scream, he let all his restrained emotions run free. The fire surged forward like an angry predator, found a suitable outlet in the torches, and blazed through the tunnels with irresistible force, driven and fed by the king's emotions. Casto didn't care that most of the men who had been there to ambush him and the others were burned alive. In his anger, he even welcomed the screams of the dying, which he felt rather than actually heard. Daran was dead, and sacrificing those men didn't even begin to cover the loss.

It was Sic who jolted his friend back to reality.

"Come, Casto. They need us now."

With a heavy sigh, the king turned away. He could feel the fire losing its vigor. The cistern as well as the tunnels were made mainly of stone, so the flames had no food to sate his fury. There was no danger of a conflagration that could destroy all of Kwarl. Casto knew it had been stupid to give his anger free rein. The Barbarian wasn't here to take control of the fire, which meant his little tantrum could have easily turned into a catastrophe. He still wasn't used to the deadly forces he was now able to evoke, a problem he would have to deal with sooner rather than later, but which he did his best to avoid. There was too much emotional baggage attached to this particular problem to make him want to deal with it. And now was definitely not the time to muse about it. It was more important to support his brothers-in-arms in their hour of need.

At the inn, Aegid and Kalad took Daran's body into their room. Sic and Casto acted as a guard of honor in front of the door. Both of them were so crestfallen, they hardly spoke to each other. For the first time since their departure from the Valley, Casto missed his husband from the bottom of his heart. The trip to Kwarl had been his chance to prove his independence to Renaldo, to show him he was fine without him. But right now, Casto would have given everything to have the Barbarian at his side. If the Angel of Death had been here, then Daran would have still been alive, Casto was sure.

Sic, too, was longing for Noran. To make Casto happy, he had agreed to come on this little adventure, but he really missed the master smith. It had been hard for him to leave with Noran so opposed, and now he regretted it deeply. Although their conversations had been strictly about business so far, he had started to feel comfortable and at ease around his former master again. It was a sense of security he recognized from the time when Noran had taken him from Dalwon. He longed for this feeling now—no, he actually craved it—but his personal needs had to wait until they got back home. Right now, his brothers-in-arms needed him. Sighing, Sic buried his face in his arms.

In their room, Aegid and Kalad had taken off Daran's clothes and started to wash him. They were silent, both of them still too shocked about this loss, which they had always known was inevitable. Aegid started speaking first. He talked in the tongue of the desert tribes, a language only he and Kalad still knew. They had taught Daran the words of their fathers as well, so it was fitting to use them now.

"I remember how we met him for the first time, here, in the market. He was so beautiful. And so clumsy. A horrible thief."

"But a wonderful lover. I remember what it was like to own him for the first time. It was a rush not even the sweetest wine can give you."

"I remember his generosity. He always forgave us, no matter what we did. His heart was pure."

"I remember his devotion. His love. He lived only for us."

"I remember his laughter. He had the same humor we do, and he never hesitated to show his amusement."

"I remember…."

"I remember…."

Until the early morning hours, they honored the love of their life. With every sentence, the love they had felt for Daran was engraved more deeply in their hearts, making the loss they had suffered more unbearable. Their union with Daran, which had grown in such a short time, had become an irreplaceable piece. And for the first time since they met, it wasn't certain whether they could be each other's strength again.

WHEN THE sun rose, Aegid and Kalad left the chamber.

"We're going to buy suitable clothes and some other items to get him home in a manner befitting his rank."

Sic smiled wistfully at his brothers-in-arms.

"I'll stay with him. He won't be alone."

In a gesture of silent gratitude, Kalad placed his hand on Sic's arm.

"Where's Casto?"

"He's looking after the horses and preparing everything for our departure."

The desert brothers nodded in acknowledgment and left the inn. Sic watched their retreating figures from the window for some time before he entered the room where Daran was resting. Sic felt himself trembling when he looked at the lifeless body of the thief. His owners had washed all traces of violence from his skin, and it almost seemed as if he was only sleeping. But something, perhaps a chilling wisp of finality, or simply the absence of life, made it clear that Daran's laughter was gone forever. Sic knelt down next to this exceptional person, who had changed not only the lives of Aegid and Kalad. Lovingly he caressed the silken black hair. He felt empty; even his grief seemed to have collapsed on itself. Without knowing what he was doing, or being conscious about it, Sic started to talk to Daran.

"That wasn't your best idea, to die now. You must know how much they need you. You're irreplaceable to them, and to be honest, I can't imagine those two without you. What were you thinking, leaving us like this? I really don't know how to console Aegid and Kalad. Their despair is like a black hole, swallowing all the light. I've never seen them like that, so completely lost. Because of this, I've finally understood how much they, how much all of us, have taken you for granted. Whenever I think about them, you're part of the thought. It terrifies me that this has to change now."

Sic hesitated. It was just so damned unfair that a person as loved and adored as Daran was forced to leave the world, causing those who had to stay behind such insufferable pain. What kind of order justified a monstrous act like this? Daran had so much to live for and had been brutally yanked from his happy dream while others, who might even pray for death, had to endure the nightmare of their lives.

Something inside Sic snapped. A pressure that had been building all of his life finally found an outlet, and it unearthed what he had been desperately trying to ignore. The Luksari stirred. The ancient power buried in his soul reacted to Sic's despair and rose to the challenge. The smith was overwhelmed by his own nature, but contrary to his deepest fears, it wasn't terrifying this time. It merely opened his eyes.

Sic blinked. Daran was wrapped in shadows; darkness cloaked his body in a loving caress. And for the first time, the smith was able to see past his own grief and perceive the peace the thief had obtained. Death really wasn't as cruel as he had thought. It was a gift. It didn't always come at the right time and surely wasn't received with gratitude in most cases, but it was a gift nevertheless. A gift he could take away again. The knowledge was suddenly there, as if a lost memory had taken on new color. Light emanated from Sic's body, blinding in its heat and radiance. Tendrils of it reached out tentatively for the darkness around Daran, making the shadows quiver. It was so easy, and yet the most difficult thing Sic had ever done. There was no way he would pry his friend from his sleep without asking his consent first.

"Can you hear me, Daran? If yes, then please listen to what I have to say. I can bring you back, I can make the shadows go away, but only if you want to. I'm not sure if I remember how it is to die. From what I can tell, it means peace, and I won't hold it against you if you wish to remain in this state. But if you truly love Kalad and Aegid, if you ever have, please consider coming back. They're lost without you."

For a seemingly long time, nothing happened, and Sic was ready to withdraw when the shadows started to flicker. The peace was disrupted by another, tiny light, nothing more than embers glowing in the dark. It was all the answer Sic needed. He felt his light exploding, curling around Daran's body, eating up the shadows, consuming them as life, glorious life, streamed back into the void. There was a pang, as if something had exploded, and then such blinding light appeared that even Sic had to close his eyes for a moment. When he opened them again, his sight was back to normal. He watched as color returned to Daran's cheeks. His chest trembled and then started to rise and fall in the ancient rhythm of regular breathing. The long, elegant fingers twitched; his eyelids fluttered like a newborn dragonfly testing its wings. He sat up and looked around the room in astonishment.

"Lord Sic? Are you here? I heard your voice."

Sic was as pale as linen. He didn't know whether he should be joyful or terrified. For a moment he contemplated the possibility that his lack of sleep and the traumatic events of the past hours had caused him to hallucinate, but no matter how he looked at it, Daran was back. Confused, but back.

"I followed your light, my lord."

Awed, Sic touched the skin that was no longer cold, but warm and soft again.

"I can't believe this. You were dead. I saw you die."

Insecure, Daran furrowed his brow.

"I remember the faces of my masters. Then everything went dark. I couldn't move and I was so tired. When you started talking, I was glad. I didn't want to sleep. Thank you very much for calling me."

Deeply moved, Sic smiled at his friend through a veil of tears. Then he suddenly remembered something.

"Could you turn around, please? I want to see your back."

Daran obeyed immediately. Where the dagger had hit him, a faded scar was visible, but it vanished while Sic was still staring at it. Daran was whole again.

"Master, please tell me what has happened. Where are my owners?" Daran hesitated for a moment. "And where is Egand?"

"You'll never have to worry about him again. Kalad and Aegid have punished him most brutally. Concerning you—you were dead. I saw with my own eyes how the dagger pierced your heart. Your masters have mourned you the entire night. Now they're out to get the things necessary to escort you home properly."

Daran winced and lowered his gaze. Only now did he start to understand the severity of his actions.

"I troubled you a lot. I'm truly sorry."

"It's okay. Once they see you're alive again, they'll be thrilled. I'm sure you'll be forgiven."

A sob escaped Daran's lips, which caused Sic to embrace him tightly.

"Shh, there's no need to cry. Be happy you're still alive. Everything else will sort itself out."

"I'm sorry. I just can't seem to stop. It's simply too much."

Whimpering, Daran held on to Sic, who caressed his back in a soothing manner while the past events finally sank in. That was how Aegid and Kalad found them.

THE DESERT brothers had walked solemnly across the market, buying all the things they needed for their slave's funeral with heavy hearts. They had bought expensive clothes, jewelry, spices, and two ornamental daggers. All these riches would accompany Daran on his last journey to the Green Lands. Buying these things had a terrible finality, but it also helped the brothers to accept the new reality. When they returned to the inn, they heard sobbing sounds that were all too familiar coming from their room. Almost tripping over each other, they rushed to the door. What they saw then made them freeze.

Sic was sitting on the bed, holding the crying Daran. Daran, who should be lying there cold and lifeless. Daran, who had died in their arms.

The thief noticed his masters. He pried himself free of Sic's embrace and staggered toward the desert brothers. Directly in front of them he stopped, his eyes full of love and hope. Then he sank to his knees.

"I'm so terribly sorry, Masters. I was disobedient, and I have disappointed you."

He couldn't speak further. Strong hands lifted him up, and then he drowned in the warm embrace of his owners. Over the thunderous hammering of his own heart, he heard and felt the anxious heartbeats of his masters. He sank beneath the love they felt for him and bathed in their affection, which generously forgave all his shortcomings. There was no doubt he would have to pay for his actions later, but at the moment, all that counted was the warmth of his owners.

Daran didn't know how long they had been standing there; he hadn't even noticed when Sic had discreetly left the room. He was completely caught in the moment, inhaling the scent of his masters and reacting willingly when they started compensating for the shock of their loss with unbridled passion. Wherever they touched him, his skin seemed to burn, their lips left blazing trails that permeated his flesh. He accepted the brothers again and again, full of hunger and longing, until he was completely exhausted. When Daran recovered, Aegid and Kalad were holding him tight while he confessed his sins to them in a monotone.

"I was disobedient, Masters. I met an old friend at the market and allowed him to convince me to go with him. I risked the consequences without hesitation."

Kalad lifted Daran's chin.

"Why? We would have never thought you capable of such disobedient behavior."

"I was afraid he would follow me if I declined his request. The idea of you finding out what kind of company I had kept and how I had lived…."

"Daran. We met you when you tried to steal from us. We don't have any delusions about your upbringing."

Aegid's voice was very gentle. Embarrassed, Daran turned his head away.

"I'm aware of that. Still, I was ashamed. I couldn't allow him to meet you."

"How does your stepfather fit into this scenario?"

"It was a trap. Egand seemed to have known I was in Kwarl and ordered Gar to take me to the tavern where he kidnapped me. I told him I'm merely a slave, but he didn't believe me at all. He thought I wanted to swindle him out of the money he deserved."

"He definitely got what he deserved. You don't have to worry about him anymore, little thief."

Lovingly, Kalad kissed Daran on the mouth.

"And we do hope you're not going to lie to us ever again. You can trust us, and we're most certainly not so shallow as to judge a man by his ancestry alone."

Crimson invaded Daran's cheeks. He was deeply humiliated by his own dishonorable behavior.

"How can you be so lenient with me? I disappointed you so badly!"

"You really are stupid, aren't you? We love you. Losing you has hurt us in a way we'll never be able to describe in words."

Despite the grave topic, Aegid's voice was heated. His eyes glinted maliciously.

"Of course, you'll be punished once we arrive at the Valley, but we're just really glad to have you back. From now on, we won't ever let you go."

STILL STUNNED, Sic stared at his best friend. "I don't know whether I find your lack of interest good or worrisome."

The news that Daran had returned from the dead hadn't seemed to move Casto at all. On the contrary, he appeared to be completely unfazed, his mesmerizing gaze focused on Sic.

"I'm mate to a god, brother to a demon of chaos who has taken the form of a horse. I've seen with my own eyes how my husband survived an explosion that obliterated an entire city wall, and my brother-in-law's wife can heal people with the power of her mind. And now I find out that my best friend is not only a creature made of magic, but can also bring back the dead. It's nice that Daran's back, but I'm not really surprised."

"Are you sure you're human?" Sic still couldn't believe it. Casto stared at him with a tense expression that made the smith shiver.

"I'm not human. Not anymore. And neither are you." He turned away, his voice softening a little bit. "To be frank, I'm mainly relieved. So much, nothing else matters to me at the moment."

Sic regarded his friend with worry. "I hope you're not blaming yourself, are you?"

Angrily, Casto clenched his fists. "Of course I don't. Perhaps a little bit. Mainly, I'm just pissed that things didn't go smoothly. After all, it was my idea to come here. I put my will against that of the Barbarian and thus created the condition for this mess. If I had obeyed Renaldo, none of this would have happened."

"Oh, Casto. It's not like you to torture yourself like that. The Angel of Death had imprisoned you. It's your nature to rebel against it."

Casto leaned his forehead on Sic's shoulder.

"It's nice of you to say that, and you're absolutely right, but that neither changes the fact that it was my temperament that brought us here, nor that the Barbarian is going to use this incident against me in future arguments. He'll have more leverage from now on, which will make it even more difficult for me to handle him. Right now I just want to go home as quickly as possible and perhaps come up with some good retorts to the discussion Renaldo and I are definitely going to have."

Sic shuddered. He had always known Casto was a ruthless, cold-blooded personality, and right now he wondered how he had managed to befriend somebody whose character was the exact opposite of his own. Then again, Sic wasn't entirely sure how much of Casto's behavior was just pretense to hide his true feelings. Understanding Casto was a task that could not be accomplished during one lifetime. In an attempt to cheer his friend up, Sic patted his shoulder.

"It's your lucky day. Aegid and Kalad feel the same. They want to leave right now. It's already the middle of the afternoon, but even with the horses you have bought, we can still put some leagues between us and Kwarl."

"Then tell them we're leaving in half an hour. I want to be out of this stupid city as soon as possible."

Still slightly worried about the strange mood his friend was in, Sic returned to the inn to tell the desert brothers. Half an hour later, they departed, right after Daran had apologized to Casto on his knees.

During the ride, Aegid and Kalad made sure Daran was always between them. They kept touching him the whole time, as if they wanted to reassure themselves he had really returned to them. Daran's expression alternated between joy and fear, for he was aware of the punishment still waiting for him. At the same time, he was simply happy to be back with his masters and willing to bear anything they deemed appropriate.

When the sun set, they chose a suitable campsite off the road and ate a light dinner. Most of the time, they stayed silent, each of the men lost in his own thoughts. It wasn't an ominous quiescence, but neither was it comfortable. Together they had experienced things that couldn't be left unsaid; still, none of them was willing to breach the topic first. It was Casto who finally lifted the ban in his usual offhand manner. The flames of the campfire threw flickering shadows on his face, making him appear more menacing than he probably intended to be when he confronted Daran directly.

"Is there a special reason why you fell into your stepfather's arms so easily, or did we risk our lives because of something petty?"

Wincing, Daran lowered his head. He had known he would be held responsible for his deeds not only by Aegid and Kalad, but it frightened him to be questioned by Casto. The king had changed since their return from Ummana. He had lost the last traces of youthful jauntiness and was becoming more similar to his mate on a daily basis, using the power his status gave with casual naturalness, expecting nothing less than absolute obedience from everybody else. Kalad slung his arms protectively around Daran, his eyes clouded by worry.

"Can't we postpone this, Casto? Daran has suffered enough for the time being."

"No, you can't."

The voice booming through the night was ripe with fury. Renaldo stepped into the circle of light, his expressive gray eyes glinting ominously. Casto got up gracefully, allowing his mate to embrace him. This open display of affection was proof enough to Sic that the events of the past day had impressed the king more deeply than he had first assumed. The Angel of Death held his lover in a tight embrace, the look on his perfect features hard to describe. Then the shadows behind Renaldo stirred and Noran stepped forward.

"Master!"

Without thinking, Sic flew into Noran's arms. He was so relieved to see his former owner, he didn't care what his brothers might think of him. He, too, felt the strain of all the things that had transpired. Compared to that, his relationship with the master smith seemed pretty easy to fix. Sic closed his eyes and inhaled the reassuring scent of the bulky man deeply two or three times before he stepped back again. Before any of them could so much as utter a greeting, Renaldo took the reins. He scrutinized Daran, who had gone pale between his masters.

"I'm still waiting for an explanation, slave. And when you're at it, I'd love to find out why I was jolted awake in the middle of the night by Casto's panic."

Aegid and Kalad exchanged a quick glance. They had been wondering what kind of business the Angel of Death might have so close to Kwarl. Obviously his connection to Casto was even stronger than they all had thought possible.

"I'm still waiting, Daran."

There was no doubt about the god's impatience. With his gaze still on the ground and his voice trembling, Daran reported what had happened. He didn't sugarcoat his motives and didn't try to make his actions appear in a more positive light, because even though he was truly afraid of the Angel of Death, he was no coward, but a man who owned up to his faults. It made his owners almost burst with pride. After Daran ended, Renaldo addressed his heart.

"Which brings me to you. Do you wish to explain to me why you endangered yourself?"

Casto's blue eyes lit up dangerously. Contrary to Daran, he didn't fear his husband, and the tone of the Angel of Death didn't sit well with him.

"What are you implying, Barbarian?"

"I think you know very well what I'm implying. Now, why did you accompany those two idiots on their mission?"

He shot Aegid and Kalad a menacing glare at these words.

"Because they are my brothers-in-arms. Because I like Daran. And because it was my responsibility. I'm the leader of this group, and I'll be damned if I'd run for cover behind their shields at the first indication of danger."

Renaldo grabbed his mate so hard, they all could hear the bones creak.

"Your first and only responsibility is toward me, slave. You are mine and mine alone. It's your duty to obey me. I had ordered you to be careful, but you simply ignored my commands. Now you have to bear the consequences."

The campfire blazed when Casto's hands connected with his mate's arms, his blue eyes darkened by outright fury.

"I'm a free member of the Pack. It was you who gave me that freedom, Barbarian. You better learn to accept that I make my own decisions."

"Casto! That's enough! I had planned to do this when we were back in the Valley, but you leave me no choice."

While he was still mercilessly holding his heart, the Angel of Death turned to Kalad.

"Get me a whip. And you," his eyes pierced Daran, "take off your shirt."

Trembling, Daran obeyed. Aegid wanted to say something, but one gaze at the masklike face of his god and he fell silent. Renaldo was beyond himself with rage. Kalad brought a whip, his eyes silently pleading with the furious god, but he was simply ignored. The orders of the Angel of Death were given in a detached tone.

"Aegid, chain Daran to the tree over there. Noran, Sic, you're on watch duty. Casto, take off your shirt."

The king shook his head. He was the only one not intimidated by Renaldo's mood.

"Forget it, Barbarian. I won't allow you to whip me."

Renaldo didn't even look at his mate when he answered.

"Do as you're told. Unless you wish to make me even more furious than I already am. Keep in mind, I'm going to punish Daran before you—and he's only human."

Casto gritted his teeth. "That's blackmail!"

The Angel of Death didn't bother to answer. With an expressionless face, he watched as Casto got rid of his shirt. Then he chained him to another tree next to Daran. Aegid and Kalad were standing at the fire, their fists clenched. Renaldo took position behind Daran, whip in hand.

"You know why I'm punishing you?"

The thief gulped.

"Yes, Master, I know."

"Good for you."

Then Renaldo started to flog the thief. He spared neither his arm nor Daran's back, and the young man's screams rang out through the night. When his back was covered in blood, the Angel of Death stopped.

"For the night, he stays like this. You can take care of him tomorrow."

"My lord."

Aegid wanted to plead with his god, who shook his head in denial.

"It's part of his punishment. Just like the pain he'll have to endure until we reach the Valley. Once we're there, I don't care if you ask Noemi to heal him, but I want him to pay for his sins. Because of him, my heart was in danger. There's no way I'm going to let this pass. Be grateful that I let him off so easily."

Beaten, Aegid lowered his gaze. "As my lord wishes."

Renaldo was concentrating on Casto now. "I assume you don't know why I'm punishing you?"

Casto snorted derisively. "Don't hold back, Barbarian, but be assured, I won't forget this in a hurry."

"Your stubbornness is out of place here. You should show a little humility."

Casto didn't respond to that. He stared fixedly at the bark of the tree he had been chained to and endured the whipping without making a single sound. When it was over, Renaldo threw the whip to the ground.

"I hope you both learned your lesson. You can spend the rest of the night contemplating your mistakes."

He made himself comfortable at the campfire. Daran turned his head to Casto.

"I'm sorry, Master. This is all my fault."

"It's not, Daran. Your willfulness wasn't good, but it was my decision to accompany your masters. You couldn't change that, so stop worrying about it. Try to get some sleep. The ride tomorrow is going to be hard."

Daran closed his eyes. Casto had it easy. His wounds would be healed come the next day, while Daran could only hope to get through the ride in more or less one piece. Daran knew he deserved this punishment; nevertheless, he still dreaded the hours of pain waiting for him.

At the place they had chosen to watch out for approaching enemies, Sic and Noran listened as Daran's shrill screams ripped the peaceful night to shreds.

Sic trembled, remembering all too well what it felt like when the merciless whip tore the skin open and the blood started to flow. Even though Ana-Isara had taken away the scars on his body, he could still feel a tingling where the worst wounds had been. His body hadn't forgotten what had been done to him. Sic closed his eyes as the memories swamped him. Curiously enough, the worst pain wasn't caused by the whip, but by the knowledge that he'd deserved the punishment, that it was still nothing compared to the agony he had caused the ones he loved. Accepting the pain just made it easier to bear, but it also enhanced the weight on the mind, the nagging feeling that the deed that had brought about this anguish could never be properly avenged.

"Sic!"

Noran's voice cut through the frenzy Daran's screams had created. Still dizzy from the emotional overload, Sic stared at the master smith, not sure if he was imagining things. There were tears in the corners of Noran's eyes, and an agony even worse than what Sic had been feeling was written all over his face.

"I'm so sorry, Sic, so terribly sorry."

Slowly, tentatively, Sic reached out for his former owner's face. His fingertips brushed over the tear-stained cheeks as gently as a butterfly's wings. So he wasn't the only one haunted by the past.

"It's me who should be sorry. I betrayed you. Even though I loved you, I didn't trust you enough to tell you the truth. Ultimately, I forced your hand."

Noran swallowed hard. Even gentler than his true love's touch, he reached for Sic's wrists.

"No. I could have forgiven you, but instead of opening my eyes to the truth, I did something unforgivable instead. And now I wish I could turn back time, and it's just not possible."

"I'm wishing for the same thing. I want this pain to end. I want to stop thinking about what I should have done, about how terribly I messed up."

They looked at each other for a long time. Daran's yells had finally stopped, and the quiet of the night returned. In the other's eyes, they both glimpsed the guilt and the pain and the regret they were harboring. It was almost like staring into a mirror. And when they had finally seen it all, after they had both bared their deepest shame to the other, the glass shattered. In the shards, something else stirred. It wasn't the childish adoration Sic had felt for the man who had saved him when he was still a kid. It wasn't the silent contentment Noran had experienced whenever his apprentice was close to him either. It was something a lot deeper and much more powerful. Something that would grow and become stronger as time passed by. It was love.

The silence surrounding them crystallized. So slowly it almost seemed as if they weren't moving at all, their lips approached, getting closer hand by meaningful hand. When they finally connected, oh so lightly, little jolts of excitement ran through their bodies, making them even more sensitive to the other's touch. Both of them took their time; it was almost as if this very first kiss they shared was a stand-in for an entire lifetime's worth of courtship. After an eternity, time flowed back into the space they had created. Sic snuggled up to Noran, and they spent the rest of the night enjoying the bliss of finally having come to terms with each other.

THE NEXT morning, Daran was woken by Kalad. His owner patted his head gently.

"Time to wake up, little thief. We're going to leave soon."

Dizzy, Daran blinked in the bright morning light. He felt stiff because he had been chained the entire night, but apart from that, he was fine. Which was astounding, since the punishment had been brutal. Amazed, he righted himself. Kalad watched him with worry in his bright eyes.

"Easy, little thief. Lean on me. Aegid has already heated some water to cleanse your wounds."

Gingerly, Daran moved his shoulders. And wondered whether he had lost his mind during the whipping. It didn't seem as if his back was hurt at all. Only the dried blood pricked at his skin.

"I'm fine, Master. Surprisingly fine."

Kalad place a hand on Daran's forehead.

"You don't seem to have a fever."

Then he skimmed over the thief's back. His eyes went wide.

"Aegid, come here! Bring the cloth with you!"

The giant handed his desert brother what he had asked for and watched in surprise as Kalad started cleaning Daran's back with forceful motions.

"Slow down, Kalad. You're only going to hurt him more."

"I don't think so. Look at this!"

"That's impossible!"

"What's going on?" Casto approached the three men. He was wearing his shirt again, and nothing in his appearance showed that he had endured the same punishment as Daran. Kalad pointed at the thief's back.

"There are no wounds."

"How can that be?"

The warriors stared at the soft, unmarred skin that shone under the dried blood.

"It seems my hunch was spot-on." Renaldo sounded strangely satisfied. "I had noticed something odd about him right away."

"You knew?" Kalad glared at his god, who answered with a menacing stare.

"I wasn't entirely sure. And before you get worked up, remember that you all earned this punishment. It's his luck the wounds healed overnight, but he would have also deserved to bear the pain until we reached the Valley. Concerning you, you suffered so vicariously with him, I won't ask for further compensation."

Kalad wanted to give sharp answer, but Aegid held him back.

"We understand, my lord. And we're grateful."

"Stop sweet-talking him."

Casto's voice was brisk; it was obvious he hadn't forgiven his mate yet. For a moment he placed his hand in a conciliatory gesture on Daran's shoulder, and then he turned away. The entire trip back to the Valley, he didn't say another word. Whenever one of his companions tried to get close to him, Lys flattened his ears and bared his teeth to keep the other horses at bay. Not even Sic was allowed to ride next to his friend. In face of Casto's dark mood, he wasn't too keen on it, anyway. He was glad to spend his time with Noran, even though they, too, didn't talk much. The Angel of Death was riding in the lead, wearing an expression similar to that of his mate. Nobody dared to approach him either.

When they reached the Valley, Casto went into the stables with Lys without sparing his husband or his companions another glance. Canubis, who had wanted to welcome them, lifted a brow but refrained from any comment.

4. MATURITY

"You've been sleeping at Lys's place for a week now. Don't you think it's time to forgive my brother?"

Mildly, Canubis watched as his brother-in-law put a saddle on a promising dun mare. The young man's movements were graceful as ever, even though his face was frozen in an angry mask.

"I wouldn't know why I should do that."

Canubis sighed. As expected, Casto wasn't going to make this easy.

"You know he did it because he loves you so much, don't you?"

Casto spun around quickly, his eyes black with fury. "I can do without this so-called love!"

His voice shook, indicating how deeply he was moved.

"I hate it when he uses his love as an excuse to imprison me. I want him to trust and respect me. I'm a king and his mate, not a cheap toy he can use as he deems fit."

"You are aware that he could force you anytime, and that he isn't doing it because of this love you abhor so much?"

"What good does this love do me if it takes away the air I need to breathe?"

All anger had gone from Casto's voice. Now he sounded desperate and terribly lonely. Canubis dared to put an arm on the king's shoulder. He knew this loneliness well, since it was the same that had tortured his brother from the day they had been born.

"I know it's hard for you. And I'm not saying he's right. But I'm asking you to understand him. My brother has always been alone. People only ever see his beauty and are blinded by it. Or they grow stiff in fear of his fire. He's gotten used to being alone, to always sticking out. Not even the Emeris, not even Hulda, have managed to truly know him. You're the first who's completely oblivious to his beauty, the first who didn't even notice Renaldo is wearing a mask, because you looked straight through it. And even though you know my brother like nobody else does, you're not afraid of him. Not even his fire frightens you, although this power is so terrible. Renaldo is deeply scared of losing his most precious treasure, and in his panic, he sometimes does things that aren't right. He shouldn't have whipped you and, believe me, he regrets it with all his heart. But for him, it was proof that you're still there, that you're still his, that he hasn't lost you. He's become so insecure, my proud brother, and it's all because of you, Casto."

The beautiful blue eyes of the king had widened during Canubis's speech.

"But I am his. I can't get away from him. I mean, he's my god. Why can't he be content with that?"

"Because he doesn't want to force you. I know it sounds like mockery given what he's done, but it's a fact. He wants you to stay with him because of love, not because it's his will. Until today, he hasn't gotten over the fact that you were his slave in the beginning."

Casto snorted derisively. "Maybe in his dreams. I only stayed with him because the Valley offered protection from my persecutors. I could have easily left him during the first winter."

Canubis grinned. "I know. But he seems to have forgotten. Perhaps you should remind him."

The king's eyes narrowed. "For somebody who always acts so aloof and dismissive, you're surprisingly empathic and shrewd, my *lord*."

Canubis laughed out loud, then put a finger on his lips. "Don't tell anybody. Let this be our little secret."

Against his will, Casto had to smile. He liked his dominant brother-in-law a lot, more than he was willing to admit. He also felt deep respect for him. Canubis was the undisputed master of the Valley, and he wore his authority like an invisible cloak.

"I'm going to talk to the Barbarian. It's getting tiresome to sleep in the straw every night."

True relief brightened the Wolf of War's eyes. He had anticipated a lot more obstinacy from Casto and was glad the problem had been solved so easily.

RENALDO LOOKED up in surprise when Casto entered their chambers that evening. He hadn't thought he'd see his capricious husband anytime soon. Considering what he had done, he wasn't even sure if the king would ever return to him. The Angel of Death was ashamed for having beaten his heart, but on that evening, he hadn't been able to think clearly. The fear of losing his mate had driven him as much as the anger over how thoughtlessly Casto had put himself into danger. Seen matter-of-factly, he had only done what was expected of him: he had acted like a leader. But when his heart was concerned, Renaldo couldn't think clearly anymore. The beast inside him, this wild, untamed part of his divine personality that was also the source of his fire, wanted to monopolize Casto completely, without regard for his personal wishes. The beast was insatiable and never content. Renaldo hated this part of himself, but he also knew there was no way to bring the monster to heel. As a form of punishment, he had forced himself to stay away from Casto until he decided to come back on his own. It had been the most terrible week in his life. And now his heart was here, looking at him with his mesmerizing blue eyes, mocking pity written all over his face.

"You look ghastly, Barbarian."

Renaldo smiled weakly. "That's probably because I haven't slept much the past few days. I'm missing you."

A sigh escaped from the full, sensual lips. "I've missed you too."

"I'm truly sorry for whipping you. I lost control."

A lazy, seductive smile was the answer. Casto's voice was now a beguiling purr.

"You know how much I like it when you lose control—under different circumstances."

When Renaldo's gray eyes lit up in plain hunger, Casto turned serious again.

"If you hurt me against my will one more time, I swear you're going to regret it to the day you take your last breath."

Renaldo took his stunning, capricious, and yet generous mate's hands in his own and kissed the palms. "I thank you, Casto. I promise, this won't happen again. I'm so sorry."

"I hope so. And now,"—the king snuggled up to his lover—"it would be nice if you started kissing me. I want to make up with you."

Full of relief, Renaldo pulled Casto closer and kissed the young man deeply. He knew there was still an uncomfortable discussion about trust and his lack of it in store for him, but at the moment, the only thing that counted was that Casto had forgiven him. The beast, which had stirred full of longing when the king entered the room, wanted to burst its bounds, but this time Renaldo managed to keep it under control. There was no way he would destroy the fragile peace they had just established. And so he concentrated on seducing his mate with all his skill.

WHILE CASTO was busy playing dominance games with his god, Sic had to face an entirely different problem. Now that he and Noran had finally reached a mutual understanding, he felt a certain urge to consummate their union. Since they both had taken such a huge detour, he thought he was entitled to be eager. In addition, concentrating on his relationship with the master smith kept him from thinking too much about what had happened in Kwarl. Yet no matter how eagerly he wished for them to become intimate, there was still the problem of his being a virgin again after Ana-Isara's kiss, and the bad experiences he had endured so far still surfaced now and then. Asking Noran was out of the question; the master smith got worked up whenever Sic so much as hinted at some nightly activities that required them to be naked. No, if he wanted to make the next step, he had to take matters in hand. After a day of contemplation, Sic ruled out every possible advisor except for one. Casto was out of the question; he hated Noran with all his heart. Talking to Hulda or Noemi was simply too embarrassing, and requesting the help of Aegid and Kalad…. Sic shuddered just thinking about the saucy smiles on their lips and the mocking glint in their eyes. Which only left Daran. He was the most logical choice, since he knew a lot about intercourse and was understanding enough for Sic to trust him. The only problem was getting hold of the thief without his masters noticing.

The first three days after they returned to the Valley, the desert brothers had locked Daran into their chambers to make sure he couldn't slip through their fingers once more. When he had finally been allowed to go out again, they stuck to him like glue, following him everywhere. Fortunately they were training the new recruits for the Pack at the moment, and so Daran was all by himself. Sic seized this rare chance.

He met the thief at the chambers of his masters, where he had just had a bath, judging from his dripping-wet hair. Daran welcomed Sic most politely and asked him in. There the two of them then stood frozen in awkward silence. Nervously, Sic tried to start the conversation.

"So, how are you feeling? Is everything all right?"

Daran winced. "I'm fine except for being sore all the time. They're overdoing it at the moment. I can only hope they'll calm down sometime soon."

"That's good."

Another gap in the conversation threatened to turn into absolute silence. This time, Daran was the first to speak.

"So, what can I do for you, Lord Sic? You know you can ask anything of me."

Sic smiled weakly and decided to tackle the problem head-on.

"It's a delicate topic. First of all, I want to ask you not to tell your masters about it. Unless they ask you directly. I know you can't keep anything from them. Do you think you could do that?"

Daran was getting curious now. "Sure. Just ask away."

Sic hesitated one more moment. Then he spoke so fast, Daran had problems understanding him.

"Can you teach me how to have fun in bed?"

Sic felt crimson invading his cheeks. Daran was staring at him as if he was a creature from another dimension. When he caught himself again, he sounded very composed.

"Am I right in assuming that you're planning to be intimate with Lord Noran?"

"Yes. If I want to get over my trauma, I have to take the next step. And this time, I want to be prepared. I've seen how you enjoy sex, and to be frank, I envy you. Can you please help me?"

Daran's features lit up. "It would be my pleasure, Lord Sic. Where do you want to start?"

"Honestly, I don't know. Consider me an absolute beginner. All I've known so far is being forced when I was at the receiving end and embarrassment when I was the active part."

"Lord Noran will be the active one, won't he?"

"Yes."

Daran took Sic's hand, a reassuring smile on his lips.

"Then we start with the most difficult part. Finding out what gets you off."

"I DON'T understand, Sic. How can you not know what you did to call Daran back? Kalad and Aegid have already mastered their talent, while you're not even able to recall exactly what happened."

Canubis's voice was sharp; he was frustrated that a talent as vital as Sic's was beyond his control. Shaken by the rebuke in his god's voice, the smith stared at his hands. The better part of a week had passed since they had returned home, and the things that had happened in Kwarl were weighing on his mind. Kalad and Aegid had embraced their deadly new asset with the excitement of children who'd been given a new toy. To show off, they had called the sand in front of an astonished audience who had the disputable pleasure of witnessing how a pig's carcass was ground into oblivion. In many ways, Sic was envious of the easygoing attitude of the desert brothers. For them, power was something so natural, they took it in stride. For him it was still terrifying, which was probably the reason why he couldn't—or wouldn't—remember what he had done to get Daran back. His recollection of the feeling when the light emanating from his body had consumed the shadows was still vivid, but how he had managed to see them in the first place remained a mystery to him. The Luksari had taken that knowledge with him when he went back into the depths of Sic's soul. All he had to show his displeased god was his inaptitude to be an Emeris.

"I'm truly sorry, my lord. I'm trying hard to remember and to understand my talent, but the harder I try, the more blurred it all gets."

Noran put his arm protectively around Sic's shoulders. Even though they hadn't become physical yet—much to the young smith's dismay— the intimacy between them was growing every day.

"Sic is doing his best. But don't forget, he's become an Emeris not even a year ago. Compared to him, Aegid and Kalad are ancient. Of course it's easier for them to deal with their talent."

"Although I find your comment regarding our age somewhat diminishing, I have to agree with you."

Kalad grinned broadly. He enjoyed being able to tease Noran again. During the time after Arja's death, the bulky smith would have reacted to such banter with fury, but now he reciprocated his brother-in-arms's smile with the same mocking openness he had shown at the beginning of their friendship. Canubis ignored this attempt to lighten the mood.

"I don't know if you've realized it yet, but this is not about Sic's personal well-being." The Wolf of War shot acidic glances around. "He's the one who can turn ordinary humans into Echend'dim—immortal warriors we're going to need for our battle against the Good Mother. I can't afford to keep on betting on luck and chance while Sic is waiting for an epiphany."

For a moment, nobody said a word. The prophecies were clear about the importance of the Echend'dim, the eternal guard that Canubis and Renaldo needed to gain their victory, but evasive when it came to explaining how those warriors would come into being. Now that they knew that an Echend'dim had to die first and then be called back by Sic, things were clearer, though not more pleasant.

Noran opened his mouth to give a sharp retort, but Sic was faster. His voice was hushed, his tone betraying how unhappy he was.

"Lord Canubis is right. My incompetence is endangering us all. I promise, I'll work even harder and will only stop when I'm able to control my gift."

"That's quite noble of you, Sic, but also kind of unnecessary."

Hulda's voice was calm, her lavender-colored eyes focused on Canubis in a condescending manner. The warrior stared back at the mother superior without hiding his irritation, angry that even she seemed to fail to recognize the seriousness of the situation. Without minding the silent threat coming from her leader, Hulda spoke on.

"Daran has been able to describe the circumstances of his resurrection in vivid detail. He said it was Sic's voice that woke him, and then he followed his light back into life. According to Noemi, Sic's true shape in the world between is pure light. For the Luksari, this seems to be their natural form. I doubt that he's currently able to influence his appearance actively. Considering this, I'd say Daran's rescue was indeed a happy coincidence initiated by the Mothers. After all, the thief is Aegid's and Kalad's reward for their loyalty. So, if we assume that calling the dead back is part of Sic's natural abilities, then this means his talent as an Emeris has still to manifest itself. And I'm almost sure this will have something to do with his ability to recognize a future Echend'dim. Enabling them to return from the world between is Sic's nature and has nothing to do with his talent."

Hulda's words were followed by a prolonged silence. When Renaldo finally spoke, he didn't try to hide his awe.

"It sounds perfectly logical when you put it like that. And we do know that the Luksari have evolved from pure magic. But because they're so unbelievably rare, we know practically nothing about their powers. Perhaps they all have this ability."

Canubis sighed. "It makes sense. But it doesn't please me, because the problem remains the same. How will we build our army when the selection of the warriors is left to chance? I don't think it's a good idea to kill all the members of our Pack in the vague hope Sic will be able to resurrect some of them."

"That won't be necessary." Aegid's voice was soft. "First, you're implying our warriors are worthless as long as they're mortal, and that's a mistake. They are the best there are and until now, none of them have let us down. And I doubt the final battle against the Good Mother will be anytime soon. Of course, we can't afford to slack off, but I'm sure we have more time than you think."

The amber eyes of the Wolf of War skimmed over his assembled counselors and stopped at Sic. Now that the Mothers had left Ana-Darasa, he felt the weight of responsibility on his shoulders even more. Hulda's and Aegid's words were wise, but still they did not manage to put him at ease. Ever since he and Renaldo had become full-fledged gods again, he could feel the threat coming from the Good Mother more intensely. Her presence on Ana-Darasa was like a malicious maelstrom that inexorably pulled all order into chaos. The longer he allowed her to feed on the power that had been set free by the departure of Ana-Isara and Ana-Aruna, the more difficult it would be to destroy her. But if he acted too rashly, he would endanger them all. Simply put, he couldn't allow himself to make the slightest mistake.

In his apprehension, he had been unjust to one of his Emeris. Even worse, he had pressured a Luksari. Canubis had only begun to realize how important Sic really was, and just the thought of what the young man had endured in the Valley until now made the Wolf of War fear he could still lose him. Instinctively he knew that without Sic, the battle was lost before it had even started.

"I'm sorry, Sic. I wasn't fair to you. Please forgive me."

Shyly, the smith looked up at him, his face a mirror of his worries.

"You don't have to apologize to me, Master. You're my god, and it's my duty to serve you well. I'm really sorry that I'm unable to ease your mind."

Despite the seriousness of the situation, Canubis had to smile. When Sic talked like that, he dispelled all fears the Wolf of War felt regarding him.

"Thank you, Sic. Now that this topic is closed, let's discuss whether we should go on a short raid during the next few weeks, or if we better stay here in the Valley."

AFTER THE counseling session ended, Sic waited until he and Noran were alone. He was so nervous about what he was planning to do, cold sweat was pouring down his back. Determined, he stuck out his chin and put a trembling smile on his lips.

"Master, I was wondering if you would like to have dinner with me today? Gweris has promised to cook something special, and I want to share it with you."

Noran's features brightened. They were getting closer with each passing day, and having dinner together was one of the things he enjoyed most. It was then he felt a real connection with his former slave, one that allowed them to meet not only as equals but also as friends. And so his answer was enthusiastic.

"It would be my pleasure, Sic. I'm looking forward to it."

Noran received a shy smile in return, which caused his heart to skip an excited beat.

"Then I'll be waiting for you tonight."

"GOOD EVENING, Sic. I hope I'm not too early?"

Noran looked into the open, yet slightly worried face of the young man. He seemed nervous, which was strange since this wasn't their first meal together.

"Are you feeling unwell? Should I leave?"

Frantically, Sic shook his head. "No, no! Please, don't leave! Come in."

He stepped aside to let his former master pass. Noran looked around. The table was already laid, and a mouthwatering scent permeated the air. Gweris had outdone herself. Sic poured some dark red wine, trying to suppress the trembling in his hands. When he offered the cup to Noran, the bulky man shot him a questioning look.

"Are you sure everything's fine, Sic? You don't look well. Are you still pondering what Canubis said today? Don't take it to heart. He's just worried."

Sic shook his head vehemently and seemed to have trouble lining up the right words.

"That's not it. I'm just…." He took a deep breath. "I'm just nervous. I want this night to be special."

Noran reared back. There was no misinterpreting those words.

"No, Sic. I can't."

The Luksari's shoulders slumped. "Why not? We love each other. Isn't this also part of love, of a relationship?"

Sic sounded so hurt, it made Noran's insides constrict with guilt.

"I love you more than anything else in this world, Sic. My feelings for you are so unfathomable, they're bordering on obsession. There's nothing I wish for more deeply than owning you most intimately. But I'm scared. Scared that I won't be able to control myself once we start. Scared that I'm going to hurt you again. You are my everything. I just can't risk losing you once more."

Sic sighed deeply. "I know. And I understand. But it can't go on like this. Don't you feel trapped as well?"

There was nothing Noran could say, for Sic was right. He did feel confined in their current relationship, but what could he do? Sic took his hands, looking at him with an expression Noran had never seen before. The smith's voice was firm, although his frame was trembling.

"I've been thinking about this for a long time, and when we got back from Kwarl, I decided to get some help. I assume we both agree that we can't leave things like they are. We have to take the next step."

He paused for a moment, his eyes glued to Noran's face.

"To make it easier for us, we'll just change roles."

When he glimpsed the slightly panicked look on the master smith's face, Sic chuckled with just a tiny hint of glee.

"Don't worry, Master. I do not wish to top you. I meant something different. Until now, you always used me to find relief. Tonight I'm going to use you. Daran has shown me how to seek my own pleasure, so I'm not clueless anymore."

The last sentence jolted Noran from the shock-induced, trancelike state he had fallen into. To find Sic so aggressive was new, exciting, and alarming. Hearing that he had sought counsel from Daran, of all people, made darkest jealousy rear its ugly head.

"You slept with Daran again?"

Sic seemed taken aback by this fierce reaction. "Are you jealous?"

"And if I was?"

Noran couldn't help it. The thought of his treasure being with somebody else…. He stared at Sic, who didn't seem to be shaken at all, but rather pleased.

"It makes me happy to think I can get such a reaction from you. Rest assured, there's no way Daran and I will ever become intimate again. Apart from the fact that he's both physically and mentally unable to cheat on his masters, Aegid and Kalad would probably kill me on the spot. Besides, for me there's only you. No, Daran just showed me how to feel good."

Noran breathed a sigh of relief. He knew he had no right to interfere with Sic's affairs, but he still felt an overwhelming surge of possessiveness whenever he laid eyes on the young man he had known since he was a boy.

"So you really want to do this tonight?"

"Yes. I want us to move on, to leave all the bad memories behind."

"What if I lose control? If I hurt you again?"

"You won't. I trust you. I trust the love you feel for me."

The absolute conviction in Sic's voice broke Noran's last resistance. The young man had risked so much; how could he turn him down now?

"Fine. Let's leave the past behind." Carefully he extended his arms, a silent invitation Sic accepted without hesitation. "And you'll show me what you like?"

"Yes. Yes."

Sic snuggled closer, reveling in the warmth of this embrace he had craved so much.

"Let's move to the bedroom."

IN THE chambers of the desert brothers, Daran was fidgeting. He knew how special this night was for Sic, and he only hoped everything went according to plan. He felt two strong hands heavily on his shoulders.

"Hey, little thief. Where are you right now? Certainly not with us."

Kalad's voice was mocking and his lips were a little too close to Daran's ear for comfort. The warrior had an agenda, something the new Echend'dim usually welcomed eagerly, but not tonight. Tonight he was preoccupied. His two lovers sensed something was off and decided to dig a little deeper.

Aegid took Daran's face in his hands. "You've been awfully secretive this week. Why don't you tell us what this is all about?"

"I'd rather not, since it's kind of private business."

Kalad's hands slid down Daran's naked torso, caressing the soft skin lovingly. "You can tell us. We're your lovers. Come on."

Daran sighed. Well, it was his own fault. If he had been better at hiding his feelings, they wouldn't have realized something was off. And Sic had given him permission to tell them when they asked directly. Plus, with any luck, the whole problem would be solved by tomorrow, so he didn't think there was too much harm in revealing the truth.

"It's Lord Sic. He's trying to seduce Lord Noran tonight."

Both warriors whistled. Then Aegid's eyes narrowed.

"How do you know about it?"

Daran winced. "I may have helped him to prepare for the occasion."

Kalad's hands froze on the thief's hips. His tone was a little more aggressive than Daran deemed comfortable. "What did you do?"

"I didn't sleep with him, if that's what you're thinking with that overly active imagination of yours. I merely showed him how to make it feel good. Gave him some tips to be prepared for something as big as Noran's cock going inside him. That's all."

Daran's choice of words made clear how annoyed he was. Kalad rested his chin on the thief's shoulder, and Aegid kissed him on the lips.

"We're sorry, little thief. We didn't mean to accuse you of anything. We're simply still shocked. Kwarl has gotten to us."

"When will you stop using this incident as an excuse to monopolize me? You've done it before without bothering to justify yourself. It's heartbreaking to see you so meek."

"You're calling us meek? Well, we've got news for you, Echend'dim. You won't have to bother about Sic and his trysts any longer, because you'll have your hands—and mouth and ass—full tonight."

Daran moaned, already slain by the words alone. When the desert warriors started touching him, he gratefully slid into the bliss of athletic, rough sex only they could give him.

SIC WAS moaning as well. He lay sprawled out on his bed, next to the bulky figure of Noran, who was caressing his entire body ever so gently. The young smith could feel his own lust slowly building up, changing from nervous anticipation to pure longing. When Daran had shown him how to pleasure himself, he had been reluctant and insecure. How could he ever tell Noran where and how he liked to be touched? In the end, it had been surprisingly easy. Noran was eager to make him feel good and had implemented his wishes so perfectly, Sic almost believed he was having a very realistic masturbation experience. To convince himself otherwise, he reached out for Noran's neck, pulled him closer, and started kissing him. For a sweet eternity, their tongues snaked around each other while both savored the spicy-sweet taste of the other.

On his thigh, Sic could feel Noran's arousal, hard and demanding, making him feel wary. The master smith was indeed well-endowed, even better than Aegid, and his cock had made Sic cringe in fear before. Tentatively he reached for this powerful weapon that could induce such terrible pain. It was hard and soft at the same time, the tip rubbing against his palm eagerly, the shaft already covered in sweat and drops of precum. Unsure what to do, he looked up at Noran, who smiled wistfully at him.

"If you don't want to get a nasty surprise, you'd better take your hands away. I'm so close, I don't think I can hold back any longer."

"You mean you are aroused?"

"Beyond words."

"Can I…?"

"You don't have to, but if you want…."

Sic's palm slid slowly over Noran's erection. The idea that he would be able to make this proud, strong man lose his composure went straight to his head. Recalling everything Daran had taught him in the course of those embarrassing days, he concentrated on this part of the warrior. As Noran had predicted, it only took a few measured strokes and he spilled like an exploding barrel of beer. Stunned, Sic stared at what he had just done, unable to decide whether this was good or bad. When the master smith finally managed to get his breath back, he took Sic's hands in his own, kissing and licking the essence away.

"Thank you, my precious. Now please, let me return the favor."

Suddenly insecure again, Sic slung his arms around the strong neck in front of him. Noran kissed him deeply before his mouth started its journey south. When Sic finally realized what his master was about to do, he stiffened.

"You can't do that, Master."

"Why not?"

"It's embarrassing."

Noran gave Sic's cock a tentative lick. "Is this embarrassing?"

Sic shuddered, assaulted by waves of pleasure. "Yes!"

"Does it feel good?"

Sic moaned, his cheeks a deep crimson.

Noran chuckled happily. "I thought so. Don't fight it."

He started licking again, completely focused on giving his lover the ultimate pleasure. Like him, Sic was close, and way too soon he spilled his essence as well. Now the air was heavy with both their scents, arousing them even more. Sic felt the last restraints falling from him. His body was pulsing, eager for the next step on this journey to fulfilment. He took Noran's hand and gently led it to the place between his butt cheeks. They were so close their foreheads were touching.

"Do you really want this?"

Sic could only nod.

"If you feel insecure, if you don't like what I'm doing, just say the word and I'll stop immediately."

"Yes. I promise."

"Good boy."

Noran put some oil on his index finger and then started massaging the tight crown he had violated so cruelly more than once and that was now twitching invitingly under his ministrations. Sooner than he had anticipated, he was able to slide into the velvety-soft channel, penetrating it first with two and then three fingers. It only took him a short time to find Sic's sweet spot, and just moments later, the young man was arching his back and thrusting his hips.

"More! Please, give me more!"

Emboldened by these words, Noran moved his fingers a little harder, causing his precious lover to have another orgasm. Panting heavily, Sic reached for his master's cock, stroking it deliberately.

"I'm ready now. I really want to feel you inside. Please, come."

Trembling, Noran helped Sic to put a cushion under his lower back. Then he lifted the young man's legs, put some oil on his penis, and positioned himself at the narrow entrance. Agonizingly slowly, he pushed into his lover, every little movement forward pure delight and deepest pain at the same time. This was what he had been craving all his life, what he had sullied and thrown away, what had been given back to him. Regret and joy filled his heart, and he found it difficult to look into Sic's eyes. When he did, he glimpsed a similar jumble of emotions. His exceptional lover was as confused as he was. Noran stopped, reaching out for Sic's face.

"I love you. I love you so much, it's tearing me up inside."

A smile as bright as the rising sun appeared on the young man's face. All doubts were gone, washed away by the power of these three simple words.

"And I love you."

Together they found their release, drowning in sweet ecstasy that made them forget the hurts of the past.

THE NEXT morning, Sic was awakened by the smell of tea and warm bread. He blinked into the rays of the sun and then jolted up. Usually he got up at dawn, a habit from his days as a slave, but judging from the position of the sun, it was already close to noon. For the first time in his life, he had slept in. Warm laughter erupted next to him. Noran was sitting upright, a mug of tea in his big hands.

"Good morning, my precious. Did you sleep well?"

Sic grimaced. "Obviously. Why didn't you wake me? It looks as if you've been up for quite some time."

Noran put the tea aside and kissed Sic lovingly on the forehead.

"How could I wake you when you were sleeping so soundly? I felt you were due, after what we did last night."

Sic felt himself blush. The memories started flooding back, and though they weren't unpleasant, he still felt awkward in front of his lover. Noran sensed that and embraced the young man.

"You made me very happy, Sic. Thank you for everything we did. Are you sore?"

Sic winced. He did feel a little uncomfortable in certain areas, but it was the kind he could enjoy.

"I'm fine. I feel sated."

Noran chuckled with a hint of male pride in his voice. Then he reached for the mug again and offered his lover some tea. After Sic gulped down almost half the contents, the master smith passed him a plate with warm bread smeared with butter and honey. At the sight of the food, Sic suddenly realized how hungry he was. He started wolfing down the slabs of bread, while Noran watched him in silent amazement.

"I'm sorry, I don't even know your favorite food. I just brought what was available."

Sic interrupted his feast to smile at his lover in a reassuring way.

"This is fine. Bread and tea are always welcome." He hesitated for a moment. "And I like scrambled eggs."

"So scrambled eggs it will be tomorrow."

Noran grinned happily. He couldn't remember when he had last felt so content and joyous. Not even with Renaldo had he felt such bliss, and they had done things in bed that would make even Aegid and Kalad blush—probably. No, being with Sic was more than just physical fulfilment. It also put his mind at ease, something he had never known before. Now his precious treasure offered him some of the bread.

"Aren't you going to eat, Master? There's plenty, you know."

Noran took a bite from the bread, chewed carefully, and thought about something that had been weighing on his mind for some time.

"Why are you still calling me master, Sic? I've told you before, you're no longer my slave, and I definitely don't deserve the honorific."

Sic took another sip from the mug, then touched Noran's face.

"Does it bother you?"

A crooked smile appeared on the master smith's lips.

"Yes. It makes me feel guilty. After everything I did to you, you still refer to me as a figure of respect. If anything, it should be the other way round."

Sic put an index finger on his lips and shook his head.

"You've got it all wrong. The 'master' is not referring to you as my former owner, but as my smith master. No matter how questionable your methods of teaching were, they made me one of the best in my trade, and I've got the money to prove it. So even if we are equals now, you'll always be the man who was my first and only teacher. Calling you master comes naturally to me."

Noran was so overwhelmed, he could only stare at the exceptional man in his arms. He had been brooding over this ever since they had started getting closer again, and here all his worries were proved baseless.

"Are you all right, Master?"

He smiled at Sic's worried face.

"I'm fine. Just stunned by my own stupidity. Now come here. I have the sudden urge to kiss you."

"Just kiss?" Sic turned toward him, a challenging look in his eyes.

"If you must know, I have other urges as well."

Both of them giggled like little boys at this innuendo. Then they started kissing again, and very soon the room was filled with their moans.

5. FOREIGN AFFAIRS

WITH A disdainful look in her eyes, Her Majesty, Queen Anesha of Ummana, listened to the rantings of Mother Venya, high priestess of the Good Mother and supposed envoy for some of the eastern kings. Right now the female was complaining about how Anesha had swept the twin cities clean of all followers of the Good Mother and how she had enacted laws that made a return of those worshipping the goddess impossible. That King Erac of Medelina, as well as the rulers of the other cities in the Confederation, had followed this example didn't please the priestess. Losing Medelina had been a blow indeed, for the priesthood had used it as a base for their schemes in the past fifty years. The audience with the new queen was her last hope to gain back some ground, but the conversation hadn't gone in the direction Venya had hoped for. Contrary to what she had been expecting, Anesha was no insecure, inexperienced girl she could bend to her will, but a self-confident, power-conscious woman whose intense gaze seemed to pierce her.

"Your reasoning, Mother Venya, is quite fascinating, but I don't see where you're headed. You have to be aware that I won't allow your followers to return to Ummana, and you're in no position to pressure me, either politically nor economically."

The beautiful young woman paused for a moment, as if she just had an interesting idea. When she resumed her speech, Venya couldn't help but think of a constrictor squeezing the last breath out of its prey.

"I, on the other hand, am able to make your life a living hell. Ummana is the head of a powerful alliance and ruler of the plains. And I'm the queen of it all. You have nowhere near enough resources to get into a fight with me, so why are you here?"

Venya closed her eyes under the scrutinizing glare. Unfortunately the queen had described her situation quite accurately. There were no aces up her sleeve with which she could threaten—or bribe—Anesha. Out of despair, the priestess tried to appeal to the queen's humaneness.

"You can't tell me you're not afraid of the bastards, Your Majesty."

Anesha leaned back in her chair.

"Of course I'm afraid. Only a fool wouldn't be scared of the Lords Canubis and Renaldo."

"You've just given the answer to your own question. If you decide to follow the Good Mother, she will protect you. I can guarantee that."

The queen smiled without warmth.

"Somehow I doubt it. Apart from the fact that I have relation to the Angel of Death through marriage that, in certain ways, makes me duty-bound to stay loyal to him and his brother, I've witnessed what happens to those who dare to oppose them. There is nothing you can do or say to convince me otherwise."

Venya hesitated. She was aware of the power the bastards wielded, but she couldn't imagine what the two had done to intimidate a woman as jaded as Anesha. As if she had read her thoughts, the queen spoke on.

"I was present when Lord Renaldo damned one of your own for all eternity. He burned her soul as casually as a child pulling off a fly's wings. And that was before the eighth Emeris was found. I don't even want to try to imagine what the Angel of Death must be capable of by now." She shuddered visibly. "No, there is absolutely nothing you can offer me. My advice for you is to accept your defeat."

Mother Venya decided to back down for the time being. The queen's body language had made it clear she wouldn't budge. It was frustrating. Despite the joint efforts of the priesthood and the aid of the visions they had forced from their seers, the bastards had managed to reclaim their birthright. Their hope to stop the gods of war before they succeeded the creators was shattered, and nobody had to spell out for Venya how uncertain the outcome of the battle between the Good Mother and the bastards would now be. Nobody knew what kind of power Renaldo and Canubis had acquired in addition to their original talents, where their limits were, and what the Emeris were capable of. The followers of the Good Mother went into this battle without being able to assess their enemy, and it almost drove Mother Venya crazy. Although the Good Mother herself had appeared to her in a vision and reassured her that they would soon have an army equaling that of the bastards, the priestess couldn't relax. In her opinion, losing both Ummana and Medelina, not to mention the other cities of the Confederation, was a bad omen.

Thoroughly beaten, she bid farewell to Queen Anesha, whose cold gaze had etched itself into her soul.

As SOON as the priestess was out of earshot, Anesha got off her throne, reached behind it, and grabbed the bucket that had been waiting there. After she had parted with her breakfast, she cleansed her mouth with some water a servant brought. Who would have thought being pregnant was such a pain in the ass? At the beginning, Cassia had assured her the violent outbursts of morning sickness would be just a bad memory once she reached her second trimester, and only few women had them throughout their entire pregnancy. As it turned out, she was one of those unlucky few. The faintest smell could trigger her nausea, which was inconvenient for a queen who had to maintain an iron façade to stay in control. Cassia was a big help, with her herbal teas, the salves and potions to make her feel better, and her seemingly limitless patience with a very difficult patient. Still, Anesha was more than happy that the days of her swollen belly would be coming to an end soon. Only a few more weeks, and yet another stone to cement her leadership would be on the playing field. Not that she could relax then—that would never be the case— but breathing would become a little easier, in more than one respect.

Practically immediately after her brother and the barbarians had left, her opponents had come from the shadows to find out whether she was prey or predator. Some of them had paid for this insolence with their lives; others merely had their fur ruffled. With the onset of winter, affairs had been more or less settled within the twin cities, which left Anesha time to deal with her foreign affairs. Erac in particular had proven to be a real nuisance, and there had been times she was tempted to settle the matter of dealing with him permanently. In the end she hadn't done it, because despite his acting as if he owned her, he was still an important ally, one she couldn't afford to lose—at least not yet.

The other members of the Confederation had been keeping a low profile until now, plotting their schemes in secret, watching her every move to determine their own course of action. Anesha employed excellent spies, so she knew the leaders of Kre and Sravrana weren't happy about her ascent to the throne. For the time being, they would follow the example of Medelina and back her up to a certain extent, but only until they found an opening to snatch power from Ummana. Well, they were in for a surprise. Alemba and Eppirat, which were ruled by military forces, were more inclined to do her bidding. They respected blunt force, something the Pack was by definition. Wa'na Atoka, the only city that elected a tyrant every five years, had remained neutral until now. They were the smallest and latest member of the Confederation, albeit not the weakest. Keeping a close eye on them was an absolute necessity. The current tyrant, Lady Allianna na Wa'ra, tended to strike when least expected, and her bite was venomous. On the other hand, she was also the most levelheaded of the rulers, with a keen eye for details and incredible foresight. If she managed to stay in power, which was more or less a given, her economic visions would make Wa'na Atoka one of the leading cities in the Confederation sooner rather than later.

Anesha sighed. She was enjoying her new position very much, almost reveling in the power she had accumulated after years of subservience to people she deemed basically incapable of properly ruling the twin cities. Watching how Nambuno, Amicia, and her own sire had made all the big decisions while she had to keep her mouth shut had been hard on the queen. Now she was the one calling the shots, with only her brother and his fearsome husband to still tell her what to do. Luckily enough they were a long way off, and even though her brother had his own spies in the cities, he wasn't interested in interfering as long as the general direction was to his liking. Which was, apart from her pregnancy, the main reason she kept Cassia close to her. As Master Sic's stand-in, Jago maintained a close relationship to the last Emeris and never failed to report everything interesting about Ummana to him. Since this information pipeline worked both ways, Anesha was keen on staying on Cassia's good side. That way she always knew what her irascible brother was up to. Not to mention that Aries, the leader of the guild of smiths, was trying to position Jago as his successor. Should the master of the royal smithy accept, she would also have a close connection to a guild that was growing in power every year.

The Queen of Ummana smiled. It wasn't a very pleasant smile, rather one that suggested trouble for anybody who dared to get in her way. Rubbing her growing belly with one hand while the other supported her aching lower back, Anesha called for Aktan to escort her back to her chambers.

IN THEIR still uncomfortably huge new house, Jago and Cassia were watching as Heljia made her first attempts at standing on her own. With the concentrated look of a young lady determined to conquer new ground this very day, she kept on grabbing the edge of a low table to get her diaper-clad rear into the air. When she finally managed to stand, a radiant smile of pure pride lit up her features. Cassia went over to her daughter and patted her head.

"Well done, my sweet one. Such a big girl!"

Jago smiled at this scene of perfect domestic bliss, thanking the heavens for these two wonderful women in his life. He held out his arms to pick his daughter up, and she started to squeal happily. When she snuggled her head against his broad chest, slinging her little arms around his neck, he felt such joy it made him dizzy. Gently he stroked her soft hair, inhaling the wonderful scent of baby lotion and milk that always surrounded her.

"She'll probably keep that color, won't she?"

Jago was referring to Heljia's hair, which was a shock of blinding white crowning her head like a halo of light. Cassia smiled a bit wistfully.

"Probably. But it's fine. It reminds me of Sic."

Jago took his wife's hand. She was still missing the young man who had entered their lives so abruptly and changed them in more ways than one. Jago was missing him as well, but he had his hands full with work these days, and whenever he touched one of the pieces Sic sent to Ummana on a regular basis, he felt connected to him. And every time the new Emeris sent a letter, it was as if he was still with them, in a sense.

"You know he had to go. The Valley is his destiny."

Cassia snorted. She wasn't the type to accept reality just because it made sense.

"That may be the case, but why is he getting back with the monster? Has he lost his mind?"

Jago pulled Heljia closer to his chest. This was something he didn't understand either.

"I don't know. He never told me anything about Noran. Back then he wanted to avoid the topic at all costs. Perhaps something profound happened? Anyway, it's his decision, and he seems to be happy, so we should respect it."

Cassia sighed deeply. She knew Jago was right, which didn't make it easier for her.

"I guess I can do that. Still, I hate the monster."

Jago couldn't suppress a smile and was glad he could hide it in Heljia's hair. His wife didn't take kindly to being patronized.

"And you are free to do so, my dear. Now let's have dinner. I'm starving."

IN MEDELINA, King Erac sat on his throne listening to the introduction of the Generals Liee and Hall'ovan, leaders of Alemba and Eppirat, whom he had invited to an unofficial meeting. Soon after he returned home from Ummana, he found out just how badly he had underestimated the young queen. It was also dawning on him that King Castolus had outmaneuvered him perfectly, getting everything he had wanted and giving nothing in return. To put it mildly, Erac was furious. Everything he had hoped to achieve was slipping through his fingers like quicksand. It was so bad, he even had to fear for Medelina's standing within the Confederation. If he didn't act soon, the things he had accomplished would evaporate into thin air while Anesha accumulated all the power and dictated her terms. His only advantage at the moment was that the other cities were wary because of the queen's youth. Kre and Sravrana, monarchies like Medelina, were on his side for the time being. Wa'na Atoka had always been difficult to deal with, and the new tyrant was dangerous enough to make Erac withdraw for the time being. Which left Alemba and Eppirat—not his favorite partners, but beggars couldn't be choosers. If he wanted to keep Anesha under control, he needed all the help he could get.

After the official proceedings finally came to an end, Erac invited the two generals into his private rooms. What he had to tell them was no business of the public. General Liee, a man in his late forties who kept his gray hair brutally short and his tall body in perfect shape, regarded Erac with a certain amount of suspicion. He had accepted the invitation more out of curiosity than anything else, since he wasn't unhappy about Anesha's ascent to the throne. General Hall'ovan, on the other hand, was still torn. Having such a young queen leading the Confederation made him uneasy, while at the same time her allies impressed him deeply. He was a man of certain principles, but not as disciplined as Liee, which also showed in his appearance. Although a few years younger than the other general, Hall'ovan had already managed to acquire two extra chins and a growing potbelly. His aquiline features had been softened by alcohol and excessive meals, and he wasn't as fast as he used to be. Securing his position in Eppirat was becoming more difficult every year, and he was already thinking about abdicating his post before some of the ambitious young officers rising through the ranks made that decision for him. Now he put down his wine and looked expectantly at Erac.

"May I ask why we were invited so courteously?"

A nerve in Erac's face twitched for a moment. Of course Hall'ovan knew, or could at least guess, the reason for their meeting.

"As I said in the invitation, this is a private gathering to discuss matters that, I feel, concern us all."

Liee tried to hide his derisive grin behind the cup he was holding but failed.

"You don't happen to talk about those matters that have left you cornered like a rat, do you? From what I've heard, King Castolus made a fool of you without you even noticing it."

Erac ground his teeth and clenched his fists in order to maintain a congenial façade. Being the laughingstock of the Confederation didn't sit well with his pride, but unfortunately there wasn't much he could do about it right now. It would take time to mend the damage Castolus had caused. He managed to force a smile on his lips.

"I've to admit, it wasn't my best performance ever. But at least I tried to negotiate with the king, while you settled for sending him delegations and presents."

"Which, apparently, was the wise thing to do. We didn't get our asses handed to us."

Liee couldn't help but rub some more salt into Erac's wound. He resented the King of Medelina as a man of low morals and more ambition than was good for him and his people. Not that he was against low morals in general; what irked him was that Erac thought of himself as a man of integrity. In Liee's opinion, a leader had to be honest at least with him or herself. Deceiving your own people was sometimes necessary, but lying to yourself was bound to end in catastrophe. And if he wasn't careful, Erac would take Alemba down with him when he took the fall. Liee was no fool. He knew Erac was planning to act against the new queen of Ummana, which ultimately meant acting against Castolus and the Pack. The general had seen Lord Canubis and Lord Renaldo in action before, and no prize in the world could tempt him to do anything that would invoke their displeasure. Coming to Medelina had been an act of courtesy and, to some extent, curiosity, nothing more. And he would make sure Anesha and Castolus were clear about that.

Hall'ovan, on the other hand, did seem inclined to give Erac's proposal some serious consideration. The two men chatted amiably while Liee sat in silence and listened to their ideas, none of which were realistic, and all of which meant certain death should they be stupid enough to act them out. Alemba's leader was relieved when he finally found an excuse to leave the unofficial and highly dangerous gathering.

BIRTHRIGHT

1. GROWING UP

"WHAT'S HAPPENED to you, Daran? You look like a cat that's had an entire bowl of cream, which is strange since you just had a lesson with Casto."

Kalad grinned at the thief, full of unbridled love. Ever since Daran had come back from the dead in such a spectacular manner five months ago, his daily routine had changed dramatically. Even though his masters didn't like it, Renaldo had insisted on treating Daran according to his new rank. His days were now filled with military training and the merciless drill all new members of the Pack had to endure. Strictly speaking he wasn't even a slave anymore, but when Aegid and Kalad had wanted to take the collar off, he had stopped them with a smile.

"You know as well as I do that I'll always be your possession. Besides, I'm aware how much it pleases you when all the world can see it as well. It's my honor to wear your colors."

And even though they knew how unfair it was toward Daran, the desert brothers accepted this generous offer without hesitation. The thief belonged to them; that was how it always had been, and it wouldn't change till the end of time and beyond.

Now the young man was beaming at his lover.

"The lesson was tiresome, as always, but afterward Lord Renaldo came to me. He wants me to lead the men who are going to the mines tomorrow to escort the caravan with the blue steel! Isn't that great news?"

Kalad's smile froze. He had known this day would come, but he hadn't thought Renaldo would start treating the thief as a leader so soon. It was nothing big—Daran wouldn't lead more than fifteen men—still, Kalad couldn't just ignore it. His thief wouldn't be in the Valley for at least ten days, and there was always the chance the caravan would get attacked, even though the road between the Valley and the mines was comparatively safe. They could no longer lose Daran to the Mothers, but he wasn't invincible. Thinking about all the things that could happen to their precious lover made Kalad shudder.

He turned to Daran with a stern face. "You're not going. It's too soon. I'll go see Renaldo and tell him you're not ready yet."

He got up to do exactly that, but Daran stopped him with raised hands.

"Master! Please. I really want to go. This is my chance to prove myself to the lords. Please don't ruin it for me."

The pleading tone only managed to stoke Kalad's anger. The voice of reason in his head scolded him for being an infatuated, overprotective fool who didn't act even one notch better than the Angel of Death, but Kalad ignored the nagging. He would not allow his precious darling to get into any danger. Determined, he shoved Daran aside and was just about to open the door when Aegid entered. One glance was enough for the giant to realize how loaded the situation was. His brows shot up in question.

"What's the matter? You two look as if you're about to go at each other's throats."

Before Daran could open his mouth, Kalad started to talk.

"Renaldo is seriously planning to let this fledgling lead the escort for the caravan to the mines. I'm on my way to end this foolishness."

"Don't do that, Master, please. I'm looking forward to it!"

Daran's voice was still pleading, but there was a hint of anger blooming in his features. He obviously didn't plan on giving in. Aegid furrowed his brows. Normally he was more levelheaded than Kalad, always having the bigger picture in the back of his mind. Yet now he could feel his emotions taking control of his decisions.

"You may be looking forward to it, Daran, but Kalad is right. You're still too inexperienced. We won't allow it."

Aegid's tone showed clearly that for him the last word concerning this matter had been said. He stepped aside to let his brother through to have a talk with the Angel of Death.

Daran shook his head vigorously. "That's my first big command! Why do you have to ruin it for me? I've already led four missions successfully, and you didn't object to those!"

Aegid's eyes narrowed. He wasn't used to serious opposition from Daran, and it irritated him that the young man didn't submit to his will as usual.

"Because those missions were minor, nothing that could have us worried. And we don't want to ruin anything for you, it's just that we have hundreds of years of experience concerning this business, and you can believe us when we say you're not ready yet."

"Lord Renaldo seems to have a different opinion than you. And he's even older than you are."

Daran's tone had become more aggressive. This, and the fact that his argument was well substantiated, made the desert brothers angry. Kalad grabbed the thief's wrist and glared.

"Watch your mouth, Daran. Our patience does have its limits."

Fiercely, Daran yanked his arm free. "You're hurting me. Concerning the limits of your patience—you no longer have the right to order me."

The words hung in the air like a curse. It was obvious how much Daran wished he could take them back, but when he became aware of the unrelenting fury in the desert brothers' eyes, he stuck out his chin in defiance.

"I think it's better if I don't spend the night here. If everything goes according to plan, I'll be back in eleven days."

He turned around and left his lovers' chambers in anger for the first time since they'd known each other. Aegid and Kalad were thunderstruck. Of course they had noticed how much Daran had changed since his training had begun, and until now it had filled them with pride to see the sometimes-precocious boy turn into a real man. But real men made their own decisions even when their lovers did not approve.

"He's growing up way too fast," Kalad murmured with a certain amount of regret.

Aegid placed a hand on his shoulder. "Unfortunately, yes. I still feel proud. He really dared to defy us. At the beginning of this year, he wouldn't have dreamed about it! He's going to be a great warrior."

"Shall we follow him?"

"And make his determination waver? No. He's made his decision, and now he has to live with it."

Kalad grinned with a hint of malice in his face. "Our pretty little thief will have a sleepless night, don't you think?"

"Definitely. But it's going to teach him about consequences. All we have to do is live through the next ten days without him."

Kalad sighed deeply. "It's going to be hard. Especially since we'd planned so many interesting things for today. Once he comes back, he'll have to take responsibility."

Thinking about how they would make Daran pay for his decision lifted the warriors' spirits considerably. They had been living long enough to savor the prospect of pleasures to come as much as the pleasure itself.

"HEY, DARAN! You're making a face as long as a fiddle! This is your first command. You should be beaming with joy!" Lukan steered his horse next to that of his leader, the brows in his open, round face furrowed. "Or are you worried? Lord Renaldo wouldn't have chosen you if he didn't think you were ready. Plus, this is routine. It's perfect for your first time."

On this innuendo, the warrior's eyes lit up mockingly. He was two years younger than Daran and could take endless pleasure from such jokes.

Daran tried to manage a smile and failed miserably. "It's not the command, Lukan. I'm confident enough to believe I can lead the escort. Unfortunately, my masters are of a different opinion."

Lukan whistled silently. He knew immediately where the problem lay. "You had a fight with Kalad and Aegid."

The pain in Daran's face was answer enough.

"For the first time since we met. I mean, we did have some minor quarrels, but nothing this big. I'm feeling so ghastly, I can't find the words."

Soothingly, Lukan placed a hand on the thief's shoulder. "It will pass. You're a free man, a warrior in the Pack, and to top it off, the first immortal after the Emeris. It's only natural for you to find your own way. Considering how possessive those two are, it's no wonder you had a run-in. When I went on my first command, Elua refused to talk to me for a week. We're still together, though."

Daran sighed deeply. Lukan had come into the Valley last winter, not as a slave but as the lover of Elua, a mercenary ten years his senior. She was an experienced warrior whom Canubis often sent where the battle was worst. About fifty men and women—like her, specializing in fighting with long daggers—obeyed her command. Her fighters were able to bring severe losses to the enemy and usually went right to the center of every skirmish.

She had met Lukan in a small town south of Kwarl and spent some pleasant nights with him. That the third son of a local noble would fall in love with her hadn't been planned, but in the end she had yielded to his persistent wooing and taken him to the Valley. Once they had arrived,

Lukan had done everything in his power to make her his own, with the outcome that they were now married. After some epic and violent arguments, Lukan had decided to serve under a different commander, since his wife wasn't very good at keeping her protective instincts under control. This was the reason Lukan was riding with Daran now, who truly liked the cheerful noble. Lukan represented everything Daran had never had: respectable ancestry and a carefree, perfect childhood in a loving home. Talking to Lukan was like a balm. His balanced personality easily soothed Daran's churning emotions. Grateful, the thief smiled at him.

"I know I shouldn't be taking it to heart, but this is the first time we've been separated. And after an argument as well. I'm feeling as if somebody has roughed me up."

Lukan sighed. "This may sound like pure derision to you, but enjoy the feeling. Believe me, once you're back, they're gonna make you pay." His blue-gray eyes lit up in mockery. "When you think you can't take it anymore, imagine the make-up sex you're going to have once they've calmed down. It always helps me to get through my quarrels with Elua."

Upon these words, Daran felt a shudder run through his body that wasn't entirely born from lust. Having two lovers, especially seasoned ones like Kalad and Aegid, meant he was driven to his limit and beyond practically every night. On the few occasions when he had had make-up sex with the desert brothers, Daran had lost consciousness during the act more than once, and afterward it had taken days until he had been able to stand on his own again. He was perfectly fine with having normal intercourse with his masters.

"I'd prefer not to waste too much thought on that. I *like* being able to walk on my own."

Curiosity woke in Lukan's eyes. "What's it like, having two men in your bed?"

"Exhausting. Terribly exhausting."

"Doesn't sound like fun to me…."

Daran sighed. How was he supposed to explain something he didn't really understand himself? "Of course I like it. But believe it or not, even lust can be too much. When those two are taking me, it's like I'm drowning. I'm completely helpless and reduced to receiving them. I don't have any control left and can only endure it because I trust them absolutely."

Lukan frowned. "But you're immortal as well now. You should be able to match them."

"That's what I had hoped, but I'm still too young. And their mere presence is simply too overwhelming. They've conditioned me perfectly. If they use a certain tone or way of looking, it's like I go into heat. My body is like an instrument they have tuned to their liking."

"And yet you love them." It was more a statement than a question.

"More than anything else in the world. They are my life. Everything I am and own, I owe to them, which is why our argument is concerning me so much. I feel like I've betrayed their generosity."

Lukan shook his head in wonder. "You're a lot more complicated than I thought, Daran. Seen from the outside, your relationship is so harmonious it could make one sick. I would have never thought you could feel anything but bliss."

The worry in Lukan's voice was so obvious, Daran had to smile. It was nice to have comrades like him.

"Strictly speaking, I am in perpetual bliss. I'm truly happy. It's just that my life is really intense. And because I was a weak mortal until not too long ago, it's a little too much sometimes. But I can assure you, if I had the chance to do it all again, I wouldn't change one thing. Even my time in Kwarl—if it's the price I had to pay for being able to live with Aegid and Kalad, then so be it."

"Seems like love turns us all into fools." Lukan grinned broadly. "But I'm happy. Everything else would be plain boring."

Daran laughed. "You're so right! And now let's end this deeply philosophical discussion before one of us starts crying."

Slightly more at ease than before and determined to make up with his masters after his return, Daran edged Rajan on.

"How does concluding your first command successfully feel?"

Lukan was grinning broadly at Daran. They were about a day's ride from the Valley, and he was looking forward to seeing Elua again.

Daran made a face. The closer they had gotten to home, the more reclusive he had become. "First of all, we're not home yet, and secondly, I can hardly think about anything but my fight with Aegid and Kalad. As you well know, Lukan."

The noble lifted his hands apologetically. "I was just trying to get your mind off it. That's what friends are for."

"I appreciate the effort, but I'd rather you don't. I don't know how to face them."

Lukan rolled his eyes heavenward. Daran's obsession with his lovers was as bad as theirs for him. It was more or less impossible to get him to think of something else. Lukan was just pondering what else he could do to lift his commander's spirits when he glimpsed movement from the corner of his eye. His hand grabbed the hilt of his sword in one fluid movement while his voice resounded clearly in the fresh morning air.

"Enemy! Get ready!"

He hadn't finished his warning when hollow clay spheres started shattering all around them. A thin, treacherous dust rose in the air, burning the mercenaries' lungs when they inhaled it. Lukan had the presence of mind to press his cloak against mouth and nose before he tried to get an overview of the situation. More and more of the strange clay spheres shattered on the ground. The beasts of burden pulling the heavy carts of blue steel were getting increasingly nervous, and their loud roaring didn't help to calm the confusion. Lukan started to blink. The ground seemed to be moving toward him; the air was filled with colored lights, and a sound like an approaching thunderstorm resounded in his ears.

"It's a drug! Try to get away!"

Daran's voice was far off. Lukan had trouble understanding him. When he finally realized what the words meant, he tried to steer his mare away from the dust with hands that were too clumsy to hold the reins. He could feel his mind getting numb and fought it desperately. In front of him he could see Daran, who was swaying on the back of his horse but somehow managed to lead Rajan away from the caravan toward clean air. Lukan didn't know how he accomplished the same feat.

Just when breathing became easier again, the main attack happened. Armed men appeared from all directions. They all had wet cloths wrapped around their mouths and noses and their eyes were protected by thin veils. With the efficiency of seasoned highwaymen, some of them killed the helpless coachmen while the rest took care of the disoriented mercenaries. Lukan gripped his sword harder. As soon as he and Daran had gotten out of the dust, his mind had started to work again. The two men exchanged a glance, knowing well that the caravan was lost. Judging from Daran's determined expression, he wasn't willing to give in so easily. He turned toward the massacre happening right in front of them. Due to the drug, the mercenaries didn't stand a chance against the well-organized attackers.

"Lukan, go and get help. Move it!"

"Daran, this is madness! You are heavily outnumbered. There's no chance you're going to survive this!"

With a weak smile, Daran turned around.

"I know. But I owe it to these—to my—men. And I'm going to come back. You know that. Now get going. The Wolf of War must know what has happened."

Lukan hesitated for one more moment before he gave in. He had received a direct order from his commander, and even though everything inside him was thirsting to join Daran, reason told him that informing the lords was even more important. Determined, he spun his horse around and started galloping. He had barely made five strides when something hit him hard below the ribcage and almost swept him off his mount. Panting, he held on to the saddle, fumbling for the arrow that had buried itself in his body. Disgusted, he broke off the shaft and threw it away, then urged his mare on.

DARAN DIDN'T see it when Lukan was hit by the arrow; he was too immersed with the task in front of him. Only a handful of his men were still alive, and they stood no chance against the superior numbers of the enemy. Whoever had planned this attack had been quite thorough and knew the Pack's weakness. The drug had turned the powerful, perfectly trained warriors into a bunch of disoriented, helpless children who were barely able to fend off the clumsy attacks from the highwaymen. Daran, too, felt the effect of the drug dust, but not as badly as his men, which was probably due to his immortal nature. The horses and oxen seemed to be completely unperturbed by the effect, a small blessing for which Daran was grateful. If Rajan had been affected as well, he wouldn't have stood even the smallest chance.

He was painfully aware of how brutally they were outnumbered, and he had no illusions that they would not all find their death here. Still, he felt the obligation toward those men who had accepted his command to kill as many enemies as possible. And even though his body didn't obey him like it used to, Daran managed to take five of the men down and wound as many before the highwaymen could finally defeat him. When the cold steel of two swords entered his body simultaneously, Daran slid into darkness with a feeling of gratitude. Once he woke, he would be faced with the anger of the Wolf of War, a prospect he wasn't looking forward to.

2. ECHEND'DIM

WHEN LUKAN was absolutely sure nobody had followed him, he reined his mare in and oriented himself. Luckily his mount had instinctively turned toward the Valley. Yet they were still too far away for him to make it alive. The arrow in his side had caused more damage than Lukan had first assumed. With every heartbeat he could feel his life trickling out of him. The saddle and the fur of the mare were already sticky with blood. At least his mind was working perfectly again, so Lukan knew what he had to do. With his own blood, he wrote the exact location of the raid and the information about the drug on his coat. Then he tied himself to the saddle with the rope that was standard equipment for all members of the Pack and patted the mare's neck, grateful she was one of the horses trained by Casto.

"Sirana!" The dun snorted when she heard her name, her ears playing nervously. She could sense that something was amiss. "Sirana! *Alan nioma! Nioma!*"

Lukan whimpered when the mare started running. No matter what happened now, or who would try to stop her, she would bring him back to the Valley or die trying. For a moment he wondered how Casto managed to condition the horses to spoken commands like this, but the pain stopped his musings almost immediately. He knew he didn't have much time left and decided not to waste his final lucid moments pondering the enigma that was Casto.

A weak smile flickered across the face of the dying man. Elua. Even though he had wished to spend more time with her, he didn't regret following her. Never before had he been as happy as with this woman. The only thing he felt sorry for was that he couldn't tell her anymore. But when she followed him into the Green Lands one day, he would do so immediately.

Sirana flattened her ears. She could feel that the man on her back was no longer alive, and had she not been trained so perfectly, she would have given in to temptation and tried to get rid of the burden. Instead, she ran on, determined to fulfill her rider's last command.

"How many men have we lost?"

The dark eyes of the leader were glinting in anger. Attacking the caravan had been meticulously planned, and he hadn't reckoned he would suffer such serious losses. As it had turned out, the mercenaries of the Valley were even more efficient than the stories told about them had made him think.

"All in all, seventeen, Ma'Duk."

The man who had spoken those words ducked in fear. He had served his leader long enough to know how unfair he could be when angry. During such moments, it wasn't a good idea to be close to him or to attract his attention. The hand of the bulky man with the wild dark eyes and the three rhombic tribal scars on the forehead darted toward his dagger. But before he could vent his anger, he was interrupted by a call from the caravan.

"Ma'Duk, this one is still alive!"

Ma'Duk frowned. Usually his men were quite efficient, and as far as he had seen, all the mercenaries had received more than one lethal blow. Slightly worried for reasons he didn't understand, he hurried to the man who had called him.

"I'm warning you, Da'Ryen. If this is your idea of a practical joke, I'll personally rip your heart out."

The thug gulped but didn't retreat. "You should know I don't make jokes about such matters, Ma'Duk."

The leader hesitated. Da'Ryen was one of the four men who had followed him from the semidesert at the northern end of the Hot Heart to this faraway place. And even though they all had sacrificed their past and convictions to this new life as outlaws, there were still some things that remained sacred. Not making jokes about death was one of them.

Ma'Duk leaned over the body Da'Ryen indicated. It was the long-haired warrior who had led the caravan and who had inflicted the greatest losses on them. His formerly gleaming equipment was smeared with blood and dirt, his long black hair was tangled around his body, and the extraordinary jewelry around his neck was dulled. Ma'Duk himself had rammed his sword deeply into the torso of this man who had come like a curse over his men. By all rights he should have been staring at a corpse, but when he looked closely, he could see the chest of the fallen moving ever so slightly. Suddenly Ma'Duk reared back and made a gesture to fend off evil powers. In front of his eyes, a cut on the man's arm closed, healed so cleanly it was as if it had never been there.

"Holy ancestors, what is this?"

Da'Ryen had turned pale. Even in the remote part of Ana-Darasa where they had come from, he had heard stories about the people from the Valley and the fact that they were immortal. The closer they had gotten to their immediate sphere of influence, the more fantastic the tales had become, until they reached a point where they had stopped believing them. He had been opposed to attacking a caravan that was so obviously meant for the Valley, but Ma'Duk hadn't listened. He was conceited enough to believe he could cope with any enemy.

The other men had realized something was going on and started to draw closer. When they saw how the wounds of the fallen man started to close with increasing speed, some of them turned and ran. Those who stayed kept their distance and tried to rush their departure. Only one man didn't seem to know any fear. He knelt next to the still unconscious man to inspect him closely. A malicious smile appeared on his lips.

"What, Elgir?"

Ma'Duk was getting impatient. The men's reaction wasn't to his liking, and he, too, felt the burning desire to leave this place as fast as possible.

"It seems as if the rumors about the immortality of the people from the Valley are true indeed. I know quite a few people who would love playing with a dainty morsel like this one. And who would pay even more for the privilege to kill him."

Da'Ryen made a choking sound.

"I knew you were a sick bastard, Elgir, but this is taking it too far. Apart from that, don't you think the other warriors are going to come to look for one of their own?"

"Pah, I'm not planning to wait for them. A friend of mine knows a thing or two about magic. It shouldn't be a problem to hide this perfect prey. Don't you idiots get it? This guy here is worth more than the entire caravan!"

Unsure, Ma'Duk stared at the man on the ground. Elgir's words did make sense, and even managed to tempt him, but an uneasy feeling remained. The fallen was the only one recovering from his wounds, which meant he was special. And even though he would never admit it, Ma'Duk had no intention of facing a man like the Wolf of War directly.

He turned away from temptation.

"We leave him here. Man the carts, then we're out."

Da'Ryen didn't hesitate to follow his leader. Elgir hesitated. Then he slowly rose to his feet.

"I think this is where our ways part, Ma'Duk. It was fun, but I'll be damned if I let this once-in-a-lifetime chance slip through my fingers."

Ma'Duk stopped him with a wave of his hand. He had anticipated this from the moment Elgir had joined them and wasn't exactly sad to part ways with him.

"Do what you have to, but don't come running to me when things go awry."

"Don't worry, I wouldn't dream of it!"

CASTO WAS on his way to his and Lys's favorite spot at the lake when he heard the howling. By now he was familiar enough with the wolves to realize instantly that something was wrong. The shrill sound, like a siren through the Valley, had a desperate undertone. Casto felt shivers running down his spine when he remembered that Daran would be coming back today. Lys turned on the spot and hurried back as quickly as the narrow path allowed.

In front of the stables, a nightmarish scene unfolded. Renaldo, Canubis, Sic, Noran, Aegid, Kalad, and Hulda were standing around a dun horse Casto recognized as Sirana, Lukan's mare. Her light fur was smeared with blood, and the king glimpsed a hunched figure on her back. When he came closer, he realized it was Lukan—Lukan who was cold and dead. Casto gulped. The noble was about his age, and although they hadn't known each other closely, he had thought him to be likeable.

"Lukan! No!"

Elua, Lukan's wife, was screaming in despair. The usually collected and unapproachable mercenary was trembling all over. Her face was contorted in pain, her voice like the screeching of a demon. Casto could sympathize with her. Full of horror, he remembered the battle of Elam, when he had thought he'd lost Renaldo. Never having to feel the terrible emptiness, the gut-wrenching despair and the paralyzing sorrow again was something he prayed for every night. He felt tears pricking in his eyes, and then Renaldo was there.

"It's all right, my own. It's fine. I'm here."

Casto managed a weak smile, pulled himself together, and came right to the point.

"What has happened?"

"We don't know yet. Sirana arrived like this. Kalad was at the stables at the time and stopped her. Lukan is dead, but he still had the strength to tie himself to the saddle."

"Renaldo!"

Aegid's voice stopped the Angel of Death in his explanation.

"We've found a message. Looks like he's written it himself."

Canubis and his brother stared at Lukan's coat, on which the events of the previous day had been written with blood.

"What on Ana-Darasa has happened?"

Noran was shaking his head in disbelief. None of them would have thought it possible that anything could happen on this routine operation. Hulda stepped forward. Her fingertips grazed the coat of the fallen man. Then she rubbed the thin film between her fingers and sniffed it. Disgusted, she shook her hand.

"I think I know. Well, it's pretty obvious that the caravan has been raided. The attackers used a drug that confuses perception, and managed to win this way. If I had to guess, I'd say it was Ishe-Ryein. It's a powder made of the pulverized poison fangs of the Ishe lizard. Not very reliable and impossible to control. Plus it only works when you inhale it directly. My weapon of choice would be something different. But it's cheap and easy to obtain." The killer wrinkled her nose. "Nevertheless, it seems to have been effective in this case." Canubis's voice was deadly calm. Whoever had dared to raid the caravan would pay a high price for this sacrilege.

"Get Lukan off and prepare everything. We're going hunting."

Nods accompanied the flatly spoken words. Two servants brought a bier, on which they placed Lukan. Elua leaned over him and kissed his pale forehead, full of love.

"I'm going to miss you, my sweet one. Wait for me on the other side."

Hot tears trickled down her cheeks and wet the motionless body of her husband. Then she suddenly felt a light touch on her shoulder. Sic had stepped toward her, his friendly face full of pity. He knelt down next to the bier to place his hand in silent farewell on Lukan's chest. The moment Sic touched the dead man's skin, he froze. His eyes rolled up until only the white was visible, and his lips started to tremble.

"Sic! What's the matter?" Noran wanted to hurry to his lover, but Hulda held him back. Her voice was like a whip.

"Noran, stay here. Elua, come over!"

The warrior obeyed instantly. When she reached Hulda, Sic started to make strange sounds, which the assembled fighters could barely hear. His entire body seemed to blur; the contours of his torso were shimmering, as if an inner light illuminated them.

"What is going on?"

Canubis's hand was at the hilt of his sword, ready to strike.

"Put your weapon away, you idiot." Hulda's voice was tense; she was concentrating on Sic and Lukan. "Don't you understand? He's calling him back!"

Awed silence descended, only interrupted by Sic's almost inaudible singsong. Then Lukan's hand started to twitch, and he opened his eyes. At the same moment, Sic fell silent. The light around him vanished as if it had never been there, and his eyes returned to normal. He seemed to be slightly dazed.

Noran came to him like an avalanche. "Sic! Are you all right?"

The smith smiled weakly. "Of course. I just wanted to say my goodbyes to Lukan, but then…."

He hesitated, composed himself in search of the right words, and then spoke on carefully, as if he was afraid his words could shatter in his mouth.

"I could still feel him. It was similar to how it was with Daran. That's why I asked him to come back. I do feel kind of bad about it. There was peace."

Insecure, he looked at Elua, who was holding Lukan in her arms. The noble winked at him.

"I heard you, Lord Sic. And I saw your light. It was surprisingly easy to follow. I thank you. Don't feel bad about breaking the peace. I wasn't ready for it yet."

Before Sic could answer, Canubis took over. "I think this can wait. Lukan, what has happened?"

The warrior's face darkened. "We were attacked, about a day's ride away from the Valley. The highwaymen bombarded us with spheres of clay that emitted a strange powder that kept us from thinking. Daran sent me to tell you. He tried to help our men. I was hit by an arrow and took some measures in case I didn't make it."

"That was very thoughtful of you."

Canubis placed his hand in an appreciative gesture on the young man's shoulder.

Suddenly Kalad appeared in front of them, his lively brown eyes clouded by worry. "What happened to Daran?"

"I really don't know, Lord Kalad. When I left he was still hale, but we were heavily outnumbered. I don't think he made it unscathed."

Aegid appeared behind his brother, forcing his voice to sound confident. "Don't forget, he's Echend'dim, Kalad. He's probably waking up right now."

"Then we should hurry and get him. I want to have a personal conversation with those thugs who dared to attack one of our caravans."

The amber eyes of the Wolf of War glinted dangerously. There was no mistaking the dark mood he was in. "Hulda, choose twenty riders. I want to be gone in an hour."

The killer nodded, stone-faced. She regarded Elua and Lukan. "Can you two be ready in an hour?"

Elua's face had returned to its usual expressionless mask. "Of course. It's going to be my pleasure to send those bastards to the Mothers."

Lukan nodded as well. "We'll be there."

SLOWLY DARAN was regaining consciousness. A hubbub of voices assaulted his ears, and he could feel that he was lying on a carpet. He tried to get up, but his hands and feet were tied. Groaning, he closed his eyes again. It seemed as if the Wolf of War was even angrier than he had anticipated.

"Seems like you're done with your beauty sleep, prey."

The mocking voice jolted Daran up. That was definitely not his god! After his masters had killed Egand, he hadn't thought he'd ever have to listen to such a derisive, hateful tone again. He opened his eyes and tried to discern the owner of that repulsive voice. The man looming over him was coarse, with a broad face, small lips, a crooked nose, and scornful eyes in which Daran could see something else as well, something that made him shudder.

Now the man grabbed him by the collar and yanked him up.

"Look, it's just like I told you. His injuries have healed completely."

In front of a fire, two men, who were obviously brothers, had been watching them. Both of them had light, ash-blond hair, gray eyes, and generous lips. They were of lighter build than the man holding Daran, yet they emanated the same brutality. Daran had lived with Egand long enough to know a pimp and oppressor when he saw them.

With a calculated movement, he threw his head back and was rewarded with a crunching sound when his captor's nose broke. The man let go of him, wailing in pain. Skillfully, Daran rolled over the ground, cutting the ropes on his feet with the knife he had taken from the belt of the coarse man. Then he turned the blade to get rid of his wrist chains as well, but before he could do so, he heard a threatening growl at his back. A shadow sailed through the air, hit him hard at the shoulder, and brought him down. A dog of roughly a hundredweight was standing above Daran, growling deeply, his lips curled back, showing sharp, white fangs.

"What a lively little devil." The voice of one of the brothers sounded amused. "Our customers are going to fall all over themselves for the privilege to play with you."

Daran gritted his teeth. He had lost the knife, and if he didn't want the dog to tear his throat, he'd better comply.

The second brother stepped closer, sent the dog running with a wave of his hand, and yanked Daran up. "But it's not a bad idea to teach him some manners, don't you think so, Drik?"

The older one laughed, a hollow sound without any real amusement in it. "An excellent idea, Druran. I also think our good friend Elgir wishes to have a talk with you. You did break his nose, after all."

The derisive laughter turned Daran's stomach to ice. He glared at them.

"It would be better if you let me go right now. You've no idea with whom you're meddling."

Druran and Drik shrugged dismissively.

"We're grown men who don't believe in old wives' tales. The mercenaries of the Valley may be dangerous, but not invincible, as you should know better than anybody else. And they should have a hard time finding you here. This place is perfectly safe."

Daran cringed. He didn't doubt his masters would find him. He just didn't want to be rescued by them again, especially after the argument they'd had before he left. Whatever the cost, he had to escape from this place on his own. Unfortunately the brothers weren't even half as dumb as Daran had hoped. After his little display, they were meticulous about keeping him chained, and they had replaced the ropes with steel. As much as he tried, he just couldn't find a way to break free.

AFTER THE blood had been washed from his body, Daran was brought into a room lit with countless candles. Cushions the size of a man and covered with purple and golden cloths were draped on the ground in a semicircle so that anybody lounging on them had a free view of the opposite wall, where countless instruments of torture, such as whips, knives, hooks, and other monstrosities were displayed. From the ceiling hung cuffs that closed mercilessly around Daran's wrists.

Druran caressed the flawless skin of his prisoner reverently.

"I've to admit, I've never seen merchandise as outstanding as you before. Even if you couldn't do that trick with the healing, you'd still be a catch. This, on the other hand"—the wandering fingers had reached Daran's collar and were tugging at it—"should be disposed of as soon as possible. After all, there's no need for you to have it here. Let me see."

Druran stepped around his helpless prisoner to open the catch of the collar. His amazement was great when he saw the complicated mechanism that couldn't be opened without a key.

"What's this? A proud warrior like you wearing a slave collar?"

Daran didn't even bother to look at Druran. "It was a present."

"From somebody dear to you, am I right? Otherwise you wouldn't be wearing it."

The pimp grinned gleefully. Like most of his kind, he called a certain amount of empathy his own, which made it easier for him to play with his merchandise as well as his customers. And just now he had found the proverbial gold mine. Slowly, savoring every second, he selected a small dagger from the wall.

"Since I can't open the catch, I have no choice but to cut the leather. Don't move—you don't want to get hurt."

Desperately Daran tried to evade the knife. "Don't you dare!"

Druran laughed in amusement. Without minding his prisoner's attempts to fight him, he cut the collar and part of Daran's throat at the same time. The thief gurgled and gulped for air. Blood streamed down his chest, forming a pool at his feet, which lost their footing on the slippery ground. The smell of iron was heavy in the air, like an ominous perfume telling of things yet to come. Just when unconsciousness was closing in, Daran could feel his body healing the wound.

Druran and Drik had watched the entire process with interest and couldn't suppress a satisfied chuckle. If they played their cards right, they would be able to make a fortune with this gift from the heavens. Drik inspected the spot where the dagger had slit Daran's skin.

"It's completely healed. Seems like we have to forgo our usual method of marking. What a pity."

Druran leaned back on the wall, the knives gleaming in the light of the candles.

"A beauty like him shouldn't be marred with a branding anyway. There are other methods. I'd say a ring in a certain place should not only serve as a sign of ownership, but also have some use as a means of maintaining discipline."

"Brother, you really are an evil genius. I'll go and prepare everything. It'll still take two days for word to get to the first customers. Until then, we can have some fun as well."

The faces of the men brightened in pure greed. Daran tried to steel himself for the things that would soon be happening to him and was determined to never beg these despicable creatures for mercy. That much he owed to himself and his masters.

ELIANA SLOWLY woke from her slumber. For a change, she hadn't been tortured by nightmares and felt refreshed. Her gaze wandered to the reason she was feeling so relaxed this morning. In a bloody heap on the floor lay the mutilated, barely breathing body of a young woman she and her sister had enjoyed thoroughly the other night. Eliana bent down to check on her unfortunate toy and quickly reached the conclusion that this one was broken beyond repair. For a moment she pondered whether she should release the slave from her suffering but decided against it. She herself had never received any mercy, so why should she bestow it on others?

Carelessly Eliana stepped over the body of the dying girl to meet her sister Arborja in the dining room. She, too, was relaxed and in a good mood, the sharp lines around her eyes and mouth softened by the cruelty she was radiating. The sisters embraced each other and kissed briefly. Eliana thought she could still taste some of the victim's blood on Arborja's lips.

"Is it dead already?"

Her sister regarded everybody as a thing, just as she had been treated after the barbarians sold them off.

"Not yet, but it can't be much longer. Do you want to watch?"

Arborja considered this proposal for a moment, then shook her head.

"No, too boring. It always ends the same way. Some twitching, a plea or a curse, depending on the personality and the defeat. I'd say we already know this by heart."

"What do we do, then? Find a new toy?"

"An excellent idea! And it so happens that I already have a candidate. This came today."

She tossed Eliana a scroll with the stylized seal of their favorite brothel, a secret hideout only a few leagues from their home. The two owners, Druran and Drik, offered high-quality merchandise to those with special needs and rather peculiar tastes, like their own. Due to the peculiar tastes of their customers, the playthings on offer changed on a regular, quick basis, since the human body could endure only so much until it broke. The latest addition to the brothel's collection seemed to be really special. It was praised as a beautiful, rare specimen with phenomenal endurance. What caught Eliana's eye was not the advertising talk that covered most of the scroll, but two rather unobtrusive sentences at the very end of the litany— "Snatched from Canubis's army" and "Offered for killing."

She reared her head up and met Arborja's burning gaze. Finally the time had come. They would get the chance to exact revenge, if not on the divine bastards themselves, at least on one of their underlings. And Arborja and Eliana had a lot to avenge. A murdered family, a lost childhood, a home consumed by flames, a youth spent in brothels as merchandise, and all in all two wasted, ruined lives that only went on because they were propelled by sheer hatred of everything and everybody. Especially anyone connected to the Wolf of War and the Angel of Death.

"I've already sent them a message to secure him for us. If we get ready now, we'll be at the brothel in time for a wild night."

Anticipation made both women's worn features almost attractive, provided one didn't care about the ugly, despicable sheen in their eyes, which were devoid of anything even remotely human.

"THIS IS where they ambushed us."

Lukan gestured toward the thicket where the nightmare had started. The Wolf of War nodded and sent the wolves to have a look. Like deadly shadows, the big predators spread all over the place, sniffing for traces. Of course, the carts with the steel were long gone, and a hideous smell hung in the air because the highwaymen hadn't troubled themselves with burying the fallen. Lukan shuddered when he recognized his comrades. Only two days ago they had been warm and alive; now the ravens and other scavengers had already started to dispatch their bodies. As a warrior, he was used to death, and usually it wouldn't have bothered him so much, but things were different this time. By any rights he should have been lying with them. Instead he was standing here, defying death and the natural order of things. At that moment, Lukan understood on a whole new level how profoundly his life had changed the moment he had decided to follow Sic's voice. He didn't really regret it, for he loved Elua too much, but now he realized there was more to being an Echend'dim than just dismissing the darkness. Choosing the pain of walking in the light over the peace of succumbing to the shadows took more courage than Lukan had initially assumed. In a certain respect, he was even jealous of his fallen friends.

After the wolves were done seeking out all the important traces, the mercenaries collected the dead and lined them up on the ground. Canubis turned to Sic, who was standing next to Noran, white as linen and fighting his tears. The bulky master smith had slung an arm around his lover and was talking to him in a soothing tone. Lukan couldn't suppress a smile. Lord Sic was the gentlest person he had ever met. It was a trait the young noble had only recently come to recognize as a form of strength.

"Tell me, Sic, is one of them Echend'dim?"

The smith shook his head.

"No, Lord Canubis. They're all gone."

"Very well. Now that we've cleared this up…." He turned to a sturdy, grim woman. "Ishia, take them home."

The female nodded. Together with four other warriors, she started preparing the fallen for transport.

"And where on Ana-Darasa is Daran?"

Kalad didn't even try to hide his worry anymore. He and Aegid had held back while the wolves had been inspecting the site of carnage, trusting that the predators wouldn't miss the faintest trace.

Canubis shared a long look with the alpha. "They say Daran died with the others and was then removed. The bad news is that the trail of the carts and the one from Daran are going in different directions. We'll have to split."

He addressed Lukan. "Echend'dim! You're in command. Follow the carts, bring back the steel, and take as many prisoners as possible. None of these men deserves an easy death, and I'm planning to set an example nobody's going to forget in a hurry. Elua, you're going with Lukan. Make sure he doesn't get into trouble again. Take all of the mercenaries with you."

Elua bowed reverently, and then she and Lukan gathered the warriors and followed the lead of three of the wolves.

Canubis watched them with satisfaction. He had no doubts that they would be successful.

"Noran, take Sic back to the Valley. He needs to rest."

Normally Canubis wasn't so lenient toward his Emeris, but he still felt guilty about the way he had treated Sic before. Cutting the Luksari some slack was definitely in order.

Noran led his lover back to the horses. The young smith smiled briefly at Casto before he was taken away by his intimidating protector.

Suddenly Lys perked up his ears and snorted happily. Casto followed the stallion's gaze. From behind the thicket, a horse approached the group. Lys whinnied a greeting.

"It's Rajan!" Casto was relieved. He had feared the gelding had died during the battle. With genuine pleasure, the brown horse started rubbing his forehead on the king's arm. "It's fine. Good boy. Now all we have to do is find your rider."

"And as quickly as possible. I have a bad feeling about this." Aegid looked miserable. Losing Daran like this worked him up more than he wanted to admit.

Hulda stepped forward, sensing how much her brother-in-arms needed comfort. "We're going to find him. Daran is strong, he will persevere."

"Of course he will." Kalad was as worried as his desert brother, and covered it with irritation. "The question is what it is he has to endure, and just thinking about it makes me want to throw up."

3. TWO SISTERS

Daran jolted awake. Somebody had drenched him with a bucket of ice-cold water. Elgir's mocking voice assaulted his ear like the barking of a flea-ridden street dog.

"Time to wake up, princess. Your first customers are about to arrive, and we do want you to look presentable, don't we?"

Daran turned his head sideways. He didn't want to see the triumph, the mockery and greed in Elgir's face. To make him pay for the broken nose and to break his fighting spirit, the three men had tortured and raped him the entire night. His body had desperately tried to mend the damage his tormentors had inflicted as quickly as possible, but when Elgir had started to hit him with an iron bar, it had been too much. He had barely registered the final blow that had shattered his nose and cheekbones and broken his skull.

While he had still been unconscious, the men had cleaned him up. The stench of cheap perfume and warm oil assaulted his nose and reminded him of his time under Egand's command. Elgir was now drying him with a surprisingly soft cloth, while his hands took liberties Daran was determined to make him pay for once he managed to free himself.

To his own surprise, he wasn't afraid but mainly furious. Mostly with himself, because he had allowed them to capture him and had been unable to take the chance for escape, but also with those despicable creatures who dared to keep and torture an Echend'dim. Daran knew he had to hold on to this anger if he wanted to get out of this mess more or less emotionally unscathed. And so he forbade himself from thinking about what his masters would have to say once they found out he had been sullied by strangers. It was a problem he would deal with as soon as he had his freedom back.

Elgir finished and stepped back with a satisfied look in his eyes.

"They're going to love you. Or, more precisely, the chance to get back at such a beautiful member of the Pack."

A smile of hateful glee appeared on Elgir's face, on which the broken nose stood crooked and swollen. "Don't hope for any mercy. The Wolf of War took everything from those two, including their freedom. All they have now, they had to fight for. You can probably imagine how thirsty they are for revenge. And you, little beauty, are going to entertain them plenty tonight."

Cackling, Elgir left the room.

"DAMN, WHY is this taking so long?"

Like an impatient hound, Kalad was riding up and down alongside his gods while the wolves spread out to rediscover the trace they had lost for the third time this forenoon. The day before, they hadn't made much progress either, which increased the head start Daran's kidnappers had to three days.

"The trace has been veiled by magic."

Grimly Renaldo eyed the uneven path stretching in front of them. Whoever had taken the thief had gone to great pains not to be found, which could only mean the young man was in deep trouble. Aegid and Kalad knew this as well, and their pain was like a knife in the hearts of all members of the group. By now everybody understood how much the desert brothers loved their partner, how irreplaceable he had become to them. Imagining how he had died during the attack was more than his owners were able to bear. Not being prone to death didn't mean the Emeris and Echend'dim couldn't feel pain. Every one of them had endured the agony of dying more than once in their long lives. It was a necessary but hardly bearable experience. It reminded those whose lives knew no end how real and inevitable death was.

Renaldo's insides turned to ice whenever he remembered that his heart had yet to go through this agonizing moment. Before he could become obsessed with this dark train of thought, howling indicated that the wolves had found the trace again.

"HE'S INDEED extraordinary."

Like starved foxes, the two females circled the chained, naked Daran. Now and then their fingers touched his skin almost lovingly. If Daran hadn't lived among the scum of society for most of his youth, he might have nourished some hope for mercy in the hearts of the women. Unfortunately their murderous intentions were obvious.

Elgir only gloated while he made something vaguely resembling a bow. "I wish the ladies a pleasant evening. You can do to him whatever you please."

He turned away, and the door to the chamber closed with an ominous click. Daran was alone with the customers. Both of them were tall, with long chestnut hair, dark eyes, elegantly curved noses, and small, haggard lips. There was no doubt they were sisters, and the way they interacted showed clearly how close they were to each other. That bond was the only thing vaguely human in those two. They moved like famished predators, and in their eyes was a feverish, flickering glint that told Daran more than anything else that these two had crossed the line to insanity a long time ago. Their entire being seemed to be solely propelled by greed. It wasn't the mundane greed for power or riches, but the more dangerous one for revenge, born from utter despair. Daran didn't want to imagine what they had gone through to develop such twisted, hate-filled personalities.

Now they focused all their attention on him. The feverish glint in their eyes increased and was almost overwhelming when they selected two knives from the wall.

The cuts they inflicted on Daran weren't deep, just enough to make him bleed. Every time they slid the blades over his defenseless skin, they whispered into his ear what the Wolf of War and the Angel of Death had done to them. Faster and faster the knives hissed through the air, until Daran was unable to distinguish between the words and the pain, until he thought the words themselves were cutting him up.

"We were still children when they came."

"They obliterated the city in which we lived just because some king had paid them."

"Our father was beheaded, our mother died when she tried to protect us."

"They made us into slaves and sold us like chattel."

"We were whores, our virginity sold when we turned fourteen."

"The Wolf of War has taken everything from us."

"The Angel of Death has damned us."

"And what for? For gold, for profit."

"Because soldiers like you serve them."

"You submit your sword and your strength to their will, not asking how many lives you destroy. We were innocent, we hadn't done anything wrong."

"We hate them."

"Hate you."

"Hate."

"Hate."

When the two finally calmed down a bit, Daran was covered in blood. He was heaving while his body tried to repair the damage. The older of the two sisters licked the blood from his cheek, her voice a hypnotizing singsong.

"The dead never return, no matter how much we wish for it. The same goes for our wasted lives. But you, you're going to expiate with your blood what your masters have done to us. Rejoice, your suffering means my sister and I can sleep peacefully tonight."

They were the last words Daran consciously heard. After that, his world drowned in unbearable pain. It was so bad, he was grateful when the knife slit open his chest and the greedy hands of the sisters ripped out his heart as a trophy.

TIRED, CASTO blinked into the dim morning light. They had ridden the entire night, always in fear of losing the weak trace connecting them to Daran. Whoever had managed to take the thief knew about the resources of the wolves—and their limits. Casto prayed to the Mothers that they would find Daran soon. With every hour passing, Aegid and Kalad became more taciturn, and their faces grew more worried. The king could barely stand seeing the normally cheerful warriors in such a desolate state.

And then sharp barking filled the air, which meant that the wolves had finally found something. Lys dashed off without waiting for a command. Effortlessly he passed the other horses, racing to the spot the wolves indicated. When they reached the predators, Casto felt his hopes evaporate. The pack had surrounded two women on tolerably good palfreys, keeping them from fleeing with threatening growls and bared fangs.

Disappointed, Casto dismounted Lys. As much as he tried, he couldn't find a trace of Daran.

Now the rest of their group arrived. Canubis reined Demon in, his predator eyes regarded the women sharply.

"Get down." Like a whip, the voice of the Wolf of War pierced the air. The females, who were dressed in long, billowing black coats, regarded him with derision.

"We'll surely never bow to the orders of a murderer."

They spoke in unison, hatred distorting every single syllable. Casto felt violent shudders running down his spine. In Ummana he had come to know all kinds of mental conditions, ranging from cold and calculating to hotheaded and oblivious. Some of them had been more dangerous than others, and he had learned to deal with them all. But nothing came close to what he was getting from these two women. They were so far beyond madness, they probably approached sanity from the other direction. Instinctively he realized there was nothing that could reach those distorted, twisted minds, trapped in a world of horrors he didn't dare to imagine.

"As you wish." Canubis seemed almost glad about their resistance. "Lysistratos!"

The stallion dashed through the line of the wolves like black lightning. With two well-aimed kicks, he brought the palfreys down while their cursing riders fell off the saddles. Lysistratos shot Canubis a strange look, one the warlord acknowledged with a slight bow. The stallion had obeyed the Wolf of War because the situation had called for it, but the god had better not get used to it. Lys did only one person's bidding unconditionally, and that person was Casto.

Meanwhile Hulda, Aegid, and Kalad had approached the women. The assassin grabbed the reins of the horses and made soothing noises until they calmed down. Then her lavender eyes regarded the prey at her feet. The look on her face sent shivers down the backs of all the men present.

"The wolves say they reek of Daran." Canubis's voice was almost casual now.

As soon as they heard those words, Kalad and Aegid yanked the women up. Violently they tore off the cloaks and froze. Both women were clad in white silk, silk that was drenched in blood. The wolves started howling again.

"It's Daran's blood." Canubis no longer sounded casual.

Without hesitation, the desert brothers put their hands on the throats of the sisters. Renaldo held them back.

"Wait! We still don't know where Daran is. And you can't want them to have an easy death, do you?"

When the two warriors stood down hesitantly, the women started to guffaw.

"Your precious little Daran is dog food since this morning. We played the entire night with him, and when his screams ceased to be sweet in our ears, we ripped his twitching heart from his chest."

A sound like a wail, suffocated by heaving, pierced the air. Aegid had his arms slung around Kalad, who was staring at the women with hatred and despair. Casto noticed the quick glance the elder female gave the horses. One of the saddlebags was darker than the others, as if it had gotten wet. Heart pounding in his chest, the king slowly approached the palfreys and opened the leather carefully. It was impossible for him not to scream, even though he was used to gory sights. Wrapped inexpertly in a silken cloth, a human heart, still heavy with blood, rested inside the bag.

Trembling with rage, Casto stared at the two culprits. He could feel Renaldo's fire blazing inside him.

Before he could unleash the deadly flames, Aegid had rushed to his side. With shaking hands he took the bloody lump, his milky eyes staring at it as if he couldn't understand what he was seeing. And then Casto felt the first, almost gentle pinpricks on his skin that heralded the sand. He shuddered when he remembered the sheer, raw force the desert brothers could call. The shock made him see reason again.

"Don't, Aegid! We need them alive! They know where we can find Daran."

The warrior glared at him through hazy eyes. He seemed to have trouble returning to the real world. Casto grabbed his wrists to anchor him, his voice urgent.

"We have to let them live—for the time being. As soon as we've got Daran back, you can do to them whatever you wish. But your lover has first priority."

Aegid's eyes narrowed. "You're right." He turned his attention to the women. "Where is he?"

The younger one spat on the ground. "We'll never tell. It's only just that you taste the same suffering as we did."

Kalad, who had finally managed to get over his shock, appeared next to his brother with hardened features. Just when he seemed about to start threatening the females, Hulda interrupted them with her melodic voice.

"You don't have to. It's child's play for the wolves to follow your track backward. I doubt you took the same precautions as Daran's kidnapper."

An affirmative howling pierced the air. The predators were running up and down, eager to follow this new, crystal-clear trail.

Derision colored the mother superior's face. "Amateurs."

Canubis had already turned Demon around in order to follow the wolves.

"Wolfstan, you take care of these two until we come back. Don't let them escape or die! I want to deal with them personally. Hulda, watch our back. I don't want any more nasty surprises!"

The armorer nodded grimly. Without heeding the wails of protest from his unwilling prisoners, he tied their wrists to their ankles, blocking any attempt at escape.

Hulda showed her consent with a nod. Her elegant hands brushed the grips of her daggers lovingly, and then she vanished.

Casto had to concentrate to not show his discomfort. Witnessing a highly skilled assassin like Hulda evaporating into thin air made his sense of self-preservation go into overload. Under his breath, he couldn't help but express his uneasiness. "That is so unnerving."

Wolfstan smiled proudly at the king. He was oblivious of the danger his beloved wife posed. "She's amazing, isn't she?"

The armorer sounded so happy, Casto didn't have the heart to answer him truthfully. Instead he returned the smile somewhat awkwardly before he followed the Wolf of War, Renaldo, and the desert brothers.

Now that the trail was clear, the wolves ran with their usual speed across the sun-dried paths. After less than two hours, they found an impressive homestead situated in a depression that was guarded from the curious glances of unexpected travelers by a thicket of mighty oak trees. Only a narrow, unobtrusive track wound down through the trees. In a small clearing not far from the homestead, the mercenaries discussed how to proceed.

"I know places like that one. It's a brothel, and an exclusive one, if I'm not mistaken." Kalad sounded so grim, none of the other men dared to tease him about his knowledge.

"Seems like the owners are selling more than just pleasures of the flesh at the moment." Aegid's voice was darkened by fury.

Before he could vent on, Casto barged in.

"I say we get a feel for the situation first. To me, this looks like a place where one can encounter some unpleasant surprises. I'll act as a customer and try to find Daran."

Renaldo shook his head violently. "I don't think so, Casto. It's way too dangerous."

The king opened his mouth to give a sharp retort, but Canubis was faster.

"I'm really sorry to say this, little brother, but Casto will go. His suggestion is reasonable, and he's the only one who can do it. Aegid and Kalad are definitely too agitated, and we are too well-known. Our first priority is to get Daran out safely."

The Angel of Death made a face. He hated exposing his lover to such a dangerous situation, but Canubis was right. Casto was perfectly suited for this mission.

"Promise me not to take any undue risks. No, promise me not to take any risks at all! You get in, gather the information, and get out again, understood?"

Casto rolled his eyes but nodded in agreement. "Whatever you wish, Barbarian." An impish grin appeared on his lips. "If something goes wrong, Lys will let you know. Then you can do your thing."

Renaldo hit the king's upper arm with more force than strictly necessary. "Get a grip on yourself. This is about Daran, not your ego!"

Instantly Casto turned serious again. His mesmerizing blue eyes caught Aegid's and Kalad's stare.

"I'll bring him back! That's a promise!"

The desert warriors bowed gratefully to the heart of their god. With easy practice, Casto wrapped part of his coat around his head to hide his wheat-blond hair and part of his face. Then he jumped into the saddle and rode toward the brothel.

WHILE LYS approached the building slowly, Casto checked his surroundings with the eyes of both a warrior and a businessman. The place was so secluded, it had to be really exclusive to be able to stay in business. Everything was very clean, starting with the perfectly raked gravel on the ground over by the neat stables with the spacious bays and broad shed where the customers could leave their carriages, and including the entrance area, which was lined with potted plants and elaborate statues. The warrior noticed the small windows built high in the walls, making it impossible for attackers to get through and at the same time allowing for an effective defense. Thick walls of neatly set stones and heavy wooden doors reinforced with steel amplified the fortress feeling. Anybody who tried to get in uninvited—or out illicitly, for that matter—was faced with serious trouble. And even though the path down into the depression wound through the trees, it was perfectly visible from the building. There was no way to get there unnoticed.

As if on cue, the gate was opened for him and Lys, and a sturdy man with the calculating look of a true pimp greeted him. Fortunately Casto knew how to deal with this type of person.

"Let me welcome you to our humble establishment, my lord. My name is Druran. I'm one of the owners here. It seems I haven't had the pleasure of making your acquaintance yet."

Though he spoke very formally, the man's eyes were already assessing Casto. They had noticed the sword and daggers as well as the heavy bag hanging on his belt. No doubt he had already classified his guest as potentially dangerous and wealthy at the same time. For a man of his profession, this was the worst combination. It meant Casto would want his money's worth and could cause Druran serious trouble should he not deliver. With customers like that, it was best to stay on the polite side.

"My acquaintance is not something you need to make. I'm the man with the big bag of gold who wants to have some intense fun with your best piece of merchandise. But I have to warn you, I like playing rough."

If Druran was affected by Casto's brisk tone, he didn't show it at all.

"Is that so? Then I'm glad to say we have just what you need. A rare delicacy you'll surely enjoy. Needless to mention, we do charge extra for serious damage to our merchandise. But a man as well-off as you are can surely afford such insignificant sums."

Casto had dismounted Lys, who now towered over him like a living death threat. Druran eyed the stallion nervously.

"I don't care about the price as long as I can have my fun. And before you ask, my ride doesn't need caring for. He loves his freedom."

The pimp hastened to reassure his intimidating guest. "Of course. As long as you say he's safe to roam around, we surely won't be adamant about having him inside a bay."

Lys flattened his ears and bared his teeth, reveling in the fear the abhorrent human was displaying so openly. Casto patted the black hide in an absent way before he concentrated on his reluctant host again.

"So what are you waiting for? Show me this delicacy you're so proud of. Once I've seen it, I'll decide whether it's worth my time and money."

Pure anger about being treated like a mere servant threatened to conquer Druran's face, but he managed to rein himself in, thinking about the money the rude customer would pay once he laid eyes on their golden goose. Bowing demurely, he led the warrior into the house, carefully closing the door behind him.

IN HIS prison, Daran was listening intently to the sounds seeping through the thick oak doors. He had managed to free himself of the chains by dislocating both of his thumbs. Thanks to this painful trick, he had been able to wiggle his hands out of the cuffs. Now he was waiting for the injury to heal. He didn't know how many people were in the house aside from his three torturers, but he was sure he would be able to deal with them as long as he had the element of surprise working for him. For that, his thumbs had to heal first.

Now he heard voices down the corridor and couldn't suppress a curse. One of them belonged to Elgir, which could only mean new customers were on their way. Daran had no inclination to get tortured to death a third time, so he grabbed two knives from the wall and hurried to sit down again as if he was still bound.

Tense like a cat before it went for the mouse, Daran was waiting for the door to open. Elgir entered, presenting Daran with a pompous gesture. The customer who stepped in behind the pimp fixed his mesmerizing gaze on the thief.

"That's supposed to be your best merchandise? Do you take me for a fool?"

Daran, who had been ready to strike and kill Elgir, froze. Never before in his life had he been happier to hear the arrogant, derisive voice of his trainer. He couldn't help but grin.

"Yes, I really am their best merchandise. I guess it only shows how low-class they are. This one is a coward, deceiver, and beguiler. It's built in his character, so no curing him."

Elgir screamed with rage. "How dare you talk to me like that, you worthless piece of shit?"

He approached Daran with raised fists, ready to strike. The thief watched from the corner of his eye as Casto closed and bolted the heavy door with calm movements. It was all the invitation he needed. Quickly he ducked out of his torturer's reach, hitting him with the hilt of one of the knives. Groaning, the sturdy man went down. Daran was just about to send him to the Mothers when Casto stopped him.

"If I were you, I'd let him live. I know two very worked-up desert warriors who'd love to have a word with this scum."

The knife fell from Daran's hand, and his heart started beating unbearably loud in his chest. "They're here?"

"Of course! What do you think? They are so out of their minds with worry, they haven't slept a wink ever since Lukan told us about the ambush."

Daran felt pure love surging through him. They had come! He was so happy, tears pricked the corners of his eyes. Then he remembered what Drik and Druran had done to him. His hands fumbled down to his penis. The tip was pierced by an iron ring the two pimps had driven into his flesh in place of branding. Never should his owners lay eyes on the offending piece of metal! Daran gritted his teeth, grabbed the ring, and tore it off with all his might.

Casto rushed over, his eyes wide with horror.

"Daran, what in the Mothers' names are you doing? Have you lost your mind?"

"They cannot see this, Casto! Under no circumstances!"

The king threw a revolted glance at the bloodstained ring, which had no lock but was welded closed. It was easy to understand why Daran had wanted to get rid of it before his lovers could see it.

"They won't, I promise. And I'm sure we'll find a way to explain all the blood on your body. Or do you see any water around here?"

"I'll think about that once we're out. Can you lend me your coat?"

"Of course."

With a mocking bow, the king handed his friend the piece of cloth. Then he returned to his post at the door, listening to the sounds from outside. Daran thought he could hear a muffled scream and the creak of a door being ripped off the hinges. Casto looked satisfied.

"They're already here. It shouldn't be long until they get us out."

"Since when do you wait until you get rescued by others?" The question slipped from Daran's lips before he could hold himself back. It was simply unnatural for the usually bold king to barricade himself.

Casto made a face while he answered in sour tones. It was obvious how much he resented having his hands tied. Nevertheless, ever since the incident in Kwarl, he had become more levelheaded in his actions. Although he hated it, he deferred to his husband's experience.

"I had to promise, otherwise the Barbarian wouldn't have let me go. And I didn't know in what state you'd be. The plan was to infiltrate the place, find you, and wait for the others to get us."

"I like the plan. But why is it taking so long?"

Casto's features hardened. Now he truly looked like a merciless king, although Daran wasn't sure whether Casto was really so coldhearted or if he was trying to protect himself.

"They're taking prisoners. Not only are your lovers enraged, the Wolf of War is furious and the Barbarian…." Casto stopped. He had thought he knew the Angel of Death, but the raging fury Renaldo had been emanating ever since it had become clear what hardships Daran had had to endure made even the king uneasy. In moments like these, the perfect mask crumbled and the unrelenting god of war showed his terrible visage.

"I just hope the Barbarian never gets that angry with me."

Daran refrained from answering. He knew from personal, painful experience how terrifying the Angel of Death could be, and if even Casto, who wasn't easily impressed by Renaldo's whims, was as meek as he was now, the thief did not feel any desire to meet his god.

The sounds of fighting drew nearer, pained screams and heartfelt curses accompanying the heavy thudding when a body went down or another door was unhinged. Then the heavy oak door trembled under the blows of the attackers. Casto made some room, his sword at the ready, just in case it wasn't their side trying to get in.

Splinters hissed through the air like angry hornets when Aegid and Kalad finally barged their way in. Their hungry gazes settled on Daran, who ran toward them with a small cry of relief. Casto discreetly busied himself with checking the ties on the still unconscious Elgir while the desert brothers held the love of their lives tightly in their embrace.

4. DIVINE WRATH

SATISFIED WITH the outcome of their mission, the Wolf of War regarded the prisoners they had taken. Aside from the two owners of the brothel and the man who had kidnapped Daran, who were already tied together so they could bring them back to the Valley, all the customers as well as the whores—male and female—had been lined up in front of him like oxen on the market. Now Canubis was contemplating whether he should show some mercy toward the innocent bystanders or if he should punish them all just to get his point across.

A sound at his back made him turn. Daran was standing in front of him, his gaze cast to the ground. He had finally managed to escape the embrace of his masters and had come to confront his god's wrath. Slowly, he went down on his knees. The movement made Casto's cloak gape open and allowed the Wolf of War a glimpse of Daran's naked, blood-smeared body.

"My Lord Canubis."

"Daran. I'm glad we finally found you." Canubis spoke in gentle tones, since he knew the expression in the thief's eyes only too well. The young man was blaming himself over what had happened. Those reproaches were superfluous, of course, but a good leader had to take them seriously if he wanted a promising warrior to develop further.

When he heard the soothing words, Daran's head reared up. It was agonizing to watch the torment in his eyes.

"I'm so sorry. I have disappointed you."

Canubis stepped forward, placed a hand on Daran's cheek, and smiled at him encouragingly.

"On the contrary, Echend'dim. Lukan has told me everything that happened. It was brave of you to stay with your men when you could have saved yourself by fleeing. I'm proud to call you the first of my eternal guard."

The expressive brown eyes widened in surprise.

"But I've not only lost the carts but also the men! I'm not worth being anything, and much less the first. I wasn't even able to free myself."

"But you were working on it when we came, isn't that so? Casto told me you were already armed. You could have escaped without our help. Regarding the men, even though losing them is painful, you can rest assured that they are now in the Green Lands with the Mothers. And the carts—Lukan is retrieving them right now. As you can see, there's no reason for you to work yourself up. You've been through some rough times, Daran, but now things are back to normal, I promise."

While saying these words, the Wolf of War extended his hands to the Echend'dim. After a short moment of insecurity, Daran grabbed them and nodded at his god in gratitude. Canubis patted his shoulder before he returned his attention to the prisoners and the question of whom he should spare. The pain he had glimpsed in Daran's face hardened his heart.

Before he had to say a single word, his brother was already by his side, his gray eyes as steely and unbending as Canubis's determination.

"They all die."

The Angel of Death nodded. He had known his brother long enough to anticipate what he was planning. Together with Aegid and Kalad, he brought the whores and customers back into the house. They were locked in the room where Daran had met the sisters. Then the warriors left the building and Renaldo let the fire loose. Straight-faced, the Wolf of War watched as even the stones from the walls turned to ashes under his brother's will. Seen from a larger perspective, it was still a merciful death he had bestowed on those who had been present when his Echend'dim had been tortured. The fire burned with such fury that the people in the house didn't have to suffer; death had come too fast. Canubis had never been one for introspection. Punishing these people was only a logical reaction to something that had been done to him and his own. Without sparing another thought for his unlucky victims, he gave the order to depart.

WHEN THEIR entourage started moving, Casto stayed back. He glanced one last time at the still-smoking black earth where only moments before an entire house had been. The power of Renaldo's fire terrified him anew every time he had to witness it, even though he was confronted with it almost every day. Knowing this power was his to command as well worried him more than he would ever admit and was one of the reasons he still couldn't submit to the Barbarian wholeheartedly. Today, though, it was not only the demonstration of raw power that had him rattled. It was also the sliver of control he had felt. For a moment he had ridden the fire together with Renaldo, had experienced what it was like to have the flames obey his will. The implications overwhelmed him.

With a snort, Lys pried him from his gloomy thoughts. The stallion had been happy about their trip, even though the reason for it had been unpleasant, and now he wanted to have a good run to get things out of his system before they had to return to the enclosed space of the Valley. And even though—or perhaps because—he knew what the Barbarian would think of it, Casto went with his brother's wish.

With a shrill, triumphant whinny, Lys started to run, leaving behind all sorrows and fears, living solely for the heady feeling when the wind ruffled their hair and his feet ate the leagues stretching in front of them.

After they had put some distance between them and their companions, Casto reined Lys in. They stopped at a thicket with some trees, about four leagues from the road that led to the Valley. Casto slipped off Lys's back, unsure if he really wanted what he was about to do but also knowing he had no choice.

He closed his eyes and concentrated on the fire inside him, Renaldo's fire. As always, it felt like a torrent, something wild and untamed. Gingerly he reached out with his mind, grabbed a single flame, and drew it out. It felt strange, the way it coiled around his body, eager to become something bigger, to consume and to kill, yet controlled by his will. Casto opened his eyes, watched as the flame spread from his fingers, became a rope of heat, then curled around a branch in one of the trees. After a moment's resistance, the branch fell to the ground with a deafening crack, where it then burned to ashes. Casto watched unblinking before he willed the fire back into himself.

When he turned to Lys, his face was an unreadable mask.

"The Barbarian mustn't know. Not yet, anyway."

Not before he had the time to ponder all the consequences of this shocking revelation.

PERCHED ON top of a thick fir tree, Lukan spied on the camp where the highwaymen who had raided the caravan were hiding. It was a good one, he had to admit. Only part of it was under the sky. Most of the living space had been built inside one of the caves that could be found in abundance around this part of the mountains. For two days they had followed the wolves, until the predators finally found the lair of the attackers. Against his will, Lukan was impressed. Judging from how they had fought, he had assumed the men were nothing but a loosely connected bunch of thugs. The camp he was staring at showed a different picture, though. It had the look of something well organized and lasting. He could even make out the hierarchical structure just from looking.

The top of the heap was definitely the sturdy, brutal man with the three tribal scars across his face. Wherever he went, he was met with the utmost fear. Given how violently he reacted to every little thing, Lukan was not surprised. There were a few other men who looked similar to the leader, with the same scars, sturdy build, and bronze-colored skin that placed them at the vicinity of the Hot Heart. Why they had chosen to come to the North, of all places, remained their secret for the time being.

The other members of the gang were from all walks of life, most of them definitely from around here, with the light skin and fair features of people from the North. Out of all of them, only one man dared to stand up against the leader, probably because they knew each other well, as far as Lukan could deduce from their body language. This man seemed to be the second-in-command and more approachable and generally more levelheaded than the leader. He, too, had three tribal scars across his face and an additional one on his throat. It made him look as if he had cheated death on purpose.

As silently as he had climbed the tree, Lukan retreated to discuss their further actions with Elua and the others. They had already decided to make their move tonight and had to work out the details. When he returned to their own small camp, Elua greeted him with raised brows.

"What took you so long? Were you caught up peeping?"

Lukan smiled broadly at his beloved wife. He could tell by her annoyed tone how incredibly relieved she was to have him back. And he enjoyed riling her up even more.

"Well, what can I say, it was kind of interesting. You know how much I love a good show."

The blow hit him before he could duck out of reach.

"If I need someone to make a fool of me, I certainly won't ask you. Now spill, what's going on?"

Rubbing his bruised arm, Lukan sat down with the other mercenaries to give his report. Although he had led the occasional troop before, it felt different this time. Now he was no longer one of them, but one of the lords, an immortal. No matter how tightly the oaths of the Pack bound the warriors and the divine brothers, there was always a certain gap due to their inaccessible, eternal nature.

When Daran had become the first Echend'dim, it had caused quite the uproar among the mercenaries. They all had been anticipating this, what with Sic completing the ranks of the Emeris, and Canubis and Renaldo becoming full-fledged gods again. It was one of the many reasons joining the Pack was so attractive—if the time was ripe, the followers of the brothers would become immortal as well, the eternal guard, Echend'dim. It was one of the few things the prophecies written by Dweian and Dria stated clearly, without the usual smoke-and-mirrors tactics where the Emeris and the hearts were concerned.

Unfortunately, the seers had forgotten to mention the little hook attached to this tempting offer—that one had to die first. As much as Lukan was glad to be among the chosen ones, he could have definitely gone without the experience of dying. It hadn't been too painful, more like falling asleep when you desperately wanted to stay awake. No, the pain was not the problem. The real catch was the span of lying in darkness, waiting for the last embers of your will to live to wink out, only vaguely conscious of what was happening, if at all, and embracing the peace the shadows offered. It had been perfect bliss, a warm, tranquil feeling that was brutally pierced by Sic's blinding light and his tempting voice. Lukan had heard before that in between the worlds, you saw things more clearly, and he prayed to the Mothers he would be able to forget one day what he had glimpsed of the Luksari then. For the first time in his life, he had been afraid of the light.

Lukan shook his head to get his mind back to the task at hand. Pondering the deeper meaning of what had happened to him had to wait until they were back in the Valley. Judging from his wife's impatient face, he had already taken too long to answer her question.

"The good news is, there aren't as many as we had thought. The bad news, though, is that they're a lot better organized than is good for our mission. They have guards about thirty paces before the camp, then three more at the margins and two in front of the cave. Which leads us to the next problem. We don't know how deep the cave runs, if it has any passageways to other caves, and how many people are hiding in there. I don't think there's going to be a nasty surprise, but we have to be ready. To top it off, you know that the Wolf of War wants them alive. Any suggestions?"

"Is there a chance to get close enough to put something into their food?"

The man suggesting this, Baldan, was the very definition of sneaky. He was also a mean fighter and trustworthy friend. His idea had a certain appeal that made Lukan inquire further.

"What do you have in mind?"

"On our way here, we passed several clearings with Green Moon flowers. Their seeds make people sleepy. Even if we can't get everyone to consume them, many of them will be unable to even hear us when we're binding them. Reduces the mess."

"How long until the seeds take effect?"

"About half an hour, depending on how much they eat."

"Sounds like a plan. But how do we get it into their food? They do have a common cooking place, but it's right at the center. I don't see any chance to get there."

Elua had listened to the men's discussion with a speculative glance on her face. Now she grinned. "Well, strictly speaking, we don't have to get there. Only the seeds. Baldan, how are your shooting skills?"

Realization dawned on the assembled warriors. Baldan flexed his fingers. "As good as ever. And I feel like putting them to the test right now."

Lukan patted him on the back. "It's a deal. Let's get the seeds and prepare everything. We still have to be cautious. I do not wish to disappoint the Wolf of War."

DA'RYEN WATCHED as Nya approached him with a bowl of soup in her hands. When she served it to him, he took her hands in his, a sad smile on his lips.

"How many times do I have to tell you there's no need for you to do this? You're not my servant."

Nya returned the smile a little awkwardly. She had just turned eleven and was way too serious for a child her age. Given what she'd had to endure, it was no surprise, though.

"But I like doing this for you, Da'Ryen. I was lonely when you were gone. You're the only one here who would play with me."

"Because I like our games. Tell me, how is your little baby doing?"

From her belt, Nya produced a bag in which a small poppet about the size of a man's hand had been resting.

"She's well. But she's sleeping a lot. I think it's because it's fall. The cold doesn't suit her."

"Oh, how I feel with her. I don't like the climate here as well. Perhaps we should go to the South where the sun always shines? What do you think? Feeling the heat on your skin would surely be great."

Nya laughed. She knew as well as Da'Ryen that there was no way they could just leave Ma'Duk, but this game of pretend was all they both had, and so she participated wholeheartedly.

"I'm sure the baby would love it. And if we pack our things right now, we can leave first thing in the morning. How about it, Da'Ryen?"

The warrior pretended to think about her suggestion, then shook his head sadly.

"Tomorrow is bad. Remember, we wanted to go hunting. What would all the deer say if we just left them alone?"

"You're right, as always. The deer come first. Perhaps we'll go for the sun on another day."

"Perhaps. But for the time being, come here. I'll warm you until you can sleep."

With a content sigh, the little girl snuggled into the bulky man's arms, reveling in the heat his massive body emanated. She remembered this kind of warmth from before, from the time she used to call the dream. Then it had come from the woman with the gentle smile and soft hair. But the woman was gone; only the memory of the warmth had persevered.

DA'RYEN WOKE from an unpleasant pressure around his wrists. It took him only a brief moment to fully understand his situation. The oppressive feeling of oncoming doom he'd been having for weeks was now overwhelming. In a certain sense, he was even relieved that the time to answer for his sins had finally come.

Wiggling like a worm caught in a bird's beak, he managed to get upright despite the ropes around his arms and feet. Next to him, Nya was lying, still fast asleep even though she was bound just like him. In the semidarkness he could see shadows moving silently around, immobilizing the sleepers. For a brief moment, Da'Ryen contemplated warning them, but by the look of it, it was already too late. Except for a handful, all of the warriors had been neutralized, so there was no way they could win over this silent, perfectly organized enemy. Deep in his heart, the tribe warrior had already realized who these people were, even though a last glimmer of hope prevented him from accepting the truth.

Now that every member of the gang was secured, the attackers lit some torches and started carrying their prey outside, where they lined them up like merchandise while some of them prepared the carts for departure. So the Wolf of War wanted them alive. The thought sent shivers down Da'Ryen's spine. Even though he didn't believe all the stories told about this powerful warlord, there was no doubt that at least some of them contained a grain of truth. Given how outrageous the reports about his cruelty were, Da'Ryen had no illusions about what was awaiting them. And they did deserve punishment, if not for stealing from other people, then for all the other sins they had committed. His own were engraved in his soul, gnawing on him like rats on a corpse, never allowing him to rest. It was almost funny, how far he had run to escape them only to meet his just punishment in the icy lands of the North.

Judging from the hard, unrelenting features of the mercenaries, Da'Ryen didn't expect his last days on Ana-Darasa to be peaceful. Next to him, Nya stirred in her sleep, reminding him of the sole responsibility he still had. When a harsh-looking woman came to load the girl on one of the carts, he risked talking to her.

"Please, I know why you're here, but she's only a child. She has nothing to do with this. Could you at least untie her? I don't want her to wake up bound like this."

The woman glared at him so coldly, Da'Ryen winced.

"Child or not, she's with you, so we have no reason to treat her differently. You can try pleading your case with Canubis once we get to the Valley, but I doubt he'll be very open to your request. And now shut up before I decide to take your tongue."

She bent down to pick Nya up. Da'Ryen watched as the mercenary with the two long daggers in her belt put the girl down very gently and even wrapped her in some furs to keep her warm. The act was so contradictory to the female's words, it left Da'Ryen completely puzzled.

CROSSROADS

1. MASKS

"Noooo!"

Panting, Daran jolted awake, trembling all over and darting panicked looks around the room. He was glad the hissing sound of the iron bar coming toward his face had obviously been a dream, but he still had trouble reining in his violently beating heart. When he managed to at least even his breathing, he dared to glance sideways to see if his nightmare had woken Kalad and Aegid. His heart fell. Both warriors were staring at him, and even though it was almost dark, he could see—and, even worse, feel—their worry for him. Embarrassed, he turned away.

"I'm sorry, I didn't want to wake you."

"Daran, come here."

Kalad grabbed the thief's hand to pull him down on the furs between him and Aegid. A determined streak appeared on his lips, and his eyes shone bright in the gloom.

"Don't you think it's time to tell us what these despicable worms have done to you?"

Violently, Daran freed his hand from the warrior's grasp. "I can't. Not yet. Please be patient with me."

Aegid sighed. "We don't want to pressure you, little thief. But believe me, the longer you wait, the worse it gets. You know you can trust us, don't you?"

Tears were staining Daran's eyes when he nodded. "I know. And I really want to tell you. But the words stay stuck in my throat whenever I want to get them out. It's as if I'm still there, unable to break free."

Kalad stroked his head in a soothing gesture. "It's fine, sweet one. Take your time. You have to forgive us for being so forward. It makes us furious to see you like this, knowing we can't help you at all. We've never felt so helpless before."

Lost for words, Daran touched his owners' hands. He knew exactly how they felt and the reason for it. The problem was, he didn't know what to feel, or what he was supposed to feel. This confusion prevented them from returning to their old ways. It took all Daran's self-control not to shy away from their touch and to bear their expectations when they went to bed together. Until now the warriors had refrained from seducing him in an attempt to give him some breathing space. But it was only a matter of time before they decided to tackle the problem in a more direct manner.

And part of him yearned to become intimate with them again, to leave all the bad memories behind. Yet another, persistent voice reminded him constantly that he was sullied and unworthy. Thinking that the two could find traces of those other men on his body made him break out in cold sweat.

What was even worse was the new face he had discovered on them. Until now he had seen the desert warriors as his benefactors, as the men who had saved him from a sad, undesirable existence. The sisters had shown Daran in the cruelest manner that Aegid and Kalad possessed a second, far less friendly face. It made him wonder if this wasn't their true nature—and if he would be able to accept it. Because even though the sisters were twisted and evil, he could understand why they had acted as they did, what had made them so utterly despicable. Imagining the kind of power the desert brothers had over normal people, people like him, made him shudder. What this revelation meant for his relationship with the gods was something Daran didn't want to think about yet.

Two days after they returned to the Valley, Lukan and Elua had arrived with the caravan and almost thirty prisoners. Among them, Daran recognized the man who had dealt him the killing blow. Being confronted with the direct cause of all his misery had made him sick to his stomach. For the time being, the prisoners had been brought to the dungeons while a furious Wolf of War contemplated how to kill them in the most gruesome way possible. Seeing his lord and god so enraged only added to Daran's inner confusion, since his ineptitude was the reason for it. The Wolf of War had given Daran to understand he was willing to give him some breathing space, but he also expected him to make up his mind in the near future. Kalad and Aegid had already demanded to be put in charge of punishing his kidnapper, the pimps, and the two sisters. As far as Daran knew, they were still arguing with Canubis about who would be allowed to send them off. It was infuriating. Touching as well, he had to admit, but mostly infuriating.

Alone and confused, the first Echend'dim stared into the dark.

"Daran! If you're not up for training, just say so and stop fooling around!"

Casto's voice had the certain aggressive undertone that showed he had not yet brought himself to getting seriously angry, but he was well on his way. Daran hurried to get off Rajan. The last thing he wanted right now was a fight with his god's heart.

"I'm sorry, Casto. I wasn't concentrating."

"I figured as much, idiot. I wonder why. It's been a week since we got you back, and you don't seem to be as fine as you said you are."

The words hung in the air like a threat, reminding Daran how foolish it was to underestimate King Castolus. Suddenly determined to talk to somebody about his doubts, he met the blond's gaze full-on. His hands were buried in Rajan's mane, as if the warmth coming from the gelding could protect him somehow.

"Nothing's fine, but you already know that. I'm having nightmares. Terrible nightmares. I'm trapped in that place again, chained, unable to free myself. I can hear their laughter, their ridicule. I can feel the knives cutting through me. I see the iron bar crashing down on my face. But it's not the sister or the pimps doing that to me. It's Aegid and Kalad."

Daran choked. Tears streamed down his face while his hands dug into the soft mane of his ride, trying to anchor himself somehow.

"They're doing this to me. And I know how utterly absurd that is. Still, I'm terrified of them. So terrified."

A warm hand touched his shoulder. With a gentleness few would have thought him capable of, Casto embraced the Echend'dim.

"It's fine, Daran. It's fine. Whatever you feel, let it be. Stare your fear and sorrow right in the face, and then let both of them go so you can think clearly again."

As if these words had broken a dam, Daran started crying. Raw, throaty sobs forced their way out, proof of a despair so terrible it had the power to break the thief. It took a long time until he calmed down again. Slightly embarrassed, he freed himself from Casto's embrace.

"This is beyond awkward. Please forgive me."

With his forefinger, Casto swept a tear from Daran's cheek. "Don't worry. You've been through a lot. I can understand how difficult it must be."

Daran grabbed his trainer's wrists, desperate to get some assurance. "How do you deal with it? With the violence, all the things Lord Renaldo has done?"

Casto sighed. This was getting ugly, and it was only the start. "Easier than you might think. Don't forget, I was raised to be a king. To me, the actions of the Barbarian and his brother are legitimate. It helps confirm their claim to power."

"So what you're trying to tell me is that it's fine?"

"No. I'm just stating how much I can relate to their actions—and that I would most probably do the same if I were in their place."

"You don't give a damn about the fate of the innocent, do you?"

Even to his own ears, Daran sounded overly aggressive. Nobody had to explain to him that in the eyes of Casto, his gods, and even his masters, he was part of the faceless masses whose well-being was of no further interest.

The clear blue eyes in which one could get lost so easily now lit up dangerously. Casto had never been one to suffer critique lightly, and the Echend'dim was probing a sore spot. Legitimizing one's actions to oneself was probably the hardest trial every leader had to face. To Casto, Daran's doubts were like echoes of his own sometimes treacherous thoughts.

"Nobody is truly innocent. There's a beast slumbering in every one of us. Just look at your stepfather or the sisters. Canubis and Renaldo do what is necessary. That's not always nice, not always comfortable, but it's their prerogative and their duty. The same goes for Aegid and Kalad. They have always been like that. You just refused to acknowledge it because there was no room for reality in the perfect little world you had built. You've created an image of the two that was disconnected from reality, and now that it has shattered, you're looking for someone to blame. But I've got news for you, Daran. You're like them—like us. The moment you fell in love with them and they chose you, you became special. You're nothing like Egand or the sisters. You're a chosen one, an Echend'dim. Get to terms with it and stop feeling guilty about things you can't change."

Taken aback by this outburst, Daran retreated a little from the king. He knew Casto was right, that his insecurity and fear stemmed mainly from his denial of the truth. Unfortunately this insight didn't make it any easier to face reality.

"I'll have to think about this, Casto. It would be very nice of you if we could cancel today's training session."

His trainer nodded. "As you wish, Daran. Get in the saddle and enjoy some fresh air. I'm sure you'll feel better afterwards."

Grateful, Daran did as he had been told. After one last reassuring glance at Casto, he steered Rajan into the Valley.

"WHAT'S THE matter with you, Casto? You look like an entire month's worth of rain!"

Lovingly, Renaldo embraced his mate and pressed a kiss on his temple. Casto put up with the gesture, a sure sign that whatever had happened this day had truly rattled him.

"I had a talk with Daran. He's not doing well."

The Angel of Death stopped kissing Casto's skin. Tension filled the air.

"I know. Has he confided in you? That would be a step forward, at least."

Casto's gaze darkened. "He did confide in me. But my advice was probably not suited to push him into the direction you might favor."

Renaldo pulled his heart down on one of the lounges, reached for a cup of wine, and held it to Casto's lips. While the king took a few sips, the Angel of Death reveled in the fact that they were so intimate. After rescuing Daran, they had had a major fight about whether Casto was allowed to go for a run with Lys or not. Two lounges, a set of heavy brocade curtains, and the door leading to the spare chamber had been the collateral in this heated argument. And the heated part had been literal.

"So what did you tell him to do?"

"I didn't tell him to do anything. I just explained to him how we all have a beast slumbering inside us. And that I can understand your actions. I can't say he liked it."

Renaldo rested his chin on Casto's head. He had seen this happen before; it was a fairly normal development when somebody who hadn't been trained to execute power suddenly found him or herself in a position where they had to. The doubts, the fears, the insecurities, they all simmered inside before they eventually boiled over. Only then did one find out whether they were truly suited for leadership, or if they had better stay part of the ranks. In

Daran's case, the sudden immortality complicated the situation even more, and he and Canubis certainly didn't want their first Echend'dim to make the wrong decision.

"Daran is going through some hard times at the moment. Being kidnapped and killed hasn't made it any easier." Renaldo emptied the wine in one go.

"It's normal for a young man to experience periods of doubt in his life, but Daran has to face it all at once. My brother and I are trying to come to terms with the fact that we may lose our first Echend'dim."

Shock written all over his face, Casto reared up. "Are you going to banish him?"

Renaldo caressed the wheat-blond hair soothingly.

"Of course not. Daran is the prize the Mothers have promised Aegid and Kalad for their loyalty. We could never take him from them. But sometime soon, Daran will have to decide whether he wants to stay a warrior or become a slave again. Canubis already told him that he is willing to accept whichever he chooses, although he'd prefer keeping Daran as a fighter."

Casto leaned against the Barbarian's chest. "What about Aegid and Kalad? I've barely seen them since we got back. Are they as relaxed as you are?"

"We haven't talked in great detail, since they're too busy worrying about Daran, but their first priority is the thief himself. They don't really care what he is as long as he stays with them. Of course, his decision is going to shape their future relationship, but those are the consequences they'll have to live with."

"Sounds pretty cold to me." Lost in thought, Casto started playing with Renaldo's fingers. "Why did this have to happen now, of all times? Only a few more months and Daran would have embraced his new status wholly."

"I've been thinking the same thing. Perhaps what has happened was in our favor. If he chooses us after everything he's gone through and leaves his doubts behind, then we have an unbelievably strong general under our command."

"And if he chooses against you?"

"Then somebody else and better suited will come to take the post. The Mothers may have left us, but that doesn't mean they're not still looking after us in the small detail." Renaldo grinned broadly. "And we do know how heavily the small detail can influence the big picture."

Casto turned around and kissed his mate passionately.

"What was that for? Not that I'm complaining."

"To keep you from ranting on. If you had become even more insightful, I may have had to throw up."

"You little bastard! I'll make you pay for this!"

Laughing, Renaldo picked the protesting Casto up and carried him to the bed.

MEANWHILE, DARAN roamed the Valley aimlessly. Rajan had taken the lead so his rider could concentrate on the emotional chaos in his head. The decision he was about to make had the potential to change his life as radically as the one he had made a few years ago when Aegid and Kalad had taken him as their slave. And time was running out. For the time being, his masters had been quite patient, one of the reasons he didn't want to test their forbearance more than strictly necessary. Moreover, Canubis would want to know when his first Echend'dim reached the conclusion that he wasn't able to serve him wholeheartedly.

Daran shuddered in the face of his dilemma. If he decided to remain a warrior, then he would turn into someone who could create monsters like the sisters with his actions. He would be doing things that made his stomach churn just thinking about them. But the worst thing was, if he fought for the gods long enough, there would inevitably come a point when the monstrous nature of his deeds wouldn't faze him anymore. Losing what he had been was hard, even though it had never been that great.

If, on the other hand, he chose to become a slave again, he could keep on ignoring reality. Aegid and Kalad would protect and pamper him like they had done until now; he would be living in bliss for all eternity. On the downside, he would remain helpless, unable to stand by their side during battle, damned to be an onlooker forever.

The two paths offered to him were so different, each of them frightening in its own way, that he simply couldn't make up his mind. Staying in this precarious in-between would only make him suffer more. He had to find his place, and he had to do it now. Daran grabbed the reins tighter, resolved to put an end to his own pathetic indecisiveness.

It was already late in the afternoon when he marched from the stables to the dungeons. The guard let him pass without hesitation or comment; they had already accepted him as one of the lords.

Canubis still hadn't decided when and how to punish those who had dared to lay their filthy hands on his possessions more or less right on his doorstep. The dreadful waiting, not knowing what was going to happen to them, was, in Daran's eyes, the most brutal part of the gods' revenge. Except for Elgir and the two pimps, no one had been tortured, mainly because the highwaymen had no information the Wolf of War deemed worth finding out about. Daran's kidnapper was an entirely different case. By now he had told the divine brothers everything about his connections to the worshippers of the Good Mother in the East and how he had managed to conceal his trail so effectively. So far there weren't any more details about the depth of Elgir's sacrilege, but everybody in the Valley knew that Canubis was now eyeing the Eastern kingdoms with the thirst for revenge in his heart.

Daran passed the cells in which the highwaymen were kept without sparing them a glance. Those men had fought against him in battle, even killed him, yet he couldn't bring himself to feel anything but indifference toward them. In front of the cell where Elgir and the pimps were kept, he hesitated for a moment. They reminded him too much of Egand to deserve more than his contempt. Behind the last door, the sisters were chained to the wall. Daran took a deep breath, and then he entered the gloomy room.

He had been to the dungeons once before, shortly after Aegid and Kalad had brought him to the Valley. It had been part of their strategy of carrot and whip to show him where he would end up should he displease them. Of course, it had never been necessary, especially not back then when his heart had been overflowing with admiration and the first tender buds of an ever-growing love. Most of what Daran remembered about this forsaken place were flash images. The rattling of a chain, the soot from the flickering torches staining the stone wall black, the chill coming up from the floor, seeking its way into his body even through the sturdy leather boots, the despair permeating every corner, oppressing any happy thought that might dare to arise. And above it all, like a king of terror reigning over an army of abhorrent slaves, was the smell. The metallic tang of blood mixed with all kinds of bodily fluids, unwashed skin, moldering clothes, wet leather, and a generous dose of rusting steel.

Going to the dungeons, no matter if it was as a free man or a prisoner, meant entering a different world, one that had seemingly nothing to do with the Valley. It was like setting foot into uncharted territory, where anything could happen, where the beasts roamed freely. Down here, everybody changed.

The first Echend'dim stared at the two women who were chained against the far wall of the cell. It was hard to discern details in the gloom, but he thought they seemed more fragile than when they had tortured him so cruelly. Back then they had been dangerous predators; now they looked beaten. Only the aura of utter madness remained the same, fueling their eyes with a feverish glance that betrayed the sorry appearance of their bodies. They were staring back at him, oozing hostility.

Daran stepped a little closer, regarding them intently. Nobody had thought of giving the females new clothes, so they were still dressed in the silken gowns drenched with his blood. Seeing the proof of his suffering made him heave. His body tingled unpleasantly in all the places they had hurt him, and his heart beat frantically. Unconsciously Daran reached for his chest, to the place where they had cut him open. It had been an even greater violation than being raped. Being treated like nothing but an object, his flesh the means for release, his sole purpose to suffer as badly as possible—it had left wounds in Daran's soul he only acknowledged now.

A soft chuckle pried him from his tumultuous musings. The elder of the two sisters glared at him with a mixture of disdain and mockery.

"Seems like the little beauty can't get enough of us. Come on, unchain us and we'll play with you the entire night."

"I have no inclination to ever let you play again with anybody. You are nothing but monsters."

"Hardly any worse than you, pretty face. Tell me, how many have you killed for them? How many people's lives have you made miserable because they ordered you to?"

"Not as many as you think. I'm new to this. Not long ago, I was nothing more than a slave in the Pack."

The younger sister stirred. Slowly her head came up, revealing a face contorted in hatred.

"A mere slave would never be allowed to wield a weapon. And he would most certainly not be adorned with all kinds of riches. We're not blind. Even though you claim to come from humble origins, you're way too comfortable in your fancy clothing. You're used to wearing it, just like you're used to getting whatever you want, because your owners have always seen to it, haven't they?"

"You're right. I've always been taken good care of."

Daran took another step forward. He could feel something inside him changing. It was as if the vicious words dripping from the sisters' lips were somehow cleansing him. Arborja and Eliana sensed it too, the shift of emotions. They both spat.

"We were right after all. You're just like them, a monster of the worst kind, doing their bidding for your own benefit. We should have tortured you some more before ripping your heart out."

"I may be a monster—I can't argue about that, not anymore. But at least I'm a monster who obeys a higher power. You two, on the other hand, simply yield to your own base instincts. Given the choice, I'd say you're worse than me. What you had to endure was terrible, I give you that, and it was most probably not something you deserved, but what you made of it is beyond comprehension. You chose the worst path possible and to justify your actions, you pin all the blame on the divine brothers. They may have been the cause for your life taking a turn for the worse, but it was you who decided to become what you are now. When we first met, I even felt some pity for you, because I thought we were the same. But we aren't. Never have been, never will be."

"And to tell us this, you've come here?"

"No. I came here to find out about myself, and you helped me plenty. I have to thank you for that."

Eliana screeched like a dying pig. Spit dripped down her chin, making her look like an imbecile. The hard lines around Arborja's eyes and mouth seemed to deepen even more while she tried to soothe her raging sister by gently bumping into her side. At the same time, she glared at Daran.

"You had your fun. Now leave us alone, monster. We do not wish for your company any longer."

Daran took the last step that had separated him from the prisoners. Almost lovingly, he caressed Arborja's cheeks; his voice had now a steely undertone he had never thought himself capable of.

"You should be happy. Thanks to you, I've found my place. And it's for your best as well. You don't want to know all the terrible things the Wolf of War or the Angel of Death can do to you. I, on the other hand, will simply return the favor you did for me a few days ago. Rejoice, your death is going to be painful but rather quick, something the gods would have not granted you."

Daran had already reached the door when the sisters finally realized what he had been telling them. Enraged, they threw themselves against their chains, trying to get free. The stench of freshly spilled blood wafted through the air. Daran hurried to get out and tell the guards to keep an eye on the two rioting females.

"Daran, what are you doing here?"

Noemi looked at the young man, slightly puzzled. After all the things he had gone through, she hadn't expected him to come here.

The thief lowered his gaze. He really liked his god's wife but still lacked the courage to look at her directly.

"I wanted to know whether Lord Canubis is here. I know it's late, but perhaps he can spare me some of his time? It won't take long."

"I can always spare time for my first Echend'dim."

Like a threatening shadow, the Wolf of War towered over his petite wife, who only rolled her eyes while asking Daran in.

A little shaken, the thief followed his god and the healer. He had never been to the chambers of the Wolf of War before and was curious. What he glimpsed was so contrary to what he had expected, he couldn't help but gape. Daran was used to the sumptuous, almost decadent interior of his masters' chambers and had somehow assumed Canubis's living space would be the same. Instead the rooms were almost spartan. The walls were lined with shelves full of books and glass jars of all sizes. The jars were filled with pieces of plants, strange liquids, and sometimes things of a definitely organic nature Daran didn't want to find out too much about. The books were all about the healing arts and had so many bookmarks, some of them had grown to double their original size. Lady Noemi did not only rely on her power to heal people; she was also genuinely interested in the basics of the craft.

It touched Daran to witness how the most powerful man in the world, a warrior who could obliterate entire cities, allowed his wife to take complete charge of his inner sanctuary, his living space. It was a side to Canubis the thief hadn't known until now, and which made it easier for him to talk to the intimidating leader. It was exactly like Casto had stated. There was a beast slumbering inside all of them, but it also had a counterpart, one with a friendlier face, to keep the balance. And seeing even his god displaying this tender side reassured Daran immensely. When Canubis gestured him to sit down, he did so with newfound confidence.

"What is it you want to tell me, Daran?"

The amber eyes regarded him seemingly unfazed, but the Echend'dim could feel his god's tension. He took a deep breath.

"I'm here to ask you to leave the punishment of the sisters to me."

Those words were followed by a long, oppressive silence. Canubis's gaze drilled into Daran as if he wanted to look right into his soul. "And why should I do that?"

Daran felt his confidence waver, but then he straightened his back and extended his chin.

"Because I'm asking you as your first Echend'dim. And because it is my right as a free member of the Pack. I was the one who suffered by their hand, so it's my prerogative to decide about their end."

Again silence descended, but it was broken almost instantly by a satisfied laugh. "Well said, Echend'dim. I'm going to oblige your wish, as is customary in the Pack." The Wolf of War got up and pulled the thief in a tight embrace. "I'm so glad you found your way back to us, Daran. Welcome to the Pack again!"

Relieved, the first Echend'dim leaned against the hard, unyielding figure of his god. A feeling of peace washed over him, the kind of peace you felt when you were absolutely sure about something.

"I thank you, my lord. I thank you with all my heart."

"It's fine, Daran. You were definitely worth the wait. And now you better go and talk to your lovers. Knowing them, they should be quite impatient by now."

AEGID AND Kalad were indeed waiting, and when Daran glimpsed the worry in their faces, he felt guilty. He had left those two in the dark for too long, had even looked at them with fear and contempt. Considering what he had just realized about himself, he suddenly felt childish and stupid. They had always given him their inviolable love, had protected and pampered him like a spoiled child. Daran had to smile. It was time to pay them back.

He took the warriors' hands and kissed them, full of love, and then led them to the lounges in the middle of the room. Since he didn't know how to start, a tense silence grew between them until Kalad broke it.

"Daran." The mercenary's voice was soft. "You don't have to force yourself. If you need more time…."

The Echend'dim shook his head violently. "That's not it, masters. Not anymore. I have reached a decision today, and I want to apologize for having taken so long."

"You don't have to apologize for anything, little thief. You're the one who had to endure so much violence. If anything, it's our fault for being so impatient."

Daran sighed. Those few words showed how much his lovers had been suffering with him, how deep their love for him ran. It made it even easier for him to talk on.

"I think you've already guessed that what has happened to me has marked me in more ways than one. To be frank, the violence done to my body was the less terrible. What really got to me was the insight into what you really are. Although I'd lived with you for so long, I had always ignored your true nature. The sisters forced me to confront a truth I had been denying for too long. It terrified me to the bone. I thought I wouldn't be able to love you the way you really are, that I was only attracted to the ideal I had imagined of you."

Embarrassed, Daran stared at the ground, unable to meet his masters' gaze after what he had just told them. The warriors were silent for a moment; then Kalad gently touched his hair.

"Daran, look at us, please."

Slowly, reluctantly, the Echend'dim lifted his gaze.

"You don't have to be afraid, darling. Whatever you want to tell us, we will accept it. It's your decision, and we're proud that you're brave enough to share it with us."

Daran closed his eyes, feeling utterly blessed.

"I've asked the Wolf of War to leave the sisters' punishment to me."

This one little sentence made Aegid and Kalad gape. They hadn't anticipated such an outcome. A little breathless, Daran resumed.

"I'm ashamed for even thinking I couldn't love you when you're not like my ideal picture. Truth is, my feelings for you are overwhelming me. No matter what you've done or are going to do in the names of our gods, it won't change anything about my emotions. I've finally understood this. There's still a long way ahead of me, and I can't promise I won't feel the same insecurities again. But I promise you, I'll do anything in my power to become a man worthy of your love."

Stunned, the desert brothers embraced their precious thief, kissing him, full of love. Aegid spoke first, his voice shaking a little from relief.

"You're more than worthy of our love, Daran. When we first met, we may have chosen you on a whim, although I'm beginning to doubt even that. It was our instinct that made us take you along, and it was dead-on. You're the one for us, the only one. And we're so glad to have you back. You had us worried for a while."

"Yes, indeed. Now tell us, what made you change your mind?"

Kalad's lips were dangerously close to the Echend'dim's ear. Daran knew where this conversation was headed and realized with relief that he no longer dreaded, but rather craved what they would be doing very soon.

"Not what. Who. I talked to Casto, and he said some very accurate, unpleasant things to me. After I had gotten over the initial shock, I started contemplating his twisted wisdom and saw how right he was. It still hurt, though. He's pretty direct."

Aegid chuckled, his nose buried in Daran's hair.

"You only realize that now? But I'm grateful to him."

"Well, then you have to be grateful to the sisters as well. I know, it was they who made me doubt in the first place, but after Casto's lecture, I paid them a visit in the dungeons. When I first met them, I thought they resembled me and the people I grew up with. None of us had many chances in life, except for going down even further. There was always the hazy knowledge of 'someone above' oppressing us, keeping us in place no matter how hard we tried. Basically, we tried to stay afloat by any means possible, nurturing hatred toward the unknown. I grew up with the conviction that everybody who had more than me was an enemy, was the reason I was so miserable. I tried getting out of it, I really did. But nobody would give me a chance. All the masters I asked for work sent me away. 'Filthy street mongrel' was one of the nicer things they called me. All my struggles were in vain. There was nothing I could do to change my fate. Just like Arborja and Elianna. I even pitied them."

Daran paused, choosing his next words carefully, sensing how important it was to bring his point across.

"Then I took a good look into their eyes. They accused me of being a monster, but what I saw inside their souls was worse, if those were even still souls and not something else. I understood then that even if they hadn't met all those unfavorable circumstances, they would have still become what they are now. Which means I am what I've always been as well. Nobody and nothing can take it away from me, and I'm definitely nothing like those two creatures."

"If that is so, then what about us?" Aegid asked tentatively, still not sure where the conversation was headed.

Daran snuggled into his arms. "You are you. The love you're giving me is real. It's what I crave most in this world. The things you do—I will learn to accept them as part of what you are."

"What more can we ask?"

Kalad grabbed Daran's head with both hands, forcing him backward to kiss him hungrily. The Echend'dim reciprocated with delight, feeling the last doubts vanish from his thoughts like fog in the morning sun. Daran was finally home again.

2. BARGAIN

"So with Aegid and Kalad taking care of Elgir and the pimps, and Daran finishing the sisters, there's only those highwaymen left in our care."

"Stop sounding so damn smug, big brother! Things went our way, which is terrific, but if you don't get over the gloating right now, I'm going to throw up."

"Pff, what's gotten your panties in a knot? Did you have a fight with Casto—again?"

Canubis was way too cheerful to let his little brother's bad mood affect him. Renaldo shot him an angry glare. Of course the Wolf of War was right—he did have a nasty argument with his beloved heart, bad enough to have him sleeping alone for at least two more nights, depending on how quickly Sic could manage to soothe Casto's anger. Even though he should have been used to it by now, he still had a hard time whenever his capricious mate decided to give him the cold shoulder. It reminded the Angel of Death of the time when he had almost lost his heart, a time he was desperate to forget. Seeing his brother so happy didn't improve his temper at all.

Canubis offered him another cup of wine, trying to distract him from his gloomy pondering. "Stop brooding. He'll forgive you eventually, as he always does. Until then, use your spare energy to help me decide how we're going to send those highwaymen to the Mothers. I want to set an example."

"Which won't be easy. Aegid and Kalad are going to use the sand— that's quite impressive. And Daran is planning to rip the sisters' hearts out while they're still alive. Even you should find it hard to top that."

"I know. And strictly speaking, it doesn't have to be too showy. I mean, the main culprits will suffer badly, but those thugs simply made one wrong decision. I almost feel pity for them."

Renaldo cocked an eyebrow. It was rare to see his brother in such a forgiving mood. Only yesterday, he would have probably sentenced the attackers to death by the wolves. Daran coming into the fold had relieved the Wolf of War more than he wanted to admit.

"So no skinning alive, then? How boring."

"Cut it out, Renaldo. They do have to pay. It's just that I don't feel like overdoing it anymore."

"I understand. And forcing them to watch while the sisters and the kidnappers die should be punishment enough. Are you going to slit their throats?"

"Sounds like a good idea. Still—"

Canubis was interrupted by a sharp knock on the door. Since Noemi was still out, he answered it himself. It turned out to be the captain of the dungeon watch, a slim, levelheaded man named Borog, whom he had chosen for this difficult post because he didn't tend toward cruelty.

Borog looked slightly uncomfortable when he entered the spacious main room. "My Lord Canubis, Lord Renaldo. Please forgive my intrusion."

"It's fine, Borog. We weren't discussing anything important. What brings you here?"

"One of the prisoners, my lord. He seems to be the second-in-command of the robbers. Ever since he was brought here, he has been asking me to bring him to you. At first I thought he was only trying to find a way out, but he's very persistent, and I'm getting the impression that this could be important. Tomorrow it will be too late, so I thought I should at least tell you."

"How long have you been brooding over this matter, Borog? Knowing you, at least the last two days."

"You know me too well, my Lord Canubis. I didn't want to bother you with the petty request of a lowlife."

"What made you change your mind?"

"His eyes. He's becoming more and more desperate, and not about his own fate."

Canubis and Renaldo shared one of their famous looks. This sounded like something interesting. They both got up.

"We trust your intuition, Borog. Lead us to him."

IN THE semidarkness of the cell, Da'Ryen stirred when he heard footsteps approaching. His heart sank. So the time to pay for his sins had finally come. The only thing he still regretted was that he hadn't been able to save Nya. Once they reached the Valley, she had been taken to a different cell, and he hadn't seen her since then. Slowly, with an ominous creak, the door opened, allowing the light of two torches to spill into his stone prison. It took some time for his eyes to get used to the sudden light, but then they widened in surprise. Right in front of him, the Wolf of War and the Angel of Death had taken position, looking at him the way a cat might regard a cheeky mouse. The man with the predator eyes spoke first.

"You wanted to talk to me. Here I am."

Da'Ryen bowed his head in a gesture of respect. His voice was hoarse, for he hadn't had much to drink the past few days.

"I thank you, Lord Canubis. I can assure you, I didn't make this request on a whim. What I wish to ask you is very important to me, and I hope you can listen until the end."

With a nod, the Wolf of War showed his consent.

Da'Ryen inhaled deeply. Being in close proximity to the two most powerful men in the world made him wonder how he could have ever been afraid of Ma'Duk. Compared to these two, the leader of the gang of robbers was nothing but a willful, notoriously short-tempered child. It took all of Da'Ryen's courage to look Canubis in the eye.

"I wish to plead for a life. Not mine, since I'm well aware of the anger you must feel toward me. I'm asking you to spare the life of a girl named Nya. She came here with the rest of us, but I can assure you, she had nothing to do with the attack on your caravan. She only has the bad luck of being tied to the wrong man in the wrong place."

The amber eyes stared at him without the faintest trace of emotion. When the Wolf of War finally spoke, it was in calm tones.

"When I discovered my Echend'dim in the brothel, tortured to death twice, I killed everybody who had been present, no matter if they even knew about his existence. The mere fact that they were there was enough for me to subject them to my revenge. So as you can see, I do not make a habit of sparing the innocent. Those who get in my way pay the price. You put your filthy hands on what is mine. How can you expect me to show any lenience?"

"I'm not asking for myself. I'm asking for somebody important to me."

"She's not your daughter, is she? That would at least explain your behavior."

"No, she's not. She's the daughter of a woman I only met once and briefly, if you understand. But she reminds me of another girl and another mother. So I'm begging you."

Suddenly, the face of the Wolf of War was only half a hand from Da'Ryen's.

"You have nothing to offer, nothing to trade. All you can do is beg. It must be an unpleasant memory, one you think of as a mistake."

Da'Ryen shuddered. It was as if the warlord was able to see right through him, as if his soul was bared in front of his merciless predator stare.

"Not only a mistake, but a sin. And the memory is not just unpleasant. Part of it is so sweet, it chills me to the bone. This is the first time in my life I've ever asked for anything from anybody. It's the first time I'm reducing myself to begging. I'm doing it for her, so please show mercy."

The Wolf of War looked at his brother, who only shrugged. He seemed to have nothing to say. Canubis contemplated his options for a moment and decided to test the man's resolve. Until now, the thug had managed to impress him with his determination, so he would get his chance.

"Let's say I do let her go. What will become of her without protection? Doing this would be even crueler than killing her. So if I grant your wish, I'll have to keep her until she's old enough to look after herself. Why would I do this?"

"What do you want from me?"

A quick smile flashed across the warrior's features.

"You're no fool. If I'm going to take her in, somebody has to earn her keep. And the only one fit to take on this task is you."

"So you're going to spare my life but turn me into a slave?"

"Certainly not. That's an honor you don't deserve. You're going to be something else, something a lot worse. Everybody in the Pack is protected by our rules—everybody except for the traitors. They are the lowest-ranked slaves, those who do the truly vicious jobs and are subjected to the whims of all our members. Normally, they don't last long. The human body can endure only so much until it breaks. But you will have to persevere to ensure Nya's well-being. That's the deal you get. Take it or leave it, it's up to you."

Da'Ryen shivered. He had never anticipated to be able to plead his case to the Wolf of War, let alone have him grant his request. If slavery was the price he had to pay, he would accept it gladly.

"I thank you, Lord Canubis. You're very generous."

There was a cold glint in the eyes of the powerful man. It lacked amusement, showing the unrelenting, hideous nature of the god.

"I'm a cruel bastard, making you live like this when you could have died so easily, but you and I, we have a deal. I'm going to hold up my end as long as you do the same with yours. Borog, you heard us. Get Nya out of here. For tonight, bring her to Frankus and explain matters to him. Then you can come back and introduce our new slave to his duties."

Borog bowed and left. So did the divine brothers. Once they were gone, Da'Ryen sagged in his chains. He didn't know where this new, unexpected path would lead him, but he was still grateful, for he sensed that he had been given a second chance.

"Don't look at me like that. I just thought it could be amusing."

"I'm not looking at all. I'd never dare." Mockery tinged every syllable coming from Renaldo's mouth. "You never cease to surprise me, brother, and I've known you for quite some time now. I guess it's useless to ask you why?"

The Wolf of War sighed. Through their connection as brothers and gods, which was growing stronger every day since the Mothers had left Ana-Darasa, he could feel that Renaldo already knew the answer, that he would have done the same for the same reasons. Making him say it was just the Angel of Death's twisted way of getting back at him for the jibe about Casto.

"Drop it, Renaldo. I'm not in the mood. Besides, I know you can sense it as well as I do. This one's journey isn't finished yet. And only a year ago, neither you nor I would have granted him anything, because we wouldn't have known. Sometimes those new powers are unnerving."

Turning serious all of a sudden, Renaldo took his brother's hand. They were both feeling it, the steady pressure of pure power pouring into them, filling them up until they thought their frames would crack. The world that had once seemed to them like a gigantic playfield was shrinking as they watched, losing significance in the face of their new responsibilities and possibilities. It was still their home, something they would protect no matter what, but it was hard to maintain focus when their entire beings were overwhelmed by everything. If this was how the Mothers felt all the time, Renaldo was inclined to forgive them quite a lot of grudges he had accumulated over the centuries. Being swamped by all those impressions, seeing things that were not really there, that were still to come or could happen if things were different—it was hard to stay rooted in reality. Without their hearts, it would be impossible. Canubis had the advantage here; his relationship with Noemi was stable, and he could fully rely on her. Casto, on the other hand, was like quicksand. At one moment he was a pillar of support thanks to his amazing empathic talent; the next he used the same ability to fight his mate with everything he had. Always being thrown off-balance was beginning to take its toll on the Angel of Death. As much as he loved Casto's unpredictable, stubborn nature, there were times when he had to force himself not to subjugate the king with force. The knowledge that doing so would destroy everything they had built between them didn't improve the warrior's mood.

"Don't look so miserable. It's going to be fine." Canubis patted his brother's back in an attempt to cheer him up. A grateful smile was his reward.

"I know. Or better, I hope. Let's drink some more, since there's no one waiting for me in my chambers."

"You sound like an old man, brother."

"Still younger than you, though."

Bickering like two old women, the divine brothers returned to the warmth of their chambers.

3. PREDATORS

THE NEXT morning dawned with splendid glory. Some last wisps of autumn fog dispersed in the brilliant light of the rising sun, making the dew on the ground sparkle like the stars in a clear night sky. It was, depending on one's point of view, either the best or worst kind of day for an execution.

Not only the convicts were dreading what was to come. In his chambers, Sic was sitting gloomily at the table, staring holes into the walls. As an Emeris, it was his duty to be present when the gods carried out punishment against those who had dared to oppose them. As a former slave and convict himself, Sic could think of a hundred things he would rather be doing. Like running through the Valley naked, or cleaning out the pits all by himself. Unfortunately he wasn't given a choice in this matter. All he could do was try to make the best of it.

Two strong arms snaked around his shoulders, pulling him into a tight embrace. Instantly relaxed, Sic snuggled closer to the warm, bulky chest behind him. Noran placed a gentle kiss on his lover's scalp.

"Don't worry so much, my precious. I'll be there with you. You're not alone."

"I know. It brings back bad memories, though. Memories I had hoped we could leave behind us once and for all."

"Perhaps it's not as bad a thing as you fear. It can also make us stronger. Deepen our bond. You said it yourself—we've already hit rock bottom. It can only get better from now on."

Sic kissed his former owner deeply. Even though he had always seen more in the grumpy master smith than everybody else, he would have never dared to imagine how caring Noran could be. It made him feel pampered and loved, and it gave him the strength to face the events of the day.

"I wonder how you always find the right words to cheer me up."

Noran lifted Sic up, a lascivious glint on his face. "I have more to offer than just mere words. Do you want to find out later?"

Giggling like a child, Sic threw his arms around the master smith's neck. "Yes. Yes, I do!"

Daran was standing in front of a mirror, trying to decide what he should wear. Given how messy killing the sisters was going to be, it was best to choose something simple and old. Only his overbearing lovers wouldn't allow it.

"On a day like this, you have to wear your finest."

Both of them had been very definite. Daran's protests about the stupidity of ruining such expensive clothes had fallen on deaf ears.

"Never mind the clothes. We can always buy you new, even better ones. This is about appearances, about your place in the Pack. You're Canubis's first Echend'dim, and you're claiming this position by taking your revenge on the sisters. You absolutely can't go there in anything but the finest getup."

Taken aback by their fierceness, Daran had given in and put on his best leather trousers, a shirt woven from the finest linen and dyed in the dark green hue that was the desert brothers' color, his knee-high boots with the white rabbit fur lining, and a jerkin made of silk with a most intricate pattern embroidered at the seams. As usual, his hair hung down his back in one long, thick braid.

Now Kalad and Aegid stepped forward, offering him a dagger they had chosen just for him. The blade was about a span and a hand long, slightly curved, and shimmering in the morning light like a pool of spring water. It was also razor-sharp. The hilt was made from black wood hardened in fire. Golden inlays followed the grain of the wood, making it look as if it were a living thing. At the base, an emerald the size of a walnut nested like a very expensive egg. The weapon was perfectly balanced, a beautiful instrument of death.

"You already know where to strike, so we won't be lecturing you about how to kill this scum. This little something is a token of our love. Wield it well, that's all we're asking."

Kalad was grinning broadly. He was in an exceptionally good mood this morning. Given what they had been doing the entire night, and that he would be able to get his revenge today, it wasn't really a surprise.

Daran looked into his lovers' eager faces, unable to voice the emotions brewing inside him. Now that his decision was finalized, he couldn't help but have second thoughts. The first Echend'dim clenched his teeth. No going back now. He had already chosen his path.

FOR THE tenth time that morning, Da'Ryen reached for the iron shackle around his neck, trying to move the collar into a more comfortable position. Experience from the previous day told him how useless the attempt was, since comfort wasn't something a traitor in the Pack had any familiarity with. Borog, the captain of the prison guard, had closed the symbol of his new subservient life around his throat right after he had taken Nya out of the dungeons. There had been something akin to pity in the man's eyes, which still puzzled Da'Ryen. As fierce as they might appear, the members of the Pack did seem to have the occasional soft spot. What other explanation was there for him being still alive?

He shifted on his feet. Like every other inhabitant of the Valley, he had to be present for the execution. The place he had been led to was at the far end of the little arena, opposite the small canopy where the seats for the divine brothers and their Emeris had been set up. Slowly the ranks were starting to fill with people of all ages, chatting amiably as if this was not about punishment but a pleasant pastime. If it hadn't been for the tense atmosphere overshadowing it all, Da'Ryen wouldn't have believed that he had walked into a den of predators. It was vexing how contradictory the members of the Pack were, and it also explained a lot about the stories he had heard. None of them managed to come even close to the truth.

A sudden hush alerted Da'Ryen. The divine brothers made their entry, accompanied by the Emeris. Since he had already met the Wolf of War and the Angel of Death, Da'Ryen's eyes only skimmed over them. Instead, they stopped at the stunning blond walking next to Lord Renaldo. Of course there were stories about the wild, stubborn, and, above all, breathtaking mate of the fearsome warlord. Only two years ago, King Castolus had been officially recognized as the heart of the Angel of Death, and the tales about him had already taken on the quality of legends. Apparently, none of the rumors did him justice.

The divine brothers were the very definition of the word "intimidating," and even the Emeris seemed to be wary of them. It was nothing obvious, only small gestures that nevertheless revealed how feared the warlords were even among their own—except for the blond with the mesmerizing eyes of the sky. If anything, he seemed annoyed about being there, and when the

Angel of Death tried to put his hand on the small of Castolus's back, the king shooed him away like a troublesome insect. To Da'Ryen's utter surprise, the Angel of Death let it happen without rebuking the young man. Instead he retreated a step to give his mate more breathing space.

Those who had witnessed the little scene reacted quite differently. The Wolf of War appeared to be torn between amusement and anger; his heart, the famed Lady Noemi Amerasu, simply rolled her eyes; while the plain-looking young warrior who was guarded by a giant of a man was clearly terrified. Unfazed by the set of different reactions he had just triggered, the most fascinating person Da'Ryen had ever seen sat down on his high chair with the frozen, impenetrable mask of a true king.

The other members of this exclusive group followed his example, and it was only now that Da'Ryen realized there were two of them missing. Before he could ponder this observation, the Wolf of War nodded slightly, and the convicts were brought in. It was a rather sad track as far as Da'Ryen was concerned. There had never been any love lost between him and Ma'Duk or their fellow warriors from the Hot Heart, not to mention the other thugs who had been drawn to their unlawful union. Yet it still hurt to see those men he had shared the past six years with walk into the arena like oxen on the way to the butcher. Behind his former comrades followed Elgir and two men Da'Ryen didn't recognize. The defiant look in their eyes couldn't belie the fear they were radiating like a fire would heat. The rear of the procession was taken by two haggard-looking females whose quick, darting glances and awkward movements only served to enhance the madness surrounding them.

Poles had been rammed into the ground in the middle of the arena. They were in two rows, with an additional five a few feet to the right, closer to the canopy where the gods were seated. The highwaymen were chained in the rows while Elgir, the two strange men, and the females were tied to the remaining five poles. The silence in the arena was deafening; not even a whisper could be heard. Just when Da'Ryen started wondering how long this surreal situation would prevail, the wolves made their entry. Sleek, powerful bodies covered by silky gray fur paraded into the circle like lethal shadows, fully aware of the impact they were making. These powerful predators had inspired almost as many stories as their masters, most of them rich with blood and gore.

Behind the pack followed two desert warriors with a third one between. Da'Ryen startled when he recognized the man he and Ma'Duk had killed. Without the grime of battle staining him, he looked even more appealing. And seeing how the two warriors were hovering around him confirmed his high status. All of a sudden, Da'Ryen felt grateful for having let the young man go. Facing the wrath of the desert men was definitely something he could do without.

The smaller one stepped forward, his countless braids shaking with every move he made. His lively brown eyes were glued to Elgir and the two men with him. It wasn't a friendly stare. He made a careless bow in the direction of the divine brothers, clearly focused on his victims.

"Lord Aegid and I thank you for leaving the punishment of these three men to us."

The Wolf of War nodded gracefully, the expression in his amber eyes impossible to read. Lord Kalad turned to the convicts, addressing them directly.

"You laid your hands on what is most precious to us. You dared to sully what is solely ours. There exists no punishment that can make you pay sufficiently for the sacrilege you have committed. Nevertheless, my desert brother and I are going to make you suffer as much as possible. We will introduce you to the worst nightmare you can imagine."

When he had spoken, the other desert warrior, a giant of a man, stepped next to him. Even though he hadn't spoken a word yet, he was more intimidating than his brother-in-arms. Shuddering, Da'Ryen recognized some of the tattoos on Lord Aegid's skin. He had seen them before, on the scrolls kept by his tribe. There was a legend about a man born to the tribe with hair and eyes of the moon, chosen to be a messenger to the spirit world. Da'Ryen had never believed in these tales, thinking they sounded too exaggerated to be true. But now the proof was right in front of him, shattering his tribe's entire system of belief. After they had injected their prayers into the skin of the messenger with blunt tools made of bone, he had been driven into the desert to die there. Everything good that had happened to the tribe since then had been attributed to this sacrifice, the first and only human one his people had ever made. Apparently the spirits had never received those prayers, since their bearer was still up and about. Only with this thought did Da'Ryen realize how old Lord Aegid had to be. The implications of this insight made him shiver.

Now the desert warriors had taken position in front of the three poles restraining Elgir and his unfortunate consorts. They didn't have any weapons or instruments of torture with them, which was puzzling, since they had just promised unspeakable pain to those men. For a couple of heartbeats, nothing happened. Then a soft breeze passed Da'Ryen, and in it, he felt something terribly familiar, something that had no place here. A nightmare, born in the Hot Heart and usually confined within it. Slowly, the sand cyclone was building itself, the small, razor-sharp grains swarming around the desert warriors like angry hornets. Knowing the fate of Elgir, Da'Ryen wanted to look away, to spare himself the carnage of what was going to happen, but somehow he couldn't. A perverted part of him wanted to see, wanted to witness the power that was about to be unleashed.

AEGID AND Kalad were standing at the center of the sand cyclone, forcing themselves to stay calm while the sharp grains sang to them how easily Elgir, Druran, and Drik could be vanquished from the face of Ana-Darasa. Daran had not yet told them what he had suffered at the hands of these dirty bastards, but what they had glimpsed and guessed so far made them seethe with rage. Only the prospect of repaying the affliction their precious lover had been forced to bear kept their emotions in check. Slowly, they allowed the sand to brush past the three men, scraping their clothes and chafing their skin every time the cyclone made a turn. There would be no quick, merciful death for the convicts. Aegid and Kalad were determined to drag this out as long as possible.

FROZEN IN terror, Da'Ryen listened to the shrieks and screams, to the whimpering and begging. What shocked him most was how long the bloody lumps of shredded skin and torn muscle tissue were still able to produce sound. It also made him realize how utterly the desert warriors had to love their mate—and how merciless they truly were. Perhaps it was because they had been with the divine brothers for so long that they were the least human of all the Emeris. When the screaming finally stopped and no spark of life could have possibly remained, the sand cyclone thickened, obscuring what was left of the bodies from view. One last time the grains whirled around in their deadly dance; then it was all gone as if it had never existed. The poles were bare; not even a shred of bone remained of the convicts, and the once gleaming chains looked battered and torn. Satisfied, the desert warriors retreated, taking up their position next to the braided man again.

Squaring his shoulders, the Echend'dim stepped forward. His bow toward the divine brothers was deeper and more sincere than the one Lord Kalad had given. A slight trembling in his voice indicated how inexperienced he was.

"My Lord Canubis, my Lord Renaldo, I thank you for allowing me to punish my tormentors personally. It is a great honor to be trusted like that."

The Wolf of War nodded gravely, reassuring his Pack member with this simple gesture.

"It is our honor that you have decided to serve us as our first Echend'dim, Lord Daran. How can we deny you what is your right by the law?"

So the young man was special, just like Da'Ryen had guessed when he had seen the way his wounds had healed. No wonder the desert warriors were so upset. He had been against ambushing the caravan from the very beginning. It seemed as if his intuition had been dead-on. They had literally thrown stones into an already angry hornets' nest.

Daran was walking toward the sisters, his right hand on the hilt of the dagger protruding from his leather belt. Like his clothes, the weapon was exquisitely made, a statement on its own. Unable to take his eyes off the strangely appealing young man, Da'Ryen watched as he drew the dagger.

ADRENALINE RUSHED through his bloodstream like a torrent as Daran approached the sisters. They were still wearing their silken robes, stained with his blood. By now, they reeked, a gut-wrenching stench of decay. As if the smell had somehow afflicted his senses, Daran slowed down, doubt entered his mind again. Made sensitive by their shared madness, the sisters lifted their heads in unison, throwing the Echend'dim feverish looks.

"Having second thoughts, little beauty? Or are you simply not up to killing?"

The mockery in their voices made Daran clench his teeth. With a flourish, he sheathed the dagger again, ignoring the intake of breath from the audience and the heated stares from his lovers. There was still one thing left to do, and he wouldn't allow anybody to rush him. He would not kill if he wasn't absolutely sure, and ending a life without its owner being able to fight back was a lot more difficult than killing on the battlefield. There it could be considered self-defense; the opponent had a fair chance, something that had been taken from the sisters.

Slowly, calmly, Daran took Arborja's chin in his hand, staring directly into the void where other people might nurture a soul. It was right then that the epiphany hit him with all its might. Taking a life was a decision, just like everything else in life. It should not be made carelessly. It was his freedom and his duty, and above all, his right, not only as a member of the Pack but also as a servant to the gods of war, as the first of their Eternal Guard. The things he did for his gods had no need to be justified. They were right because they were done in the names of Canubis and Renaldo. His leaders were the most dangerous predators on Ana-Darasa and by choosing them, he had become one as well.

Daran felt as if a weight had been lifted from his shoulders. He was finally free to embrace his true nature. At one with himself, he unsheathed the dagger again.

DA'RYEN FELT the hair on his back rise when the warrior drew out the weapon again, a smile on his lips. When he first approached the sisters, Daran had given the impression of someone in doubt, as if he didn't really want to be there. Then suddenly something profound had changed, and it wasn't only the young man. Da'Ryen could feel the shift in the course of the world itself, as if this single person had just changed the future of them all. On the surface, a reluctant servant had turned into a determined fighter, but on a deeper level, something even more arcane had happened, and judging from the smug expression on the Wolf of War's face, he was fully aware of it.

Without hesitation, the first Echend'dim ripped out the heart of the older female, holding the still twitching organ high into the air while the blood trickled down his hands, smearing his face and expensive clothes. Like an afterthought, Daran tossed the heart to the alpha wolf, who devoured it with a satisfied growl to the background of the younger sister's howling. She had slipped completely into madness, foam dripping from her mouth, her eyes rolled back until only the whites could be seen. In a matter of seconds, she followed her sister into death, her heart feeding the wolf again.

Slowly, deliberately, Daran cleaned the dagger on the robes of the corpses before he sheathed it. When he turned to face his gods again, he looked like revenge personified, the blood of his enemies clinging to him like a second skin. Under the canopy, the divine brothers had gotten up from their chairs, honoring the former thief with a bow. The First of the Eternal Guard had come into his own.

AFTER ALL the violence and emotions displayed, the execution of the robbers was almost anticlimactic, like an afterthought to something that had already been exhausted. Compared to the fate of Elgir, the pimps, and the sisters, they had merciful, quick deaths, their throats slit and the bodies fed to the wolves. Once the predators had started their meal, the crowd dispersed. An overseer came to fetch Da'Ryen and introduce him to his duties in the pits.

4. AFTERMATH

Back in his chambers, Sic fell heavily on a chair. The open display of violence had exhausted him to the point where he wasn't able to feel anything anymore. He was vaguely aware of Noran busying himself with pouring two cups of wine, but he couldn't bring himself to turn around. The master smith sat down next to his lover, offering him the wine. Sic took it with a sad smile, fully aware of the tension between them. Before the silence could become even more awkward, Sic started to talk.

"It was even worse than I thought. Although I do have to admit I'm glad Kalad and Aegid didn't have their powers back then. It gives me the creeps."

"Says the man who could kill us all with a single thought."

"Please, don't mention it. I really want to forget what I'm capable of."

Noran pulled Sic into a tight embrace. His next words would lead him into uncharted, dangerous territory, and he was already prepared for rejection.

"Perhaps that's the problem, my precious. You're so scared of yourself, it taints everything else."

Sic froze in his lover's arms but, much to Noran's delight, didn't pull away.

"You're right. Of course you're right. And I know it. Still, I'm unable to fight it. And seeing what is becoming of us—I'm not only afraid of my own power. Even before I ascended to the rank of Emeris, I thought Lord Renaldo and Lord Canubis were terrifying. Now that they're regaining all the talents they had lost, I'm paralyzed with fear."

"You have to trust them. They are our gods, the leaders we have chosen and sworn to follow. There is no backing out now. Not anymore."

Sic whimpered. "I know. And I could never betray them. I just wish I could be less confused."

Noran hugged the young man even tighter. There was almost nothing he could do to help Sic except for being there and not letting their difficult past weigh him down even more.

WHEN DARAN finally returned to the chambers, Aegid and Kalad were already waiting for him. They were in their "predator mood," as he secretly called it, their eyes shining with a hunger he loved and dreaded at the same time. Killing Daran's kidnappers had aroused the desert warriors and made them restless.

Kalad extended a hand toward Daran. "Come here, Daran." His voice was oddly gentle and in stark contrast to his agitated body language.

Daran obeyed immediately, already captivated by the intense mood. Aegid's fingers brushed lightly over Daran's cheek.

"You're covered in blood."

His voice sounded dreamy. Daran took Aegid's hand into his own. He felt a strange thrill running through his body, a sensation he hadn't known before.

"I'm going to wash right now."

"No! We like it!"

Daran shuddered at those urgent, needy words. Kalad was standing behind him, sniffing his bloodstained clothes and skin.

"You smell of the blood of our enemies. It's so erotic, I can hardly restrain myself."

For the blink of an eye, Daran froze. This one sentence exposed what Kalad and Aegid really were; it showed their true, lethal nature. Only two days ago, he would have retreated from them in fear, but now he straightened his back and met their hungry, demanding gazes. This was what they were, and ultimately, this was what *he* was. His lovers had confronted him with their predatory nature only twice before, and each time Daran had been their helpless victim, only able to deal with the intensity of their assault because he had ignored the truth. Now he accepted and embraced it, knowing he would love them no matter who they were, what they did, or who they might become.

From the depths of his soul, his own predator reared its head and woke from its slumber. It greeted the other two with the same fierce gaze, challenging them to make the first move. Aegid's answering grin threatened to cut his face in half.

"You're beautiful, little thief, beautiful and irresistible."

He wanted to pull Daran close, but the Echend'dim stopped him. "Not today."

A growl emanated from both men's lips, their lust open and unveiled. Daran stood tall. He felt heady with newfound strength and wanted to test his power.

"Take your clothes off."

For a moment he thought the two would punish him for his cheekiness, but when he held their gazes, unperturbed, they finally complied. It was strange, watching them get undressed while he was still fully clothed. Usually it was the other way round. When Aegid and Kalad were naked, Daran pointed with his chin toward the bed. Again they obeyed, watching him hungrily.

Daran took his time to feast on their perfectly sculpted bodies, to enjoy the sheen on Kalad's dark skin, and to savor the whirling, endless tattoos on Aegid. While he was still engrossed in ogling them, he took off his own clothes without really noticing it. Daran's erection stood out proudly in front of him. His lovers on the bed smiled, their own manhoods rising to the challenge.

Daran knelt between them, pushing each man down with one hand. While he was still restraining Kalad, he started kissing Aegid, licking the corners of his mouth, grazing with his teeth along the steely jawline and nipping at the tender skin at his neck. Aegid groaned under these playful ministrations. His hands reached out to close around Daran's hips, but the Echend'dim stopped the motion.

"No. Today, you do as I say."

A frustrated grunt was the answer. Aegid let his hands fall down on the bed again, shooting Daran feverish looks. Smiling, Daran bent down to kiss him on the mouth. For this, he had to let go of Kalad, who sat up immediately. Instead of commanding him down again, Daran guided Kalad toward his back.

"You can stimulate me while I'm busy with Aegid. You know what I like."

Kalad's eyes widened in shock, for Daran had never before spoken to him like that. Then a smile crept on his lips, and his erection hardened even more.

"As you wish, Daran. It's my pleasure."

Daran felt his own cock straining as well. He began to understand why Kalad and Aegid enjoyed subduing him so much. It felt incredibly good to have someone at his beck and call. He started kissing Aegid anew while Kalad busied himself at his back. Daran felt Kalad's strong hands parting his asscheeks and inserting two fingers slick with oil to stretch him. In an attempt to tease Daran and regain some control, Kalad started licking Daran's already twitching anus. He turned his head, shooting Kalad a poisonous look.

"If you don't slow down right now, Aegid's going to be the only one to get some loving today."

Under Daran, Aegid began to chuckle, while Kalad pulled back in haste.

"Take your time. Search for my good spot, but only with your fingers. Once you find it, make me feel good."

Kalad nodded and concentrated on Daran's back again. It didn't take him long to find the spot Daran had been talking about. Kalad rubbed it until Daran spilled with a content groan, his lips still fastened to Aegid's. Daran broke contact only for a brief moment, directing another set of orders toward Kalad.

"Fuck me. Do it slowly, with long, deep thrusts."

Panting heavily, Kalad complied. While he took Daran the way he liked it, the Echend'dim reached for Aegid's erection and stroked it in the rhythm of Kalad's thrusts. All three got lost in the game, prey to a lust that was new and exciting, if somewhat wary, for it marked a profound change in their relationship. They were no longer slave and masters; they had become equals all of a sudden, brothers-in-arms. Thinking about the deeper implications of this change was too much to bear at the moment, and so they sealed their still-growing love with carnal sex.

Kalad was the next to release, closely followed by Aegid and Daran. The air was heavy with their scents now, arousing them again almost instantly. Daran turned around, shifting slightly to allow Aegid's still-hard cock to slide into him. He was facing Kalad, who knelt in front of him, waiting to be kissed and caressed like his desert brother. Daran smiled. He enjoyed this game immensely. Having the upper hand was indeed something to be desired. Extending his arm, he gave Kalad permission to come closer. Their lips met and Aegid started moving beneath him. Since he was so big, Daran had to hang on to Kalad to keep his balance. It didn't take long until they reached the greatest heights again, drowning in the ecstasy only they could evoke in each other.

For the better part of the night Kalad and Aegid indulged Daran, doing his bidding even though he was already weakened by their games and, technically, no longer in a position to order them around. When he finally lost consciousness during one especially athletic act, Kalad and Aegid carried the limp Daran to the bath. They washed off the blood of the sisters still clinging to his skin, as well as their own fluids plastering his body like very special markings. Daran didn't wake up once, and so they brought him back to the bed and made themselves comfortable with their precious lover between them. Kalad looked thoughtful while his fingertips drew lazy circles on Daran's chest.

"He's grown into a fine man."

"Indeed he has. Better than us, I'd say."

There was a certain undertone in Aegid's voice that aroused Kalad's suspicion.

"You think we're not good enough for him?"

"We love him more than anything else in the world. I doubt there will ever be somebody who feels deeper for him than we do, so we are good enough. Nevertheless, what he said before, about us being beasts, is not wrong. To call our actions questionable is serious downplaying. And if it weren't for us, he would have never tasted this kind of life."

Kalad frowned. There was just enough truth in Aegid's words to make him uncomfortable.

"If it weren't for us, he would be dead by now."

The two warriors stared at each other over Daran's sleeping form. Introspection had never been their strong point. Only since they had met Daran had they started to reflect on their actions a bit more. Love could be a real bugger sometimes.

"We would have never met him."

Aegid's voice trailed off. The implication alone was enough to make them both miserable. Kalad extended his chin with a determined expression. It wasn't like them to ponder things that could not be changed.

"He's ours. Our reward for being loyal servants to Canubis and Renaldo. Daran was born to spend his life wreathed in our love. Nothing is going to change that."

Aegid grinned broadly. He liked what he heard.

"So we're going to do it?"

"Of course. We've been planning this for months! There's no way we're going to back out now!"

Reassured, the two warriors slung their arms around Daran, sated in the knowledge that he would always be theirs.

NEW PATHS

1. SIRA

Far out in the vastness that was Ana-Raina, the Big Sea, a vortex had formed in which the waters had turned black and seemed to be boiling in some places. In others, it was as hard as the ice on a glacier, under which it was bubbling like lava from a volcano. A closer look revealed that it was not the water that had turned black, but the background that sucked in even the tiniest speck of color. What was growing in the depths of the sea was like a cancer, an unholy, deviant connection between Ana-Darasa and the domain of chaos. Untamed powers were crashing against the dam the Mothers had created to give life a safe place.

The Good Mother smiled coldly. She had chosen this place with meticulous care. Though still unable to take solid form on Ana-Darasa due to the barriers Ana-Isara had placed all over the world, she could feel her powers grow. Now that the Mothers were gone, it was only a question of time until she would be able to break through. The magic stream was strong here, and even though it was already tamed, she could draw enough power to weaken the dam and give chaos a chance. Soon the borders would break under this constant assault, and then she would use it to destroy the sons of her enemies.

Sira was concentrating on a knothole in the ceiling above the bed on which she had been forced. The grunting of the man who had just entered her body in the most brutal manner was deafening. She tried to tell herself that this was nothing, that this business partner of her owner was nothing but a nuisance who would go away if she wished for it hard enough. She could feel him tensing, his movements became more rapid, and then he finally released inside her. Sira hated this man, just like she hated all men. It was an emotion life had taught her in the cruelest way.

Her owner's voice violated the walls of protection she had built around herself. "What do you think? Not too bad, eh?"

The business partner laughed. "She's okay. A bit unresponsive. And even though she's got such a nice face, she doesn't know how to use it. You should train her a little more."

"Don't worry, she's going to learn her lesson soon."

Her owner's voice was now menacing, and Sira shuddered since she knew too well what he had in store for her that very night. Her master wasn't known for his patience. She would bear this lesson like all the ones before and keep on waiting for her chance to either kill this despicable man or herself. By now she was so desperate, she didn't care which happened first.

The business partner was already fully dressed again and threw her one last, taxing look. She was still young; her breasts hadn't reached their full size yet and were pointing upward. Her limbs reminded the onlooker of a boisterous foal and not a grown woman, but there were already hints of the sensual curves she would soon develop. Her hair was short. It had been sheared when she was sold to her current owner. Her skin was of a light bronze tone, and soft with long, thin scars in some places, proof that she had been punished before.

That night, she became intimately acquainted with the small whip, and even though she had sworn not to give in to her tormentor, she begged for mercy in the end. Mercy she had only received after showing what an obedient, subservient slave she was. Now she was lying in the shed her owner called a room, crying and trying to ignore the burning pain of the welts on her back. Unfortunately it seemed as if her suffering wasn't over yet. The door to the shed opened, and one of the men working for her owner dragged her outside.

"Get up, stupid slut. We have customers who wish to inspect the merchandise."

Sira was dressed in a white tunic and brought to the exhibition room. The other slaves were already gathered, standing in a row, not making the slightest sound, their gazes cast downward. The first thing you learned in this man's possession was to show nothing but absolute obedience. Resistance was weeded out without mercy.

After Sira had taken her place, another door opened and her owner entered with two customers. The older of the two was like a bear; he filled the door completely with his powerful frame. His dark skin, the tattoo on his cheek, and his dark aura made Sira shiver. She didn't want to imagine what it meant to be at the mercy of such a brutal man. His companion was almost two heads smaller and by far more likeable. His green-blue eyes sparkled in a friendly way in his open face, and his hair was even shorter than Sira's. The young man stayed close to the massive one who had slung his arm around his shoulder.

"Relax, Sic. We agreed that it's important for you to learn how to choose your own slaves. A lord must be able to do this, as well as teach them respect. The merchandise here is famed for its good training and obedience."

Sira's owner bowed deeply to thank the customer for his praise.

"What does the young master need?"

Out of the corner of her eye, Sira saw Sic looking at his companion for reassurance before he turned to the slave trader.

"I'm looking for a slave who's good with tasks concerning the household and has a gift for needlework."

"Male or female?"

"It doesn't matter. I don't care about the age either. All I need is someone skilled."

The owner made two men and Sira step forward.

"Those two are quite mature, as you can see, but well-versed in all matters concerning the house. The female is still young but good with her hands and can also sweeten your nights. Her training isn't completed yet, but I'm sure a determined young master like yourself should be able to break her in in no time."

Flaming red rushed into the young man's face, and he averted his gaze.

"Thank you, but that won't be necessary."

Again he looked at his companion, who nodded encouragingly. Sic stepped forward to inspect the three slaves. The last one was Sira. With an apologetic smile, he started feeling her body. His hands were muscular and callused. Unlike the regular customers, he seemed to know what hard work meant. He furrowed his brow when Sira flinched as he touched the fresh welts on her back. Abruptly he turned away from her. His voice was raw when he made his decision known.

"I would like to take the woman, Master."

It was a statement that sounded like a question. A gentle smile appeared on the fearsome man's face and made him less intimidating.

"It's your decision, Sic. I think you chose well."

Again the young man blushed, this time not because he was embarrassed but because he was happy about the praise. Sira wondered what kind of relationship those two had. Since she was going to be the younger one's possession, it was a valid question. The companion turned to her former owner.

"You heard his decision. How much?"

Sira barely registered the haggling; she was too occupied with the fact that she had changed owners again. The three men agreed quite fast, and then her new owner led her out into the street. His companion looked at the dawning sun and placed his hand on Sic's nape.

"It's too late to go home now. We'll take a room and ride tomorrow."

"As you wish, Master."

In one of the inns they got a room with two chambers and had their dinner served there. Sira was tense. Until now, neither of the two had spared her more than a casual glance, but she knew this would change once they had sated their hunger. Insecure, she stood a few feet away from the table where the food was. Sic beckoned her closer.

"Please, sit down. You must be hungry and there's plenty. By the way, my name is Sic and this is my Master, Lord Noran."

The respect in Sic's voice told Sira clearer than words who was the dominant one in this relationship. As subserviently as possible, she bowed to this man who would from now on have the last word about how she was treated.

"My name is Sira, Master."

"Fine, Sira. Sit down and eat. Afterwards, you can go to sleep. Tomorrow we'll ride as early as possible. I want to get home."

Sira nodded, still insecure. That didn't sound as if the two men wanted to test their new acquisition this very night. After she had eaten in silence, she hurried to get into bed, not giving the men a chance to change their minds. Even though nothing was asked of her, she couldn't find rest. Her bed was standing at the same wall as that of her new master, and so she could hear every word they spoke.

"You chose her because of the welts, didn't you, my darling?" Noran's voice was deep and gentle.

"Yes, I did. Are you displeased, Master?" Sic sounded strained. It was obvious how important Noran's opinion was to him.

"Of course not. I already told you I would respect your decision. Apart from that, this is not what this was about. The crucial point was that you chose freely and on your own. It's your first step toward becoming a reliable owner. And with time, it'll get easier."

"Was it that obvious?"

"How uncomfortable you were? For me, yes, but I do know you pretty well."

"Master!"

It seemed as if Noran had heightened his words with a gesture, because Sic sounded indignant.

"What, you're not interested?"

A breathless silence followed those words, and Sira didn't have to be a seer to know that they were kissing. When Sic answered, he sounded agitated.

"How can you even ask, Master? You know very well that one look from you is enough to make me burn."

A deep, sensual laugh was the answer, then silence descended once again.

"I know, my precious. Please forgive me for teasing you."

"Already done. And now, please take me before I lose my mind."

It was the last coherent sentence Sic managed to utter. Sira pulled her blanket over her head and tried to ignore the lusty groans and stammered pleas for more. She would have never imagined that those two shared a bed. Of course, she was aware that men could have sex with each other, but her experience in this regard was limited. For her, intimacy was something she abhorred deeply, since it was always connected with force. She thought it almost despicable that Sic and Noran so obviously enjoyed their lovemaking. Still, she was relieved. When her masters had sex with each other, they wouldn't bother her.

"WHY DO I have the impression that you two are up to something?"

Daran shot Aegid and Kalad a suspicious look. Not even a week had passed since the execution and their steamy first night as equals. Since then, they had spent most of their time in bed, trying to find out how to reshape their relationship in order for it to fit their new needs. Daran was happy they had established a balance that allowed him to indulge his newly found dominance when he wanted and, at the same time, preserved the playful connection they'd had before, where Kalad and Aegid spoiled him rotten. Both scenarios had their charm, and getting it all sat well with the predator Daran had discovered inside himself.

He had hoped to go on experimenting this night, but his lovers seemed to have different plans. The room was lit with countless candles throwing flickering shadows on the walls and making the scenes displayed in the tapestries look real. On the table, a sumptuous feast was laid out, and it didn't take Daran long to determine that these were all his favorite things.

The heavy, sweet wine with the dark red color he loved to sip in the evening. Freshly baked bread, still warm by the smell of it, accompanied by a creamy mountain cheese spiced with herbs. A small pot with chicken broth and sour dumplings, and some generous slices of lamb roast. Daran raised a brow.

"What, no red berry cake? You're disappointing me."

Kalad grinned saucily, reached for a plate on a smaller table, and presented it to Daran.

"Ta-da, red berry cake, made according to Gweris's secret recipe. We have it all covered!"

"Which brings us back to my initial question: what are you planning?"

Aegid placed his hands on Daran's shoulders, leading him to the table.

"Let's just say we do plan something, and we need you to be relaxed and in a good mood for it. It's nothing bad, so don't be alarmed."

Daran let himself be seated in front of the mouthwatering meal.

"I hate to point this out, Aegid, but there have been several occasions on which your and my interpretation of 'bad' diverged so vastly, they were almost opposites. So excuse me if I'm a little… wary."

Kalad blew Daran a kiss across the table.

"We do excuse. Nevertheless, it would be nice if you could trust us a little. We're pretty sure you're going to like this."

With a sigh, Daran admitted defeat. Whatever they were planning, it would happen anyway, judging from their determined body language. He might as well enjoy the food first and face the future with a full stomach.

Dinner reminded Daran of the time right after he had come to the Valley. Kalad and Aegid fed him the best pieces of every course, offering him the wine so often he soon started feeling dizzy. They pampered him as if they were courting him again, and when Aegid presented him the first bite of the cake, Daran finally realized that this was their intent—to woo him. He shook off the dizziness from the wine and glared at them.

"What unspeakable evil do you want to try out in bed?"

Dumbfounded, Aegid and Kalad stared at Daran, unsure whether they should laugh about his assumption or be offended because he had interrupted the mood. They decided to take it from the funny side and broke out in roaring laughter.

"What do you think of us?" Kalad managed to sound wounded.

"It doesn't matter what I think of you. I've been with you long enough to know my suspicion is well-grounded."

"Point taken. Although I wish to stress that we have become quite harmless under your influence. As for the evil bed thing—we do have some ideas we wish to discuss with you sometime soon, but this is not the reason for our hard work tonight."

Aegid gestured vaguely toward the table.

"No, we want something entirely different from you, something we have been thinking about for some time. Will you listen?"

Sensing how serious his normally carefree lovers had gotten, Daran nodded. He couldn't think of anything important enough to rile them up like this, and so his curiosity got the better of him.

"Of course I'll listen. I always do, in case you haven't noticed."

Kalad got up from his chair and stepped next to Aegid, his lively brown eyes trained on Daran like a hunting falcon's. He took Daran's left hand in both his own while Aegid did the same with the right hand. Kalad started to speak.

"I think you already know how much we love you. Words are too weak to describe the emotions you evoke in us. From the moment we met you, our relationship was special. You accept us as the unity we are, and not even once did you try to pry Aegid and me apart. How you do this, how you manage to love us both equally, we don't know and will probably never understand. What we do understand is that you're a gift from the Mothers, and we have every intention of keeping you forever."

"What Kalad wants to say is that we would be deeply honored if you chose to tie yourself to us officially."

Daran gaped at his lovers. It took him some time to get his composure back.

"We're talking about marriage here, aren't we? I just don't want to get this wrong."

Kalad kissed Daran's hand reverently.

"We are. And we would be beyond happy if you would accept our proposal."

Daran felt tears streaming down his cheeks. He had trouble speaking clearly so that his lovers could understand him.

"Why do you even ask? Of course I accept. You two are my everything. The center of my being. So yes. Yes. I do want to be yours forever."

For an eternity hidden between heartbeats, the three men stared at each other, savoring a love that had stopped asking questions and harboring doubts and was now mature and invincible. It was a fleeting moment, yet it cemented a relationship that was meant to face the centuries.

Kalad broke the spell with a grin and a deep kiss on Daran's mouth.

"I guess this means we're officially engaged now." Aegid's voice boomed with pride. Daran pulled him closer and kissed him as well.

"Could be you're right."

He made a face.

"That's a mouthful. Engaged. Almost as big a chunk as 'married.'"

"We'll get to that soon enough. What do you think about a winter ceremony?"

Kalad looked eager; he didn't want to lose any time. Daran could hardly suppress his chuckle.

"Winter sounds good to me. Anything sounds good to me. As long as you two are there, I don't care when and where the ceremony is held."

"That's good to know. We've already done some preparations, but there are a few things we would like to discuss with you first."

Aegid, too, sounded eager. Daran got up from his chair, his tongue wetting his lips in an almost unconscious movement.

"You've just proposed to me in the sweetest of manners, and now you want to discuss wedding details? I thought you'd take me to the bed for sure. You know—to celebrate."

Growls emanated from Aegid's and Kalad's throats. Plain hunger lit their features, making them look like a pair of starved wolves. Kalad grabbed Daran's wrists while Aegid embraced him from behind. His voice was guttural and reminded Daran of a beast.

"You want to celebrate? Then let's celebrate until you can't remember your name."

With a contented sigh, Daran abandoned himself to his future husbands' lust.

"SIRA! HEY, Sira! Would you be so kind as to listen to what I have to say?"

The biting sarcasm in Gweris's voice pried Sira from her musings. Since it wasn't a good idea to make Gweris mad, Sira hurried to apologize.

"Please forgive me, Gweris. I was distracted."

"That much I realized."

Gweris regarded her latest charge with worry. Sira was the first slave Lord Sic had bought by himself, and it was important for Sic's further development as a lord of the Valley that everything went smoothly. He was still terribly insecure about how to handle his slaves, and that he was now living with Lord Noran had only worsened the situation. Even though the slaves had been anxious to fulfill their tasks since Sic and Noran moved in together, they still lacked respect for their lord. Their sudden obedience stemmed from fear of Lord Noran, whose strictness was almost as legendary as that of Lord Renaldo.

Gweris had taken over the task of helping Sic after Lord Casto had asked her to, and she had managed to discipline them quite well, but true respect was something different. The main problem was not Sic's own past as a slave, but his lack of rigor. He was gentleness personified and had never learned to impose his will. Gweris had hoped Lord Noran would influence him in a positive way, but instead of taking his lover as an example, Sic had left all business regarding the slaves to Noran. After she had watched for some time, Gweris had decided to put her foot down. Luckily, Lord Noran shared her worries, and so they had resolved that Sic had to learn how to behave like a true Emeris. The outcome of their efforts was this young woman who rarely went to the trouble of concealing her displeasure about being a slave. On the contrary, she seemed to be getting more recalcitrant with every passing day. The entire situation was undesirable, and Gweris already regretted the path she and Noran had chosen.

"Would you please pay attention? Lord Sic may be a lenient master, but that doesn't mean you have to test his patience to the limit. If you go too far, you'll have to answer to Lord Noran, and I do hope that even so foolish a creature as you would have figured out by now how incredibly stupid that is."

Sira blanched in anger. She hated that Gweris was bossing her around, always trying to make her a model slave in the name of the precious Lord Sic, who was the most indifferent master she had ever met.

"I don't have to listen to you!"

Gweris sighed. She was getting weary of Sira's constant obstinacy, so her voice had a steely undertone.

"Yes, you do! And I'd advise you to listen closely. I'm responsible for you, and I'm fed up with listening to your whining and effrontery."

"Are you trying to frighten me? You're a mere slave yourself! You can't threaten me!"

"She can."

Both women spun around when they heard these words. Gweris immediately curtsied, but Sira could only stand there and gape with her mouth hanging open. The man standing in front of her was simply awesome. His wheat-blond hair was tied up in a ponytail, his mesmerizing blue eyes were piercing her, and his noble face showed the first signs of anger.

"Apparently this slave doesn't know the simplest rules of courtesy, Gweris."

Gweris rammed her elbow into Sira's ribs.

"Please forgive me, Lord Casto. She's new and inexperienced. I didn't have the chance to show her all the lords in the Valley."

"It's fine, Gweris. I know you're doing your best. This is the slave Sic has bought?"

"Unfortunately, yes."

Hearing those two talk about her as if she were nothing but a puppy that had still to be trained made Sira seethe with anger.

"Stop talking as if I'm not even here! And just for the record, I would have preferred not to be bought by your precious Lord Sic. I'm nobody's property."

Panting, Sira stared at Gweris and Casto. The man looked back at her, his gaze drilling into her very being, sorting through her mind like a merchant would go through his goods and then throw away most of the bits with a certain disdain. Sira felt completely naked and humiliated by his stare, especially since she wasn't able to read anything from him. Only one thing was for sure: angering this man was even dumber than defying Lord Noran. Casto radiated something she couldn't name, danger paired with intransigence and spiced with a hint of sorrow that made shivers run down her spine. Sira was just about to bow to this intimidating man when he suddenly started to laugh. It was a mocking guffaw that made her tense up again.

"She sounds a little bit like me back in the day, don't you think so, Gweris?"

The slave started laughing as well.

"She does, my lord." Then Gweris turned serious. "But she's not you, and if she goes on like this, Lord Sic will be troubled."

The amusement vanished from Casto's face. Again he sized Sira up.

"Gweris is right. I'm expecting you to show more effort from now on. It's important for Sic."

For a moment, Sira didn't know what to say. She felt the anger inside her bubbling up like water in a cauldron, and she let it erupt.

"I couldn't care less even if he grieved himself to death."

Sira only needed a heartbeat to realize she had gone too far. Lord Casto's eyes darkened like the sky before a storm, and his voice was steely. While one part of Sira froze in terror, another cheered her on into destruction. After all, what did she have to lose?

"That's enough. You're coming with me."

Casto reached for Sira's arm, and she felt all her reason drowning in anger and despair. Never again would she allow anybody to push her around or give her commands. Her hand shot upward and left three bloody welts on Lord Casto's flawless skin.

The deed was followed by a breathless, bewildered silence that was finally broken by a furious roar. Sira was grabbed and flung away from Casto with brute force. She landed heavily on her back, her arm hurting as if it had been burned.

"How dare you?"

Sira stared into the face of a man who was even more regal than Casto. She had been in the Valley for only three days, but she already knew whom she was facing. In reality, the Angel of Death was even more intimidating than in all the stories she had heard about him. And his anger was aimed at her. His gaze didn't allow so much as blinking on her part, and his voice sounded flat, as if he was restraining himself with all his might.

"Gweris, go and get Sic. Right now!"

"Yes, my lord."

Gweris bowed and hurried to fulfill the Angel of Death's command. He reached for Casto, who stepped forward into his arms. Renaldo tried to inspect the wound, but Casto shook him off.

"It's just a scratch, Barbarian, nothing big."

"This may be the case, but I'm not going to accept it—not even when it's about Sic. Especially not when it's about Sic. He has to learn how to deal with this kind of situation."

Frozen in terror, Sira waited for her owner to appear. She didn't have to be a seer to know she was in deep trouble now. What she had done was a capital offense that justified killing her, and the way Lord Renaldo was sizing her up didn't bode well for her future.

Finally Gweris returned with Sic. The young Emeris looked from Renaldo to Casto and back to Sira with worry in his eyes.

"My lord. Casto. What has happened?"

Renaldo stared at him coldly.

"Your slave has shown improper behavior. She dared to raise her hand against my heart. I expect a fitting reaction from you. An offense like that must be punished severely."

Sic blanched.

"I apologize for Sira's behavior, my lord. Casto, I'm truly sorry. Please tell me how I can reimburse you for this incident."

Casto's stern features softened considerably and gave Sira some hope.

"It's fine, Sic. She's new, so I'm willing to let it slide."

With a grateful smile, Sic bowed to Casto. Then he turned to Renaldo, whose face showed no sign of forgiving. Sira's heart sank.

"I won't let you get off so lightly. I demand that you punish this slave according to her crime."

"My lord, please. Sira has come to the Valley only a few days ago. She has yet to learn the consequences of her actions and the rules governing our lives."

"Ignorance doesn't protect from punishment. Besides, I haven't gotten the impression that she would have acted differently if she had known who Casto is. Take care of this mess, Sic. It's your responsibility."

Renaldo grabbed Casto's hand and led him away from the scene.

For a moment, absolute silence ruled while Sic stared into nothing. Then a determined line appeared on his lips and he held out his hand to Sira.

"Come."

His tone was unrelenting, with a hint of resignation. Insecure, Sira got up and followed her owner back to his chambers. Nobody had to spell out to her that the lenience Sic had shown until now was coming to its end. Now that she had calmed down, she realized how incredibly stupid she had been. It was one thing to be obstinate against being a slave, and an entirely different one to challenge a man like Lord Renaldo, who was rumored to be a demigod in addition to being the most powerful and fearsome warlord on the continent. She had dug her own grave, and lowered her head in anticipation of her punishment. To her surprise, Sic didn't beat her, but started talking in a monotone.

"Casto is my best friend. At a time when I deserved death for what I had done and hated myself to the bone, he reached out for me and bestowed the mercy of his forgiveness on me. Everything I am, I owe to him, and you just hurt and insulted this incredibly precious person."

Sic paused, his gaze focused on something only he could see. Sira shuddered, for she hardly recognized the man standing in front of her. Normally Sic radiated innocence and friendliness, so much that he bordered on being a pushover. Sira had secretly labeled him as a harmless puppy, unable to do any damage. Now he seemed threatening and distant, no longer the Sic who had bought her but somebody else, somebody she shouldn't mess with. It was as if he had taken off a mask, a thin veneer that hid something even more frightening than the Angel of Death was. That Sic himself was afraid of this other creature as well didn't help at all.

"I chose you because I felt pity for you. You reminded me of myself, and I had the feeling I could pay back some of the good that happened to me by taking you. Apparently, you're not keen on being saved."

When Sira opened her mouth to answer, Sic raised his hand.

"I'm well aware of how undesirable it is to lead a life in slavery. But even the wish for freedom should be guided by some decency. If you can't accept me as your master, fine. I'm not even asking for gratitude because I saved you from your owner, since I'm well aware that this was my own decision. What I do ask of you is some respect. Not as your master, but as a fellow human being who has done you a favor. I also don't think the work you have to do is hard enough to merit complaint. You have consciously spurned my outstretched hand, yet I'm still willing to leave you a choice. You have till tomorrow to decide whether you want to serve me. Should you think you can do it, I'm going to punish you, and then we'll forget about this whole incident. Should you feel you can't give me the respect I do expect from you as your owner, then I won't insist on you staying here and will return you to your former master. It's your decision."

With this ultimatum hanging in the air, Sic left his slave alone.

MEANWHILE, CASTO was glaring at Renaldo, who pretended to be unaware of his lover's foul mood.

"Isn't it a fine day? Too warm for the season, but definitely nice."

A low growl escaped from Casto's throat.

"Stop it, Barbarian. You know damn well that I'm not in the mood for chitchat."

Renaldo sighed. He'd known Casto long enough to tell from his tone alone that this was going to be nasty. Unwilling to give in, Renaldo faced the storm.

"I am aware, Casto. And we've been through this before. Sic has to learn to embrace his new status, otherwise he's useless to us. Even Daran is more of a lord than Sic, and he's had less time to get used to it."

"Daran is a completely different case and you know it! I'm talking about you ruining all our efforts just because you felt like making a point."

"Hah, what efforts? Are you talking about the heroic deed of buying a slave with the aid of Noran? Or are you referring to Sic's absolute inability to keep order among his servants? No matter how I look at it, he hasn't made any progress at all. I've been very patient until now, but this woman has hurt you, and that is definitely his responsibility!"

"It was just a scratch, nothing near as bad as what you've done to me, and it healed almost immediately, so don't even think about using this as an excuse for your irrational behavior. Sic is on the right path, but he needs time, not a pushy god who teases him whenever he feels like it."

"You just mentioned the key word here, Casto. I'm his god. Of course he has to do whatever I want when I feel like it. Just like you. Just like everybody."

Renaldo and Casto were standing so close, their noses were almost touching. Much to Renaldo's dismay and secret thrill, Casto didn't budge in the least. He neither lowered his gaze nor reined his tone in. Fearless in the face of absolute power, Casto still spoke his mind.

"Never! I may accept you as my lover, but I will never be your servant. And stop pushing Sic or I may contemplate leaving you again. Just to get *my* point across."

Abruptly, Casto turned around and stormed off in the direction of the stables. Renaldo had to suppress the urge to run after him and beat him up. Nothing would come of it anyway.

2. DECISIONS

Sira was trembling all over. When Sic had given her the ultimatum so relentlessly, she had realized for the first time that he, too, was a lord of the Valley and could act accordingly. That his words had also hit the mark didn't make it better. Shuddering, Sira decided to get some fresh air to put her thoughts in order. Deep down she knew she had no choice, because there was no way she would ever return to her old life.

She wandered around aimlessly until she beheld a man cleaning a horse in the vicinity of the stables. The animal had its eyes closed and was clearly enjoying the caress. When she regarded the man more closely, Sira realized how handsome he was. His long black hair was hanging over his shoulder in a thick braid, and his finely sculpted upper body gleamed in the sun like polished bronze. He was wearing two golden bracers with emeralds on his arms, and another emerald was resting in the dent where his collarbones met, right under his chin. It was held by a thin golden necklace that was close enough to his throat to give the impression of a collar. The man was talking to the horse in a low drone Sira couldn't understand, but she felt herself relaxing while watching the peaceful scene. Suddenly the man turned around and looked at her. He must have felt her stare at his back, yet he still smiled politely with only a hint of mockery. If he thought her behavior to be rude, he hid it well.

"Do you need something?"

Slowly, Sira approached. Her tumultuous emotions made her blurt out a question before her brain had the chance to filter the words.

"Are you a slave?"

Taken aback, the man dropped the brush he had been holding. After retrieving it, he smiled at Sira again, this time with open challenge. There was no doubting it, he was enjoying himself.

"You could call me that."

Determined to get to the point without letting his attitude get to her, Sira pressed on.

"Do you like it?"

Now the man was grinning.

"Of course I like it. It's the best thing that's ever happened to me. I mean, look at me. When my owners found me, I was a luckless thief on his way to the gallows. Now I'm a splendidly dressed, well-fed, and deeply loved man. I'll never be able to repay their generosity."

Sira's eyes widened. She had trouble believing his words. All the slaves she had met had been miserable.

"Are all slaves in the Valley like you?"

"Most certainly not. Most of them long for their freedom, but I'm not like them. I'm leading a good life and have no reason to complain. Are you asking me because of your master? Whom do you serve?"

"I belong to Lord Sic."

The young man stared at her in disbelief.

"And you're dissatisfied? I dare say you've won big. There's no lord in the Valley who's gentler and kinder than Sic."

"This may be the case." Sira hesitated. "How long have you been here? Do you know Lord Sic well?"

"I've been living in the Valley for some years. Sic was already here when I came. Lord Noran bought him from a brutal drunkard when he was still a boy and made him his personal slave. He had to endure a lot before he rose to the rank of Emeris."

"Lord Sic was a slave?" Sira couldn't hide her surprise.

"You didn't know? I'd thought this would be the first thing the other slaves told you."

"No, they didn't. But it explains a lot."

"What did you do?" The young man's voice was so casual and relaxed, Sira didn't even think about not answering him.

"I have humiliated Lord Sic in front of the Angel of Death and a man named Lord Casto. He was very angry."

The young man whistled.

"Sounds really bad. Be grateful that Noran doesn't know of it, otherwise your skin would be in scraps by now."

When she heard those words, Sira started feeling uneasy. Since she didn't want to go back to her old master, she would have to endure the punishment Sic imposed on her. That the terrifying Lord Noran would have a say in it horrified her.

"When Lord Sic punishes somebody, how bad does it get?"

The young man shrugged.

"I don't know. You'd be the first. As I said, he's a very gentle man who forgives generously. Some time ago I made a mistake regarding him, but he relinquished punishing me even though I deserved it."

"You forgot to mention that we made you bleed for it."

The two men approaching them seemed highly amused. The smaller one, especially, looked as if he was going to burst with laughter at any minute. He extended his arm and the slave stepped forward to receive a kiss on his mouth. The other warrior stepped closer also, with a mocking glint in his eyes. After he had kissed the slave as well, he held up his index finger as if he wanted to scold the young man.

"If you have time to dally with slave girls, you better hurry back to our chambers."

Laughing, the slave took the lord's hand and kissed it. He wasn't impressed by the stern words.

"Whenever I go there, you take me until I'm completely exhausted. As much as I love our trysts, I do have some responsibilities besides you, so it's more than enough when I go back in the evening."

"Come on, we'll behave! Besides, we have a wedding to plan, and we can't do that without you."

The smaller warrior slung his arms around the slave's hips, caressing him between the legs. Sira's presence didn't faze him at all; he was too engrossed in touching his slave. The young man retreated with a gleam in his eyes that betrayed the resistance he was faking.

"I understand. Let me get Rajan back, and then I'm yours all day."

"A tempting offer." The bigger warrior stepped back, dragging the smaller one with him. "Come on, Kalad. The sooner you let Daran go, the sooner we can indulge ourselves."

Kalad let go of Daran. Plain hunger was written all over his face. While he reached for the horse's bridle, Daran addressed Sira once more.

"If I were you, I'd apologize to Lord Sic and accept the punishment. Knowing him, whatever verdict he speaks is probably still too lenient, given what you've done. Please excuse me now. As you can see, I've got my own problems to deal with."

Kalad snorted. "Don't act all innocent here! I wonder what this slave would think about you if she could see your shameless behavior in bed."

Heat flushed Daran's cheeks and made him even more attractive.

"And who made me so shameless? I wasn't born like that. There were two smooth desert warriors who turned me into someone who can outdo even the most experienced courtesan."

The two warriors took Daran in their arms, their faces suddenly serious.

"You do know you're our most precious treasure, don't you? We won't allow anybody to talk about you like that, not even yourself."

Daran patted the warriors' arms in a soothing manner.

"I know. It sounded worse than I intended. Let's go before one of us starts crying."

Grinning, the warriors slung their arms around Daran's hips and led him away, Rajan trailing behind them like a lost puppy.

"WHAT HAVE you done now?"

Gweris's dry voice pried Sira from her trance. Guiltily, she turned to the older woman, whose eyes showed a gentleness Sira hadn't anticipated.

"I haven't done anything. At least, I don't think so. I just wanted to talk to that slave, but when his masters appeared, he was distracted."

A grin flashed over Gweris's lips.

"That's normal—they can't get enough of Daran. And he's not a slave, by the way. He's Lord Daran, the first Echend'dim, and soon he'll also be the husband of the Lords Aegid and Kalad."

Sira's eyes widened in shock. So she had made a mistake again.

"I asked him if he was a slave and he said yes! Why did he lie to me?"

Gweris sighed. How should she explain a relationship as complicated as Daran's with the desert warriors to somebody who rejected the mere idea of slavery out of habit?

"He didn't lie to you. Not really. When he came to the Valley, he was indeed their slave. They had acquired him in Kwarl. As it turned out, he wasn't the only one who got enslaved back then. These three are so close, it doesn't matter if the chains they're bound with are visible or not."

Even though Sira had thought Daran to be handsome, she suddenly felt repelled by him.

"How can anybody fall in love with the person who enslaved them?" Gweris patted Sira's shoulder.

"You'd be surprised. Now tell me, why are you out here, unscathed, when Lord Renaldo made it clear that he wanted your blood?"

Sira hung her head.

"I have till tomorrow. I've to decide whether I want to serve Lord Sic or go back to my former owner. Which I won't. Never. So I guess I have to bear whatever is coming."

"Lord Sic is a good man. He won't hurt you more than absolutely necessary. He doesn't take pleasure from cruelty."

"I know. I still don't like it. If you would leave me alone now? I have a lot to think about."

With another deep sigh, Gweris complied. She could relate to Sira's feelings, although she wasn't able to completely understand them. Gweris was the kind of person who always made the best out of a situation. Sira's focus on how miserable she was annoyed the older slave, especially since an owner like Sic made it easy for any slave to have a good life. Apparently there was no helping some people.

SIC STARED at the crouching figure of Sira with a certain reluctance and a feeling of fatalism. He had spent a long, unpleasant night learning from Noran how to wield a whip to cause suitable pain without inflicting too much damage. Since he couldn't ask Noemi to heal Sira after the punishment—Renaldo had been crystal clear about that—he would try to keep the worst from her. Of course, Noran didn't understand at all. He even offered to do the punishing himself, but Sic declined. This was his problem. He had chosen Sira and neglected his duties as her owner. As much as he wished he could turn his back on the situation and leave it all to Noran, he knew he had to face it. In the back of his mind, Sic was already toying with an idea to solve the whole slave-keeping conundrum, but before he could exercise it, he had to get through the punishing first.

"So you've made up your mind?"

"Yes, Master. I wish to remain in your service, and I apologize for my behavior."

Sic sighed. Sira sounded surprisingly sincere, but since she had no real choice, it was not exactly a revelation.

"I accept your apology. I do have to punish you, though. Get up, undress, and put your hands against the wall."

Sira did as she was told. When she turned around, she caught a glimpse of Sic's face. Her master was absolutely miserable, and for the first time in her life, Sira understood what it meant to hurt somebody. Sic clearly hated what he was about to do. Sira shuddered. She had forced his hand, had made him do something that went against his very nature. Tears pricked the corners of her eyes.

"I'm so sorry."

A weak smile appeared on Sic's lips.

"Me too. Let's get this over with."

3. WEDDING PLANS

"Casto, Sic, I need your help."

Daran was sitting with the other two men on the south wall of the stables, enjoying the relative heat of the midday sun. The first snow was covering the Valley two ells high, and the cold air hurt in the lungs. Winter had successfully claimed the North again.

"Are you talking about the wedding?"

Casto shifted his weight slightly to stay in the middle of the sun's rays. As always when the cold season began, he was in a foul mood. By now Daran had learned to ignore Casto's temper and just act as if nothing were amiss.

"What else should I be talking about? It's in four weeks, and Aegid and Kalad are driving me nuts."

"Get used to it. I wanted to throttle Renaldo during the last few weeks before we married. Sometimes I wonder if that wouldn't have been for the better."

The speculative tone made Daran shiver. He never knew when Casto was serious and when he was just joking. Sic came to the rescue.

"It's fine, Daran. You can always put it down to nerves. They are simply thrilled to make your relationship official. As for you, Casto, stop adding to Daran's tension. You enjoyed your wedding, I know it."

"The wedding, yes. We were talking about the time before. And that, I hated. It was plain horrible."

Sic punched Casto playfully on his upper arm, then focused on Daran again.

"What do you need from us? Your wedding jewelry is almost finished, so what else can I do for you?"

"It's about my present for Aegid and Kalad. I don't have any money, but I don't want to stand in front of them empty-handed."

"Oh no!" Sic groaned, clapping his hands over his head.

"I'm not going to make another branding iron. It was bad enough doing it for Casto. What is it with you guys, that you always resort to drastic measures?"

Casto laughed, not entirely amused.

"It's our nature. Otherwise we wouldn't be able to bear our lovers."

"Whoever said I wanted a branding iron? I'm not completely insane."

"Hey, that hurt! I'm not insane either. Just firm in my convictions."

"Stop it, you two! As for you, Casto, I think we can all agree that your stubbornness is close enough to insanity to make them indistinguishable. Daran, if you don't want an iron, how can we help you?"

Daran fidgeted a little, clearly embarrassed by his request.

"I don't want a branding, I want a tattoo. I already have a vague idea about the design, but I need your help to make it look good. Please?"

Sic patted Daran encouragingly. "No problem, I'm glad to help you. A tattoo is definitely better than a branding iron. Is Frankus going to do it?"

Daran nodded, oozing relief. "Yes, I already talked to him. I wasn't sure if it would even work, because of the whole Echend'dim thing, but apparently, tattoos are possible. Frankus has done one for Wolfstan when he married Hulda. He said he could do a design for me as well, but after we discussed it in detail, we agreed it would be better if you did it. Our connection is deeper."

Silence followed those words. Neither Sic nor Daran were keen on talking about the consequences of what had happened in Kwarl. It had been too disturbing. The one thing they couldn't deny was the link they shared now. It was not conscious, but on a feral level, they were able to feel each other. It was the same with Lukan, who tried to ignore it as well. Soon they would have to talk it out, since it was significant, but none of them was yet ready to face those depths. Sensing that the situation was becoming awkward, Casto barged in.

"If you have the design and the tattooist covered, what do you need me for?"

"You're going to be my cover. Getting the tattoo will take three to four days. Since it's meant as a surprise, I'll get it right before the wedding."

Casto's brows furrowed. It wasn't clear whether he was amused or annoyed.

"You need me to deceive them, don't you?"

"I bow to your wisdom, Your Majesty."

Casto shot Daran a nasty look that warned him not to take this joke further. Even though he appeared unwilling, he was already pondering the problem. Casto had never had friends before. The experience was new and exciting for him, although he would never admit it openly. Helping Daran just because he liked him, and not for some twisted, hidden agenda, made Casto happy.

"I'll come up with something. They're not going to like it, though."

Daran sighed. "I know. But the outcome is worth the trouble, or so I hope."

"Then let's get to work and create something outrageous!"

Sic sounded enthusiastic, dragging Daran behind him as if he were a little child. Casto waved them goodbye, glad that he could now occupy the entire bench.

"WHAT IS it you wish to discuss with me, brother?"

Renaldo took a sip from the wine Canubis had offered him and sat back in his chair. Canubis was still standing, seemingly in two minds whether he should get some wine as well. In the end, he sat down without the wine but with a weary expression instead.

"Are you still pondering our next campaign?" Renaldo sounded disbelieving. He wasn't used to a hesitating Canubis.

"Yes, I am. I'm still not sure if we should take it on."

"What's there to be unsure about? Elgir told us that he learned his tricks from a rebel group in the Dark Forest. Queen Xe'lien wants us to hunt down a rebellious splinter group in the same area. The chances that they are one and the same are quite high, which means we get paid for indulging in personal revenge. And even if they aren't, we have free range within the forest to find our target. I really don't understand where the problem is."

"I do admit it fits neatly and suits our needs perfectly. Except for one thing—it's going to be a guerilla war. You know they can drag on endlessly. We might be stuck in the East for the next five or six years, depending on the contract. Since Xe'lien is no fool, she will see to it that we can't back out before we've done a thorough job."

Renaldo made a grunting sound. Canubis's worries were well-grounded. The Dark Forest stretched seemingly endlessly between the northeastern plains and the fertile lands of the East. The Umman had its source somewhere in the northern part, where the forest covered the flanks of the Wolf Mountains. In countless little streams, some of them underground, the water flowed through the forest until it reached the southwestern end, where it united into one huge river that was the source of life for the entire continent.

It was a huge area where it was easy to hide. Even if the rebels didn't have any military training—and chances were they had—they could easily withstand the Pack. The question was whether they could afford being stuck in the East for so long.

Renaldo drained his cup. "It's a wager, but I don't think we have a choice. The magic Elgir used to disguise himself was strong. He didn't have any talent, so whoever gave him the power must have known what they were doing and why. I don't like the idea of somebody as dangerous as that lurking at our back."

"Neither do I. Still, I don't like it. I can feel the Good Mother's strength growing. Being scattered throughout the Dark Forest to end a guerilla war isn't an ideal tactical position."

"I agree. But even though the Good Mother is becoming more powerful, she's still unable to strike. Until now, she had to resort to schemes to fight us, and we have all the Emeris and our hearts. She's undoubtedly gathering her troops, but like us, it will take her time. And the Dark Forest is one of her strongholds. If we obliterate it, we have the advantage."

"I never thought I'd say this, but from a tactical point of view, you're right, little brother. We have to go."

"I'll just pretend I didn't hear the condescending part of your words and agree with you, big brother. You'll see, it's going to be fun."

Canubis made a face.

"It's going to be tiresome, running around in the woods, chasing shadows, looking out for the next ambush while catching the rebels one by one. I hate guerilla warfare! Speaking of which," Canubis reached for the wine, "how is your mate doing?"

Now it was Renaldo's turn to make a face. Casto was a sore point at the moment.

"It has started to snow, so his mood swings have taken a turn for the worse. He doesn't like it when he freezes."

"You're finding excuses for him again. Are you still fighting?"

"You mean the big one from last week? We resolved that, more or less. We had some intense fun last night, so I think he has forgiven me."

Canubis grunted. He didn't like how Casto played Renaldo.

"You should teach him some manners, brother. He's getting out of hand."

Renaldo leaned back in his seat. It was a difficult topic, made worse by the fact that Canubis was right. If Casto didn't learn to bow to their will, he could quickly become a curse for the Pack.

"How should I do that? I don't have your authority, and even if I did, I promised not to use my divine powers to subjugate him. If I ever do, he probably won't forgive me. You've seen what he's capable of. I want him on our side, wholeheartedly."

"I do as well. You know I like him. But he's too dangerous at the moment. You have to find a way, brother, or else he has the potential to blow up in our faces. Knowing him, he'll choose the most inconvenient moment as well."

The divine brothers shared a grim smile. Having somebody like Casto in their ranks sure kept things interesting. To lighten the mood, Renaldo addressed another, equally important but far less explosive topic.

"What are you going to give Aegid, Kalad, and Daran for their wedding?"

"First I thought I'd go with something kinky, knowing Aegid's and Kalad's preferences, but that wouldn't be fair to Daran. He already has his hands full without me adding to the burden."

The mocking smile playing around Canubis's lips betrayed the care he pretended to have.

"You just want your first Echend'dim to be able to walk properly, that's all."

"You got me there. In my defense, I have to say that I also want to strengthen his position in the Pack. So I decided to make him rich."

Renaldo grinned.

"We're definitely brothers. I was thinking the same. So the little thief is going to be a rich mercenary soon."

Canubis nodded. He liked how his and his brother's minds were getting more and more attuned. It was a good sign.

"Rich and powerful indeed. Speaking of which, how is Sic doing?"

Renaldo made a face. The Luksari was another sore topic he'd rather avoid.

"Not well. I'm starting to have doubts whether he will ever be able to become a true lord of the Valley. He's too hesitant and way too soft."

"He did punish that female, though. The one who hurt Casto."

"Yes, but only because I pressured him. Afterward, he set her free. Now she's working for him for money! Can you imagine that? Noran told me Sic is thinking about doing the same with his other slaves."

Canubis sighed. This was indeed unheard of—yet it suited the Luksari.

"He can do that. It's his right as their owner. And perhaps it's for the best. If he's truly unable to become a master, it's probably better for him to pursue different paths."

"Since when are you so lenient, brother?"

Canubis regarded Renaldo with half-closed eyes.

"You know why. We can't afford to lose Sic, it's as simple as that. And we know next to nothing about his true nature, except that he's able to intimidate even the Mothers. If keeping him means making a few minor concessions, I'll gladly do that. So far we have only two Echend'dim. Once the Good Mother has reached her full power, we're going to need a lot more."

"I know, brother. I know. I share your worries. So we leave him be for now."

Renaldo took another deep sip from the excellent wine. Things were progressing fast, and he was not sure whether he should desire or dread the speed with which they were moving toward the end. To get his mind off such gloomy thoughts, he turned back to the most pleasant topic at the moment.

"Daran is planning something interesting for the wedding, or so Casto has told me. I think we can look forward to another gripping ceremony."

The grin the divine brothers shared now was tinged with unbridled joy. Seeing their oldest companions finally claiming the reward for their loyalty made the gods of war happy.

"TELL ME again who had this stupid idea?"

Daran spoke the words between labored intakes of breath while Frankus calmly tattooed him with a needle made of blue steel and a green ink he had concocted just for this occasion. Casto only smiled at him, full of malicious joy, while Sic used a wet towel to wipe the sweat from Daran's face.

"It's fine, Daran. This is one of the worst places, and I'm almost done there."

Frankus sounded a little absentminded. He was concentrating on the pattern he had to inject into Daran's skin.

The Echend'dim groaned. "You've said so before. Twice, if I recall correctly. Damn, this really hurts!"

"Of course it does. But look at it this way. It's meant to be a proof of your undying love for Kalad and Aegid. If you didn't feel any pain obtaining it, it would be meaningless, am I right?"

There was a hint of sadism in Frankus's voice, proof that he enjoyed torturing Daran at least a little bit. Now he looked imperiously at Casto.

"I need more ink, Your Majesty."

Casto rolled his eyes and shot Frankus a warning glance but did his bidding nevertheless. They had been holed up in this little cave deep in the southern part of the forest for two days now. Although the four of them would have preferred leaving the Valley to find an inn where they could stay for the next three days, they had finally settled for this cold, damp place inside the Valley instead. Convincing Renaldo, Kalad, and Aegid to let them leave had proven impossible. Casto's initial reasoning—that Daran wanted to spend the days before the wedding with his friends in order to get a clear head for the ceremony—had met with a surprising amount of understanding from the three warriors. It was the "not staying in reach" part that had almost turned into a catastrophe. Sic had finally managed to negotiate this compromise, since Casto had refused to talk to Renaldo anymore—or Aegid and Kalad, for that matter. Since the desert brothers were notoriously nosy, they couldn't stay in one of the houses of the mercenaries, or even the sheds that were scattered around the Valley. At first they had made jokes about this being a great adventure out in the "wild," but now, Casto was convinced he would never feel warm for the rest of his life. Winter was upon the Valley, with all the drawbacks it always brought. There was simply not enough firewood in the world to get the cave warm.

He retrieved another bottle of ink from Frankus's saddlebags, glad they would be going back to the comfort and warmth of brick-built rooms tomorrow. Until then, Daran still had some pain to endure. Even Casto had to admit that the image Sic had designed was stunning, the only problem being its size. It was a tree with three roots whose tips started at the highest points of Daran's hipbones and right above his penis, meeting about two fingers under his navel, where they intertwined into a trunk that spread into a tree crown at the tip of his breastbone and reached as far as half a hand below his collarbone. As beautiful as the tattoo was, getting it was agony. Listening to Daran's pained intakes of breath and hissed curses when Frankus hit an extra-sensitive patch of skin had made Casto grateful for the probably more brutal but a lot quicker sting of the branding iron.

The only thing he truly enjoyed were their evenings together. Sitting around the fire with men he had come to call friends was a novel experience for Casto, as well as the conversations they had. Being this intimate in a nonsexual way with anybody besides the Barbarian made Casto nervous and wary and, at the same time, thrilled. He was still careful about what he revealed to the others; nevertheless, he reveled in their trust. The part of him that still thought like an Ummanian politician marveled at how easily Sic, Daran, and Frankus revealed information that could be used against them at any time, until he suddenly realized this was another, subtle way of strengthening their relationship. Since they all knew something secret about the others, they were in the same boat.

Because this was the last evening before the wedding, the topic was of course Daran's relationship with the desert brothers.

"You tamed them pretty well." Frankus patted Daran on the shoulder. He was pleased with the outcome of his hard work. The tattoo looked absolutely fabulous, and the dark green ink was the perfect contrast to Daran's light skin color.

The Echend'dim grinned back at him. Now that the pain of tattooing was over, Daran could finally relax. "I wouldn't say I tamed them." A shudder ran through his body. "They're truly savage."

Frankus laughed. "Oh, I wasn't talking about their sexual—well, let's call it preferences for lack of a more befitting term. I meant their sudden fidelity. It's even more astounding than Lord Renaldo's change of heart after he met Casto."

Daran's features displayed his curiosity. "How were they back then? They don't tell me a lot about the time before we met."

"Yes, tell us! I'm dying to know what kind of men they were." Casto sounded almost as eager as he looked. Only Sic, who had known the desert brothers for almost ten years, held back.

Frankus took a sip from his hot tea and stared musingly into the flames.

"You just want to know because you're going to use it against them."
The accusation was made in a light tone. Still, Casto looked a tiny bit contrite.

"And if so?"

Frankus grinned. He liked teasing Casto. "I fully approve. They do deserve it."

"Hey, you're talking about my future husbands here!" Daran was by far not as indignant as he tried to sound, and it showed on his face, so Frankus ignored the reprimand.

"It's hard to choose the best story from such a vast treasure chest. Of course, there are all those lovely rumors about their trysts with Lady Hulda, but that was before she met Lord Wolfstan, and *that* was long before I was born. As you may know, they used to change their partners quite often, due to reasons only they know."

Daran closed his eyes. He knew exactly why Kalad and Aegid had done this, and he still felt his heart constrict with pity when he thought about it. Not wanting to spoil this evening with sad thoughts, Daran focused on Frankus again.

"So many partners do provide quite a lot of stories, but the best one, I think, happened two or three years before Casto came to the Valley. There had been a minor campaign against Ta'li'en, a city on the western border of the Plains."

Casto furrowed his brow. "Isn't that the city of whores? It's famous for its courtesans."

"Indeed it is. You're well informed, Your Majesty." Frankus looked pointedly at Casto, who was not fazed in the least.

"Knowledge is the key to power. Always." The short sentence made Sic and Daran shudder, for it showed once again how differently Casto had been raised compared to them.

Frankus ended the slightly awkward silence by resuming his story.

"Ta'li'en's main merchandise are the whores who are trained by the five main houses. Once their education is completed, they are sold to the biggest brothels all over the continent, as well as to private households. A whore trained in Ta'li'en is an exclusive and expensive item, perfectly versed in every matter concerning the bed. When Lord Canubis appeared with his army, the city elders opened the gates for him, knowing they had no chance. Since the contract was about getting a certain type of whore for a very greedy and rich customer, the Wolf of War accepted their offer. He told the elders what he wanted, and they gave him the requested females without making a fuss. The contract was fulfilled, but it had all been kind of anticlimactic. So when the leaders of the city invited the Pack to a night of fun, they did not say no.

"It was during that feast that Kalad and Aegid met the Doll."

Frankus paused for a moment, took another sip from his tea, and enjoyed the anticipation coming from his audience.

"The Doll was really special. She, or he, was a hermaphrodite, male and female at the same time. Of course the desert brothers were fascinated, like everybody else in the Pack. The Doll chose them for the night, and they somehow managed to convince him to come with them. He wouldn't accompany them to the Valley, but he agreed to stay with Aegid and Kalad until they reached the Umman River. From there he would go back to Ta'li'en to claim the more than generous amount of money they had deposited for him there."

"So far this doesn't sound outrageous. Just Aegid and Kalad being their usual selves." Casto wasn't impressed by the story so far, except for the hermaphrodite part, which had woken his curiosity.

Frankus shot him a scathing look. "That's because you're not letting me finish my story. The good part comes now. No need to say that they fucked the poor creature raw every night, so he had to travel in a carriage during the day. On the fifth night, the Doll vanished, taking with him everything valuable he could get his hands on, and that was quite a lot. The wolves didn't stop him since he was a free man, and once they realized that he had stolen from Aegid and Kalad, he had already covered his trail by smashing a bottle of Nerula perfume. Outraged, Aegid and Kalad rode back to Ta'li'en, to either catch the Doll or at least reclaim their money, but neither was there. The Doll had managed to deceive them completely. Even his soreness had been an act. The entire winter, they stayed away from whores and brothels and concentrated on slaves alone. It was almost heartbreaking to see them struggle so bravely to regain their courage." Frankus tried in vain to suppress a chuckle. "Then they met you, Daran, and I have to admit, I find it highly amusing how monogamous they have become."

"You are a wicked man, Frankus!" Casto was holding his sides. Whenever he pictured the faces of the desert brothers when they had found out they had been tricked, he felt laughter welling up inside.

Daran shot his trainer a nasty look before he turned to Frankus. "And they never found the Doll?"

"No, they did not. But they received a letter the following spring, thanking them for their generosity by helping a 'poor double-faced creature' to find freedom. Strangely enough, that seemed to help them to find closure, because after that, they returned to their old ways."

"Kalad and Aegid are good men, Daran. I don't think Frankus meant to belittle them." Sic spoke in a soothing tone. Because of their connection, he could feel Daran's distress more intensely than the other two men.

The Echend'dim smiled at him gratefully. "Thank you, Sic. It's very nice of you to say so. I'm aware of their many faults. And to be frank, I love them because of it, not despite."

"Blah! You do know how nauseating that sounds, don't you, Daran? Sometimes I get the impression that they brainwashed you. Or, to be more precise, fucked you senseless."

Daran reacted to Casto's banter with a saccharine smile. He knew how to get back at the king. "Just because my relationship with Aegid and Kalad is so healthy compared to the complicated mess you have with Lord Renaldo doesn't mean I was brainwashed. I hate to tell you this, Casto, but the weird one is you."

Casto put his hand on his chest in feigned consternation. "An insult! How dare you! Sic, Frankus, did you hear that?"

The two men grinned broadly. It was Sic who answered.

"We did. And he's so right, there's nothing we can add."

"So, you too? I think I'd better ride home right now. Obviously there's no place for me here."

"Do as you please, Your Majesty. If you leave now, there's more of the honey cake for us."

Frankus had started to unwrap a parcel with four generous slices of the delicious sweet. The rich scent filled the air and made the men's mouths water. Casto, who was already standing, sat down again.

"On second thought, I don't think I'm as deeply insulted as I should be. For the sake of this wonderful cake, I'm willing to forgive you all."

"You're so generous, it almost makes me cry." Daran bowed slightly in Casto's direction. Frankus handed out the slices of cake, and when they all had their share, Daran addressed his friends in a more serious tone.

"Thank you. Thank you for what you've done for me, and thank you for being the way you are. I never had real friends before, but if the loneliness I had to endure is the price for meeting you, I'd gladly suffer it again."

"Damn it, Daran. You almost made me cry!" Casto glared at the Echend'dim in an attempt to hide how deeply he was moved by his words. He, Sic, and Daran had all experienced the desolation of a lonely, wasted childhood spent in constant grief. It was a bond that connected them on a deep, semiconscious level. To get over his embarrassment, Casto took a bite of the cake. The others followed his example, each of them contemplating similar thoughts and coming to the same conclusion—that they were indeed lucky to have obtained such great friends.

4. VOWS FOR ETERNITY

The following morning, the four of them rode back to the center of the Valley as quickly as possible. Frankus took Daran with him to prepare him for the wedding. Sic and Casto returned to their own chambers to get some rest before the ceremony started.

Renaldo greeted his mate with a deep kiss when he entered the room. "Welcome back, my own. Is everything all right?"

Casto snuggled closer to Renaldo, glad for the heat his mate radiated.

"Everything's fine. I'm just miserably cold. Sleeping in a cave at this time of the year is a bad idea."

Renaldo chuckled while he pulled Casto closer. "I don't understand it. I mean, you can tap into my fire, and yet you're still unable to withstand the chill."

"I know. It's strange. To be frank, I'm too tired to think about this mystery right now. Please help me undress and get me into the hot water. Perhaps I'll regain some feeling in my toes then."

"Your wish is my command." A saucy smile appeared on Renaldo's lips. "If you're a good boy, I'll warm up more than just your toes."

Casto winced. "Sounds tempting. Unfortunately it'll have to wait until after the ceremony. If we start now, there's no way we'll be in time for the wedding, and you're an integral part of it."

Renaldo nibbled Casto's nape. "Fine. After the ceremony. You won't be able to escape me then."

"I'll take you at your word, Barbarian."

When Sic entered the main hall, it was already bursting with people. Together with Noran, he approached the table where the other Emeris were waiting. Even Cornelia was there, standing next to her brother. She greeted Sic with a wistful smile on her lips, and he felt his heart constrict when he imagined how hard this had to be for her. Then the great doors opened once again, and Canubis, Renaldo, Kalad, and Aegid entered. All four of them looked stunning in their black, blue, and green tunics, with their ceremonial swords around their hips. There was a special connection between those two pairs of brothers who had known each other for more than eight hundred years, and on this special day, it showed clearly. The men radiated superiority, a certain lethal arrogance, and a closeness born of centuries of trust. They approached the table, turned around in front of it, and aimed their gazes back to the door where Daran had taken position.

Sic had to admit the former thief had never looked more alluring. His long black hair flowed freely down his shoulders, and his expressive brown eyes were highlighted by black kohl and full of love for the two men he was about to marry. Like Kalad and Aegid, Daran wore a dark green tunic and a ceremonial sword with an emerald at the back of the handle. He also had a cloak slung around his shoulders that was dyed dark blue on the inside and black on the outside, with the rune of the Mothers embroidered on the back. It was a gift from Canubis and Renaldo to their first Echend'dim. Lukan, who was standing left of the four men, wore the same. Behind Daran, Casto had taken position. Since Aegid and Kalad had been the ones to bring him to Renaldo on his wedding day, he had gladly accepted when they had asked him to do the same for Daran. Casto whispered something into Daran's ear before he hurried to take his place next to Noemi. All eyes were now glued on the Echend'dim, who stuck out his chin proudly and walked up to his waiting lovers. Kalad and Aegid took Daran between them before they turned to Canubis and Renaldo. When he saw them standing there, Sic couldn't help but feel envious. Even though the desert brothers were insatiable in bed, they still had managed to build a healthy, mature relationship with Daran. A relationship that was grounded in trust and love and didn't need games for dominance, because the three men felt mutual respect. It stood in stark contrast to the unpredictable, wild, and violent connection Renaldo and Casto shared, and it made Sic's relationship with Noran look like a bad joke. Sic knew he had to be patient, that the love between him and Noran needed a lot of time and nourishing to become the dependable pillar of trust he wanted it to be. Still, he felt a pang of jealousy when he thought that Daran had obtained seemingly without effort what was still out of reach for him. Having such unseemly feelings on the day of his friend's wedding added a good deal of guilt to the contradicting emotions in his heart.

At that moment, Sic felt Noran's hand engulf his own. The reassuring pressure helped him to gain his focus again. Determined not to let anything ruin this day, he concentrated on his joy about the union that Daran and the desert brothers were about to enter into.

Renaldo slung a green silken cloth around the intertwined hands of the three men, while Canubis started to talk.

"Standing here again so shortly after my brother has found his heart to tie the knot between our eldest Emeris and their chosen one is an honor and a joy that words can hardly express. I still remember the day when Aegid and Kalad brought Daran to the Valley as their slave because he had tried to steal from them. In the beginning, we all thought he would last only for the winter, as a substitute for yet another brazier."

Chuckles erupted in the hall. The desert brothers' need for warmth during the winter was legendary.

"I have to admit, I was rather surprised when they kept you, Daran, throughout the following summer, but it became quickly apparent that you were more than just a meaningless fling for them, and nobody besides Aegid and Kalad is happier than me and Renaldo that you also turned out to be our first Echend'dim. To make it short, this day is as perfect as it can get, and it is my honor to marry the three of you. Would you now please say your vows?"

Daran was the first to speak. His voice was shaking slightly, and the happiness he emanated made him glow from within.

"Ne, Daran, ana Echend'dim te elendio remaro net elendio muoro, renosor aremao net tarenar nelen memosos Aegid net Kalad."

I, Daran, Echend'dim to the Wolf of War and the Angel of Death, swear to love and respect my mates, Aegid and Kalad.

The desert brothers gazed at their precious lover with so much love, it forced some of the mercenaries to avert their eyes. They spoke in unison, thus expressing how interwoven their personalities were.

"Ra, ana brestere eltame, ana rieto La'id net ana mearo La'id, Emeris te elendio remaro net elendio muoro, renosor aremao net tarenar raes memoso, Daran."

We, the kindred of the heat, the unbending man and the spirit man, Emeris to the Wolf of War and the Angel of Death, swear to love and respect our mate, Daran.

Renaldo and Canubis placed their hands on top of the silken cloth. They, too, spoke in unison, their voices booming through the hall like drums of war.

"Ra, elendio remaro net elendio muoro, karenar ana lerindo. Alte ana rodono anoso te'li."

We, the Wolf of War and the Angel of Death, bless this union. May it prosper for all time to come.

Applause broke out among the mercenaries when Canubis undid the cloth and the newlyweds turned around. Kalad allowed his brothers-in-arms to cheer for a few moments; then he held up his hand, a broad grin on his face.

"Time for the gifts."

Sic stepped forward, an open box in his hands. Inside were three identical bracelets, about a hand's breadth, the gold hammered so thin it felt like a second skin. Etched into them were the names of the three men and a complicated pattern of stylized runes telling the story of their love. It was another masterpiece from Sic that had cost him a couple of sleepless nights and a splitting headache when he had sketched the runes. Seeing them on the wrists of the three warriors reimbursed him for his trouble, since they looked more than just stunning. They were the perfect jewelry for the three men, who wanted to show their union openly. Sic retreated with the empty box to make room for the slaves who carried the trunks filled with the gifts Aegid and Kalad had chosen for their beloved mate. It was a shower of riches similar to the one Casto had received, with the exception of slaves. Daran hadn't wanted any, his reason being that it didn't make a difference to whom they belonged. After the last trunk had been brought in, Daran thanked his husbands with a deep bow and an even deeper kiss. Before things could get out of hand, Renaldo declared the feast opened.

At MIDNIGHT, Kalad, Aegid, and Daran left their drunken, high-spirited brothers-in-arms and returned to their chambers for the three days of seclusion. The desert brothers were a bit miffed, since Daran had declined having sex with them in front of all the mercenaries. He smiled when he pictured their faces once they found out the reason for it. Aegid closed the door, and for a moment, an uncharacteristic silence spread. It was Daran who ended it.

"So we're married now. Feels unreal."

Kalad smiled. "It does. As if everything has changed while still remaining the same."

Aegid stepped forward, pulling both his desert brother and Daran into a tight embrace. "I've never felt so content in my life. We're home."

He bent down to kiss Daran, while Kalad started fumbling with the belt around the Echend'dim's hips. With considerable difficulty, Daran managed to free himself from their grasp and to retreat a few steps. When he saw the hunger in their eyes, he treated them to a seductive smile. Slowly, he opened the belt and let the sword clatter to the floor. Then he reached for the fasteners on his tunic. The cloth fell with a soft whisper, exposing Daran's naked, tattooed torso. Aegid and Kalad stared at him, wide-eyed.

"This is my gift for you, my mates. I hope you like it."

"Like it? We love it!" Kalad sounded breathless, his excitement already showing clearly.

"So that's what you've been doing the past three days. You really managed to surprise us." Aegid's voice was so deep and guttural, Daran had trouble understanding him. Without warning, both men pounced on Daran and dragged him to the bed. How they got rid of their own clothes so quickly was a mystery Daran had no inclination to solve. He was too busy groaning while they licked first the tattoo and then his entire body. It didn't take them long to make him climax the first time. The almost four days of abstinence as well as the tension from the wedding made Daran easy prey. Aegid, who had sucked him when he came, flipped Daran on his belly and spread his legs. Daran felt Aegid's fingers entering and stretching his hole, and then a warm sensation when the giant let the semen from his mouth dribble into Daran's body. He moaned, hardly able to wait for the wonderful feeling when Aegid would penetrate him.

Kalad reached for Daran's head and kissed him deeply before he pulled him upward. Daran realized Kalad was propped up against some cushions, his penis hot and eager at Daran's thighs. Aegid helped his desert brother to position Daran right over his cock. While Kalad slid into the Echend'dim, Aegid bit him playfully on the neck. Then Kalad was completely in, but instead of starting to thrust, he slung his arms around Daran's chest and pulled him close.

"Do you trust us, little thief?"

Daran shuddered. He felt a feverish anticipation growing inside, a heat that spread like wildfire. Knowing what they wanted to try, he gave his consent without thinking twice—not that thinking was still an option in his current state.

"Yes, I do."

He could feel both men tensing. Aegid reached for a bottle of oil and applied the contents generously around Daran's stretched hole. Then he started massaging the taut ring, slipping in first one finger, then two, slowly accustoming Daran to the additional strain. When all Daran was able to utter were moans and lustful whimpers, Aegid positioned himself between the young man's legs and slowly pressed his massive erection against the creamy, twitching hole. For a moment it seemed as if it was too much, but then it went in with a soft, wet sound that almost drove all three men crazy. They paused, savoring this new, most intimate feeling.

Kalad's voice was hoarse. "Are you all right, little thief?"

Daran groaned, unable to muster a coherent sentence. To express his consent, he licked Kalad's lips while at the same time shaking his hips, albeit carefully. He liked the feeling of being so completely stuffed, of owning both his lovers at the same time. Over Daran's shoulder, Kalad's and Aegid's eyes met. They had always been connected in ways most people would never understand. Now they suddenly realized that the thing they had been looking for, the goal they had been trying to reach since the day they had first met, was finally there. It was Daran, forever and always Daran. He was the part of their union they had been missing, the final piece. They both smiled and started to thrust.

IT WAS already noon the next day when Daran finally woke. Even though he was Echend'dim, he still felt sore and exhausted from the previous night. His husbands had taken him four times in the new position, and each time they acted greedier, their lust so insatiable that Daran drowned in it. With a groan, he sat up. Aegid and Kalad had obviously cleaned him and the bed, but he had no memory of it. Daran had swung his legs over the edge of the bed to get out of it when Kalad's voice stopped him.

"Where do you think you're going, little thief?"

Daran looked up. His mates were standing in the door to the chamber, stark naked, hunger plain in their features, and obviously ready for another round. Daran shook his head.

"Forget it. I need to go to the bathroom and then I need to eat. You did me pretty hard."

There was a hint of contrition in the desert brothers' eyes, yet not for long. The memory of what they had done only added to their arousal. Daran's shoulders slumped. He knew that look; it meant he wouldn't have breakfast anytime soon. Somehow he managed to fend them off long enough to make a trip to the bathroom, but then there was no escaping them anymore.

5. SHATTERED TRUST

"In two days we'll be holding the Spring Ceremony as the sole masters of Ana-Darasa for the first time. I hate to admit it, but I'm actually giddy."

Canubis sounded so overly smug and content, Renaldo couldn't help but grin. He, too, was excited. This Spring Ceremony was indeed a very special one. The only thing that diminished his good mood was the contract they had signed with Queen Xe'lien. Neither Renaldo nor Canubis was entirely sure whether a guerilla war was a good idea at this point, but given the circumstances, they had no choice. Since the bargain was struck, there was no use pondering the wisdom of their decision any further. Renaldo rose from his chair.

"I've got to go now, brother. I need to get Casto's present."

Canubis made a dismissive gesture.

"So you're doing it again? Rewarding him for being stubborn and disobedient?"

Renaldo shrugged. As close as Canubis and he usually were, they would never reach an understanding concerning Casto.

"I'm open to suggestions that don't involve beating him into submission. Which would never work, as we both know."

Canubis leaned back in his chair, the expression in his eyes slightly mocking. "Somehow I'm glad that this is your problem and I'm just the one who points it out to you. I would hate it if I had to deal with a heart as difficult as Casto."

"I love you, too, brother. A lot."

Renaldo went to get his mate's present while the Wolf of War stayed in his chambers, wondering about the nature of love and the necessity of Casto being just the way he was.

"You really are an idiot."

Casto glared at Daran, who was covered in silver dust, the bracelet from the wedding and the golden belt Sic had given him the only clothing he wore.

"You're an Echend'dim, husband to two of the most powerful members of the Pack, and you still behave like a slave. I just don't get you!"

Daran smiled sheepishly. He had known Casto wouldn't approve of him going to the Spring Ceremony as a favorite and had been prepared for some harsh words, but the utter fury he felt from his friend was far worse than he had anticipated. For various reasons, he had pondered the wisdom of going as a favorite again. In the beginning it had been a joke between him and his husbands, nothing any of them contemplated seriously. The longer Daran had thought about it, though, the more torn he had become. When he had discussed his musings with Aegid and Kalad, they had been opposed to it first, for political reasons similar to those Casto had just voiced. At the same time, Daran had sensed how much they longed for him to take on the role of slave once more. All three of them enjoyed their new, more mature, and balanced relationship, but there were times when they missed the straightforward connection they had shared in the beginning. In the end they decided to treat it as a very kinky role-play game, something Daran would never tell Casto. It had been bad enough to see the salacious grin on Canubis's face when he had asked his permission to go as a favorite. Explaining to Casto why he found it highly erotic to submit to his husbands in such a spectacular manner was a place Daran did not wish to visit. In fact, he would rather bite off his tongue than discuss this intimate topic with Casto.

Noemi stepped next to them, her golden skin glittering in the light of the torches.

"Leave Daran alone, Casto. It's not his fault that you hate the Spring Ceremony. He's doing it out of love for his mates, and even Canubis respects his decision. It's not your place to criticize him."

Daran flinched. He wasn't sure whether Noemi truly believed he was doing this out of love and not for purely carnal reasons, or if she just wanted to tease her brother-in-law. The impact of her words was clearly visible, though.

Made even angrier by the reprimand, Casto glared at Noemi. "I'm not a child, Noemi, so cut it out."

"But you do behave like one, and unless you stop, I won't either."

Just when Casto was getting ready for an acid retort, Kalad, Aegid, Canubis, and Renaldo appeared. The desert brothers kissed their mate lovingly and with a telltale glint in their eyes before they chained and led him away. Renaldo approached Casto, a radiant smile on his lips that did nothing to improve the king's mood.

"My own. You are beyond beautiful."

"Cut it out, Barbarian. Just let us get this over with."

Renaldo and Canubis shared a long look behind Casto's back, but neither of them commented any further. Instead they led their hearts to the main hall in silence, filled with nervous anticipation of what was to come.

After Canubis and Renaldo had spoken the traditional blessing, the mercenaries sacrificed their blood. It was when the first drops hit the floor that the divine brothers registered the change. It started slowly, like the first hesitant drips of rain after a particularly long drought, and quickly turned into a torrent when the assembled warriors started to engage their lust. The two gods felt as if they were struck by lightning. All the raw energy from the countless pairings that had previously gone to Ana-Isara and Ana-Aruna hit them full force, filling them up to the point they felt as if their bodies would just dissolve. Everything they had thought made them what they were was drowned in the sheer power of their natural right. For the first time, Canubis and Renaldo truly understood what being a god meant. Reality turned soft under their glare, turned into something they could mold the way they wanted it. They were the only substantial things in a world made of shadows. They and their hearts. Noemi and Casto appeared like beacons in the blur, drawing the gods in, anchoring them to the real world. The light Casto emanated was the most beautiful thing Renaldo had ever seen. And it was his.

Full of hunger, the Angel of Death turned to his heart. His vision was focused on Casto alone, and he was no longer able to think at all. The beast had woken, eager and determined to have it all tonight, because if it did not, Renaldo would drown in the energy directed at him. Possessing Casto was no longer just a whim: it had become an absolute necessity.

Because of his perfectly honed instincts, Casto sensed immediately that something was off. The Barbarian stared at him with a strange look in his eyes, one Casto had never seen on him before. It was so intense, he felt shivers running down his spine. Dread pierced through the haze the Nerula oil had created and made him wary. Casto was about to retreat a few steps, ready to escape from Renaldo, who looked as if he had taken some powerful drug himself, but the god was faster. With a grip like steel, he grabbed Casto's upper arms and pulled him close to force a kiss on him.

Casto, who had by then completely shaken off the effect of the Nerula oil, bit down on Renaldo's tongue with all his might. They both felt the coppery taste invading their mouths like a curse. The Angel of Death winced; the grip he had on Casto hardened. The beast was now fully awake and furious. How could this worm dare to defy him? How could he go so far as to draw blood from him? He was *elendio muoro*, the god of death. His will was law, and his heart had the duty to obey. Without thinking, Renaldo entered Casto's mind, telling him exactly that, forcing him to submit. Casto fought against Renaldo with all his might, his iron will enabling him to withstand the Angel of Death for a few heartbeats.

Renaldo roared when he was confronted with such utter defiance. The energy coming from all their followers burned through his body in search of an outlet, an outlet only his heart could provide. That was Casto's main and most important task, the reason for his existence— to shield his god from the void that lurked behind the power, ready to consume those not strong enough to bear it. Casto had to share both the power and the burden. If he did not do that, they both would perish.

As quickly and swiftly as a sword cut through flesh, Renaldo's will overwhelmed and subjugated Casto in an attempt to save them both. It left the king defenseless and unable to fight his god anymore. Almost bursting with lust and longing, Renaldo bent his prey over the table, exposing his firm asscheeks and the hole hidden between. He thrust inside with all his might, enjoying the sensation of tightness almost as much as the knowledge that he had Casto completely under his control. And it felt so good to channel the power, to let it flow through his body and pour into his heart, where it was purified before given back to him.

Beneath the raging Angel of Death, Casto dug his fingers into the table until splinters of wood pierced the skin. He focused on that pain in order to endure the rape of his mind. He had always known that Renaldo was not only physically but also mentally stronger than him, which was one of the reasons he had been so shocked the first time the Angel of Death had used his mind to make his wishes clear. Being prey to Renaldo's strength was his worst nightmare come to life. He also felt the stream of power Renaldo forced into him with every thrust. It felt as if he was stuffed until he would break, as if he had eaten too much and would start throwing up at any moment. When Casto thought he couldn't endure it anymore, the energy started flowing back to the Angel of Death. In the rhythm of their violent pairing, they also exchanged power. Being used as an outlet as well as a whore and a possession made Casto seethe with rage, yet he realized that there was nothing he could do, that he had to accept what his god demanded of him, simply because Renaldo was beyond reason at the moment. The injustice of what was done to him filled Casto with helpless rage and humiliation. Beaten by the man he loved, his mind screamed in despair.

Renaldo sensed that his heart had finally given up. Basking in his triumph, he took what was exclusively his the entire night.

IT WAS already afternoon when Casto woke. He could sense Renaldo's presence next to the bed, and before he could stop himself, a surge of heat blasted the god's way. Instead of reprimanding him for it, Renaldo started to speak in hushed tones.

"Casto. I'm so sorry. Believe me, I never wanted things to turn out like that. Please, just listen to me, let me explain."

"I'm not talking to you, Barbarian. Not for a long time."

Renaldo sighed. He knew he had messed up badly; still, he wanted Casto to at least understand the reason.

"It was just too much, all that power filling me up. I couldn't think clearly anymore—it was all a blur. And when you resisted even though I needed you so badly, I lost it."

"So it's my fault, then?" The words came out biting; there was no doubt about Casto's point of view and his current mood.

"Of course not. I'm just asking you to understand."

Pointedly, Casto turned his back to Renaldo, ignoring his pleading mate.

Sighing, Renaldo took a small box out of his pocket and placed it on the nightstand. "This is for you, Casto. I'll be leaving you alone now."

When the door had closed, Casto reached for the box. For a moment he considered not opening it, for it felt too much like the payment a whoremonger would give after a heated night. Nevertheless, some kind of perverse curiosity made him peek inside the box. A seal ring with the rune for "rider" lay on a silken cushion. Something was etched into the gold on the inside of the ring.

To my own. R.

The inscription undid Casto. With a scream of rage, he threw the offending piece of jewelry against the wall, and since he was at it, he did the same with everything he could get his hands on. Letting out his helpless fury in such a destructive manner helped him cool his head. When he looked at all the destruction he had caused, he even felt a certain satisfaction. Some of the items that now lay broken and scattered on the floor had been dear to the Barbarian.

When Casto looked out the window, he saw it was already getting dark. As if he was in a fever, he hurried to put on his warmest clothes and the thickest boots he possessed, and then filled two leather pouches with gold and jewels. In the kitchen he obtained a bag full of provisions, and in the armory he took a sword, four daggers, and two knives.

Lys was waiting for him in front of the stables. Since the sun was already down, Casto hurried to put the saddle and bridle on his brother. The stallion whinnied softly, a comforting sound meant to reassure Casto. The king patted Lys's neck.

"Thank you, my friend. Let's get out of here. This time forever."

Gracefully he leapt into the saddle, and Lys started to run. His body became one with the shadows, so the few people who were still out did not see him. The wolves realized they were leaving, but since Casto was no longer a slave, they had no reason to stop them. Once Lys and Casto had left the Valley behind, the stallion called a storm to hide their tracks, just like he had done when they had fled this place for the first time. Given what Renaldo had done to his rider, Lys was sure they would never return, no matter how much Casto loved the Barbarian. The Emperor of the Storms was satisfied. He did not like the Angel of Death for various reasons; that he had almost killed Casto was only one of them. When all was said and done, he was still a creature of chaos, while the divine brothers represented order. Because of Casto, he had put up with them until now. Casto's happiness was the most important thing for Lys, and as long as he found it with Renaldo, Lys had accepted that. Things had changed, though. The Barbarian had broken his vow last night; he had hurt Casto so deeply, it made Lys shiver with rage when he thought about it. His determination to protect his rider at all cost grew with every league they put between themselves and the Valley. He would definitely not allow Renaldo to haunt Casto in his dreams as he had done before.

SPEECHLESS, RENALDO stood amidst the chaos that had once been his chambers. He had dared to return this morning to see if Casto was still holed up or if he had gone to Lys, as was his usual reaction when they had a fight. Casto was gone, and the room was torn apart. In his rage the young man had not only destroyed every breakable item he could get his hands on, but he had also thrown the chairs against the wall and broken the table. Feathers flew up whenever Renaldo moved, because Casto had also slit all the cushions. The destruction worried the Angel of Death. Never before had his heart reacted so harshly. There had always been a last vestige of control that prevented Casto from doing something irreversible. Making such a mess only showed how terribly Renaldo had hurt him.

The Angel of Death was just about to call for some slaves to clean up when Canubis entered the room. He looked so worried, it alarmed Renaldo.

"What?"

Canubis put a hand on his little brother's shoulder. "He's gone. I just talked to the wolves. Casto and Lys left the Valley last night."

Renaldo didn't know what to say. Blood roared in his ears. Torn between anger and worry, he could only listen to what Canubis had to say.

"I told you he would blow up in our faces! You need to get him back right away, and this time, I want him punished severely. Even though we are his gods, even though he has witnessed our strength, he still dares to defy us. He needs to be broken, Renaldo. It's too dangerous otherwise."

Slowly, Renaldo shook his head. "Witnessing our strength is what drove him away. Of course I'll call him back, but brother, breaking him should be our last resort."

Canubis leaned his forehead against Renaldo's.

"I know, little brother, I know. It pains me to see how much he's hurting you, and I want him to pay for making you so miserable."

Renaldo managed a weak smile.

"Thank you, brother. I really appreciate your care."

THAT VERY night, Renaldo tried to establish a connection with Casto to call him back. Unlike the first time he had run away, Casto did not reach out for his mate this time, and so Renaldo had considerable problems finding the king. Once or twice he thought he had tracked Casto down, only to realize that he had seen nothing but shadows. The Angel of Death kept running around in circles, chasing phantoms as insubstantial as a dream and as hard to catch. Three nights he struggled in vain to find Casto. On the fourth night, the king finally allowed him to come closer, and once Renaldo thought he had managed to get Casto at last, he had taken control of the dream.

And so Renaldo found himself standing in the throne room of the palace in Ummana, trying his hardest to regain control over events. He still couldn't believe Casto had managed to drag him here, to this place Renaldo had hoped to never see again. Casto was sitting on the throne with a golden crown on his head. The throne itself was surrounded by shadows that were dancing and coiling like living things. Between them, Casto's past unraveled in a series of flickering images. The day he had been born, scenes from his earliest childhood that seemed almost happy if one ignored the fact that the friendly governess had been a spy Queen Isiris had skinned alive once she found out about her treason. Or that the servant who was singing Casto a lullaby had been poisoned by an assassin from the Donai family because they wanted to place one of their own slaves there. Then Renaldo saw the day Queen Isiris died, and what came afterward made him heave. Casto had told him everything that had been done to him, but now, in the dream, Renaldo could also feel it. The realization of what his heart had endured without breaking forced him to his knees.

Casto's voice cut through the images like a knife.

"This is what they did to me. I was constantly forced against my will, and all I could do was bear it with gritted teeth, not showing anybody how deeply I was hurt. Then you came along and you forced my trust. You made me rely on you, only to betray me even worse than they did. How dare you follow me into my dreams and try to get me back? How dare you?"

Renaldo swallowed hard. Everything Casto had said was right. He had betrayed him, had done to him what he had sworn would never happen. There was no excuse for it, no sugarcoating it with nice words. He had broken his vows to Casto, had hurt his precious heart on more than one level. All he could do was beg.

"Casto, please."

The king rose from his throne and started to walk away.

"Goodbye, *Lord Renaldo*."

When he realized that his heart was about to leave him, that he would lose the one thing most precious to him, the Angel of Death panicked and reached out for Casto with his power, forced him to turn around and face him again. What he then saw made Renaldo recoil. The clear blue eyes had gone cold, the sensuous lips were pressed into a thin line, and the noble features had hardened. It was as if Casto had turned into a statue. When he spoke again, his voice was like icicles.

"You went back on your word, Barbarian, so there's no need for me to keep mine."

While the deeper meaning behind those words slowly sunk in, Lys suddenly appeared next to Casto. The stallion seemed to be taller than usual; his presence was suffocating, like the air just before a summer storm set in. Renaldo realized Lys was the reason he hadn't been able to reach Casto, and that the Emperor of the Storms would take the young man away from him again. The shadows slithering around the throne started to expand, hugging the horse and the man. Like a wall they solidified around Casto, obscuring him from Renaldo's view. Driven by fear and utter despair, Renaldo roared. His fire exploded and hit the shadow wall with full force. He could feel his power burning the dark and ripping it open. When the blaze subsided, the shadows were gone, shattered by the Angel of Death's will.

Casto was gone as well. For a heartbeat, Renaldo thought he could hear a condescending snicker.

Then he was all alone.

XENIA MELZER was born and raised in a small village in the South of Bavaria. As one of nature's true chocoholics, she's always in search of the perfect chocolate experience. So far, she's had about a dozen truly remarkable ones. Despite having been in close proximity to the mountains all her life, she has never understood why so many people think snow sports are fun. There are neither chocolate nor horses involved and it's cold by definition, so where's the sense? She does not like beer either and has never been to the Oktoberfest—no quality chocolate there.

Even though her mind is preoccupied with various stories most of the time, Xenia has managed to get through school and university with surprisingly good grades. Right after school she met her one true love who showed her that reality is capable of producing some truly amazing love stories itself.

While she was having her two children, she started writing down the most persistent stories in her head as a way of relieving mommy-related stress symptoms. As it turned out, the stress relief has now become a source of the same, albeit a positive one.

When she's not writing, she translates other authors' manuscripts to German, enjoys riding and running, spending time with her kids, and dancing with her husband.

Website: www.xeniamelzer.com
Email: info@xeniamelzer.com

CASTO

GODS OF WAR

XENIA MELZER

Gods of War: Book I

All is fair in love and war. Renaldo has lived happily by that proverb his entire life. But he has finally met his match, and he's about to discover how unfair love and war can be.

When demigod and warlord Lord Renaldo takes a beautiful stranger captive during an ambush, he is delighted to have found a distraction that will keep him entertained during the upcoming siege. Little does he know, Casto is keeping more than just one secret from him. Slowly, Renaldo gets sucked into a turbulent roller-coaster relationship with his mysterious prisoner, one that begins with hatred and soon spirals into a whirlwind of conflicting emotions. And when it seems that things can get no worse, an old enemy stirs right in the heart of his home.

Determined to keep Casto by his side, Renaldo has to find a balance between the capricious young man and his own destiny as a ruler and god to his people.

www.dsppublications.com

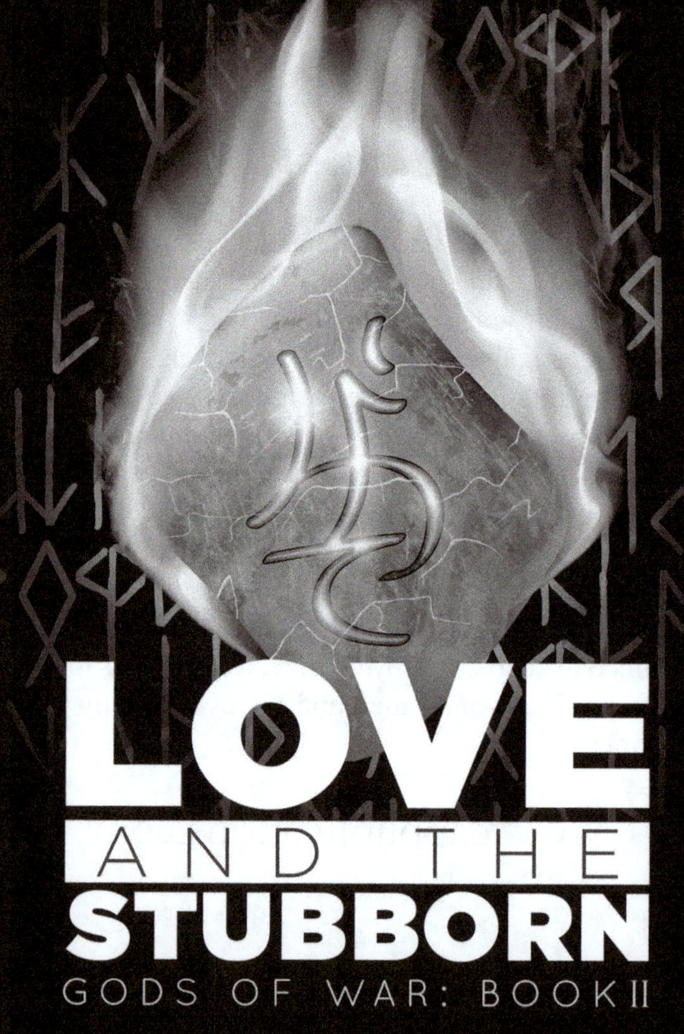

LOVE
AND THE
STUBBORN
GODS OF WAR: BOOK II
XENIA MELZER

Gods of War: Book II

All is fair in love and war. By now, Renaldo has found out the hard way how utterly stupid this statement is once you've met your match. And Casto won't give an inch in their ongoing war for love.

After a tumultuous start to their relationship, Renaldo and Casto seem to have finally reached calmer waters. But just when Renaldo starts getting comfortable and thinks he can relax, things get out of hand again. His old enemy, the Good Mother, is dangerously close to defeating the divine brothers by reaching out to what is most dear to him. Casto still clinging to his stubborn pride is all the plotters need to drive him and Renaldo apart. Burdened by the secrets of his past, Casto fights with everything he's got not only to save his life, but also to secure his future happiness. Facing the destruction of everything they have built together, Renaldo and Casto must choose between pride and love.

www.dsppublications.com

UMMANA

GODS OF WAR: BOOK III

XENIA MELZER

Gods of War: Book III

In war, loss is the price of victory, and the cost of love is sometimes pain.

After Renaldo and Casto finally celebrate their marriage, the time has come for revenge against the followers of the Good Mother who tried to kill Casto—though this time, the gods of war won't use bloodshed to take Medelina.

As a member of the Confederation of the Plains, Medelina answers to Ummana, the head of the alliance… and Casto is heir to the throne of Ummana. Accompanied by their most capable mercenaries, Canubis and Renaldo travel to Ummana to make Casto king.

They'll face the Council of Elders; Lord Aran, Casto's father; and Princess Anesha, Casto's sister—none of whom are happy about the king's return. For Casto, the city is a reminder of a terrible childhood, and Renaldo can only helplessly watch his beloved fight a seemingly hopeless battle.

Through trickery and political scheming, vengeance against the Good Mother is finally within their grasp—but their success might be bittersweet. Not everyone will return to the Valley with Casto and Renaldo.

www.dsppublications.com